HOPE REKINDLED

HOPE REKINDLED

An Historical Novel of Central Pennsylvania
During the Late Eighteenth Century

Wayne E. Taylor

Word Association Publishers
www.wordassociation.com

17,962

Printed in the United States of America.

Cover painting and design: Linda Kay Whitesel

Softcover ISBN: 978-1-59571-199-1
Hardcover ISBN: 978-1-59571-211-0
Library of Congress Control Number: 2007931516

Word Association Publishers
205 5th Avenue
Tarentum, PA 15084
www.wordassociation.com

To

my little schoolmarm,

Lucy,

who made all this possible

"No man can have a
peaceful life who thinks too
much about lengthening it."

—Seneca

"Hail to the hardy pioneers
The men that cleared the forest
And built log cabins crude;
The wives that shared the hardships
Of toil and solitude.
Founders of institutions,
Upholders of the right,
Reformers brave, and leaders
From darkness into light.
Hail to those hardy pioneers!"

—Rev. Robert E. Flickinger,
a native of the Tuscarora Valley

CHAPTER ONE

Early 1760

The Tuscarora Valley that Robert Taylor inhabited in early 1760 was drab and life was tedious. The labor that he and his frontier neighbors endured was heavy and constant—from daybreak to back-break. It had been proven time and time again that to survive on the Pennsylvania frontier a person had to be courageous, energetic, ambitious, resourceful, ingenious, and independent-minded.

Hacking a home out of the wilderness with an ax and rifle developed strength, self-confidence, individualism, and a spirit of independence. Robert Taylor appeared to possess all these attributes, but his mind never gave him any relief from his loneliness.

The new year and a new decade had opened on a bitter note in the valley. The month of January had recorded one significant snowfall after another. These heavy snows had made travel quite difficult, almost impossible for several weeks.

The banks of the Tuscarora Creek proved to be a bleak and solitary place during the cold and snowy months of January and February. Robert simply had too much downtime at this time of year. His main occupation was attending his line of traps, a job that he did not particularly enjoy. All too often his traps contained suffering animals, because they were not designed to kill an animal outright.

Skinning the animals, and stretching and drying the pelts involved considerable time and skill, but these chores still left far too much time for him to think, and think he did. With the fall of

Quebec last autumn and the anticipated surrender of Montreal this spring or summer, Robert visualized a flood of liberated white captives returning south to their homes. Among that mass of white humanity would just have to be his Ann, Robbie, and Elizabeth. It just could not happen any other way. They had to be together once again in the near future.

Across his mind marched the great phantoms of the images of his family in all their form and outline, and their details. There was no way that he could avoid the constant reminders of those three absent souls who meant the world to him. It was with great relief that he greeted those first days of February that washed his cabin's surroundings with lean sunshine. A new spring was waiting to be welcomed in a few short weeks. Moreover, spring could not arrive soon enough for Robert.

The dreariness of his cabin and the grimness of his work left Robert depressed. Although he was not a pious man, Robert would sit by the light of his fireplace and read his Bible aloud during the long evenings of the bleak winter. This was a violent and lonely land, and when night came it appeared to last an eternity.

This was a time of pseudo-peace and promise, the lull after the past several years of turmoil. He and his neighbors had come to stay, and against all adversities, they would continue to possess this valley.

While Robert was struggling to survive another bleak winter in Central Pennsylvania, the British army and navy in Quebec were also suffering dreadfully. The troops lacked adequate clothing for the harsh Canadian climate. Diseases, such as typhus, typhoid, scurvy, dysentery, hypothermia, and frostbite, took the lives of over a thousand men. Inadequate nutrition contributed to the death and disabled tolls. The anticipated victory might not come as easily and as soon as most observers envisioned.

About a day's ride west of the Tuscarora Valley is the Conococheague Valley, which allegedly was protected by the garrison at Fort Loudoun. During this same period in early 1760, a young man by the name of James Smith returned to the Conococheague. He had been spared suffering through the devastating winter in the St. Lawrence Valley. Eventually Smith would have a monumental impact on frontier-trader relationships, which in turn would lead many of the settlers in this section of the frontier to support the Patriot cause during the American Revolution.

James Smith was born in what is now Peters Township, Franklin County, near the site where Fort Loudoun was later constructed. In May of 1755, when Smith was only eighteen years of age, he was involved in construction of a road from Fort Loudoun to Fort Bedford and beyond, which would join Braddock's road near Turkey Foot. He had left the arms and charms of his sweetheart for what he believed would be a period of short duration. At the end of their separation, a frontier wedding was planned. These plans were shattered in May of 1755 when James Smith and his companion, Arnold Vigoras, were ambushed by three Indians about four or five miles from Bedford.

Now, nearly four and a half years after the ambush and Smith's abduction, James Smith reappeared unannounced in the Conococheague Valley.

Not far from Fort Loudoun on the road to Chambersburg was MacDougal's Tavern, where a man could fill his belly with liquor and good food, and his mouth with swearing. A few of the locals were engaged in some early afternoon imbibing when James made his appearance.

As James made his way to the bar, none of the tavern patrons paid him any heed. Even the barkeep did not break his customary routine, and habitually filled Smith's request for more whiskey without giving him more than a glance. James listened to the bantering among the clientele for a short time until he could no longer keep his silence or his secret as to who he was.

Finally, he spoke jokingly. "Well, Will Henry, I see your tall tales haven't lost any of their luster in the last four and a half years. The bears just keep getting bigger and your conquests greater in number."

Will Henry and the other four patrons whirled around in James's direction, and Will took exception to James's words. "Stranger, around here we measure our words a mite closer. If you are looking for trouble, you have come to the right place and have insulted the right man. Now if you'd like to step outside, I'd like to teach you some manners."

James kept his composure. "Even when we were kids you couldn't take a joke, Will. Guess you never got over us calling you Brownie, as to what you did in your pants the day that bear jumped us down on the West Conococheague back in '52."

"Just who the hell do you think you are bringing that up? I'm really going to teach you a lesson now."

"Just stop and take a good, long gander at who's pulling your leg, Will. Of course, I always thought you were blind, the way you shoot and the unattractive girls you used to chase."

"There's only one man that could make fun of me that way and get away with it, but he's been gone nearly five years."

"Was gone, Will, and hopefully not forgotten by you and the good people of this valley, especially Becky."

"Oh my God! It's James Smith! Back from the dead. Holy Cow, James, you are some sight. You're more Indian than some of the Delawares I've seen lately."

It finally dawned on the rest of the customers that it truly was James Smith, back from captivity and God only knew where. MacDougal and the rest all began to jabber at the same time, while pumping James's hand and slapping him on the back.

MacDougal jumped over the bar and yelled, "The drinks are on me. We're going to do some serious celebrating. Sarah! Sarah! Go spread the word that James Smith is back in the valley. Invite everyone to come to the tavern; we're going to have a good old-fashioned frolic."

Within a short time, the tavern filled to overflowing with well-wishing friends and neighbors, overjoyed that one of their own had survived such a long ordeal. Men and women of all ages joined in. The Smith clan was especially well represented, as they were overwhelmed at his return.

After a period of serious celebrating, which of course involved some earnest drinking, James was persuaded to answer some questions and give a short discourse on his missing years from the valley.

"I promise to make this as short and simple as possible," he began. "Arnold Vigoras and I were working under my brother-in-law, William Smith, near Raystown, in helping to build the road from our fort to Fort Bedford to link up with Braddock's Road, coming up from the south. We were ambushed by three Indians about four or five miles above Bedford. Poor old Arnold was killed and scalped. My horse threw me and I was taken prisoner. After several days' travel westward, we arrived at the outskirts of Fort Duquesne.

Before we entered the fort, I was forced to run the gauntlet, during which I was knocked senseless. When I recovered, I was informed that I would not remain in the fort, but would be taken by the Indians and made an Indian.

On July 9, I watched the victorious Indians and French soldiers return from overrunning Braddock's army. I was then forced to witness the terrible torture and the burning to death of many British prisoners.

"A few days later I was taken up the Allegheny River to the Indian town of Tullihas, about twenty miles above the fort on the West Branch of the Muskingum. Here I was given a proper Indian haircut, as they not only cut my hair, but also pulled much of it out of my head." At this, James removed his floppy hat and exhibited his unusual hairstyle.

"They bored my nose and ears and gave me earrings and nose jewels. They stripped me and gave me typical Indian attire. After this makeover, I was guided through an unusual adoption ceremony and was turned over to my Indian family.

"Eventually I will divulge more details of my time spent in captivity, but for now I'm going to give only an abbreviated version of my stay with the natives.

"About October my Indian family moved to the shores of

Lake Erie, where we built a winter cabin. Food was scarce and the winter was a difficult one. Near the end of March, we moved to the valley of the Canesadooharie.

"The next few years I lived in the area west of the Allegheny, north of the Ohio, and around the Great Lakes. In the winter of 1758-59, we hunted up the Sandusky and the Scioto Rivers and went to Detroit sometime in April of 1759. Shortly after this we headed east to the ancient Indian town of Caughnawaga, about nine miles upriver from Montreal on the St. Lawrence River.

"I learned that a French ship that housed English prisoners was anchored in the river. I developed this wild scheme, whereby I stole away from Caughnawaga by canoe, paddled near the ship, and boarded it to become a prisoner in the hopes that I would be exchanged for a French prisoner and sent home.

"This scheme went awry when General Wolfe blocked the river, and the ship had to unload the prisoners in Montreal. I was a prisoner in Montreal for about four months. Last November, we English prisoners were sent to Fort Crown Point in New York, where we were exchanged. Since then I have been through Albany, New York City, Philadelphia, Lancaster, Carlisle, Shippensburg, and Chambersburg, and finally home at last here in the Conococheague."

James then fielded a few questions about his treatment by his captors. While he talked, he searched the festive crowd for one special face, the angelic face of his adored Becky. However, his scrutinizing gaze never stared into her sky-blue eyes. She was a no-show.

The crowd was overjoyed with his return and showed their enthusiasm for his liberation by shaking his hand and slapping him on his back until his hand and his back were quite sore. He continued to explore the faces for the one that meant the most to him.

Finally, MacDougal inquired, "Who are you looking for, son? As if I didn't already know. I'm sorry, James. She's not going to show."

"What do you mean, she's not going to show? She has to!

She's the only thing that kept me going all these years. Without her to think and dream about, I wouldn't have survived. Where is she? Is she sick? Was she captured too? Was she killed? Come on, give me the answer. Don't torture me!"

"Well, you're not going to like what I have to tell you. She's alive as ever. Still as beautiful as ever, but she's no longer a free woman. About a week ago, she got hitched. She waited and waited for you to return, but she finally gave up. Everyone was telling her to get on with her life. That she was never going to see you again. You were dead and gone. Finally, she believed all this advice. A young man moved in from Chester County about a year ago. Six months later he began to call upon Becky, and he eventually won her heart. They had a real big wedding. Everyone was there and we certainly ate and drank our share. I'm sorry, James. Sorry.

"It's sad, but you really can't blame her. Four and a half years is a long time to wait without ever hearing a word. If you had just sent word once you got back to civilization. From New York, Philadelphia, even Lancaster—you might have been in time."

James shook his head in disbelief. "Since May of 1755, she's been the center of my thoughts. I can't believe my rotten luck. A week too late! What's one lousy week in a period of four and a half years? Well, in my case it was everything. I have nothing more to celebrate this night. Thanks for the party, but it's over for me."

With that, James left the tavern and was not seen for over a week. When he came back, he was a changed man. For a long period, he rarely spoke. He simply immersed himself in hacking out a farm and didn't associate with anyone in the valley. This went on for about six months, and then he reemerged as his old gregarious self, a leader in the valley, and a man that people looked up to and respected. The old Jim Smith had returned, and the valley would be a better place because of this.

Over the next several decades, James Smith would earn a prominent position in frontier Pennsylvania history with his exploits against unscrupulous Indian traders, Indian marauders, and the British government and army.

CHAPTER TWO

February 1760

In mid-February, during a break in the weather, Robert decided to take a pack full of furs across the mountains to Carlisle to trade for some needed supplies. He did the neighborly thing by stopping at the Ennis cabin to inquire if the family needed anything, or whether one of them might want to travel along with him. To his amazement, the cabin was empty, and it appeared that it had been uninhabited for at least a month. On the door was scribbled a hardly legible note: "Gone home back across the Susquehanna. Will return in the spring." It seemed strange to Robert, but something urgent must have come up, for the Ennis family had left in a hurry.

Robert continued southwestward, past the remains of the fort, which was now being resurrected by Ralph Sterrett, although not much had been accomplished yet. Then he rode over the mountain to spend the night at Robinson's Fort on Sherman's Creek. The inhabitants of the fort area greeted him warmly, and several of the men decided to join Robert on his trek across the mountain. The group left the fort shortly after dawn the next morning, and they arrived at Carlisle by late afternoon.

As usual, they quickly booked a room in Buchanan's Inn. The party from Sherman's Creek spent the evening in animated discussion with the other patrons of the inn. About eight o'clock a newcomer joined their group around the wall-wide, pleasantly burning fireplace.

The newcomer introduced himself as Joseph Bailey of the Conococheague Valley. Robert was utterly amazed at this man's bleak appearance. Although Bailey was barely in his midthirties, his hair was snowy white, the hair of a man twice his age. Joseph's eyes were sunken deep into his skull, and he was drastically underweight.

"Glad to meet a fellow survivor of our friendly neighbors to the west and the north," Joseph Bailey said half-jokingly when he was introduced to Robert. "Don't be taken back by my appearance. I just thank God that I'm back in this good old Cumberland Valley. I'm sorry to say that many of my fellow captives will remain in the St. Lawrence permanently."

"I'm sorry if I looked shocked," replied Robert. "I just have to pause and remember how people reacted to me when I showed up at Fort Bedford in the spring of 1758. I was a sorry sight, and some people wouldn't believe who I said I was.

"I hope you don't mind my abruptness, but your captivity is the subject I would like to approach. My wife, Ann Taylor, was supposed to have been taken to Caughnawaga on the St. Lawrence above Montreal in the late summer of 1757. I was hoping you might have some information about her. Just anything about her would sure help me to deal with my loss."

Joseph Bailey cast his eyes downward; he just couldn't bring himself to look Robert straight in the face.

"Yes, I remember talking to an Ann Taylor from the Tuscarora Valley shortly after she arrived in Caughnawaga. I was interested in making her acquaintance once I learned she was from a neighboring valley in Pennsylvania.

"If you won't take offense, I'll have to tell you that you would have been real proud of the way she handled herself."

Robert winced at Joseph's use of the past tense. He realized that he might not want to hear the rest of the story.

Again, Joseph Bailey spoke in the past tense. "Your wife was a comely woman, downright beautiful, even with all that she had experienced the previous year before I met her. She had that business-like gait in her walk, always had a defiant expression on her face.

"I saw Ann several times during the fall and winter of 1757-58. Like most of us, you could just tell that the lack of nourishment and severity of the weather had taken its toll. It's hard to believe that weather exists as we experienced in the St. Lawrence Valley. If you weren't healthy enough to maintain a certain body temperature, your body just shut down, and you went to sleep and never woke up.

"We thought that the first winter was severe, but we soon learned that we hadn't really experienced any real hardships. As the population of the town enlarged and the pressure from the British increased, supplies were prevented not only from moving upriver from the Gulf of St. Lawrence to Quebec and Montreal, but also downriver from the Great Lakes region. The amount of food and other supplies dwindled to almost nothing.

"We captives made a concentrated effort to produce more food during the short growing season, but the climate and weather didn't cooperate. The growing season is so much shorter in Canada than here in the Cumberland Valley.

"The second winter, 1758-59, was worse than the first. It appeared that each winter increased in severity. How any of us survived is a miracle.

"Your wife survived the first two winters, but when spring came in 1759, her beautiful face disappeared just like the winter snow. She no longer existed in that Indian town. I'm sorry; she just disappeared from our midst, like so many other poor souls."

Tears streamed down Robert's leathered cheeks as the cruel words began to sink in. There had always been some hope, but now this stranger was informing him that there was probably no reason to have any more.

Robert eventually was able to speak. "Isn't it possible that she was taken elsewhere, maybe even downriver to Montreal?" His voice trembled. "I just can't accept the fact that she simply disappeared from the face of this earth."

"I don't want to upset you anymore than I have already," Joseph said, "but you can't imagine what it was like up there. Each day, each night, people succumbed to the elements. It would be 30 to 40 degrees below zero. There was no way of disposing of the bodies. They would be frozen almost immediately. The captives who survived to the next day were required to take the frozen bodies to the edge of the village and stack them up.

"When the spring thaw occurred and the river opened up, we survivors had to struggle to push, shove, or carry the bodies to the banks of the St. Lawrence and shove them into the current. The bodies disappeared instantly into the murky waters. That sadly was the end of many of the unaccounted-for white captives.

"It was a ghastly scene straight from a frozen hell. I'm sorry to have to describe this to you. It's something that will torture me forever. I have horrible dreams about it every time I close my eyes."

A thoroughly shaken Robert regained enough composure to extend his right hand to Joseph Bailey. "I want to thank you for telling me of the probable fate of my beloved wife. I know it has to be extremely difficult for you to try to describe what transpired. I remember all too well what I experienced in captivity, and your captivity was of much greater length and undoubtedly under much worse weather and climate conditions than mine."

Robert patted Joseph on his left shoulder. "Welcome back to Central Pennsylvania and good luck in reestablishing your life in the Conococheague Valley."

Robert retreated to his room in a somber mood and began to reflect on Bailey's description. He thought to himself, "How can I accept Joseph Bailey's account of his ordeal and the alleged demise of Ann? It just doesn't seem possible that she would meet her fate in such a morbid manner. She was such a fighter; she just wouldn't give up so easily. What am I thinking, *so easily?*

"I have to face reality and realize that for her to have survived that length of time is a tribute to her legacy. My Ann was one of a kind. A real gem!

"It's certainly not the type of closure I've been seeking. However, look around you, as time goes on you have to recognize that the rate of survival on this frontier is not very high. You can't fool yourself. You've always suspected that things would end this way—not a complete ending—always room for doubt!"

Robert decided that he didn't want to spend the rest of the

evening alone. There would be plenty of time to be alone back on the Tuscarora. He finally regained his composure and headed for the tavern part of the inn.

Throughout his life, Robert had never sought the false refuge of liquor; it was part of his staunch Presbyterian upbringing. But tonight, there appeared to be a chink in his religious armor, and he sought the solace of demon rum. Only once had he given in to this temptation. That was when he celebrated with the Chippewa braves after the baggatiway match on the shores of Lake Erie during his second summer of captivity.

When Robert awoke the next morning, it appeared to him that it was almost a repeat of the morning he had experienced at Conneaut. His head appeared to be exploding, and his stomach demanded that it be emptied immediately—and it was, several times.

Robert's head still was not clear as he and the men from Sherman's Creek Valley gathered in the morning and took their furs to the trading post to exchange for the supplies that they desired. None of the group was very happy about the amount their furs brought. However, these were hard times, and the traders in Carlisle enjoyed the benefits of a monopoly in the fur trade at this time of year.

The over-the-mountain group spent a second night at the inn, but this time Robert did not yield to temptation and so did not touch a single drop of alcohol—although, after spending several sleepless hours tossing and turning, as he couldn't escape the impact of Joseph Bailey's description of life at Caughnawaga, he almost wished he had tipped a few mugs again.

When Robert and the Robinson's Fort group mounted up the next morning, they knew that they had better not dally crossing the mountain, for the nip in the air forecast snow in the near future. About a mile before reaching Sherman's Creek, the first snowflakes began to drift earthward. Within an hour, it began to snow vigorously, and the men urged their horses to increase their pace. The men were quite thankful when their noses picked up the first scent of smoke, indicating that they were just a short distance from a warm cabin and hot food.

Robert was in no hurry to return to the Tuscarora and his solitary life. Instead, he spent three days enjoying the companionship of the families within Robinson's sturdy log walls. Later, as he swung up on his horse, he promised his hosts and himself that he would return soon to enjoy their company.

Life became almost unbearable once he returned to his cabin, as it became a bleak and solitary abode. Robert became despondent. He asked himself repeatedly, "Is life worth living?"

His inner self fought back. "You can't be afraid of life and what it offers. There is no way that you can be mad with despair and simply give up. What if Joseph Bailey's assessment of Ann's plight was inaccurate and she survived? Do you want to end up like John Gray? Remember, John gave up and Hannah returned only to find that her husband gave up too soon. You can't make that mistake. Ann is a survivor and you are too. Somehow, you're going to see this through. You need to think only positive and good thoughts!"

CHAPTER THREE

March 1760

Many times during this bleak period before spring arrived in 1760, Robert thought about giving up and going home to Pineford. Going home to Pineford? Pineford hadn't been his home since the winter of 1755. "The Tuscarora Valley was my real home now and I'm staying."

He could not endure the solitude and detachment any longer. During the second week of March, he loaded up a cache of furs and headed for Robinson's again. As before, several of the men of the fort eagerly joined him in his journey across the Blue Mountain to Carlisle.

When he walked into Buchanan's, the innkeeper greeted Robert heartily. "You're in real luck! There's another Conococheague man just liberated from up on the St. Lawrence. His name's James Smith. If I were you, I would detour west to the Fort Loudoun area and locate this Smith fella. Maybe he will be able to give you more insight into what is going on in Canada. Anything is worth a try.

"From what I understand, Smith was captured clear back in 1755, while building a road for the Braddock disaster. Apparently, he was adopted by the natives just like you. Word has it he spent time in the Ohio Valley, on the Great Lakes and the St. Lawrence. So it's hard to tell what he's seen and heard."

Robert nodded. "You're absolutely right. As soon as I unload my furs, I will be heading west to Shippensburg, to Chambersburg, and on to Fort Loudoun. Perhaps this James Smith won't be able to give me anything new about the situation on the St. Lawrence, but it will be interesting to talk to someone who experienced a similar existence with the natives."

Again, sleep was difficult to achieve, but finally Robert was able to log a few hours. He was the first one up to eat a quick breakfast and bound out the door to wait until the trading post opened its doors. He quickly made his transactions and headed for Shippensburg, even if it might mean arriving there after the sun had gone down.

Robert spent an uneasy night at Fort Morris and then headed for Loudoun via Chambersburg, knowing that it would not take him a full day's ride to arrive at Loudoun. The soldiers at Fort Loudoun were well aware of the now famous James Smith, and several old-timers also remembered Robert and his travels. Everyone had an interesting morsel to share about Smith.

Directions to Smith's cabin were easy to obtain. Within an hour after sunrise, Robert guided his horse to the ford on the creek and headed for Smith's claim. It was a shorter ride than what Robert had imagined, and he soon crossed the creek again and sighted a muscular man hard at work clearing more land, actually what Robert should be doing.

"Hallo, the cabin! It's Robert Taylor from the Tuscarora looking for James Smith."

"Come on in, Robert Taylor! I'm the fella you're looking for! Welcome to the Conococheague settlement. I need a break from this boring job anyways."

Robert alighted from his horse and vigorously shook hands with James. Robert stepped back and observed, "It seems to me that I've seen a haircut like that before. About a year after you were taken, some of my neighbors, my family, and I were taken at Bigham's Fort on the Tuscarora. We were conveyed to Kittanning, and we were there when it was destroyed. After Kittanning's devastation, we were taken to the Forks of the Ohio and dispersed. I was separated from my family and then spent time at Pymatuning, Conneaut, Niagara, and finally I escaped from Buckaloons on the Allegheny River in March of 1758. The reason I have sought you out is that I have good reason to believe that my wife was at Caughnawaga. I am hoping you might be able to give me some information about the situation on the St. Lawrence."

Smith nodded politely. "Yes, I was in that vicinity for a short time. I certainly sympathize with you. A good woman is a commodity that is almost impossible to replace here on the frontier. Probably the good soldiers gleefully told you about my alleged sweetheart. My Becky said she would always wait for me. Well, she did. Up until about a week before I returned; then she couldn't wait any longer. She married some newcomer, a greenhorn. Poor bogger doesn't know the first thing about living on the frontier. Probably get himself killed by some renegade Indian.

"Sorry, I didn't mean to bring that subject up. It's just that after you survive for that period of time, you think things will be the same when you get back. I don't know what I was thinking, and nothing ever stays the same. Unless you have experienced the pangs of disappointed love, you could never understand how I feel."

"Please don't apologize," Robert said. "I know a little of what you're going through. I just figured that when I got back, my wife and kids would have returned also. Until now, I've had no such luck. Someday maybe it will happen; I just have to keep hoping for the best."

James Smith regained his composure and began to answer Robert's inquiry about Caughnawaga. "I'm not going to be much help in this area. I spent most of my captivity in the Ohio, Illinois, Indiana and Michigan territories. During the early months of last year (1759), we hunted up on the Sandusky River and down the Scioto. About April, we returned to Detroit.

"Soon after arriving at Detroit, we paddled down the Detroit River into Lake Erie. We followed the northern shore of the lake and eventually entered into the flow of the Niagara River. Very cautiously, we portaged around the falls. Once we had circumvented that dangerous portion of the river, we also avoided Fort Niagara and reentered the river above its mouth. We adhered to the southern shores of Lake Ontario as we continued eastward.

"Once we entered the flow of the St. Lawrence River our tiresome chore of paddling became easier because the river was at a good level and supported a rapid current. Around the middle of June, we arrived at our destination of Caughnawaga, an ancient Indian town about nine miles upriver from Montreal.

"I was given a significant amount of freedom to move around the area. About the first of July, I heard a rumor about a French ship with a cargo of British prisoners of war being located near Montreal. These prisoners were to be taken across the Atlantic to Europe where they were to be exchanged for French prisoners.

"Under the cloak of darkness and a summer rainstorm, I stole a canoe and paddled into the river. Once I was close enough to the ship, I abandoned the canoe and swam to the ship. I clambered up the ship and became a British prisoner of war on my own. I was quite elated with my little ploy, but General Wolfe and his forces undid my plan. Wolfe had his naval forces blockade the St. Lawrence, and the ship's captain decided to unload his human cargo at Montreal.

"I was held in Montreal for almost four months. Sometime in November, we were ferried across the river, taken overland to Fort Chambly, and loaded into a bateau. We were involved in a race with Old Man Winter because we needed to float down Lake Champlain before it froze over. We arrived at Fort Crown Point where we were officially exchanged. Again, they had to continue to move us south so we could use the Hudson River for transportation. Eventually we disembarked in New York City, and within a few weeks we were conveyed to Philadelphia. From there it was an easy journey to Carlisle and to the good old Conococheague Valley.

"I'm sure it was the same with you. During my absence, people could never determine whether I was killed back in '55 or taken captive. With my return, just about everyone in the vicinity received me with great joy. Some were taken back as to my new mode of dress, my hairstyle, my manners, my speech, and my approach towards life in general. It will take me a long, long time to erase my Indian ways. Maybe I will never lose them, and sometimes I believe some of my new ways are better than my old ones.

"The most difficult adjustment is the one that I alluded to earlier in our discussion. When I left the Conococheague in the spring of 1755 to help in the construction of a road for Braddock's ill-fated army, my sweetheart and I had decided to tie the knot once I had earned enough money. When I arrived at Loudoun, one of my first questions was about Becky. The silence that I was greeted with told me that I was not going to like the answer to my inquiry.

"No one really wanted to answer me. They couldn't even make eye contact with me. Finally I demanded an answer. 'Is she alive or dead?' 'Alive,' they said. 'Then what's the matter? I want an answer and I want it now,' I commanded.

"From the back of the room, a meek voice croaked, 'She got married last week.'

"'Last week?' I screamed. 'Why couldn't she have waited just one more week?' Now I wished I were still back on the Ohio, the Lakes, or even the St. Lawrence. My knees almost buckled, and I slammed my fist into the table with all my force.

"As I bolted out the door, some wag yelled, 'Why in heaven's name didn't you send word ahead that you were returning?' That really hit home. I just never figured that she would not wait. We were made for each other. It's too late now. What has been done is done. She is a married woman, out of bounds for me. I'll get over her, but it will take time. My mother used to tell me that time heals all wounds.

"Now, to get back to the subject of Caughnawaga... I'm truly sorry. I wish I could give you some useful information, but I was there such a short time that I really didn't get to know anyone. I wish I could be more helpful, but I don't know anything about your wife."

"That's all right," Robert replied sadly. "It was just a wild idea, a shot in the dark, that you would have made contact with her. Earlier in the year I met a Joseph Bailey from this valley; he also had been at Caughnawaga. He had seen Ann over a year ago, but said she just disappeared. He wasn't very optimistic about her survival. I can't give up; I'll never give up.

"Thank you for your time and effort, James. I hope I didn't open too many old wounds about your former sweetheart. Good luck in getting reestablished here on the Conococheague. Maybe we'll soon have peace and not have to worry about the possibility of Indian attacks."

Robert spent the night at Fort Loudoun and was on the Tuscarora Path at daybreak heading northeast and home. It took him the good part of two days to arrive back on the Tuscarora, and now he was as depressed as ever.

CHAPTER FOUR

Summer 1760

In early June, while Robert was struggling with the daily chores involved in producing his subsistence crops, a messenger approached, following the path from across the creek. The man was a stranger, but Robert welcomed him warmly, since company was a real treat.

"I'm sorry to interrupt your labor, Taylor. I am Charles Saunders. Buchanan sent me from Carlisle with a message that had arrived at his inn, and he knew you would want to hear its contents immediately."

"Thanks for making such an effort on my part. Let's go up to the cabin and refresh ourselves, and I'll see what's so important for Buchanan to send you across the mountains."

Almost immediately, tears began to trickle down Robert's cheeks as he read the short letter from his brother William:

> I know I should have written you sooner, but I just couldn't bring myself to burden you with any more grief. Mother became quite ill in mid-January, and on March 3rd, she joined our Maker. Father never was the same afterwards. He just seemed to give up, lost his zest for life. He joined Mother the afternoon of May 25th as we were working down in the pasture next to the creek. One moment he was talking and joking, and the next he was gone. There was no struggle, no apparent pain or discomfort. We just looked around, and he was on the ground—silent.
>
> We realize that due to your crops, it probably won't be

convenient for you to come to Pineford until late fall or early winter, but I wish you would consider returning across the Susquehanna for a period of time. Please consider this seriously; there is plenty of room for you here on the Swatara.

The letter went on to address other matters, but Robert couldn't focus on them. Eventually he remembered that he had a guest. "Please excuse my manners. I just got carried away with the depressing news contained in this letter. Would you care to spend the night under my roof? I have some stew I can warm up quickly if you're hungry."

Saunders smiled. "Thanks for the invite, but I'm going to head over to the fort to talk to Ralph Sterrett about some land he might want to part with. Sorry, I brought you bad news. Seems that just about all one hears anymore is bad news. Well, good luck. Maybe someday we'll end up being neighbors in this valley."

"Thank you for making the trip and thank Buchanan for sending you. Tell him I'll be across the mountains sometime in the late fall unless something else occurs."

Much of the summer went by in a blur for Robert. It was the same routine, day after day, from sunup to sundown. He faced nothing but tremendously hard and boring labor, and worst of all, no contact with other humans. One day was the same as the preceding one, and he never knew what day of the week it was or what day of the month it was.

Finally the monotony was broken on a hot, humid afternoon in late August. Robert was engaged in building an alleged animal-proof corncrib to rest on stilts about ten feet off the ground. He had labored diligently to dig eight post-holes about three feet deep, and he was involved in setting the fifth locust pole when he was alerted by a startled flock of crows that intruders were crossing the creek.

He dropped his digging iron immediately and thrust his trusty rifle on his right shoulder, just in case unfriendly humans were approaching his cabin clearing. He instinctively leaped behind a large oak tree, propped his barrel against the tree, and aimed the sight of the weapon so that it covered the path up from the creek.

A voice with an Irish brogue bellowed from near the bank of the creek. "Halo, Robert Taylor! It's Corporals Mehaffee and Kelly from Fort Lowther. Our good captain sent us with an important message."

"Come on in! It will be a real pleasure to talk to two fellow Irishmen. Let's continue up to the cabin, and I'll find some suitable refreshments for you."

Once the soldiers had begun to quench their thirst with some of Robert's good cider, Robert quizzed them about the message.

"What's so important that you gentlemen are ordered across the mountains to find me?"

"Sorry, but neither of us can read. It's all written down for your eyes only," Mehaffee answered contritely, handing the neatly folded message to Robert.

To Robert Taylor of the Tuscarora Valley, formerly of Pineford Plantation:

This is to inform you that a group of newly liberated captives has just recently arrived in Philadelphia. One white female claims to be Ann Taylor, the wife of Robert Taylor of the Tuscarora Valley of Central Pennsylvania.

Unfortunately, this white female is in very poor health. She is extremely malnourished, underweight, and appears to be suffering from either consumption or tuberculosis.

We are sorry that we have to report that she is in such poor condition. We thought it best to portray an accurate description of the alleged Mrs. Taylor, so as not to give you a great deal of hope in her recovery.

It is imperative that you arrive in Philadelphia immediately so that you can supervise her recovery efforts and arrange for better living conditions and better medical care.

The rest of the message was obscured by tears as Robert wept openly, and his mind reeled from the impact of the harshness of the meaning of the words. The message-bearers looked on in disbelief, having no idea of what the message contained.

Eventually Robert regained his composure and spoke to the two soldiers once again. "I'm sorry about my reaction. A woman recently liberated from captivity with the Indians and in very poor health claims to be my wife. I'm overjoyed with the news of her return but deeply troubled by the description of her health.

"I hate to rush you on your way, but I'm packing immediately and heading east to Philadelphia. I shouldn't leave my claim at this time of year, but I have no choice. My wife's health is more important to me than any piece of land. If it's all the same with you fellas, I'll head across the mountains with you at the break of dawn. Let's get a good night's rest and be on our way bright and early."

Robert was torn by the message. He was elated that Ann had survived and was back in civilization. This is what he had dreamed about since June of 1756. On the other hand, he was worried about her condition. It would be cruel if she were to survive all these years of captivity only to lose her struggle for life back here in civilization.

Robert pushed the men and their horses harder than what they were used to, but he was in a big hurry to get to the provincial capital as soon as possible. At Carlisle, he hurriedly thanked the fort's commanding officer for sending the two men with the message, and he went quickly on his way to cross the Susquehanna River.

Luck was not with him when he arrived at the western terminal of the ferry, because the ferry was still en route to the eastern shore. This meant a delay of several precious hours until the ferry returned to the western shore and then transported Robert across the river.

The ferry's crew made a big fuss over Robert, and quickly accommodated him, despite the lateness of the hour. When the crew arrived on the eastern shore in record time, Robert paid his fee and thanked them for their extraordinary effort.

He pushed his horse almost to its limits and covered the almost ten miles to Pineford under the cover of darkness. Then it hit him. He was arriving at a Pineford that no longer housed the elder Taylors. The property had passed into the hands of his older brother, Henry, and his wife, Isabel, but he realized that was no problem. His siblings and their spouses and children would welcome him warmly.

Robert realized that he would be rousing his brother's family from their sleep, but he figured that anything as important as his mission would be easily excused. His assumption was correct; everyone in the Taylor family and Ann's family quickly rallied and assembled at the old Taylor farmhouse.

More questions than what Robert had answers to were thrown his way, and he attempted to answer as many as he could. Before too long, exhaustion caught up with the whole Taylor clan, and they returned to their own homes and beds, vowing to meet again early the next day.

With the dawning of a new day, arrangements for Robert's journey were laid out. In addition to the plans, more questions were posed: Where exactly were the liberated captives? How long would they stay? Where would Robert stay? Would he be able to find a doctor to treat whatever ailments plagued Ann? Would she be able to be moved back to the Swatara and eventually to the Tuscarora Valley?

Most of these questions could not be answered until Robert arrived in Philadelphia and was able to assess the situation. One thing that was settled quickly was that Robert would not travel by horseback, but instead in a borrowed buggy. The family would try to make Ann as comfortable as possible whenever she was able to travel.

CHAPTER FIVE

Late Summer 1760

A messenger was immediately sent to Cousin John Taylor, with whom Robert had stayed back in 1758 when he appeared before the Provincial Council. The Taylors knew he would use his considerable influence to aid his western cousins in their hour of need.

Anticipating that travel by horse and buggy would prolong the journey, Robert left two days later as dawn was breaking. He only stopped to feed and water his horse and arrived at John Taylor's late in the evening.

The Taylors were well prepared for Robert's arrival, and his horse was immediately attended. They quickly addressed Robert's needs and knowing his state of weariness, soon escorted him upstairs to a bedroom. Before he was ready to leave the comfort of his mattress, they notified him that breakfast awaited him downstairs.

During the course of the meal, Cousin John outlined the remaining details of Robert's journey. John Taylor had arranged lodging for Robert near the Pennsylvania Hospital, where Ann was convalescing.

"I'm arranging lodging for you at the establishment of one of my business associates. It's located at High and Water Streets, near the Indian King, and is called "Le Trembleur," meaning "The Quaker." Its owner is Obadiah Bourne, a sea captain who owned a privateer (a merchant ship authorized by the government to attack and capture enemy vessels) by the same name. During King George's war, Bourne struck terror into the hearts and minds of the French and Spanish.

"If you're really hungry some evening, I suggest you continue down High Street to Biddle Alley, just east of Third Street, and dine at John Biddle's Indian King. Many believe that Biddle serves the best meals in town. Since they don't dispense liquor after eleven at night, you might observe the mayor and corporation leaders there at dinner. Somehow I don't believe that food will be an issue for you while you are in Philadelphia."

John Taylor then handed Robert several letters of introduction in case he needed additional services. "I wish you the best of luck. And if you need anything, and I mean *anything*, just ask and we'll do everything within our power to be of assistance."

Robert thanked John Taylor and his family and then headed east, retracing his route of July of 1758. He soon recognized that the City of Brotherly Love had expanded tremendously since his previous visit. The increase in population led to a great increase in the traffic, noise, and pollution in the city's busy streets.

He arrived at Le Trembleur in late afternoon and quickly registered.

Although Robert was anxious to join Ann's side, he realized he was nearly exhausted. After a filling meal, he climbed the stairs to his bedroom and soon was fast asleep. The arrival of his bedmate at a late hour went unnoticed by Robert as he slept soundly until his need to eliminate bodily fluids awakened him.

After a quick breakfast, he headed down towards the riverfront. Robert attempted to report to the commanding officer of the military installation known as the "British Barracks." These army quarters had been constructed in 1757 in the area known as the Northern Liberties, around the present Third and Green Streets. The Assembly had originally called for the new Royal American Regiment to be quartered in inns, but the innkeepers refused to house the soldiers at the fee legislated by the Assembly.

The Royal Americans had processed Ann's official reentry to the civilized world. Major William Carpenter, the commanding officer of the British Barracks was not available, and Robert was directed to Lieutenant Martin Draper.

After brief introductions, the young officer attempted to impress Robert with his ability and his considerable knowledge of the military operations that aided in liberating the captives from the St. Lawrence Valley.

"The liberation of your wife and her fellow captives is the result of the British army's perseverance, discipline, tactics, superior numbers, and superb military leadership.

"The British victory at Quebec in late 1759 was not completely decisive for the control of Canada. French General Chevalier de Levis took advantage of winter's descent on the St. Lawrence Valley, which ice-locked the river and left the scurvy-ridden and outnumbered British under Brig. General James Murray in a precarious position. On April 20, when the spring thaw was well along, Levis led a force of over seven thousand men towards Quebec. He moved downriver and unsuccessfully attempted to retake the former French stronghold. It appears that this second battle of Quebec was a much bloodier affair than the first battle.

"Once the ice broke in the spring, reinforcements arrived with large amounts of supplies. In the early months of this year, three superior British armies converged upon the final French citadel, Montreal.

"General James Abercrombie had unsuccessfully attempted to invade Canada in 1758, which had earned him the nickname "Mrs. Nabbycrombie, but due to Lord William Amherst's victories in July of last year over Fort Carillon and Fort St-Frederic at Crown Point, the central route to Canada had finally been opened. General William Haviland took advantage of these victories and followed the Lake Champlain route north through Fort Chambly to the outskirts of Montreal.

"Lord Jeffery Amherst left Fort Oswego, located on the southeast corner of Lake Ontario, across the lake to Fort Frontenac, which had been captured by Lieutenant Colonel John Bradstreet in 1758, and started down the St. Lawrence River. Fort Levis and Fort La Galette, on opposite banks of the river, fell to the British.

"One important objective was met when Amherst's troops captured the Indian town of Caughnawaga located on the opposite bank and upriver from Montreal. It appears that during the course of the French and Indian War, many white captives were guests in this formidable Native American haven. Lachine, just downriver from the mouth of the Ottawa River, fell to Amherst's onslaught as well.

"The third British army, supported by strong naval forces under Murray, moved up the St. Lawrence Valley from Quebec. Along the way, this army surrounded Chevalier de Levis' relief forces and forced them to surrender.

"Currently (September 1760), Governor General Pierre de Rigaud de Vaudreuil de Cavagnial, marquis de Vaudreuil, is hard pressed to end the struggle and allow Montreal to capitulate. When the signing of the copies of surrender is accomplished, all of Canada will surrender as well.

"Our conquering general, Jeffery Amherst, attributed our sensational future victory to military efficiency as he proclaimed, 'I believe that never have three armies, that set out from different and very distant parts from each other, and later were joined in the center, as was intended, did better than we did. These armies' movements could not fail of having the effect of which we have just now seen.'

"The capture of Caughnawaga and Lachine and, of course, Montreal itself has led and will lead to the liberation of huge numbers of whites who had been taken captive after hostilities broke out in the fall of 1755.

"From what I have been able to piece together, Ann Taylor was originally held at Caughnawaga. In the winter of 1758-59, she was moved to Lachine. This relocation perhaps saved her life, because food and shelter were apparently in greater supply than that found in Caughnawaga. Perhaps it was because Lachine was closer to Montreal, and it was easier for this town to receive food and supplies from the outreaches of the province of New York, especially the Lake Champlain valley.

"When Lachine was liberated this spring, those captives who were able were routed back to the English colonies for processing as soon as transportation could be secured. Due to Ann Taylor's poor health, the army doctors felt it was in her best interests to keep her under their care in the north until she had recovered satisfactorily. Unfortunately her condition did not improve rapidly, but a decision was made for her to be transported southward in the hopes that the warmer weather and climate would speed her recovery.

"From Lachine, Ann Taylor was ferried across the St. Lawrence River to La Prairie and overland to Fort Chambly, located just below where the Richelieu River begins to flow northward to the St. Lawrence River. The group then headed south, using the waters of Lake Champlain, to Fort St-Jean, Isle-aux-Noix, Isle La Motte, Grand Isle, Valcour Isle, and Split Rock, and to Fort St-Frederic, now renamed Crown Point. Newly named Fort Ticonderoga was her next destination, followed by Rogers Rock, and then Fort George at the end of Lake George. She was taken overland to Fort Edward, which allowed her to use the Hudson River, through Albany and on to New York City.

"When it was ascertained that Mrs. Taylor had resided in Central Pennsylvania, she was sent overland to her present residence of Philadelphia. She has experienced a tremendous amount of hardship over the last four years. I am so sorry that she is not in better health. Perhaps when she arrives among her own people and familiar surroundings, she will respond and her condition will improve.

"I want to wish you and your wife the best in reestablishing your lives back in Central Pennsylvania. If it were within my powers, I would offer greater assistance, but we are limited in what we can do. I will instruct Corporal Wilson to escort you to the wing of the building where your wife is housed. How soon she can be moved will be in the hands of her attending doctor."

Robert was grateful for the information. "I certainly thank you for your time in explaining in such great detail my wife's path from captivity to her present surroundings. My expectations of my wife's condition are somewhat diminished; it is a miracle that she survived. Earlier this spring I was informed by another Caughnawaga survivor that Ann had just disappeared, and that she probably was just another wintertime casualty. He gave me no hope for her survival whatsoever. Seeing her alive is more than I ever dreamed. Again, thank you for your efforts."

The young lieutenant then bellowed, "Corporal Wilson, please escort Mr. Taylor to see his wife in the east wing of the Pennsylvania Hospital. Stay with him and see if he needs anything."

As the corporal guided Robert through the streets, he acquainted Robert with the background of the Pennsylvania Hospital.

"Dr. Thomas Bond first conceived of a charity hospital for Philadelphia, designed after those found in London and Paris. Ben Franklin publicized the concept in his *Pennsylvania Gazette* and many leading Quakers of the city backed Bond's project. In 1752 the Hospital opened its temporary quarters in the residence of the late Justice John Kinsey, located on the southeast corner of Fifth and High Streets.

"In 1754 the permanent site for the hospital was acquired between Eighth and Ninth Streets on the north side of Pine Street. The construction of the east wing where your wife is located began in 1755 and was completed in 1756.

"Well, here we are, just across the street. I'll escort you to your wife's room, and wait to see if there is anything else I can do for you."

Robert was apprehensive about this first contact with Ann. He knew that under no circumstances must he show any shock or any undue concern so as not to upset her. This first encounter would be of utmost importance to them both. He needed to convey to her that no matter what her condition was or how she looked, he still loved her very, very much.

The corporal led Robert through a labyrinth of halls and passages until they arrived in a large, high-ceilinged, depressing-looking room, filled to overflowing with women lying on what passed as cots. The soldier pointed to the next to last cot on the right side of the room, indicating that this was where Robert would find Ann.

The room reeked of illness and death, and Robert's nose and stomach rebelled against the unsavory odors that greeted him as he unsteadily approached Ann's cot. He struggled to formulate an appropriate greeting, but his thoughts would not coordinate into an intelligent sequence filled with sensitivity. Everything that he thought of seemed too rehearsed, and before he was prepared, he was standing over the woman he loved.

The figure on the cot had her back to Robert, and in the dim light it was difficult to ascertain just who occupied the bed. The form stirred slightly, as the soft footsteps apparently had been perceived, and turned to acknowledge the intruder, although the eyes did not open immediately.

Shock permeated Robert's entire system at what he immediately observed. His knees almost buckled and his head wanted to spin, but he fought off these weaknesses. There was no way he could show that anything was out of the ordinary. This person was extremely emaciated and ghastly-looking. Her beautiful chestnut hair that once shone so radiantly in the sunlight had lost its luster and was a dull, premature gray. Her hair looked as if it had not seen a comb or brush for several days. This simply could not be his beautiful Ann. However, deep within, he knew it was she. In his worst nightmares, he could never have dreamed such an immense calamity could have fallen upon his loved one.

The form in the cot began to shake and cough convulsively. A deep, hacking cough projected deep pain and suffering. Robert winced as he watched her catch the bloody phlegm in a rag and dispose of it.

He waited until the hacking and convulsions subsided; then he moved closer and around to the other side of the bed so they could view each other once Ann had recovered.

Robert recuperated from the initial shock and looked down lovingly upon his very infirm wife. She seemed so vulnerable that he wanted to take her into his arms and comfort her. Instead he took her hand and whispered, "Ann, my darling, it's Robert. I'm here to take you home and make you well."

Just barely, he observed a flicker of her eyelids. He smiled as he stroked her hair and gently caressed her once beautiful face. Some time lapsed before Ann realized there was a visitor in her midst. She reacted slowly, uncertainly, in her attempt to focus on the figure that hovered over her. Her lips trembled, and slowly she spoke in a barely audible murmur, "Oh my God, Robert! Where did you come from? Oh, Robert, at last we're together." She struggled to gain a more advantageous or more comfortable position on her bed and then hesitantly continued. "I never thought I'd hear your firm voice again. God, how I have missed you, I love you so."

"Oh, Ann, my wonderful Ann, how I've missed you too. I love you so very much. I never thought I would have the pleasure of holding you again." Impulsively he went to his knees, and ever so gently, squeezed her to him. Uncertain and trembling, he drew her frail body to his chest.

He withdrew from her so that he could observe her. She attempted to smile, a very weary smile, but one that Robert would have recognized anywhere.

When Ann winced with pain, he realized that what they both desired was out of the question now. Robert relaxed his grip on her but continued to hold her as gently as possible. For the longest time, they were satisfied, but at the same time, overjoyed, just to gaze into each other's eyes. Her eyes held steady on his own eyes, and Robert broke into a huge smile.

Her eyes continued to absorb him, enveloping him. She spoke quietly, "Let me look at you, just look at you." She feebly reached for his head and ran her fingertips over the scar that he had acquired that terrible day at Bigham's. "It looks as though you're going to carry that little memento to your grave." Then she withdrew her hand as though the effort had exhausted her.

"Just lay back and relax, just enjoy the moment," Robert told her. "I'm going to get you out of here and we'll have all the time we want to just look at each other."

"Oh, Robert, I'm afraid I'm beyond salvage. I'm in such dreadful condition; I don't know how I'm ever going to survive."

Robert took her face in his hands, "Don't you ever talk or

think like that. You are going to live. We're going to live to an old age together back on the Tuscarora."

Then he noticed an irritated grimace on her face. He realized that something was bothering her, and immediately guessed what it was. This was the moment he had dreaded and he was not sure how to react. Then the question came, and he wanted to ignore it, but he knew there was no way out. Robert had the crazy urge to ease her mind and tell her the children had returned and were waiting for them back at Pineford with their families, but he knew that it would be far worse for her when she found out the truth later.

Her lips trembled as she asked, "What about Robbie and Elizabeth? Are they well? Are they at home waiting on us?"

Fear and bewilderment remained in her eyes. Robert's eyes began to well up with tears, and she knew immediately what the answer was going to be. Through his own sobs, Robert was barely able to vocalize, "I'm sorry, so very sorry. I have traveled as far as the Forks of the Ohio and unfortunately, I was not able to find them. I've tried and tried, but no luck. I haven't given up and I never will. George Crogan and some of the army personnel are keeping their eyes open for them. But I'm sorry, I haven't had any luck."

Ann dropped her head, and Robert reached out to hold her. Her body went limp as the deep, terrible sobs began. The sobs became incessant, and then she began to wail. "The prospect of seeing you and the children was what kept me going all these years. I didn't want to let you down. I promised you and them that I would return. It's so useless, so hopeless, I don't want to continue without them."

Robert held her as she wept convulsively. It was all he could do, all he really wanted to do. Eventually two of the hospital staff arrived and concluded that it would be best if Robert were to leave and return tomorrow.

Robert did not argue with them. He thanked them for their attendance and excused himself. Before taking his leave, he gently stroked Ann's hair, and whispered, "I love you, Ann.

Please don't give up the fight and leave me. I need you." He hesitated for a moment, and then added, "I'll return tomorrow, and we'll discuss plans for getting you out of here and back home."

Robert then ran down the hall, down the steps, and out the door into the street. He quickly left the street and found the solitude of a garden in the back of the hospital.

He muttered to himself, "There must be something I can do. I can't lose her, not again, not ever again. I can nurse her back to health if she'll just give me the chance. Why, oh why, did she have to ask that question so soon? But I guess if I were in her place, I would have done the same."

Robert sat on a bench for a long time. Then he realized the sun was about to set. He had not eaten since early that morning and even under these forlorn circumstances, he knew he had to eat in order to maintain his strength. It was going to be a long up-hill battle and he would need all the strength he could muster.

Before sliding into bed, Robert dropped to his knees and prayed a prayer of thanks for Ann's return. Her return had been his ardent prayer since they were separated on that bleak day at the Forks of the Ohio in late 1756. Sleep eluded Robert for most of the night; finally near dawn he collapsed into a nightmarish slumber, which lasted only about forty minutes. It wasn't much rest, but he arose ready to meet the challenges of a new day. On this day he would begin the struggle to return Ann to a life of normalcy.

CHAPTER SIX

September 1760
Pennsylvania Hospital

After a brief breakfast, Robert headed for the hospital. He wanted to meet Ann's attending physican as soon as possible to arrange for an individual treatment schedule to accelerate her recovery.

This time, when he arrived at the hospital, he was bombarded with a flurry of queries by the matron who manned the front desk. Robert handled the inquiries as best he could, but was simply unable to answer many of the questions. When the matron appeared satisfied with the information she was able to glean from him, she stated flatly, "Come with me and I'll introduce you to your wife's attending physican, Dr. Lawrence Henry."

Dr. Lawrence Henry was a portly man, probably in his late forties, who, judging by his complexion, was unaccustomed to enjoying the radiance of sunlight. Dr. Henry greeted Robert heartily and asked him to take a seat.

"I understand you saw your wife yesterday. As you readily observed, she is in a very fragile condition. How she has survived this far is almost unbelievable. You have a remarkable wife, Robert. She has undoubtedly just willed herself to overcome all odds in order to return to her home and family. Any lesser being would now be with her Maker.

"Modern medicine doesn't have many answers in regards to preserving an emaciated human in the deplorable condition that Ann is currently facing. We are doing everything possible to make her comfortable and to hasten her convalescence. However, we must caution you, there are times when the body's physical capacity to overcome extreme adversities is limited.

"The practice of medicine can hardly be classed as an exact science. Owing to the limitations of present medical knowledge, absolute precision in the effectiveness of the measures employed in therapy is impossible. We have to be flexible in anticipating unpredictable changes in the patient's therapeutic requirements.

"Thus far, we have taken measures designed to provide relief from Ann's discomfort and to improve her resistance against her afflictions and to minimize their effects. She needs total bed rest. A modified diet with the inclusion of nutritional elements and dietary supplements has been provided. A normal fluid balance has been introduced for the reduction of excessive dehydration. Provisions have been made for bathing and the use of other facilities for maintaining cleanliness of all areas of her body.

"Ann tends to be uncommunicative regarding her discomforts and disabilities. We have attempted to draw her out and have diligently questioned her in regards to obtaining information of diagnostic value. However, we have avoided overzealous questioning in that it is distinctly disadvantageous to Ann's morale."

Robert had listened in silence as Dr. Henry had articulately described his efforts to save Ann's life. He drew in a deep breath, exhaled sharply, and then acknowledged, "Dr. Henry, I greatly appreciate all the exceptional efforts which you and your staff have performed these last few weeks. Besides acute malnutrition, serious weight loss, and chronic fatigue, what other ailments confront Ann?"

"Robert, I fear that she suffers from an acute infection of the lungs. Unfortunately, her symptoms are insidious and the early stages seldom suggest the lungs as the seat of the disease. Ann has lost considerable weight. Although in most cases she feels very well upon rising in the morning, she fatigues a little more easily than previously, especially in the afternoon. She has become a trifle pale. Her appetite has gradually begun to fail, and at times she suffers from indigestion. Although her temperature is normal in the morning, it is elevated each afternoon. Before long, the clearing of her throat every morning, will develop into a full cough."

Robert interrupted, "You're informing me that Ann has galloping consumption, aren't you? She just can't have that terrible disease! She just can't!"

"I'm sorry, Robert. All the early symptoms are there. As the disease progresses, the indigestion may increase markedly. Abdominal pain or even vomiting may occur after meals. The cough gradually will become more troublesome, and the sputum will increase. Ann will develop night sweats, and will rapidly lose more weight and strength."

Tears welled within Robert's eyes. "Isn't there anything that can be done to save her?"

"I wouldn't give up hope, Robert. The course of this chronic disease is marked by ups and downs. When the healing process gains the ascendancy, Ann will feel better. When the ulcerative process progresses, she will feel worse. Therefore, it might go on for months or even years, until either the disease stops or an acute exacerbation of the trouble, such as tuberculous broncho-pneumomia, enters the scene.

"In some cases the cavity formation is arrested and the patient is able to continue a fairly normal life for many years. But I must caution you, you must be very patient, very diligent, in your activities concerning certain contacts with Ann, because the disease could spread to you, or anyone else who doesn't take the necessary precautions."

"I think I know what you're attempting to tell me. I'll do anything within my power to prolong her life. Anything!"

"I knew that would be the attitude that you would take. Now, let's get down to basics.

"Ann will need to live in an environment where complete relaxation and rest are possible. Sanatorium treatment for several months until the lesion is quiescent is the most desirable situation. Our principal objective will be to put the infected lung at rest as long as the infection is active. As long as fever persists and for several additional months, complete bed rest is mandatory. Mental rest is as important as physical rest. Proper posture in bed will ease the difficulty attending motionless existence.

"Ann should be segregated because of the production of infective sputum. She will have to be cared for by individuals trained in the practice of isolation techniques. Precautions are necessary for the protection of others, including covering the mouth and nose while coughing or sneezing. Most important is the careful and quick disposal of materials contaminated by sputum or other secretions.

"The individuals involved in Ann's care should always practice protective precautions against open contact with contaminated materials. They should wear protective masks when in her vicinity and take pains to avoid unnecessary contact with Ann or any of her objects. When such contact is necessary, individuals should use a protective gown and perform a careful lavage of their hands after the removal of the gown and the conclusion of contact."

"I realize it's going to be a long hard road to recovery," Robert conceded, "but I know I can make the necessary sacrifices to bring her back. I've gone through too much to give up now."

"I believe you, Robert Taylor. Anyone who has been able to overcome and survive what you have been through will be able to see this through also.

"One more important factor: if Ann should hemorrrhage while she is up and about, she should be put to bed immediately and immobilized as completely as possible. She should lie on the infected side, and any movement should be limited as much as possible. If the blood is bright red, the bleeding is probably venous in origin and very likely will cease spontaneously.

"Her cough may be alleviated by warm poultices on the chest and by steam inhalations. The inhalation mixture can be prepared by boiling at bedside a solution containing creosote, turpentine, and benzoic tincture in equal parts, and one teaspoon of this mixture should be added to one pint of water.

"The advent of high fever may be relieved by the application of cool sponge baths. Of course, her diet is of the utmost importance in the maintenance of her general health and her resistance to infection. She should benefit from the stimulation of cold, fresh air. Her bed should be wheeled outdoors during the day, and adequate ventilation of the bedroom should be provided during the night.

"I know that you will not be able to remember everything that I have been bombarding you with, so I'll have one of the matrons write the instructions down, and then you'll have them to follow and refer to."

"Is it possible for me to see Ann at this time?" inquired Robert.

"I see no reason not to. Just don't excite her. Be very patient, and if she begins to sob uncontrollably, call for an aide to assist you. We can't afford for her to become too upset.

Now, get upstairs and see her, and good luck. Just be careful and try not to make contact with her nose or mouth."

As Robert was about to enter Ann's ward, an attendant approached Robert and provided him with a crude gown and mask. He thanked the attendant for the preventive clothing and entered the ward. Ann was again lying on her side, which allowed her to face the window, and she did not see Robert approach.

He hoped she was sleeping and not lying there agonizing and grieving over the disturbing reality that her babies had not been liberated as she had been. During his almost sleepless night, Robert had rationalized that the monumental challenge facing Ann's recovery was not to conquer the dreaded disease that she had contracted, but surpassing any mental aberrations that might develop, and to reverse her negative thoughts about her survival since the children had not returned yet.

Any abnormalities of mood or unusual behavior, especially acute anxiety, must be addressed as a grave situation. Robert concluded that the correct interpretation of these manifestations was very important, for he surmised that it might well determine the success or failure of treatment.

Robert deduced that it was important that Ann be informed adequately regarding her medical problems. Such information should be wholly reliable and easy for her to comprehend. In this early stage of her illness, she should not be bombarded by a wealth of medical data, but informed just enough to ensure her cooperation and confidence in the procedures.

Pushing all those thoughts from his mind, he knelt beside her bed and whispered her name. He attempted to be upbeat. "Hi there, blue eyes. It's your friendly Irish frontiersman, back to tell you how much he loves you."

Her reaction was immediate. She had not been sleeping as he had hoped, but rather, reflecting about her circumstances. With some labor she shifted on her bed from her right hip onto her left hip, so that she was now facing Robert.

A smile slid across her face. Just for a moment, Robert saw some of the old Ann emerge through her pain. The blue eyes did not flash as they used to, but they widened in recognition, and it stirred him to see her react in this manner.

"Oh, Robert, you're back. During the night, I was afraid that your visit was all a dream and you weren't here. I was so afraid that I was losing my mind. Thank God you returned today."

He leaned forward and kissed her on the forehead. "I wish I could taste your sweet lips, but the doctor told me that I have to wait a few days before we have such intimate contact. We'll just have be patient and enjoy just holding each other and gazing into each other's eyes."

Robert stroked her hair, wrapped his arms around her, and gently held her close. Very softly, she murmured, "Oh, Robert, it feels so good to have you hold me. My darling, why didn't you come sooner?"

"I stopped to confer with your physician," he explained. "I needed to get an exact diagnosis of your condition and to find out what remedies he is recommending. We concur that we need to remove you from this place and get you where we can speed up your recovery."

"And what did he tell you of my chances for recovery? How

long do I have to live? I know quite well that most people do not recover from this type of illness. To tell you the truth, I am not sure that I really want to recover. Without my children beside me, I don't really care what happens to me."

"Ann, please don't talk like that. I need you—doesn't that matter to you? We will have each other. Remember, the war is almost over. When it ends, the British will force the Indians to return their white captives. George Croghan has been working towards that end over the past several years. Just don't give up. Don't give up hope. You and I have returned—why not our children as well?"

"I've been through too much. I just can't continue forever. Time is running out for me." She lifted her chin towards him. A few drops of sweat formed on the bridge of her nose and her forehead. He saw the once glorious blue eyes fill up with tears, and she began to tremble and to sob uncontrollably.

When the tremors had subsided into a low sobbing, Robert got up from the bedside and summoned an attendant, who in turn sought the doctor. About an hour later Dr. Henry arrived. His examination was brief. He searched briefly in his bag and produced a vial of white powder. "Mix this with water and give it to her," he said. "It will make her sleep soundly through the night. I'll come again in the morning to check on her."

Robert walked Dr. Henry to the door. Robert spoke softly so only the doctor could hear. "Doctor Henry, the one therapy that you haven't mentioned is bleeding. I will tell you right now that I will not allow you to induce that barbaric practice for my wife. I lived with the natives for nearly two years, and for all their alleged savagery, I never saw that fiendish remedy utilized. "

The doctor replied, "I'm glad that you have taken that stand because I am not an advocate of that antiquated practice, although some physicians in this colony, in this very city, such as the esteemed Dr. Benjamin Rush, are strong proponents of this remedy. To me, bloodletting is a folly of the past. Bleeding has been used to reduce excess circulation, to slow the pulse, and to reduce irritation. One of the reasons that this practice has been continued is that the procedure actually is beneficial in some circumstances, including reducing fluid overload to avoid heart failure. None of these circumstances pertain to Ann. So put your mind at ease. I assure you that bleeding will not be a part of Ann's recovery program.

"I'd suggest that you take her out of this place as soon as you can make arrangements to find a quiet, isolated situation for her. It might work wonders for her. Anything is worth a try."

The distraught husband turned and walked back into the darkened room. He mixed the vial of white powder in a tin of water and gave it to Ann. She drank it slowly. A few minutes later, her breathing diminished, then evened, and she was asleep.

Robert sat by the bedside watching her for a long time. He leaned over Ann's prone form and kissed her lightly on her forehead. "Sleep well, my love," he said and went out into the hall and down the stairs. After closing the outside door, he descended the steps and went out into the street.

Nightfall had come, and the moon was just on the rise. He began walking, moving quietly and aimlessly through the streets, attempting to conceive a plan. He was confused. Before he realized it, he was down on the waterfront, walking along the docks. Being there helped to clarify his thinking process as his mind left behind his current problems and took him back to July of 1758 when he first observed this setting. He spent about an hour walking along the waterfront, and finally he decided he should walk west and find some food at his city abode.

This night was a repeat of the previous one, as he tossed and turned hour after hour. He awoke in a state of frustrated weariness, in dire need of a good night's rest. He wouldn't allow himself to dwell upon his own problems. Ann was the one facing the real demons, the trials and tribulations of a very serious illness. It was up to him to remove her from the hospital and arrange for a quiet, peaceful, sanitary, isolated locale where she could recover and begin to lead the good life that they had always dreamed of.

He penned letters to John Taylor, Ann's parents, his sisters, and brother William. He informed them of how he found Ann and what type of care she would require, and asked whether they could aid him in finding a quiet spot where Ann could convalesce and if they could set up travel arrangements for them to return to the Swatara. He wanted to remove Ann from the hospital as soon as he could, not because they weren't treating her properly but because he felt that her recovery process would accelerate if she were in different surroundings.

This time she was watching the door when he entered the ward, perhaps an indication that her mood was changing. They greeted each other warmly. Then he began to unfold his plan. "I'm getting you out of here as soon as possible. It will be a long, uncomfortable journey and a few unfortunate things could happen, but we're going back to the Swatara soon."

He could tell that something else was on her mind. "But what about returning home, to the Tuscarora?"

"That will come, but it will take time. We must be patient. We can't overdo it and harm your chances for recovery. I'll tell you all the plans later. There are still some details to be worked out. It probably will be at least another week. In the meantime, you will improve and become stronger, making it easier to make the trip."

He held her briefly, feeling the warmth and the hope each gave the other. It was good therapy for him; he hoped it was the same for her. As he held her gaunt body next to his, he wondered, "How had she maintained the stamina to withstand the trek from the St. Lawrence region?"

In his mind, he went over the many details of the proposed trip to the Swatara Valley. He struggled with the thought that he might be upsetting her by pushing the idea of returning home so soon. He vowed no matter what, they would return home together.

Eventually she drifted off to an uneasy sleep. He sat by her side, holding her hand, wishing he could do more, but thankful that he was able to be with her after all those miserable, frustrating years of separation.

This was how they spent each day. He knew she needed deep,

uninterrupted sleep, so when she went to sleep, he refused to bother her and allowed her to sleep most of the day away. He wouldn't allow her to wallow in self-pity, but there were times when the tears came, usually welling up slowly. To him, they were the balm that meant that healing, both physically and mentally, had begun.

Occasionally the thing he feared the most would occur: Her incessant sobbing would lead to a coughing spell. She knew the dangers involved in expelling those tissues, and guarded her nose and mouth with great care. The production of infective sputum and the careful disposal of the contaminated materials were of paramount importance, and Robert attended to the task diligently. He attempted to use his protective mask throughout most of his visitations, but there were times when it limited his intimacy, and he removed it.

In due time, he received answers to the letters that he had sent to the west. All the arrangements were in order, so it was just a matter of determining when Ann was stable enough to make the trip. He confronted Dr. Henry about setting a date for Ann's departure. The doctor was hesitant to do so, but eventually advised Robert to take her home as soon as the weather was favorable.

Then another miracle unfolded in the war against France. One afternoon in late September, when Ann had just fallen asleep and Robert wasn't too far from following her into dreamland, huge explosions erupted near the British Barracks and down near the wharves, startling them from their naps. The explosions continued for a lengthy period. Before long, Robert and Ann could hear cheering and celebrations coming from the streets below them. Robert's curiosity finally got the best of him, and he went down the stairs to inquire as to what caused the commotion.

He returned with a huge smile on his face. Well, at last it happened. The British forces had taken Montreal. The French dominion in Canada ended on September 9 when Vaudreuil's forces surrendered to Amherst. Maybe this would help the situation with Robbie and Elizabeth. Surely, this surrender would mean the liberation of more white captives, not only from the St. Lawrence region, but from the Lakes and the Ohio as well.

The celebration continued well into the night. Huge bonfires blazed until dawn; the smoke from the fires often blotted out the moon. The taverns stayed busy throughout the night, because the usual mode of conducting business was cast by the wayside. Many a man was unable to function normally the next morning, as headaches were the norm that day.

The surrender of Montreal and all of Canada prompted many anxious moments and thoughts for the Taylors. The pressure would be placed on all Indian allies of the French in all of North America to give up their white captives. The Taylors could only dream about what might lie ahead. The news cheered Ann and improved her overall condition. But he hoped she wouldn't build herself up too much for their return. It could prove to be detrimental if the children weren't liberated in the near future.

But for now, the main concern was removing Ann from the hospital and returning her safely to her home and family on the Swatara.

Slowly, very slowly, as the month of September ran its course, Ann gradually progressed. Her breathing improved, the coughing spells became less and less frequent, the ashen color was replaced by a semi-healthy glow, she began to gain weight, and most important of all, her mental attitude towards life itself lifted.

With Ann's steady improvement, Robert set in place the cautious steppingstones to reunite her with her family. This would be a joyous homecoming, but Robert wanted to be certain that Ann was equal to the task of making the formidable journey to her family's plantation on the Swatara.

Finally, Dr. Henry agreed that Ann was capable of meeting the challenges of the bumpy, uncomfortable buggy-ride that would encompass nearly a weeklong trek just east of the Susquehanna River.

CHAPTER SEVEN

October 1760

On the first Monday of October, everything was in readiness. Robert hitched the lone horse to the buggy, loaded their few belongings, and very, very painstakingly lifted Ann into the back of the horse-drawn vehicle.

Robert glanced at the face of his wife as she lay in the back of the buggy. He had covered the floor with a thick coating of straw and placed two thick blankets over the straw to soften the impact of the uncomfortable ride facing them as they headed west over a heavily rutted road.

When Robert came to the fork in the road, which could have taken him to Pikeland Station, located on the Pickering Creek and the home of the German immigrant Zachariah Rice, he wondered how the fine German millwright was progressing. Robert had fond memories of his visit to Pickering Creek and the vast amount of knowledge he had acquired concerning the construction of millraces and production of gears to produce waterpower to turn the huge grinding wheels within a mill.

He still dreamed of constructing a significant mill on the Tuscarora. That particular dream would have to be postponed because he had more pressing problems facing him at this moment.

The difficult part of the trip was to arrange for lodging where they could be isolated from the rest of the population. Robert didn't want to risk spreading Ann's affliction to other people along the way. Again, Cousin John Taylor had come to his rescue. Once John had been informed of Ann's condition he sent word that Robert and Ann were quite welcome to spend a night, or as many nights as they might need, at the John Taylors'.

John Taylor fully understood the ramifications of the disease that threatened Ann's life. He instructed his servants in the special precautions that were needed in caring for Ann, and they performed them to the utmost of their abilities. Again, John Taylor informed Robert that whatever he needed, it would be at his disposal. Therefore, so as not to tire Ann too much, they spent two nights at Cousin John's, and then they headed towards Lancaster.

Robert was uneasy about this next stop. It was at Uncle James's farmhouse. He had wanted to decline his uncle's invitation to stop over at their farm, but he knew to do so would be an immense insult to his beloved ancient aunt and uncle.

Upon dismounting from the buggy, and before he removed Ann from the back of the buggy, he took his aunt and uncle aside and explained what exactly would be involved in caring for Ann. His aunt simply shook her head. "James and I have withstood all kinds of illnesses and diseases. When our time comes, it will be God's will. You'll always be welcome here, no matter what the circumstances." That ended any arguments, and they spent two enjoyable evenings with the elder Taylors, who reminded Robert so much of his own departed parents.

After another long day's travel, Robert finally turned the weary horse into the winding lane that led to Ann's home. Ann seemed to sense their location and lightheartedly requested, "Robert, could you please reverse my position and raise my head so that I can see all the familiar sights as we pass down the lane?"

He immediately halted the horse and walked to the back of the buggy, where, with a little effort, he carried out Ann's requests. He kept looking back over his shoulder to watch her reactions to each well-known scene as she renewed her acquaintances with old, familiar views that Ann had not observed in over five years.

Robert continually glanced at the face of his wife. She was composed, almost cheerful. He thought to himself, "She will recover. She will be well again soon. I must always be on guard to protect her and guard against any relapses."

The buggy lurched around the final bend, and the farmhouse of Ann's parents came into view, nestled in a grove of pines. Robert heard Ann gasp and attempt to raise herself into a better viewing position. "Robert, please stop. I want to sit beside you on the seat. I don't want anyone to know exactly what condition I'm in. I want to return to my former home riding like a lady, not an invalid."

Again Robert halted the horse and went around to the back of the buggy. Without much effort, he lifted Ann off the blankets, transported her to the front, and gently placed her on the seat. She propped herself up with the help of blankets which Robert removed from the back of the buggy. The smile that emerged across her face was worth all the money in the world, as far as Robert was concerned. That smile certainly lifted his spirits, and undoubtedly hers.

Robert had written to Ann's family and his own about what to expect upon their arrival on the Swatara. They had determined that the best location for Ann was probably their old, small house back on Pineford where they first lived when they were married. Robert worried about this location. This is where Robbie and Elizabeth were born. Would those memories be too much for Ann? He had never mentioned to her where they would live, so the moment of truth would soon be upon them.

He had simply requested that the two families, neighbors, and friends not overwhelm Ann with their kindness and best wishes. He knew this might be difficult for them to understand, harder yet to carry out. Ann needed her space and isolation most of the time. He had sent a complete set of rules regarding physical contact with Ann. He didn't want them to be responsible for spreading her affliction to others by not following the guidelines for prevention of this dreaded disease.

The buggy ground to a stop in front of the farmhouse. Ann's parents walked hesitantly across the yard and for the first time in nearly five years beheld their once beautiful daughter. They had been warned by Robert of Ann's appearance, and had coached each other in how to react.

Ann's parents were not very good actors. Their true feelings were transmitted to their daughter, but she simply cast them aside and ignored her mother's gasp and her father's wincing in pain when they came within a few feet of her. They had been instructed that they could gently and quickly hug her, but kissing her was strictly forbidden. Robert could understand their despair in not being able to make full contact with Ann, but those were the rules and they had better adhere to them.

Robert tenderly lifted Ann from the seat of the buggy and assisted her to the porch of the farmhouse. They moved inside to the kitchen where refreshments and an evening meal awaited them. After the meal, nightfall began approaching. Even though the travelers were weary, Robert commented, "I think we better continue our travels to Pineford where we can spend the night and not bother you."

Mrs. MacIntire responded, "There's been a change in plans. The Taylors, MacIntires, and their friends and neighbors had an old fashioned house-raising and constructed you a nice, solid, little clapboard house over on the rise overlooking the creek. We thought it would be more convenient if you were closer to our home, and we could look after you somewhat easier."

Robert and Ann looked at each other in surprise, but in a way they were probably relieved that they didn't have to continue their travels. Robert was pleased that this news eliminated the problem of Ann's reaction to returning to the birthplace of Robbie and Elizabeth.

Father MacIntire said, "Come on, I know you're both exhausted. Earlier in the day I built a fire to take off the chill, so it should be nice and comfortable in there by now. We constructed the bedroom so that its two windows would provide good cross-ventilation and give you nice fresh air whenever the need arises.

"We tried to think of everything you would need, but there have to be items that we omitted. Whatever your needs are, just state them and we'll try to resolve them. Now try to get a good night's rest, and we'll see you in the morning for breakfast. I'd imagine if Ann is up to it, some of the family will be dropping by to say hello."

The MacIntires returned to the farmhouse, and Robert and Ann gave their new home a quick inspection. "This makes me feel like a bride all over again," Ann sighed. "If I weren't afraid of the consequences, I would like to treated like a bride again. But that's only wishful thinking. I do love you, my darling."

"And I love you too. You must be exhausted. We can't allow you to become too tired. You seem to be feeling quite well. We don't need for you to suffer a relapse. Now, off to bed. Notice there are two beds, so we won't even be tempted to perform what you were alluding to a while ago. See you in the morning, unless you need something during the night. Please don't be afraid to summon me if you need anything."

Robert slept well that night, although on two occasions he did leave his bed to check on Ann. She appeared to be resting quite well, and when he awoke in the morning he allowed her to continue in bed until she awoke herself.

CHAPTER EIGHT

October 1760
England

Another major event of 1760 that would affect Pennsylvania, all the colonies, and the rest of the world was the death of King George II, who had ruled Britain since 1727.

He was the king who had appointed William Pitt as prime minister, and it was Pitt's strategy that had brought victory in the war against the French and Indians in the American colonies.

King George's successor was his grandson, George William Frederick. This new monarch was born on June 4, 1738, and was the third British monarch of the House of Hanover of Germany, but he was the first of his line to be born in Britain and to use English as his first language.

Prince George of Wales inherited the throne upon the death of his grandfather on October 25, 1760. As George III, he was King of Great Britain and King of Ireland, and concurrently Duke of Brunswick-Luneburg, and thus Elector (and later King) of Hanover.

At the time of his coronation the new king was a bachelor, although rumors had it that he had married a Quakeress named Hannah Lightfoot on April 17, 1759. In fact, he would marry Princess Sophia Charlotte of Mecklenburg-Strelitz on September 8, 1761, whom he had not met until his wedding day. It is recorded that the king winced when he first saw the homely Charlotte, but he went ahead with the marriage anyway. To his credit, George III did not follow in his predecessors' footsteps by taking a mistress. Instead, the union produced fifteen children, more than any other in British history did. Two of his sons would become kings of the United Kingdom, one King of Hanover, and a daughter became Queen of Wurttemberg.

Unfortunately King George III's reign would be marked by bureaucratic instability and hostility of the part of rebellious American colonists. This unrest would lead to the American Revolution and the Declaration of Independence wherein King George was held personally responsible for the political and economic problems faced by the American colonies.

CHAPTER NINE

Early Winter 1760

It soon was decided that Robert would quickly return to his holdings on the Tuscarora and harvest his corn crops and any other products that had been able to withstand his absence of care and the probable ravaging of the crops by various members of the valley's animal population. Two younger members of the Swatara Valley's families joined Robert. Their prerequisites were quite simple: hard workers who could handle a rifle if the need arose.

The small expedition made the round-trip in three and one half weeks. Robert did not tarry along the path; also, the crop was not in great abundance, so the trip did not take long. He certainly didn't want to be away from Ann any longer than necessary.

Robert pitched in and aided with all the pre-winter chores on the Taylor farms and also on Ann's family farm. Most of his time was spent close to Ann. Even though she appeared to be progressing, anything could go wrong at any time.

During Robert's absence, a neighbor girl who lived two farms on down the creek had begun to come several days a week to aid in Ann's care. She too was an Ann, but her name was spelled Anne.

As the last days of November passed and the calendar moved into December, Robert at times felt somewhat uneasy in Anne's presence. The young girl's eyes seemed to follow him throughout the room, and later Robert heard her mention to Ann, "Your husband is certainly different from most of the men of this valley. I'm impressed with Robert's devotion, gentleness, and the loving care that he is administering to you."

One afternoon when the Taylors were alone and Ann appeared in an upbeat mood, she teasingly mentioned to Robert, "My handsome husband, I think you have an admirer in our midst."

Robert retorted, "What do you mean by that?"

"Our neighbor, Anne, she seems somewhat taken by you. Although she is not our maidservant, if she were, she certainly goes against the third attribute of Ben Franklin's advice about what you should find in a maidservant. 'Let thy maidservant be faithful, strong, and homely.' You have to admit she is very attractive."

"I don't want to hear any more of this nonsense. You must be running a fever and hallucinating. Never again do I want to hear any idle chatter on this subject."

"Why, my dear husband, I think you're embarrassed. But I still think she's infatuated with you."

For the majority of the Taylors and MacIntires the Christmas season on the Swatara in 1760 was a merry one. The two united families were still in a celebratory mood over the return of Ann and the fact that Ann and Robert were in the valley for Christmas for the first time since 1755. The lone exception was the Robert Taylor cottage. Even though the Taylors were surrounded by loving nieces and nephews enjoying a festive holiday atmosphere, Robert observed that what Ann was displaying concerning the celebration was all a sham. The absence of Robbie and Elizabeth tore at her heart; outwardly, she carried her despair with stoutheartedness, but inwardly she was a calamity.

At night, Robert could hear Ann sobbing and he could recognize that she was sinking deeper and deeper into depression. This was what Dr. Henry was worried about and he had warned Robert that such a condition could arise. Deep depression could be Ann's undoing. It could lead to reversing her gradual progress to normal health and instead produce an ominous reoccurrence of the dreaded pneumonia.

Robert held his breath and prayed that she could weather the tumult of depression. Then in mid-January, he was rudely awakened by a hacking cough that sent chills up and down his spine. He had heard that same despicable sound when he first saw Ann back in the hospital in Philadelphia. Robert shuddered and arose to prepare the warm poultices that Dr. Henry had suggested be administered on Ann's chest. He also anticipated the use of the steam inhalation advocated by the Philadelphia physician. These measures would be the first line of defense against the affliction.

Would this be the beginning of the end? Robert prayed and prayed that it would not be the case. Ann had fought arduously to rebound from the initial effects of the infirmity; she just couldn't give up at this stage of her recovery.

Robert had noticed the slightest change in Ann's attitude after the Christmas holidays, as had her sister; although neither of them was inclined to discuss the change, the apprehensive facial expressions between the in-laws was recognition enough.

Unfortunately, just after the Christmas celebrations, a deadly influenza had been delivered to the shores of the New World upon a ship that had docked in Philadelphia. The deadly virus spread rapidly throughout the City of Brotherly Love, out through the three original counties, and westward into Lancaster County. The Swatara Valley was not spared this virulent scourge. Everywhere in its path, the infirm, the aged, and the young were the most susceptible to its contamination.

Ann never stood a chance. In her venerable infirmity, she was one of the first to fall prey to the incurable malady. The female members of the family, and Robert, battled around the clock in a final effort to keep Ann Taylor among the living.

By the end of January, it appeared it was just a matter of time until the grim reaper claimed another infirm victim. Ann recognized the inevitable as well. Finally, on a bleak, snowy afternoon, as her mother, sisters, sister-in-law, Robert, and the neighbor Anne, were all in attendance, Ann very feebly addressed her audience.

Tearfully and haltingly, Ann endeavored to scrutinize each one as she shifted from one face to another. She finally paused when she came to Robert. "This is very difficult for me to say and probably just as difficult for you to hear, but I have several last requests to submit.

"Foremost, it is my desire to be taken back to the Tuscarora Valley to be buried. I would like my final resting place to be on the little knoll just east of our cabin so that I will be facing the Tuscarora Mountain. I enjoyed that view like no other I ever witnessed. Unfortunately, I just did not get to enjoy that panorama as many years as I would have desired. If and when the children return, they will be able to find my resting place and know that many of my final thoughts were of them.

"Secondly, if Robbie and Elizabeth do return, please look after them for me, and tell them I'm sorry I had to leave them behind, but our Maker has his own plans for me. Tell them all the good things that you can remember of me, so whatever they do carry throughout their lives, they will think fondly of me.

"My last request is that you all help Robert in this dire time for him. A woman could not have asked for a better man than my Robert. Robert, I do not wish you to live alone the rest of your life. You have many good years ahead of you, and you should have a loving companion to live with you into your old age."

Ann's eyes then shifted to Anne's tense and emotionally overwrought face. "Anne, I know that you look with great favor upon my husband, and I do not begrudge you that. Even with his scar and the remnants of his Indian hairdo, I still consider him a handsome devil. So, Anne, if you are in any way desirous of my Robert, you have my blessings. These good women are all witnesses to this statement, so that if my prophecy holds true, this man should never feel any guilt."

All the female eyes in the room fell on Robert. Robert was extremely embarrassed by his wife's assertion, and his head dropped so that his own eyes observed only his own feet. There was no way he could make any eye contact with the women in his midst.

After a few minutes of hushed silence, Ann continued, "I want to thank you from the bottom of my heart for all your kind deeds and your thoughtfulness these last few months. I know that I have been very difficult to contend with at times, but you have to remember that I am not myself, for which I am heartily sorry. Again, I thank you for everything. Now, please excuse me, but I need to rest for a while."

CHAPTER TEN

Ann's Final Days

A few days later, when Ann and Robert were alone, her great blue eyes clouded over, and she looked as if she would burst into tears. She spoke in a low, measured tone. "One of the greatest benefits God ever gave me is that he sent me you, and I thank him."

Robert nodded. "And I feel the same about you. You've been my inspiration since I first laid eyes on you."

Ann tossed feverishly and turned her head away. "I am as hot as fire—it is the fever."

He leaned over her and felt her pulse, which was certainly throbbing, and then he felt her head which was extremely warm.

The dimly lit room began to swim around her. Robert saw her face whitening, sharpening with animal fear, her eyes scanning him in turn, flashing the thoughts she did not speak. Then she looked blankly at him through her tears with the candid grace of a bewildered, disillusioned girl.

Robert's breath caught in his throat, and he attempted to keep his voice calm. "Please, don't give up. Don't leave me. I love you and need you by my side. I have loved you since I first saw you." He then realized that she was not able to hear him, and every muscle in his body was screaming to be able to aid her, but it was not to be.

Ann hemorrhaged heavily in the aftermath of a coughing seizure later that night. Additional hemorrhaging occurred intermittingly the next few days. During the following weeks, Ann grew weaker and weaker. She died quietly in her sleep.

Death apparently occurred silently, as no one heard a last gasp or cough. Robert arose from his bed to check on her just before daylight, but immediately recognized that she was no longer breathing. There were no signs of any tossing or struggle. Her eyes were closed; she looked as though she was sleeping. She was at peace with her Maker. She had passed on with dignity and grace.

Robert sat in silence for a long period, holding her hand. Eventually her sister and mother awakened and saw him sitting beside her, and they knew that the end had come. Reluctantly, the other family members were informed of Ann's passing. Two days later a simple funeral was held in her parents' home, and Robert then began the preparations to make good on his promise to return her to the Tuscarora Valley for her final resting place.

A simple coffin was constructed along with a cradle-type apparatus that would carry the coffin on the back of a horse. Care was taken to pad the cradle so that it would not dig into the horse's back.

Once Robert ascertained that the weather would be satisfactory for several days, he, his brother John, and Cousin George made the sad journey to the Tuscarora. They took with them three shovels and three picks to break through the frostline and create a suitable grave for Ann.

They followed her request, laid her on the knoll east of the cabin, and made sure that her face would be towards the gap in the Tuscarora Mountain. Robert withdrew his Bible and read several passages, which he remembered that Ann particularly enjoyed. Reverently John began to sing a traditional Scottish rendition of the Twenty-third Psalm:

The Lord's my Shepherd, I'll not want.
He makes me down to lie in pastures green.
He leadeth me the quiet waters by.
My soul he doth restore again, and me to walk doth make
Within the paths of righteousness,
E'en for His own name's sake.

My table Thou has furnished in
The presence of my foes.
My head with oil Thou dost annoint
And my cup overflows.
Yea, though I walk through death's dark vale,
Yet will I fear not ill,
For Thou art with me
And Thy rod and staff me comfort still.
Goodness and mercy all my life
Shall surely follow me,
And in God's house forever more
My dwelling place shall be.

As the last notes reverberated down the valley, John and George retired to the warmth of the cabin while Robert remained behind and spent the remaining daylight with his departed wife.

Robert delivered one final prayer over his wife's solitary gravesite. "O dear Lord, claimed by Christ and filled with God's grace and hope, I offer this enduring prayer for my dearly departed Ann. I pray for authentic and lasting peace among nations and in families, that kindness may replace intolerance and war, so that the grievous circumstances we now face will not be repeated.

"I pray in thanksgiving for all who have died in Christ, as we anticipate the day that we too will dwell with Christ in the kingdom that has no end.

"God of love, holy and mighty, hear these petitions from one of your faithful people, and by your grace, you will grant us those things you see for our need, for the sake of our redeemer. Amen."

The next morning they left the cabin early and headed towards Carlisle and the Swatara. When Robert returned in a month or so, he would erect a suitable grave marker for Ann, but for now as he took one last look back at her grave, all that was visible was a simple cross with her name on it.

CHAPTER ELEVEN

Spring 1761

Robert felt extremely uncomfortable in the clapboard house that he and Ann had called home the last few months of her life. After destroying Ann's clothing and bedding in a fire, he moved back to Pineford for the remainder of his stay in the Swatara Valley.

As soon as the first signs of spring began bursting forth, he said his farewell to Ann's family and his own family. He wanted to return to the Tuscarora and deal with his suffering by working himself from morning to night. At least he would derive some satisfaction out of clearing more land and planting more crops than he ever had before.

When Robert began the ascent from Laurel Run and headed east on the Tuscarora Path towards the site of the old ruins of Fort Bigham, he was astonished to hear voices and the sounds of construction activity in the vicinity of the fort. His curiosity was greatly aroused, and he spurred his horse and packhorse into a gallop up the rest of the rise to the junction of the path to the fort.

There in the clearing stood the log walls of a fort. A little more land had been cleared surrounding the new walls, but it could very easily have been 1756 again. It took Robert some time to adjust to what he was observing, but then he realized that, rightly so, someone was utilizing the old site to reconstruct a formidable haven for the people of the valley.

Robert dismounted and slowly approached the work party that was raising the walls of a structure inside the outer walls of the fort. He was somewhat dismayed that the work party was not vigilant and should have noticed his approach of the fort.

Someone needed to change some policies or the walls will not make much difference in defending these industrious folks.

In order not to create complete chaos, he called out a greeting. "Hallo, the fort. It's Robert Taylor returning to the valley."

Startled, the workers dropped their tools and grabbed their weapons. Had Robert been someone who intended to do these people any harm, their reactions would have been too late. Robert hoped that these good folks would learn quickly or they would face the consequences.

The construction activity was initiated by Ralph Sterrett, an Indian trader and land-jobber who was as at home in the woods as anyone. Later he would claim tracts of land on both sides of the Tuscarora Creek. Robert was introduced to the members of the work party, some of whom Robert had met earlier.

Mrs. Sterrett was soon to become a new mother. The unborn child would be named William and his birth would be recorded as that of the first white child born on this side of the Tuscarora Mountain.

Robert spent several days at the fort, helping to raise the roof on the inner structure of the fort, which would protect the inhabitants of the fort from the spring rains. All the while he couldn't help remembering what occurred on this ground on June 11, 1756. Once the roof was in place, Robert headed for his own secluded cabin.

Robert immediately began to prepare his small vegetable garden and corn patches for spring planting. This labor consumed all his energy from dawn to dusk. By mid-May, he had successfully planted all his available acreage in corn, flax, rye, and vegetables. With adequate rainfall, he felt that his endeavors should be highly successful.

Then one afternoon, his work schedule was interrupted. Long before Robert detected any movement on the western edge of his field, he heard a "Hallo, Robert," and immediately recognized Francis Innis's deep voice. As Francis approached, Robert could see that Francis was upset.

"What's wrong, Francis? Is something wrong with Margery or James?"

"No, thank God. However, there is something brewing that could have far-reaching ramifications.

"I hadn't the time to really walk the boundaries of our property since we returned this spring. The other day I decided to explore to the westernmost edge of our claim, and to my surprise I found that a very crude lean-to had been constructed about fifty yards from the creek. In addition, a small plot of ground had been cleared and it looked like someone was going to plant some crops.

"I swear it's on my property. I'm going to have to spend some time investigating who this squatter might be and ask him to remove the lean-to. Surely, he will be able to concede the fact that we've been here since 1755."

"What if he refuses to leave peacefully?" Robert asked. "Be careful. You know how ornery and possessive people can get over a piece of property. Make sure you avoid any direct confrontation that could lead to violence. If he doesn't listen to reason, you'll probably have to travel to the land office at Carlisle or, worse yet, all the way to Philadelphia, to make sure you have a clear title."

Francis continued, "It doesn't appear that anyone has been staying at the lean-to permanently. It will undoubtedly be a hit-or-miss situation for me to find the squatter. I guess I'll attach a note to the lean-to in the hopes that he can read and will take my claim seriously. I certainly don't want any type of violence over this situation."

Robert nodded. "If you want me to ride with you to the lean-to someday soon, I'd be glad to tag along, just as a backup. Surely, the squatter wouldn't challenge the two of us.

"Keep yourself keenly aware of any smoke or noise coming from that area. If you notice anything out of the ordinary, come and get me immediately. We'll ride over there to see what is taking place."

Francis eventually settled down and headed home. Two days

later, Robert observed him approaching; this time he was pushing his horse at a rapid gait.

"Margery and I are both sure that we smelled smoke last night and early this morning. I'd like to take you up on your offer to ride along with me to investigate the situation. I would certainly appreciate having you to back me up if this man doesn't listen to reason."

Francis and Robert pushed their way through the grove of huge maple and oak trees to the west of the Innises' cabin. When they came to a small stream, they headed north towards its source. Sure enough, every once in a while, their noses would sense the smell of a fire, and they quickened their pace in the direction they assumed it was located.

Soon they observed the crude lean-to that Francis had described, and a small cooking fire just outside its open entrance. Their ears then detected the thud of an ax on a tree. Robert and Francis glanced at each other in concerned anticipation and, by old habit, quickly checked the pan of their rifles to make sure that they had powder in them. They certainly didn't want to have to use their weapons, but they learned a long time ago that it was always better to be prepared.

They swung off their mounts and carefully picked their way towards the sounds of the ax. Within twenty-five yards of the lean-to, they detected movement and began to hold their rifles at the ready. They quickly closed the distance between themselves and the intruders.

Through the trees, they observed a man and what they at first identified as a teenaged boy, but as they moved closer, they realized it was a young woman instead. The couple was so involved in their work that they never realized they had company. Robert could have easily touched the young woman on the back but did not, and instead called out to them.

They were completely startled, and if Robert and Francis had been unfriendly natives, the two would never have stood a chance. The man made a sudden movement towards his weapon, but Francis grabbed it well in advance of the squatter's late attempt to arm himself. The two strangers immediately recognized their dilemma and made little additional effort to defend themselves.

Francis spoke abruptly, "Just what in the world are you two youngsters doing out here? You can thank your lucky stars that my neighbor and I aren't a raiding party looking for easy scalps, because we would have had two without any struggle."

The young man, no more than a boy, looked wild-eyed at them and stuttered slightly as he attempted to explain his position. "I'm John Farley and this is my wife, Bridget. We're fixing to establish a homestead on this land. I came through this area at the beginning of last winter and there wasn't anyone living here. Therefore, I went back to Carlisle and filed a claim to this land. I've got papers to prove it."

Francis shook his head. "I'm sorry, son, but we've been on this land since the spring of 55. Of course, we haven't been on it continually. King Beaver took us on a little trek out to the Forks of the Ohio, and eventually we ended up in Canada, but we've always maintained a claim to this piece of land."

The young man shook his head in disagreement. "I've got a valid claim to this land...says so right here on this piece of paper I got back in Carlisle."

Robert looked John Farley straight in the face. "I don't want to insult you, but can either of you read? Do you really know what this piece of paper says?"

The young couple looked at each other in bewilderment, then back to Robert. "No, we can't read or write. But that doesn't mean that this land isn't ours."

"Look, I'd like to help you two youngsters out," Francis said, "but I have to be concerned about my own interests. If you'd just move on up the valley, I'm sure you can find uncontested land."

The young girl began to cry, which seemed to give John additional confidence. "You've upset my wife. We're not leaving unless someone of authority makes us."

Francis held his ground. "I can understand your not wanting to abandon this land, but I've spent too much time and effort to allow you to simply take it. I'm not going to force you off, but I assure you the authorities from Carlisle will in due time."

Francis and Robert withdrew and returned to the cabin. Margery quickly made a decision to rectify the situation. "James and I will journey to Carlisle to acquire the proper verification of our ownership. If we can't secure it in Carlisle, then I will journey all the way to Philadelphia to secure our warrant."

Mother and son left the next morning, via the newly reconstructed Fort Bigham, where they were fortunate to accompany some other travelers to Fort Robinson and over the Blue Mountain to Carlisle. There she had no luck in clarifying the disputed land claim. Once again, this woman would not give up her dream of owning her own farm. Therefore, she traveled to Philadelphia in an endeavor to secure an undisputed warrant and deed to her piece of the Tuscarora Valley.

Finally, on June 3, 1762, the records in the land office in the colony's capital indicated that 283 acres had been warranted to Francis Innis in the Tuscarora Valley. Once the young Farleys were convinced that they had no legal claim to the land, they packed up and headed west.

The other frustration facing Francis and Margery was the plight of their other children, Jane and Nathaniel, who were still missing. Finally, early in 1763 they sent the following petition to the Governor of Pennsylvania, James Hamilton, which was later recorded in the *Pennsylvania Archives*:

> That in June 1756, your petitioner, his wife and three children were taken and carried away from Tuscarora by Beaver King and his company; that your petitioners' youngest child was put to death in December following. Your petitioners were bartered away for French goods, etc., and your petitioner's son and daughter are still prisoners left behind. They, therefore, humbly beg leave to remind your Honor, and pray your wanted care in enquiring for your petitioner's children, and your distressed petitioners, as in duty bound, shall ever pray.
>
> (Signed) Francis and Margery Innis[1]

CHAPTER TWELVE

The Rise of Pontiac

In October 1758 during the Grand Council at Easton, the Delawares had promised to abandon the French as allies, while the English had vowed to accede to Delaware desires for a boundary between Indian territory and English colonial settlements.

The British officials abandoned the concept of a line between Indian and British domains as soon as the French vacated Fort Duquesne, and the French fortress was quickly replaced by Fort Pitt. The Delawares viewed the new English fort on the forks of the Ohio as abhorrent, just as the Senecas perceived Fort Niagara as dominating their territory in New York.

Sometimes prophecies become reality. During testimony before Pennsylvania's Provincial Council on July 14, 1758, Robert Taylor speculated that the native unrest to the west of the Alleghenies would eventually be led by chieftains who had not yet emerged as leaders.

Some of these young, untested chiefs would vent their anger through ranting and fiery orations; others would display their hatred and frustrations by performing unique brutal deeds against ancient tribal enemies or against the increasing white menace located between the Alleghenies and the Atlantic seaboard.

One such young, charismatic chieftain was Pontiac, a war chief of the Ottawa Nation.

He was born to an Ottawa chief and a Chippewa woman on the banks of the Maumee River in Ohio about 1720. Pontiac had assumed the role of war chief of the Ottawas due to his skill and bravery in battle, his dominance of situations, and his logical thinking ability. This situated him as the second most powerful figure in the tribe, next to Mackinac, the principal chief of the tribe.

Pontiac possessed no love for the Iroquois League or his ancestral enemies, the Cherokees, and least of all, the white English invaders who had just driven his French friends and comrades from Canada, the Ohio and Mississippi Valleys, and the Great Lakes region.

Since Pontiac had been born the son of a chief and possessed great personal merit, vehement ambition, a commanding energy, and a dominant personality, his power and influence extended from the sources of the Ohio and Mississippi to the farthest boundaries of the Algonquins.

This Ottawa war chief was slightly better than medium height, well built, and in prime physical condition. Paint usually adorned his face and body, as was the custom of his tribe. His father had taught him to cut his hair so that it was shaved close to the skin at his nape and crown of his head and gradually tapered to a brushy length of nearly an inch or so high above his forehead. This type of hairdo would not allow an enemy the advantage of grasping him by the hair and plunging a knife into his breast.

During the French and Indian War, Pontiac had fought valiantly for the French. It appears that he led the Ottawas during the memorable defeat of General Edward Braddock in July 1755.

Many of the French officers treated Pontiac with great respect. General Louis de Montcalm held him in the highest esteem and presented the war chief of the Ottawas with one of Montcalm's own full dress uniforms.

Montcalm honored Pontiac even further when he asserted, "Accept this French general's uniform from me. Since I am a French general, you should be a general among your own people."

Extremely proud and honored by this extravagant display of respect and comradeship from the French commander, Pontiac responded, "I, Pontiac, give you my word that I shall never desert you as long as a breath remains in one or the other of us."

Pontiac was as good as his word. On September 14, when Montcalm died at dawn after being struck by an English lead ball on the Plains of Abraham, Pontiac and his warriors were still involved in the defense of Quebec.

When Pontiac learned of Montcalm's demise he vowed, "I will never accept English control over Canada. I do not think the English are strong enough to take Canada, but if they should take it, I do not think they can hold it for very long. If the English prove me wrong, it will be at Quebec where they will hold on. They will not be successful in the west, I will make sure of that."

The fighting in North America was virtually suspended with the capture of the citadel of Montreal on September 8, 1760. Sir Jeffery Amherst sent British troops and Rogers' Rangers to occupy the forts in the Ohio Country and the Great Lakes region that had been garrisoned by French forces. Within a year, the Indians living in the previously French occupied areas became dissatisfied with the new policies implemented by the victorious British.

The British dispensed with the carefree and benevolent trading policies of the French. Instead of cultivating alliances with the Indians, the British treated them as conquered subjects. In an attempt to reduce expenses, General Amherst curtailed the customary distribution of presents and provisions distributed to the natives. Amherst did not attempt to conceal his contempt for the tribes; thus, the Indians felt greatly insulted.

To add to the insults, Amherst restricted the distribution of gunpowder and ammunition, which the natives needed to secure food to eat and skins for trading purposes. The general also outlawed the sale of alcohol, especially rum. These were strong indications that Amherst did not trust his old adversaries and wanted to restrict their movements and ability to strike at the British.

If Amherst had had the opportunity to read what Peter Kalm wrote about the Indian's sense of values and the effects of the white man on Indian culture, he might have wisely chosen a different route. "The Europeans have taught the Indians the use of firearms, and so they have laid aside their bows and arrows and use muskets. If the Europeans should now refuse to supply the natives with muskets, they would starve to death, and they would be irritated to such a degree as to attack the colonists."

Kalm further noted, "It is likewise certain that the colonists gain considerably by their trade in muskets and ammunition."

The first to take action against these insulting policies were the Senecas. They sent a red wampum belt of war to the Shawnees and the Delawares and eventually to tribes of the Ohio Country and the Detroit region. The Detroit tribes were not ready to take to the warpath, and the uprising did not gain momentum in 1761.

The English quickly forgot their promises and treaties as soon as they were enacted or spoken. On the other hand, the Indians lived up to their agreements. The natives never forgot a signed treaty, an act of kindness, or an injury inflicted upon them.

Eventually in 1762, the Indians of the Detroit region came to the realization that the British policy as suggested by the Senecas was indeed insulting and a serious threat to their well-being, causing food shortages and epidemic disease. Adding to this discontent was the emergence of a strange religious figure known as Neolin or the Delaware Prophet.

This evangelistic visionary preached that if the natives were to return to their old ways of living and reject the bad habits of the whites, they would be able to drive the white men from their midst. The Delaware Prophet urged the tribes to follow a doctrine of self-sufficiency and not depend upon English trade goods, alcohol, and weapons. He warned that sickness, smallpox, and alcohol would destroy the tribes. "We should eliminate the English in the old manner. We should return to the old ways of waging warfare, as did our fathers and grandfathers. Our salvation is to abandon firearms and make use of the bow-and-arrow, the spear, the tomahawk, and the knife. Our Divine Master will lead us to victory if we follow the old ways and give up the influence of the whites."

Pontiac, the Ottawa war chief, heard Neolin's message, which had a profound effect upon his campaign to redress the grievances imposed upon his people by the arrogant General Jeffery Amherst.

In June of 1762, Pontiac held a secret meeting that was not well attended. Late that summer, on September 15, the Ottawa war chief held another meeting at his village on the Detroit River.

This council was attended by all of the western Great Lakes tribes, with representatives from the Shawnees, Miamis, Senecas, Hurons, Wyandots, Potawatomies, Mississaugas, Chippewas, Weas, Kaskaskias, Peorias, Cahokias, as well as Old Shingas representing the Delawares. Also on hand were three Frenchmen. In all, there were about eighty or more chiefs and sub-chiefs in attendance.

Pontiac's opening remarks were a customary thank-you for attending and a brief summary of the secret meeting held in June. He spoke of his support by the Kings of France and Spain and how the English would be conquered. Then his voice gained in volume, and he became more animated.

"It appears that some of my brothers fear that we are not strong enough to rise up against our white conquerors and that destruction will fall upon us. However, if all our tribes joined together, how could the English stand against us?

"What, besides harm and broken promises, have the English brought us? How can any of you believe that it is beneficial for them to be on our land? All of us have suffered greatly for lack of ammunition for hunting. The French shared their powder and ammunition with us, but the English look upon it as their private property, and give us very little.

"My brothers, another winter is coming and we need all our skills and efforts to provide food for our families. Therefore, we will do nothing for now. Return to your villages and lands and wait for the message that we will hold another, and final, grand council in the spring. In the spring we will make the decision. Then we will drive the whites from our lands!"

CHAPTER THIRTEEN

Return of Captives 1762

While Pontiac was making his moves, Christian Frederick Post was diligently striving to arrange for a treaty with the western Indians. George Croghan had received nearly 380 white captives from June 1759 to October 1761 at Fort Pitt. Since Post's mission to the Indians in 1758, he had continually labored for better relations and the return of more captives.

Through Post in early February 1762, Pennsylvania's Governor James Hamilton had received a letter from Shingas and King Beaver who were living on the Tuscarawas. Previously, the two chiefs had been reluctant to travel to Philadelphia, because they feared that the whites would retaliate against them for the atrocities they had performed during the French and Indian War. In their letter they stated that they desired to hold a treaty conference with the governor in the spring of 1762.

The governor replied through Post in March. He invited Shingas and King Beaver to come to Lancaster that summer because Philadelphia was undergoing an epidemic of smallpox. Post was dispatched to the Tuscarawas to begin the preparations for the journey of the chiefs, in addition to the numerous returning white captives. The chiefs of the Western Delawares had displayed their good intentions by having already returned seventy-four captives to Fort Pitt.

The news of the peace conference and the subsequent return of white captives spread renewed hope across the frontier. Robert Taylor and the Innis family made immediate plans to make the journey to Lancaster. July was not the best time for them to leave the valley due to the harvesting of their oats, flax, and wheat. However, Mother Nature was very cooperative, and they were able to reap their crops prior to their desired departure time.

There had been no time to advise Robert's family at Pineford that he and the Innis family would be arriving unannounced in early August. Robert knew they would be elated about his return and would welcome Francis, Margery, and James with open arms. Their arrival set off a huge celebration and a holiday with a huge picnic on the next day.

As usual, the whole Taylor clan, along with their neighbors and friends, joined in the festivities. Robert was hoping that one certain person would have other plans during his short stay at Pineford. Sister Janie was at her teasing and taunting best. "I guess you know who will be here. She talks about you all the time. I know it might be too soon for you to consider looking at another woman, but at least be civil to her. She's an awfully nice young woman, and she certainly aided us when we needed help last year."

"I realize that Anne Sample is your best friend and that you apparently believe she would be good for me. However, right now a woman is the last thing on my mind. I'm too excited about going to Lancaster and the possibility that one or both of my children might be returned—I have no desire to think about anything else. If this young lady is interested in me, she's just going to have to bide her time. Please try to understand and explain that to her. I wish her no ill will, nor do I wish to offend her. My mind is just preoccupied."

Shortly after Anne and her family arrived at the picnic, Robert noticed Jane taking Anne aside and entering into a lengthy discussion with her. Later in the day, Anne approached him apprehensively. "Robert, it's so good to see you once again. I want to wish you the best of luck at Lancaster. I'm sure that you are going through a tremendous amount of turmoil and anxiety in preparation for attending the peace conference. I wish I could share some of your burden, but Jane has explained your situation and I will honor your desires. Later, if I can be of any comfort or sustenance, please allow Jane to indicate your needs to me."

"I indeed thank you for your kind consideration and understanding. Jane has a very special friend in you. I can appreciate why she believes that you would be very good for me. Just understand the time is not right. It wouldn't be fair to either of us. If you're patient, perhaps the situation will change. Again, thank you for being such a good friend."

The news arrived that Post was having the usual difficulty in keeping the captives from running away and returning to their adoptive homes. Also, Shingas and King Beaver had second thoughts about traveling to Lancaster. Finally, the news was spread that Post and his delegation would arrive at Lancaster on August 8.

When Robert, Francis, Margery, and James arrived in Lancaster, they were informed that the conference would be a lengthy one. The exchange began with great anticipation, and as Robert had observed previously, not all the captives were willing to be exchanged. The usual guarding and restraining had to be employed to keep the former captives from bolting, even after they had been exchanged.

King Beaver reluctantly turned over settlers who had been captured in Virginia, Maryland, and Pennsylvania. The governor played a significant role in the ceremony. James Hamilton arose from his seat at the conference circle and walked to greet the prisoners, one by one.

Thomas King, the Oneida chief of the Six Nations, assisted in delivering captives from the Munsee Clan of the Delawares on August 19. In his speech, he spoke about the reluctance to return these adopted people, especially those who had become wives. He also mentioned that the reason there weren't more returnees was the white practice of making servants out of returned prisoners.

As at the other ceremonies involving the return of adopted captives, Robert and the Innis family were unsuccessful in recognizing any of their children. With saddened hearts they made the stopover at Pineford for two days; then they headed back across the Susquehanna to Carlisle and across the mountains to the Tuscarora Valley. The corn harvest season would soon be upon them, and there would be all the preparations for another difficult Central Pennsylvania winter, so there was little time to dwell upon the cruel situation of their absent family members.

CHAPTER FOURTEEN

Early 1763

In the meantime, the English strengthened Forts Bedford and Ligonier, erected Fort Pitt and fortifications at Stony Creek and Bushy Run, and replaced the French forts at Presqu'Isle, LeBoeuf, and Machault, which the English renamed Venango. Upon the erection of these forts, garrisons were stationed for defense and for maintaining a line of communication to Carlisle.

On February 10, 1763, France and England signed the Treaty of Paris that officially ended the Seven Years War or the French and Indian War. This treaty erased every sign of French sovereignty from the map of the North American mainland, except around New Orleans.

This tremendous transfer of territory opened vast opportunities to colonial investors, traders, and land speculators. For a period before the signing of the treaty in Paris, English settlers had been migrating west of the Alleghenies and the Ohio River and taking possession of these lands without purchasing them or gaining the consent of the natives residing in this area. The original French forts were either occupied by the English or replaced by even stronger forts than those the French had surrendered.

The English settlers quickly laid out plantations or farms west of the Alleghenies even though the lands were not open to lawful settlement, just as they had done in the Juniata Valley prior to the Treaty of Albany in 1754.

Many settlers followed George Washington's advice: "Any person who neglects the present opportunity of hunting out good lands…will never regain it."

Beginning in 1753 with the French invasion of the Ohio Valley until the signing of the peace treaty in February 1763, the Iroquois and the Shawnees and Delawares never ceased in their demand that both the French and the English remain east of the Allegheny Mountains.

The actions of the English settlers were in violation of their ten years of promising to the contrary and against the Indians' protests. The Indians had learned what to expect—a horde of land-hungry settlers from Eastern Pennsylvania and Virginia.

Examples of these broken promises can be found in the words of Lieutenant James Grant while speaking for an ill General John Forbes. "The General knows that the French have told the Indians that the English intend to cheat them out of their lands on the Ohio, but this, he assures you, is false. The English have no intention to make settlements in your Hunting Country beyond the Allegheny Hills, unless they shall be desired for your convenience to erect some store houses in order to establish and carry on a trade, which they are ready to do so on fair and just terms."[2]

Later, at a council at Fort Pitt on August 12, 1760, held by General Monckton with the leaders of many of the tribes of the region between the Alleghenies and the Mississippi, Monckton told the chiefs, "I do assure all the Indian Nations that his Majesty has not sent me to deprive any of you of your lands and property."[3]

Britain's official victory over the French in February 1763 did not bring peace to Western Pennsylvania. With one broken promise after another, the Indian allies of the French still hated and feared the victorious English. Some of the Indians decided to drive out and destroy the promise- and treaty-breaking English.

The Ottawa war chief Pontiac had reluctantly consented to the occupation of the Detroit region after the French had been defeated, but he eventually formed a confederation of the Shawnees, Delawares, the Senecas of the Iroquois, and all of the important Algonquin tribes in an attempt to drive the English into the Atlantic Ocean. Pontiac was joined in his efforts in Western

Pennsylvania by the Seneca Chief Guyasuta, Custaloga of the Munsee or Wolf Clan of the Delawares, and Shingas and King Beaver, also of the Delawares.

CHAPTER FIFTEEN

March 1763

In late March, a letter arrived from Robert's sister, Jane. On the other occasions when he had received any news from Pineford, it had been bad news. Therefore, he began to read his sister's precise handwriting with some hesitation.

Dearest Robert,

I know that I'm probably overstepping my sisterly bounds, but I'm urging you to return east of the Susquehanna and back to the valley of the Swatara. With Mother, Father, and Ann gone from our midst, there is a huge void in our family relationship.

I constantly fear for your physical and psychological safety. We hear constant rumors that the tranquility of the Indian problem is about to cease and warfare will once again plague the frontier.

We know and recognize that you want to be self-sufficient and create your own destiny on the Tuscarora. I also recognize your desire and need to stay on just in case one or both of your children should return.

However, let us face the facts. It has been over six years since the incident at Bigham's, and the likelihood of your children being liberated becomes more remote with each passing day. You need to move on and maybe find a new woman to share your life and begin a new family. You are still young and quite handsome. You will have no problem persuading a woman to become part of your life.

While I'm on that subject, I must remind you that you left quite an impression on the neighbor girl, Anne, who helped to care for your Ann during her final days. You also have to remember that Ann urged you to consider this young woman as a future mate. I know I shouldn't be trying to play the role of cupid, but this young woman has it all. You can't expect her to wait forever for you to see the opportunity that awaits you.

We've discussed your circumstances, so any interest that she has displayed is not without her knowledge of what you have experienced. I've teased her that you are the most handsome of my brothers, and she readily agreed.

Please don't delay in pursuing this young woman. On the financial side, you should consider the fact that someday she will inherit a substantial amount of land, that even if you decide not to live in the Swatara Valley, you could sell it for a considerable profit and reinvest in land on the frontier.

Keep in mind that she is of marrying age and that she certainly doesn't lack for suitors who await her beck and call.

Robert, I hope that I haven't offended you by bringing up this subject of seeking another wife. Just give it some consideration, some sincere thought.

Maybe you should surprise us with a visit and investigate the possibilities. It won't do any harm, and we would all enjoy your company once again.

I've often thought that perhaps you are unnerved by the fact that the young lady in question is also an "Ann," but you must remember she spells her name with an "e" on the end. On the lighter side, at least you won't ever make the mistake of calling her by the wrong name. Maybe it would be best for you to call her by a suitable nickname.

There I go again, overstepping my sisterly boundaries once again. I know you'll forgive your sister for putting her thoughts down on paper.

Hope to see you in the near future.

Your loving sister, Jane

After reading the letter, Robert sat and looked across the valley at the Tuscarora Mountain for a long time. Before he knew it, he had wasted several hours, just allowing Jane's words to sink in. Her words stuck with him, hour after hour, day after day. Finally, he realized there was a great deal of merit in what she had written. "Maybe if all goes well, I'll make a trip back east after all the crops have been harvested in the fall. However, that is a long time off; I have a lot of work to do before then."

CHAPTER SIXTEEN

April 27, 1763

On April 27, 1763, Pontiac held a grand council on the banks of the Ecorse River, not more than six miles from Fort Detroit. Pontiac was filled with tremendous pride and exultation in that his influence had persuaded nearly twenty thousand Indians from numerous tribes to come to hear his inspiring speech. Several Frenchmen were also on hand, including some of the most important Canadians from Detroit.

When Pontiac decided the time was right, he moved so that he was visible to the entire audience on the steep little knoll beside the Ecorse River. He had stripped down to a loincloth and a pair of moccasins, and three eagle feathers were attached to a silver disk on his right temple.

Pontiac began slowly, "Friends and brothers, it is the will of the Great Spirit that we should meet together this day. He orders all things and has given us a fine day for our council."

The Ottawa war chief spoke at great length about the injustices of the English and the friendship of the French. He reminded them of their great victory over Braddock and how they would perform similar deeds in the future. He explained in detail the role of the Great Spirit in directing him on his path against the English. In doing so, he presented himself as a disciple of Neolin.

Then he became quite passionate and appeared to be a man possessed. "My brothers! My friends! My children! Give me your ears: We must cast away the anger among us and join as one people whose common purpose is to drive out the English dogs who seek to destroy us and take our lands."

This was met with a tremendous roar of approval that grew in volume and eventually died away. However, it was nearly five minutes before it was quiet enough for Pontiac to continue.

"Go now. Let us now return to our homes. Watch and study the English in your lands and learn how best to attack them and destroy them before they can prepare to defend themselves. Deceive them! Allow them to accept you as friends and when the moment is right, we will strike them all in the same instant. Leave here now, but when the word comes to you that I, Pontiac, have attacked Detroit, raise then your own war clubs to crush the English in your own land. You will not be alone. We are all united to this cause. We will have coming to us the great army of men from our good white father in France. Go! Go, and prepare!

"Say nothing of this so that an Englishman can learn nothing of our plans. Return to your villages and remain quiet. In the meantime, prepare your weapons for war. After four more days have passed, I and some of my young men will go into Detroit. When we have learned what we need to learn to take advantage of the English dogs, we will leave, and then I will summon another council of our tribes to determine the best method of attack."

On May 5, Pontiac sent all the women out of his village and informed the warriors what his spies had learned earlier in the week about the interior of the fort at Detroit. Two days later, Pontiac and about three hundred men entered the fort with weapons concealed under blankets, hoping to catch the garrison unprepared. The pretense was that the Indians sought to hold a council. Unfortunately for the Indians, Major Gladwin, the fort's commander, had been informed of the plot to assault the fort and had his 120-man garrison well prepared.

Another two days passed, and the Indians tried again, but once again Gladwin's men were ready for the sneak attack. Pontiac realized he had to take some action. He exhorted his warriors, "Attack every Englishman you can find outside the walls of the fort. We will make sure that Detroit is cut off and receives no help from the east."

Pontiac's warriors laid siege to the fort. Before too long more than nine hundred warriors joined the siege. The siege would last until late July, when reinforcements finally arrived to help lift the stalemate.

While the siege of Detroit continued, war parties throughout the frontier began to attack other British forts and white settlements in an earnest attempt to eliminate the whites from the region, which the natives felt the British had promised not to occupy.

The attack on Detroit was a signal for violence to flare up all along the frontier.

CHAPTER SEVENTEEN

George Croghan's Warning to Robert Taylor
May 1763

On the first day of May, Robert Taylor's daily working routine was interrupted by the arrival of two young frontiersmen who appeared to be pushing their mounts to the limit. Robert observed that they were probably under pressure not to waste any time as they delivered a message.

"Sorry, but we're under orders to hand over this message and get over the mountains to Carlisle as soon as possible. Croghan gave us specific orders not to dally. We are to give you the pouch and keep moving."

The older rider added a verbal piece of advice from the Buck. "George says for you to give ear to his warning and follow us over the mountains as soon as possible. He seemed rather agitated by the way things were playing out in the Ohio Valley. Best you heed his warning. Things are going to get hot again on the frontier, and soon."

"You sure that you don't want some nourishment or drink before heading off?"

"Thanks, but we've got to be in Carlisle by tomorrow."

With that, they left Robert alone to read and ponder the recommendation from his old friend.

Robert, my young friend,

It has been quite some time since I last communicated with you. For this, I apologize. Nevertheless, as you can well guess, my work here in the west has kept me occupied.

Right after we first met back in '55, Montour and I

warned you that the time was not right for you to move your young family into the Tuscarora Valley. I know you had valid reasons for not following our advice, and unfortunately, much to my chagrin, my warnings of bloodshed held true. Sadly, you and your family suffered severely.

Once again I am sending a warning of alarm back east. I implore you not only to heed my urgings, but also to spread the word, not only throughout the Tuscarora Valley, but also to every white settler west of the Susquehanna River.

As before, the land is going to run red with the blood of white settlers. I know that most of you back east feel secure in your present situation since the signing of the Treaty of Paris earlier this year. But please do not be misled. I realize that many settlers are streaming back into the valleys that were depopulated beginning with the hostilities in the fall of 1755 and escalating the following summer. I happen to believe that this second wave of attacks will be much worse than the first wave.

Not only are the French still stirring up and instigating the natives, but the policies of the British and Pennsylvania governments are woefully inadequate and absolutely insulting to these people.

The Indians have been extremely disappointed in the trading wares that we have brought to them. Most of these goods have been geared to please the French inhabitants of the region, rather than the Indians. Our esteemed commander, General Jeffery Amherst, while located in the haven of his headquarters in New York, seems to have deliberately calculated to offend and deprive the very Indians with whom I have been attempting to develop friendly and peaceful relations.

After the end of hostilities on the frontier, His Majesty initiated a program to ensure that the Indians would receive great amounts of presents that would entice them to be subservient, thus averting possible bloodshed. Amherst has apparently reversed the earlier policy established by General James Abercrombie.

Under Amherst's program, the Indians would no longer be provided with ample supplies of lead, gunpowder, clothing, blankets, food, rum, tools, and tomahawks. The English were the conquerors of all Canada and all its inhabitants, and the general expected complete subjugation.

General Amherst's polices have deprived the Indians of their very means of survival by placing unbearable pressure on their traditions and imposing a harsh economic situation upon the natives.

Sir William Johnson, my boss, has been instructed by Amherst to discontinue the practice of buying the good behavior of the Indians by bestowing presents upon them. The good general has no concept that these so-called presents are looked upon by the Indians as being a form of tribute. Tribute is not the correct term. More accurately, they considered the gifts as a form of rent.

This concept of rent gives us the privilege to enter their land in peace and to set up trading posts. The French perfectly understood this tradition and gladly paid without any questions.

Slowly, the tribes have learned the truth of our new policies, and great anger has arisen among the various villages. There has developed a dangerous lack of supplies and trade goods. This is destabilizing the economy of the area. If the Indians don't receive the goods they need and desire from the English peacefully, they will take matters into their own hands.

I know that Captain Donald Campbell at Fort Detroit and Captain Simeon Ecuyer, the new commander of Fort Pitt, do not fully support the new policy and attempt to circumvent it by bestowing upon the natives in their areas what few supplies they can afford to part with.

I feel that I have established remarkably good relations with the Ottawas, Potawatomies, Chippewas, Mississaugas, and Hurons, and at times, with a few Delawares, Miamis, and Shawnees. The tribal leaders have repeatedly asked that traders be permitted to come among their villages and supply them with ammunition, weapons, tools, clothing, and other needed and desired goods. I promised that this would happen, but I was unable to keep my word under Amherst's new policies.

Fort Pitt is perhaps the finest English-built fortification in America, but it does have its shortcomings. The barracks are drafty and cold, and the garrison is plagued with lice and bedbugs. The men of the garrison and those who inhabit the small village at its walls are a coarse and rowdy group. Many are escaping from the law from across the mountains, and are often guilty of immoral and drunken behavior.

If the necessary supplies and an upgrading of the garrison don't soon become a reality, it will be very difficult for Ecuyer to hold out. If Pitt can't survive, I don't think I need to explain what will happen to the lesser forts on the frontier. This also applies to the forts between Fort Pitt and Carlisle. All these forts are undermanned and short on supplies.

Also, there are new, young, ambitious, and power-hungry war chiefs and tribal leaders who are quite anxious to prove themselves in a new war to drive out the English from their traditional lands.

To be quite blunt, prepare youself and your neighbors for a resumption of bloody warfare this summer. It's coming! Get out of the valley now before it's too late. Don't repeat your mistake of June 1756. Persuade all your neighbors to leave now. Spread the word! It's going to be a bloody hell from Detroit to the Susquehanna. It may well spread east of the Susquehanna.

If I were you, I'd head across the Susquehanna to Pineford tomorrow. I don't care about your pride, but I do care about your scalp. Just rub your hand over the side of your head and remember how close your scalp was to be hanging from some warrior's belt.

I'm heading east immediately. Hopefully I'll see you on

the other side of the mountains, or better yet, east of the Susquehanna.

Your friend and servant, George Croghan

With the arrival of this message, along with the letter he had received from his sister, Jane, back in March, Robert knew that it was time for him to pack up and head across the mountains and the Susquehanna. There was a certain type of insistency in George's message. He thought to himself, "The Buck knows that things aren't right out at the Forks and beyond. Something bad is going to occur. I didn't listen the first time he tried to warn me, but this time it's going to be different. It's time to go, and apparently now, not later."

It took Robert several days to move some of his possessions to an underground storage container located towards the ridge to the north of his cabin. His few animals he simply turned loose to fend for themselves. When he returned he hoped to find all kinds of wild pigs, chickens and cattle roaming the banks of the Tuscarora.

His first stop was at the Innis cabin to warn them of the impending danger lurking far to the west. They also agreed it was time to go. When he stopped at the fort, the Sterretts weren't convinced that it was time to head over the mountains. Robert didn't plead his case to any great length; he recognized that everyone had to make his or her own decision on this matter. Within less than four days he was back on the familiar banks of the Swatara, not quite sure what his future might be.

CHAPTER EIGHTEEN

Return to Pineford
June 1763

Robert was unsure about what he should do first when he returned to Pineford. With the death of his mother and father, the ownership of the lease of Pineford had passed on to his older brother, Henry. Back when Robert and Ann had begun their relationship, Henry had assumed that he and Ann would be the ones united in marriage. However, the relationship between the older Taylor brother and Ann never materialized because Ann had never been informed of Henry's intentions, and in the meantime, she and Robert had fallen deeply in love.

Ann's marriage to Robert left Henry bitter and resentful. But later, upon Robert's return to Pineford after nearly two years in captivity and Henry's good fortune in finding a suitable spouse, all the acrimony was left behind.

If only Robert and Ann had been sensible enough to have returned to Pineford in the spring of 1756, their lives would been dramatically changed. Nevertheless, that was all hindsight; he alone had to face what he hoped would be a temporary stay back on the banks of the Swatara.

His sister, Jane, had been the one to urge him to return to the Swatara until the new Indian problem had been resolved, but she was unmarried and still lived at Pineford.

Robert's brother William had married, as had his sister Catherine, but the invitation to return had come from Jane, so it would be from Jane that he would seek guidance. The main house at Pineford would be his first stop, and he would allow events to unfold on their own.

Henry's wife, Isabel, and his sister, Jane, greeted Robert warmly when he hitched his horse to the post in front of the house on a warm June afternoon. Jane explained, "Henry and the rest of the men are out working in the fields and probably won't return until dusk. In the meantime, you might as well clean up, partake of some refreshments, and visit with us women until the men return. I'll send a message to the rest of the family that you have arrived. In the meantime, feel free to make yourself at home. You can stay here as long as you want."

After Robert had washed up and eaten, he joined the women on the porch where they were involved in catching up on some long overdue sewing. As always, Jane greeted him with a huge smile, but this smile had mischief written all over it.

"I hope you won't be upset. I took the liberty of informing a certain young lady of your whereabouts. I told you I was going to play cupid."

"Look, Janie, I know you mean well, but I don't think I'm ready for any affairs of the heart. Your friend Anne is a fine young woman, but please don't push too far and too fast. Please don't pursue this matter in front of your brothers."

Nothing more was mentioned about Jane's friend the rest of the afternoon, and the women followed Robert's wishes and didn't broach the subject that evening when the whole family met after dinner. It was all joviality and merriment, a reunion of much celebration. Hopefully, it was a sign of better times ahead for the Taylor clan.

Two days later it was the Sabbath, and Robert attended the services with his brother and sisters and their families. The one person that Robert had hoped would not attend was there with her family as well. Robert remembered all too well the words of his wife, Ann, during her last coherent days regarding his future and who she hoped would look after Robert once she had passed on.

Robert could not even force himself to look in Anne's direction. As he thought about the situation, it was almost impossible for him to focus on Reverend Elder's fiery sermon. He was beginning to have all kinds of doubts about why he left the Tuscarora Valley.

As was the custom after the service, the small congregation sat down to a meal of thanksgiving. It was during this meal that what Robert was hoping to avoid occurred. He glanced down the table, and there she was, staring directly at him. He quickly moved his eyes to the other end of the table, but the damage had been done. It wasn't long before he felt a presence at his elbow, and there she stood, in all her radiance.

"Hello, Robert. I just wanted to welcome you back to the valley. We were beginning to think you would never return for a visit. It's certainly good to see you again."

In no way did he want to look at her directly. He realized that he was afraid of her. Better yet, he was afraid of how he would feel if he ever weakened and looked into those alluring blue eyes. Why did he allow himself to become trapped in this position?

He slowly turned on his seat on the bench and looked at her. The magnificent smile on the fascinating and delicate face was overwhelming; he was speechless. After an awkward moment, Robert regained his composure. "Hello, Anne. It's nice to see you again. Once again, I would like to thank you for all that you did for me in my time of need."

"It was something that any neighbor would have been happy to do. If there is anything else that I can do for you during your stay in the valley, I would be more than happy to comply." She abruptly turned on her heel and hurried away.

Robert looked around to try to determine if anyone had observed this exchange. Once he was assured that no one had paid them any notice, he followed the swift-moving girl down towards the banks of the creek. He observed that once she came to the bank of the creek, she veered downstream for another fifty yards. He reluctantly pursued the fleeing girl, until he overcame her.

She turned to face her pursuer. Robert observed the wetness of her tears streaming down her cheeks.

"You're crying," Robert said gently, "but why?"

"You…you took so long to return! I thought you weren't coming back."

"And that made you cry?" he quizzed.

Fire ignited in Anne's eyes. "Don't you understand anything? Don't you realize how I feel about you?" she said, her blue eyes sparkling with excitement and anticipation.

"No," he answered evasively. "No, I don't know. I'm not sure I want to know."

"Then you are a fool! I've admired you since the first time I saw you, even when you still belonged to someone else. Your poor, suffering, departed wife recognized how I felt back then. I realize my feelings showed through in a shameless manner, but I arrived at the point where I just didn't care. Now you are a free man. You have been for some time. I know your sister wrote you about how I feel about you. Nevertheless, you still didn't make any response. Do I have to throw myself at you?"

"Back then things were different. I had strong feelings for my wife. I still do, and I always will. I do remember that there were times I felt that you were watching me, but I just passed that off as curiosity. If anything is ever to develop between us, you will have to realize how I feel. I remember very well the words my wife spoke in reference to you and the request that she made. You weren't much more than a mere child."

Anne swayed towards him, raising up on her tiptoes, so that he could clearly take in her lush lips and luminous eyes. Her voice was filled with sweet innocence. "But now," she whispered, "I'm grown up. Quite grown up. I'm not just admiring you from afar. I'm here looking you straight in your face. I'm not just the neighboring girl from two farms down the creek. And I know what I want—and who I want as my husband."

Robert gazed down at her. "Yes, you are quite grown up. That's my problem...."

She cut him off. "It's not a problem. I was always grown-up to you. I was never too young to fall in love with you."

"Love me?" he asked. "What can you know of love?"

"This!" she blurted as her arm moved so rapidly that it was a blur in his eyes. It encircled his neck, tightened, and drew down his head. Her mouth moved on his, lighter than a soft breeze, soft and warm, and unbearably sweet. Her head rotated upon the slim column of her neck, a slow half-motion, so that her wide, sensuous lips lingered upon his.

In no way was Robert prepared for her zealous sensuality. He attempted to back away, but she continued her advance.

"Robert, do you have any idea how your absence has affected me? I would wake up in the middle of the night whispering to myself, 'He'll come back. He must come back!' There were times I walked about in a daze, stunned, not answering when spoken to.... Oh, Robert, please don't reject me."

She hurled her slim body towards him, her lips seeking his once again. Light kisses, brushing his mouth, his cheeks, and his throat. Robert's hands tightened upon her shoulders, thrusting her away from him.

"You mustn't," he pleaded, attempting to avoid her. "You must not love me."

"I must not?" She echoed in a half-hysterical note of laughter. "Ask me to do something easy, Robert. Ask me to stop my heart.

"Do you have any idea how many suitors I have turned away? All with the belief, the faith, that one day I would win your heart. I figure this will be my only opportunity to do so. If not, my parents are placing tremendous pressure on me to do something about my unmarried status. They're afraid they'll have a spinster on their hands. Do I look like the type of female to spend my life as an old maid?"

She snuggled back into his arms, and she laid her soft, luxurious cheek against his.

Robert gazed at the splendid creature swaying ecstatically in his arms, and his breath slowed and evened. He was suddenly conscious of a feeling of immense peace. All the weary miles he had traveled, all the hunger, all the pain, all the loneliness, died down into nothingness. He drew her gently to him, his hard, sinewy frame permeated with tenderness. He realized it was of no use for him to reject what he was feeling for this exquisite young woman.

"We'll...we'll have to do this properly. I'll have to call upon you in the customary or conventional manner. I'll be required to seek permission from your father. At least we don't have to go through all the prudish, strait-laced protocol of the Old Country. Have you ever really discussed me with your family? You know, they could reject me as a potential suitor."

"Don't you worry for one moment about any objections to your being my husband! If there are, we'll simply run away. I've waited too long for you to come to your senses. No one, nothing, is going to stand in the way of our spending the rest of our lives together."

He felt hopelessly out of control; he was no match for her. He was unable to utter another word.

Then swiftly her face moved towards him. The generous, sensitive mouth turned expertly, parted slightly, until it caught upon his once again. The lips caressed his, softly, and lingered there, slowly drawing out his consciousness, suspending him in time and space. She aroused in him the breath-stopping agony of desire. Something he had not felt for nearly seven years.

He withdrew from her arms and charms. "I'll go talk to your father tomorrow night after dinner. Until then, we'd better return to the church or some people might notice and I certainly don't want to spoil our relationship with people gossiping about what we were doing out here."

CHAPTER NINETEEN

The Big Decision

Robert was as good as his word. After the evening meal the next day, he appeared at the Sample farm to approach Anne's father for permission to call upon his daughter. He could tell that the Swatara farmer was reluctant to give his approval, because of the age difference between Robert and Anne and the fact that Robert had been married previously. But during the conversation, Robert ascertained that the daughter and mother had persuaded the hesitant father to give his endorsement.

After what Robert regarded as an inquisition, the new couple was allowed to meet in the living room and take a short walk down the lane. Once they had covered about one hundred yards beyond the house, she put out her hand and clasped his fingers. They stopped for a moment and embraced.

She went up on tiptoes, her lips slightly parted, just inches from his lips, and he could feel the soft rustle of her breath. He realized he was going to enjoy the next part immensely.

"Go ahead," she taunted, "I know I'm going to delight in what you're going to do. Not only that, this is something we are going to continue to do the rest of our lives. And you, you didn't want anything to do with me. So, I was too young for you. Now I'm going to be your wife."

"I've learned that we men can't always control our fate when it comes to dealing with your gender. You hold too much influence over us, you are able to sway our judgment in your favor. I know I have a lot to learn about you, but so do you about me."

They continued to embrace and converse while strolling down

the lane. Soon they recognized that the dusk was disappearing into darkness and that they should return to her home.

"I don't want to sound threatening or ominous," Robert said, "but there are a number of concerns that I would like to discuss with you before we become too deeply involved. There are certain things you should know about me. Maybe they would even change your opinion of me."

"There is nothing that you can divulge or disclose about your past or future that will change my mind about my feelings for you. But I will warn you, Robert Taylor, I promise you that before too long, you will learn to love me. I realize how fondly you loved your wife, and I am jealous of that affection. But I assure you that, in due time, we will have a similar relationship. *I will teach you to love me.*"

As the courting process progressed, the couple began to ignore some of the conventional obstacles to gaining access to each other's likes and dislikes.

Shortly into their courting, Robert brought up the subject of Anne's name and whether she would mind if he called her something just a little different. "I have to admit that I find it somewhat unnerving to call you Anne. Even though your name is spelled with an 'e' on the end, its pronunciation is the same as that of my deceased wife's. Would you object to my calling you Annie? I call my sister Jane, Janie. Somehow it seems a little more affectionate."

She laughed. "I would love to have you call me Annie. It gives me my own identity. You can call me Annie or any other term of endearment that you would like.

"Now on the same note, what should I call you? I don't want it to be something artificial or inappropriate. It should be something that no one else has called you. I want it to be unique."

Robert shrugged; he had no idea what nickname or term of endearment she could use. He thought of his adopted Indian name, but quickly discarded the idea. He was at a loss for ideas.

"I know!" she said. "I'll use part of your last name. I'll call you Tay. That's certainly unique. I've never heard it used for any of the Taylor family. What do you think? Is it affectionate enough?"

Robert laughed heartily. This young woman was making every attempt to achieve what she warned that she was going to do. It echoed in his ears, *I will teach you to love me.* Tay and Annie it would be.

It didn't take long for the news to spread throughout the Swatara Valley that the two were a'courting. A number of young men in the region were disappointed that Anne or Annie was being won over by the frontiersman from the Tuscarora Valley.

As the summer wore on, the couple spent as much time together as they could. Almost every encounter began in the same manner. Annie would go right to Tay as though she was magnetized to him. Her sensuous mouth sought his mouth, her eager body clamping against his, and they would struggle to get closer.

The kisses would continue for a long time, and when they broke, the couple had to step back abruptly, betraying the desire of their bodies. Tay's mind would be scrambled; he would keep telling himself he wasn't ready for these types of feelings and at times would feel outright ashamed of his reactions to her. He began to enjoy the encounters immensely, and soon realized there was no turning back. He found himself in an awkward position, but knew that he was thoroughly smitten.

"Tay, I know that the heat of the summer is not conducive to our old custom of bundling, but there are some evenings that are pleasant enough for us to practice such intimacy—unless you think we would lead ourselves into the temptation to engage in unchaste activity. Perhaps you feel it is too naughty?"

Robert tilted his eyes down to meet hers. "I guess I'm somewhat naïve. I haven't become accustomed to how far our relationship has developed, and just never considered the civility to request your permission to bundle.

"I consider the custom to be quite innocent and virtuous. I just hadn't realized it would be prudent in our situation. I do not see it as an indecent action, but I didn't want to appear unseemly towards you."

"Unseemly towards me? Ever since the first day that I observed you treating your extremely ill wife so tenderly, I've had a deep feeling towards you. I know at the time it was just a teenage susceptibility, but your very smile would have melted me into a fit of passion if I had allowed it. I felt so ashamed of myself at times. I had the feeling that Ann and your sister both knew how a simple little teenaged neighbor girl felt about you. Those feelings about you have grown considerably over the last two years.

"I know I'm not a model of virtue and modesty by expressing these deep feelings to you, but I want you to know exactly how I feel. Over the two years or so there has been a virtual parade of suitors calling at my door. Some perhaps would have been a proper match as a spouse, but I never considered any of them. My heart and mind were set on waiting for you to return to our valley.

"Don't get me wrong, I never prayed or plotted that Ann's life would be cut short, but we all knew that she would never be able to recover from her affliction. She was a beautiful, courageous woman, and I can easily see why you loved her so much. I admired your deep love for her.

"I know I never will be able to replace Ann in your heart, but given time, I think I can fill part of the void in your life and help you to reconstruct your life on the Tuscarora. We don't have to be in any hurry. Please give me the opportunity to be by your side for the rest of my life."

It took Robert quite some time to react to her confession of her true feelings for him. He just didn't know what to say; he was at a complete loss for words. Finally, he awkwardly addressed the situation. "I appreciate your openness, but I must admit that it never occurred to me until now that a beautiful, young woman like yourself could possibly be attracted to me. I'm extremely flattered, but you're going to have to give me some time to figure out this new development.

"You know that I can't stay on the Swatara indefinitely. I must return to the Tuscarora as soon as this new Indian threat is under control. The Tuscarora is my home, my future."

Annie smiled. "And I want to make my life and my home with you on the Tuscarora. I'm ready to become Mrs. Robert Taylor. Whenever you feel it is appropriate, we can be wed. I don't want to rush you into a decision. It will be done on your time schedule."

When she added, "I don't want to pressure you," he perceived that she didn't really mean that. Then she continued, "But the middle of November would be a beautiful time of year to have a wedding, right after the corn harvest."

Robert's breath caught in his throat; he knew that he had to keep his voice calm. She recognized his hesitancy and caught a flicker of concern crossing his face. He concentrated on his breathing so that he could fight off the rising panic that threatened to block his courage.

After a brief period, he was amazed that when he began to speak, his voice was soft and his motions slow and precise. He attempted to avoid her keen blue eyes, but he took one peek and her chin went up, and he noticed that her eyes were beginning to fill with tears.

He clenched his fists, relaxed them, and impulsively squeezed her close. Uncertain, trembling, he pulled her body against his. "You will have to be patient with me. I am overwhelmed that you feel this way about me, but you have to realize that your feelings about me were much further advanced than mine about you. So, I have a little catching up to do."

Waves of sexual pleasure surged through their bodies as he drew her even closer. "How could I not want you? I certainly desire to make you happy. Yes, a mid-November wedding would be a wonderful time of the year to begin our lives together."

They embraced for a long time, then withdrew and exchanged a secret and satisfied look. "I've dreamed of this for so long," Annie whispered. "You have no idea how happy you've made me. I promise to make you happy. I must warn you that I desire to raise a rather large family, at least five, maybe more."

Robert grinned. "I think we'd better notify some others about our big decision." Since her parents had observed how happy their daughter was with Robert and had come to understand why, they received the news with enthusiasm. Her mother could hardly wait to begin the planning. When they informed his family, Janie danced up and down. Her role of cupid had been successful.

While the two Swatara lovers were planning their future, the situation on the frontier became grim. Robert didn't know how fortunate he was to have heeded Croghan's advice and deserted his claim on the Tuscarora for a temporary period of time.

CHAPTER TWENTY

The Western Frontier
May–June 1763

Even though the fort at Detroit was able to hold off the attacks by Pontiac's braves, many of the other British forts were not as fortunate. One by one, the small British garrisons succumbed to ruses and direct attacks. By the end of June, the Indians had overwhelmed nine forts.

The first to fall was Fort Sandusky on May 16. A group of Wyandots gained entry to the fort under the pretense of holding council, a similar ploy to the one that had been foiled at Detroit. The fifteen-man garrison was seized and killed, and the fort was burned.

On May 25, the Pottawatomie at Fort St. Joseph used the same pretense successfully, and most of the fifteen-man garrison was killed.

Fort Quiatenon fell on June 1. The commander of the fort was lured outside the stockade by his native mistress and fatally shot by the attacking Miami Indians who had surrounded the fort. The small nine-man garrison surrendered without a fight.

Fort Michilimackinac stood on the southern shore of the Straits of Mackinac, which separate Lake Michigan from Lake Huron, and was the largest fort taken by surprise. Entrance into this fort was gained by a ruse during a baggatiway game or, as the French called it, *le jeu de la crosse*. The baggatiway match was staged between the Chippewas and the Sauks, and the garrison was invited to witness the match.

Baggatiway is a violent and noisy game. There are two posts planted in the ground a considerable distance apart, and the object of the game is to propel a ball to the post with the use of a curved stick resembling a type of racket. High wagers are placed on the outcome of the match.

The wagers and the intensity of the match enticed many of the garrison, including the commanding officer, to go outside the walls of the fort. In the meantime, many Indian women had slipped inside the gates with weapons concealed under their garments.

The ball was hit into the fort through the open gate, and the teams rushed inside on the pretense of securing the ball. Once inside the women handed the weapons to the warriors, and the slaughter of the garrison ensued, while the French Canadian inhabitants of the fort looked on. Therefore, on the King's birthday in June 1763, the British lost an important military post and a center of the fur trade.

At Venango around June 16, a large body of Senecas pretended to be friendly and gained entrance to the fort. The Senecas quickly closed the gates and commenced to butcher the small garrison, except for Lieutenant Gordon. Gordon was tortured over a slow fire for several successive nights until mercifully he expired. Once this task was completed, the Senecas burned the fort to the ground and then left the scene.

Fort LeBoeuf was garrisoned by Pennsylvania Germans of the Royal Americans under the command of Ensign Price. (The Royal Americans were recruited in the colonies, and their officers were commissioned by the king of England.) A large body of Indians struck this fort on June 18, and eventually burned it to the ground. Price and seven soldiers were fortunate to escape out the back of the fort and made their way south to Fort Pitt and safety.

Ensign John Christie had been placed in command of Fort Presqu'Isle with a garrison of twenty-seven soldiers of the Royal Americans. The fort surrendered on June 22, following a two-day battle against a force of about two hundred Indians. Benjamin Gray was lucky enough to escape to Fort Pitt; the rest of the defenders were either killed or taken to the Detroit region as captives.

Captain Simeon Ecuyer commanded Fort Pitt in the spring of 1763. Ecuyer had a force of 330 soldiers, traders, and backwoodsmen in his command, and the surrounding village of Pittsburgh was composed mostly of traders and their families. Major Gladwin of Detroit had warned Ecuyer in early May of the activities of the Shawnees and Delawares in the vicinity.

A party of Indians camped on the shore of the Allegheny River opposite the fort on the evening of May 27, 1763. The next morning the Indians crossed the river and demanded bullets, hatchets, and gunpowder for the great amount of furs they produced. These demands aroused Ecuyer's concern. Two days later, Ecuyer ordered the inhabitants of the village of Pittsburgh to be moved into the fort, and he had the cabins and houses leveled outside the rampart so that an attacking force could not use them for protection.

The beleaguered defenders were kept in a state of restless alarm as the Indians fired at sentinels twenty-four hours of the day. On the afternoon of June 22, a party of Delawares drove off the horses and cows that had continued to graze in an open field outside the fort. The Indians were showered with bursting shells from the fort's howitzers, but they suffered few casualties.

The next morning Turtle Heart and Shingas approached the fort for a council. Turtle Heart addressed the garrison. "Six nations of Indians are on their way to destroy Fort Pitt as they have already done to Prequ'Isle, LeBouef, and Venango; however, you whites will be spared if you leave the fort and return to the white settlements to the east of the mountains."

Captain Ecuyer stared Turtle Heart straight in his face and stated flatly, "At this very moment, an army of six thousand soldiers are on the march from Ligonier to relieve Fort Pitt. Another three thousand are on the march to attack the Ottawas and Ojibways of the Great Lakes. It is you who had better be concerned about being spared."

The parley ended on that note. Many of the Indians, visibly shaken by this information, withdrew from the vicinity of the fort the next day. Fort Pitt was spared for the moment and for several weeks no further substantial attacks were mounted.

Shingas, Turtle Heart, and a few lesser chiefs approached the fort on July 26 under a flag that had been given to the Indians a few months before. The Indians were allowed to enter the fort, and this time Shingas addressed Ecuyer. "We wish to hold fast the chain of friendship—that ancient chain which our forefathers held with their brethren, the English. You have let your end of the chain fall to the ground, but ours is still fast within our hands. Why do you complain that our young men have fired at your soldiers and killed their cattle and horses? You yourselves are the cause of this. You marched your armies into our country and built forts here, though we told you repeatedly that we wished you to leave. My brothers, this land is ours, and yours."[4]

Captain Ecuyer replied, "I have warriors, provisions, and ammunition to defend the fort for three years against all the Indians in the woods; and we shall never abandon it as long as a white man lives in America. This is our home.... If any of you appear again about this fort, I will throw bombshells, and fire cannon among you, loaded with a whole bag of bullets."[5]

The Indians began their attack the night after the conference. Under cover of darkness, the Indians dug holes that sheltered them from fire from the fort and from which they could fire their muskets or launch fire arrows. A general attack was launched at daybreak; it continued until nightfall, and the same strategy was employed for several days.

Chaos and terror reigned inside the walls of the fort as the fire arrows set the roofs and sides of buildings ablaze. The attack lasted five days and five nights and didn't cause much physical harm or damage, but assuredly caused great psychological trepidation.

Suddenly, on August 1, to the relief of the harassed and exhausted defenders, the attackers withdrew from their siege of Fort Pitt. The Indians had learned of the advance of Colonel Henry Bouquet, who was pushing his army westward to relieve Fort Pitt, and they moved swiftly to attack Bouquet at Bushy Run.

The small forts at Redstone and Bushy Run were abandoned due to the lack of soldiers to garrison them. At the same time that Fort Le Boeuf to the north was being destroyed, Fort Ligonier on the Loyalhanna came under attack. Ligonier was commanded by Lieutenant Archibald Blane of the Royal Americans who were small in number. The few settlers located near the fort hurriedly abandoned their plantations and sought the refuge of the fort. Pontiac's and Guyasuta's warriors attacked the post in early June, knowing that the elimination of this outpost would open the path to Carlisle.

Captain Ourry of Fort Bedford sent a relief party of twenty sharpshooting woodsmen, who arrived at Ligonier about July 1. Colonel Bouquet sent thirty Highlanders accompanied by keen-eyed backwoodsmen from Carlisle. These additional defenders allowed Blane to resist being overrun until Colonel Henry Bouquet arrived with his small army on August 2.

A siege of Fort Bedford began around the time of the attack on Fort Ligonier. Louis Ourry, the commander of Fort Bedford, ordered that the small posts at Stony Creek and Juniata Crossing were to be abandoned and their defenders quickly advanced to Bedford to enforce it. The garrison of three men stationed at Fort Lyttleton abandoned their post and marched to Bedford.

The settlers in the region of Fort Bedford attempted to reach the alleged safety of the fort, although many were unsuccessful and were overtaken and killed. On June 3 Louis Ourry wrote to Colonel Bouquet: "No less than ninety-three families are now here for refuge, and more hourly are arriving. I expect ten more before night."[6]

Colonel Bouquet's relief force arrived at Fort Bedford on July 25, to the great relief of all those within the walls of the fort. Here Bouquet was informed of the dire situation to the west.

CHAPTER TWENTY ONE

The Tuscarora Valley
Summer 1763

With the apparently simultaneous attacks on the frontier spreading across the mountains to the east, many frontier families did not receive the news that the comparative freedom from Indian incursions had vanished. The frontier of Pennsylvania suddenly was overrun by Indian war parties attacking traders, secluded cabins, border settlements, small farms, and villages.

The inhabitants were surprised and murdered with similar cruelty and barbarity as had been witnessed in the earlier French and Indian War. Those people who were not killed were taken captive. The terrified population attempted to escape eastward to the safety of forts, while others sought shelter in Shippensburg, Carlisle, York, and Lancaster, or as far away as Philadelphia.

The frontier was dotted with abandoned plantations and farms. The roads, such as they were, were overrun with panicked people without any of the necessities of life. This great influx of humanity placed a great strain on the supplies of provisions, housing, water, sanitation, and other necessities.

Some people decided against fleeing. In many areas, a rich harvest of wheat and rye awaited the reaper, and some farmers gambled that they could reap their crops before the wrath of the Indian attacks struck their areas. Some gambled and lost, while others barely made it across the mountains in time to save their scalps.

The Tuscarora Valley that Robert Taylor had abandoned in May was left unscathed until July of 1763. Ralph Sterrett, the old Indian trader, had rebuilt the fort at Bigham's that had been destroyed in 1756. Earlier in the spring of 1763, Sterrett had displayed extraordinary humanity, which, unbeknownst to him at the time, would deliver his family and many of his neighbors from certain death or captivity

Just after dawn on a day in early April, Ralph was involved in removing a stubborn stump in a field along the approach to the fort. Out of the corner of his left eye, he noticed some movement. His old instincts kicked in, and he immediately dropped his pick and grabbed his gun, just in case he would need to defend himself.

Upon further investigation, he observed that the movements were halting and unsteady. He approached the originator of the disturbance with his gun at the ready.

A raspy voice, speaking in a heavy Delaware dialect, croaked, "Friend! No enemy!"

Ralph did not let down his guard until he saw that at the end of his gun barrel was an exhausted, apparently starving Native American. Once Ralph recognized the plight of the Delaware, he brought him to the safety of the fort, where the Sterrett family and the other inhabitants of the fort gave him some venison, bread, a dram of rum, and some tobacco.

The Sterretts allowed the Indian to rest the remainder of the day. Once he seemed to have recovered, he thanked his white hosts and headed west on the Tuscarora Path, a revived man.

With all the problems involved in hacking a living out of the forest, the incident with the destitute Indian was soon forgotten. Even with the news of the renewed outbreaks of hostilities, the episode was far from eveeryone's mind.

The notion of fleeing across the mountains had not embedded itself in the minds of the inhabitants of the Tuscarora Valley until several bloody massacres and conflagrations occurred in early July.

On the Sabbath day of July 10, the Indian hostiles, under the leadership of Shamokin Daniel, caught four harvesters and a boy observing the day of rest in the cabin of William White near Patterson's fort. The boy, John Riddle, was shot in the arm and captured in a rye field. His father, William Riddle, was fortunate enough to escape through the roof. Others in the house were shot and burned.

The raiding party moved up the Tuscarora Creek to the mouth of Licking Creek where six men were in Robert Campbell's house enjoying dinner. The Indians rushed the house and of the six in the house, only George Dodds was successful in escaping across the mountain to Sherman's Valley.

The attackers continued up the Tuscarora Creek to near what is now Spruce Hill. Near dusk, they shot and killed William Anderson who apparently was seated at his table with his Bible in his hand. They summarily dispatched Anderson's son, Joseph, and adopted daughter with their tomahawks and war clubs. Fortunately, Anderson's wife, Mary, was residing at their former home in Middleton Township, Cumberland County. Before moving to Middleton Township and the Tuscarora Valley, the Andersons had lived at Fagg's Manor in Chester County.

Anderson's neighbors, William and James Christy and William Graham, heard the shots and the fracas, and not waiting to investigate the disturbance, hastily fled the valley, arriving at Robinson's about midnight. William Graham had warranted a tract of one hundred acres on September 20, 1762, and another hundred acres on March 3, 1763.

When the marauders arrived at the gates of the rebuilt Fort Bigham, they approached it cautiously, believing that it possibly could be well defended. Much to their astonishment the fort was deserted. To show the whites that they had been there, they burned the fort to the ground. In front of the gate, they laid a red war-club across the path, declaring a war to the death against the whites.

Fortunately for the former inhabitants of the fort, the humane treatment of the worn-out Indian earlier in the year by Ralph Sterrett saved them from the same fate as those poor souls trapped in the original fort back on June 11, 1756.

On Saturday night, the inmates of the fort had been alarmed by a disturbance at their gate. Through a benevolent moon, they were able to ascertain that a lone Indian made the noise. Their inclination was to shoot first and ask questions later, but Sterrett yelled out in the Delaware dialect, "What do you want of us?"

The flustered Indian replied that earlier in the spring, the good inhabitants of the fort had aided him in his time of need, and now he wanted to repay these good people. He went on to warn them, "The Indians are as plenty as pigeons in the woods. They will arrive at your gates before the next moon and plan to murder, scalp, and burn all the whites found in their path."

A collective decision was quickly made to pack as rapidly as possible and head across the mountain to Robinson's and on to the safety of Carlisle. The families of John Hardy and Alexander Robison were two that made the wise decision to leave the valley on that night. Thus, the history of Fort Bigham of June 11, 1756, was not repeated.

Another family that made the correct decision to abandon their tract of over three hundred acres was that of William Cunningham. Cunningham had come into the valley almost two years before, and in the summer of 1763, he and his daughters had returned to cut his grain and pull at some flax. On the night of July 10, one of their roosters repeatedly came inside their door and crowed so vigorously that the Cunninghams fled over the Tuscarora Mountain that night.

When the terror-stricken settlers from the Tuscarora Valley spread the news of the attacks in their valley to the men in Sherman's Valley, a volunteer force of twelve men led by the three Robinson brothers, William, Robert, and Thomas, decided to cross over into the Tuscarora Valley and attempt to rescue the remaining harvesters farther up the valley.

Early on Monday morning the volunteers crossed through Bigham's Gap and immediately discovered traces of Indian activity at James Scott's. As they progressed, they found homes that had been pillaged and burned to the ground, and livestock that had been slaughtered and consumed. It appeared that at William Graham's another force of Indians joined the original group, increasing their numbers to about twenty-five.

Upon examining the intruders' tracks, it was evident that they were heading across the mountain by way of Run Gap. The frontiersmen followed in hot pursuit, without regard for the possibility of ambush.

At the crossroads at John Nicholson's near Buffalo Creek, the Indians struck from ambush and killed five of the pursuers in the initial assault. Daniel Miller, William McAllister, and John Nicholson were killed outright. William Robinson was struck in the abdomen with buckshot and died about half a mile from the site of the attack, although the Indians didn't find his body and mutilate it. After firing his rifle three times, Thomas Robinson was hotly pursued and later found scalped and horrifyingly mutilated. John Graham was found dead on a log a short distance from the attack scene.

The attack continued along the creek; Charles Elliot and Edward McConnel were overtaken and shot just as they were attempting to ascend the bank of the creek. The Christy brothers were able to elude their attackers and hid from them for about a week before they could make their escape. Seventeen-year-old John Elliot was also one of the lucky ones who was able to make an escape. The other lucky survivor was Robert Robinson, although he was shot and wounded.

The Indians were flushed with success and continued their harassment of the inhabitants of the lower portion of Sherman's Valley. When the news of the attacks reached Carlisle, a force of nearly forty men marched across the mountains to disperse the Indians and bury the dead settlers.

Upon reaching the banks of Buffalo Creek and the scene of the attack on the Robinson expedition, the relieving force lost its nerve when they were confronted with the mutilated bodies of the slaughtered white settlers. The commander immediately ordered a retreat back across the mountain to Carlisle. The group was so unnerved that the bodies remained unburied and left to the forces of nature.

Captain Dunning led a second force of men from Carlisle with the purpose of overtaking and punishing the marauders. Part of the force attacked the Indians at George McCords's barn, which proved to be a major blunder. Alexander and John Logan, Charles Coyle, and William Hamilton were killed in this engagement, while Bartholomew Davis made good his escape and rejoined Captain Dunning and his command.

Believing that the Indians would strike Alexander Logan's house seeking plunder, Dunning had his force wait in ambush. Three or four Indians were dropped during the first volley, and the rest fled towards the mountain. Dunning and his small force were able to extract some satisfaction by dispatching the Indians.

Colonel John Armstrong and Thomas Wilson took a force of between thirty and forty men into the Sherman's Valley to reconnoiter and assist in burying and returning the dead. They buried the dead in the best manner possible and returned in two days.

Another unfortunate Tuscarora Valley settler was John Allen. Prior to turning in for the night, John had hobbled his horse and hung a cowbell around its neck when he turned the horse out to graze. Upon awakening in the morning, John simply followed the clanging of the cowbell to locate his steed, just as he had done morning after morning.

Unbeknownst to John Allen, during the night a Delaware had slipped the cowbell from the horse's neck. The brave hid in a hollow buttonwood tree and deftly clanged the bell, just as if it was still on the horse. When John approached the huge tree, the Delaware waited patiently until John's back was in front of the opening in the tree. At the opportune moment, the brave nimbly vaulted from his hiding place and struck John with a brutal blow to the head with his war club.

The vicious wallop knocked Allen senseless. The brave made one swooping slash across Allen's throat with his knife, and the white settler's life came to an abrupt end. With four arching slashes with his knife, the warrior expertly severed Allen's scalp from his skull. In defiant triumph, the interloper fluidly and mockingly twirled the blood-soaked hairpiece above his head. As he performed this savage ritual, the young native yelped an air-splitting, "YA-HOODOO!" He announced to the world that he indeed was a better man than poor, desecrated John Allen was, late of the Tuscarora Valley.

Shippensburg and Carlisle were soon filled with former inhabitants of the Sherman's, Tuscarora, and Conococheague Valleys. All available buildings—sheds, fruit cellars, barns, houses—were filled to overflowing with refugees. The frontier was shrouded in gloom and anguish. There was no good news from any part of Pennsylvania's outlying regions. The flood of refugees continued throughout the summer, with no relief in sight.

The congregation of Christ's Church of St. Peter's in Philadelphia attempted to provide some of the frontier inhabitants with relief by raising a sum of 662 pounds. That relief effort was greatly appreciated but made little impact on the urgent situation.

All along the frontier, there was an escalating hatred against all Indians and a burning thirst for vengeance. The terror of the citizens increased as news of the western forts, either under siege or having fallen to the Indians, reached Carlisle. Rumors persisted that in due time the Indians would be here.

In desperate times, desperate men will use desperate measures. It became acceptable that any means of killing an Indian was a good one. General Jeffery Amherst issued orders to give a group of unsuspecting Indians some contaminated blankets from a smallpox hospital. Captain Simeon Ecuyer executed this type of germ warfare on June 24, 1763, at Fort Pitt. An epidemic raged among the tribes all that summer and autumn and into the next year when this tactic was employed, although the disease could easily be spread by warriors returning from attacks on white settlements already infected. Colonel Bouquet agreed with Amherst in using the smallpox method of warfare against the tribes.

The Spanish had developed the use of killer dogs as an instrument of war in their conquest of the Indians. The English were quick to adopt this method of warfare. They bred English mastiffs for the specific purpose of killing Indians. Many weighed a fearsome one hundred fifty pounds and stood two and a half feet tall. They were capable of ripping a person apart with ease. Some called these mastiffs "unstoppable engines of war."

Eventually the use of mastiffs to bait bears and bulls was declared illegal in most colonies, but Indian baiting continued to be considered legal and moral. The colony of Massachusetts allowed the breeding of mastiffs to provide for "the better security of the frontier." Surprisingly, Benjamin Franklin endorsed Indian baiting. He recommended that the dogs be locked up immediately prior to their being used against the Indians so that "they will be fresher and fiercer, and confound the enemy while being very serviceable."

During the renewed Indian uprising, orders were issued that every soldier would receive three shillings a month if he brought a strong dog that could be judged proper to be employed in pursuing the savages.

Colonel Henry Bouquet was in Philadelphia when the outbreak of insurgencies occurred, and he was dispatched to Carlisle. Unfortunately, Bouquet had only a remnant of his Royal Americans under his command. When he arrived in Carlisle on July 1, his army consisted of a few Highlanders, several companies of his Royal Americans, and a small detachment of Rangers; he was expecting about thirty experienced woodsmen to join him at Bedford. Much to Bouquet's consternation, nothing had been done in Carlisle for him to transport provisions to relieve the western forts. Bouquet found himself giving help instead of receiving it.

Bouquet's little relief force left Carlisle and soon arrived at an overcrowded, terrified, and starving group of refugees at Shippensburg. He followed the route to Fort Loudoun, and then the empty posts of Fort Littleton and Juniata Crossing. Along the way, they passed many scattered cabins that were now either abandoned or destroyed.

Captain Ourry welcomed the small army at Fort Bedford on July 25. Bouquet's numbers increased when thirty woodsmen joined them. Ourry sadly informed the colonel that all communication with Fort Pitt had been severed; all he knew was that Pitt was under siege similar to Detroit.

After three days' rest, Bouquet's relief army headed west on Forbes Road hoping to arrive at Fort Ligonier in time to save Lieutenant Archibald Blane and his small beleaguered garrison. When Bouquet appeared on August 2, the Indians fled from the river valley. As at Fort Bedford, there had been no communications with Fort Pitt for several weeks.

Bouquet's march resumed two days later, but he left all his wagons and most of his cattle at Ligonier and pressed on. The following day the relief force was on the march early in the morning, and at a little after noon they were approaching the resting station at Bushy Run.

Most of the Delawares and Shawnees involved in the siege of Fort Pitt had broken off their assault on August 1 in order to attack Bouquet's relief forces. Mingoes and Hurons from Sandusky, plus some Mohicans, Wyandots, Miamis, and Ottawas had reinforced these Indians.

The exhausted soldiers were attacked just as they were expecting to rest for a few hours. The soldiers were quickly surrounded, and Bouquet drew his men into a tight circle on the top of a hill just off the road, and they withstood the onslaught until night fell.

At daybreak, the attack was resumed, but the disciplined soldiers kept the circle unbroken. About ten o'clock, Bouquet deployed a deceptive scheme of withdrawing two of his companies from the circle and using them to attack the Indians' flanks and rear.

With a devastating fire pouring on the Indians from several sides, the Indians broke and ran.

After the nearly two-day bitterly contested battle, the army buried its dead, rested a short time, and slowly proceeded towards Fort Pitt. Captain Ecuyer and his embattled garrison joyfully received Bouquet's force on August 10. After the Battle of Bushy Run, the Delawares and Shawnees abandoned their villages on the Allegheny, Beaver, and Ohio Rivers, and retreated westward to the Tuscarawas and Muskingum River Valleys.

CHAPTER TWENTY TWO

The Proclamation of 1763

Prior to the French and Indian War, and continuing through the current Pontiac Uprising, the restless people living on the frontier who had their origins in the Highlands of Scotland, the wild moors of northern Ireland, the hill pockets of Wales, England itself, or the Rhine Palatinate had developed a voracious land hunger. This group was cantankerous, proud and insistent with a great capacity to endure and an insatiable desire for land. Many of these people became perpetual movers, with a self-renewing quest for a piece of land for themselves.

Land warrants had become a major means of penetrating the forbidden Indian country. A land warrant was a document that permitted the holder to locate a specified number of acres, survey them, and register the claim in the land office. This warrant did not convey title. These western lands were worthless until inhabited.

Not only individual settlers were lured to these western lands, but also a group known as speculators. These speculators formed a company that obtained a reasonably sound title to a section of the wilderness from the colonial governors or from the king. After advertising the section of land and luring settlers into the area, the holdings were divided into small parcels and sold at a large increase in price. These speculators unabashedly manipulated colonial administrators in order to increase their profits.

The British government in London sought to control the buying of vast tracts of land for insignificant sums and then enjoying increased increments for selling the land. Other concerns were the forcible removal of Indians from their lands, the huge cost of keeping troops in America to maintain its new conquests from the French, and defending the colonies from Indian attacks and possible attacks from foreign enemies.

The British answer to its problems on the frontier was the Proclamation of 1763. This action attempted to resolve the Indian problem by separating the Indians from the white population in the American colonies. This decree was published on October 7, 1763, while the colonists, especially in Pennsylvania, were facing the onslaught of the allies of Pontiac.

This proclamation was designed to aid in placating the Indians and erase some of the main causes of the furious resistance under Pontiac's leadership. It was meant only as a temporary resolution. It set down stringent regulations for the conduct of the fur trade and prohibited the purchase of Indian lands by private citizens. Its most important provision made it illegal for the colonists to buy land or settle land west of the crest of the Allegheny Mountains. The entire region between the Alleghenies and the Mississippi was reserved for the Indian tribes, except for white traders who were licensed to sell their goods to the Indians and buy the highly prized furs from them.

This proclamation was issued without any warning to the colonists. In due time this action by the British Parliament would help to set the stage for a violent family quarrel. It deeply embittered many Scotch-Irish settlers who, when they first arrived in Pennsylvania, had found the best acres already taken by Germans and Quakers. The Scotch-Irish had pushed onto the frontier, and many of them had illegally but defiantly squatted on unoccupied land, and had quarreled with both red and white owners.

The Scotch-Irish settlers had felt the full brunt of the attacks on the frontier during the French and Indian War and continuing during the ongoing Pontiac Uprising. Pugnacious, lawless, and individualistic, and having already undergone the experience of colonizers and agitators in Ireland, they proved to be superb frontiersmen and Indian fighters. In addition, they cherished no love for the British government which had uprooted them on the Old Sod, and now they were greatly agitated by the Proclamation of 1763.

Countless Americans, frontiersmen, and land speculators were dismayed and angered when news of this action by the British Parliament reached the frontier, especially on the Pennsylvania frontier.

Wherever people on the frontier gathered, the agitation, hostility, irritation, and bewilderment was vented in disapproval of the Crown's action. Reactions in the Swatara Valley were similarly expressed all along the frontier.

The colonials repeatedly expressed the following sentiments: "Have we not purchased the region beyond the Alleghenies with our blood in the recent war?" "Is not the land beyond the mountains our birthright?" "Since the recent victory over the French, the British have swollen heads." "The British claim that the Proclamation is not designed to oppress us, but what is fair about it?" "The British treat us with no respect; it seems they are in no mood for backtalk." "It appears that the Parliament is annoyed with us unruly colonials, just because we desire a little piece of land." "They think that we Irish are used to a tradition of flouting royal authority; if they keep this up, they haven't seen anything yet."

The group of people termed Scotch-Irish were not really Irish at all but turbulent Scot Lowlanders. Over a period of decades, these Scotch Presbyterians had been transplanted to Northern Ireland where they were resented and hated by the Irish-Catholics who were already established there. The economic life of these Scotch-Irish was severely hampered, especially after the government placed burdensome restrictions on their production of linens and woolens.

Many of the Scotch-Irish vowed that they would not be treated here in America as they had been treated back in their homeland. They would refuse to be maltreated by an absentee government. The French and Indian War and Pontiac's Uprising had caused these colonial peoples to catch a new vision of their destiny. The testing of royal authority lay just around the corner.

The Proclamation of 1763 blasted the hopes and dreams of plantation owners in the South of reestablishing their fortunes through the usual procedure of land speculation. The Southern planters would easily take a leadership role in the rebellion against increased British interference in the American colonies.

CHAPTER TWENTY THREE

The Broadening of Attacks

The attacks upon white settlements didn't occur only in the region west of the Susquehanna River during the summer and fall of 1763. Tribes throughout much of Pennsylvania seemingly had taken up the hatchet and were making a concentrated effort to drive the whites from the hinterlands of the province of Pennsylvania.

During late August, a force of volunteers ventured up the West Branch of the Susquehanna to carry the war against the Indians in that region. On August 26, the volunteers successfully encountered the enemy at Muncy Hill Creek. The next day another group killed some Indians who were returning from Bethlehem.

On September 20 Colonel John Armstrong led a force of volunteers from Fort Shirley to attack the Indians in the vicinity of Grand Island. They found the Indian town abandoned and moved on downriver to Myonaghquia (Jersey Shore) and destroyed a large amount of grain.

In the meantime, the Delawares were attacking settlers in Berks County. These massacres led to the desertion of all the white settlements beyond the Blue Mountains. In October a band of Delawares led by Captain Bull committed atrocities in Northampton and Lehigh Counties.

Also in October, a band of Indians killed a group of settlers in the Wyoming Valley. In early November, a blockhouse was unsuccessfully attacked in Damascus Township in Wayne County. On November 15, three men were murdered on the north side of the Blue Mountains at the forks of the Schuylkill River.

During the fall, Reverend John Elder became recognized as the "Fighting Parson" because he organized a militia called the Paxton, or Paxtang, Rangers. The Paxton Rangers carried on an aggressive type of warfare against the tribes near their region. The Rangers attempted to deprive the enemy of their food supply by destroying the villages and cornfields of the Indians living in the Wyoming Valley of the Susquehanna River basin.

Back on the western frontier, the war was not going well for Pontiac. British reinforcements had arrived at Fort Detroit in late July, and the situation continued to be a stalemate. With the resumed siege of Detroit and the relief of Fort Pitt, many of the tribes began to defect or lose faith in Pontiac's cause and leadership.

The Potawatomies forsook Pontiac in September, and in early October the Mississaugas, Miamis, Chippewas, and Ottawas sent peace delegations to confer with Major Gladwin at Detroit.

On October 20, Pontiac made one last desperate gesture to retain his dwindling forces by calling another council. The weather became a determining factor in the tribes' decision to attend. On October 29 a hard frost occurred while several inches of snow fell. To make matters worse, a messenger from Major Villiers, the commander of Fort de Chartres, arrived. The message called upon the Indians to bury the hatchet and seek peace. He emphasized that the French would not abandon them and would continue to supply them.

With the threat of more winter weather and little time left to hunt, Pontiac lifted the siege of Detroit on October 31 and moved to the Maumee River to spend the winter. Throughout the winter, he laid plans to renew his attacks upon the English when spring arrived. He was counting on the Delawares, Wabash, Miamis, Shawnees, and possibly the Illinois Confederation to back him one more time.

CHAPTER TWENTY FOUR

The Wedding

Due to all the attacks taking place on both sides of the Susquehanna River, many of the white settlers believed that no isolated areas were safe from attack. Only the inhabitants of established towns like Chambersburg Shippensburg, Carlisle, York, and Lancaster could perhaps feel somewhat secure. Robert and his family and neighbors lived under a nerve-racking vigilance twenty-four hours of the day.

The pressure that they lived under was no less than what he had encountered while living on the banks of the Tuscarora. Guns were always loaded and never out of reach. No one traveled alone. Children were kept within the confines of the cabin. While working in the fields or in the woods, one man always stood guard.

The fall harvest in the Swatara Valley progressed in the normal manner without any problems. So did the preparations for the wedding. As the wedding date approached, Robert had some trepidation about whether he was doing the right thing for Anne. However, whenever he was in her company, all those doubts were erased, and he realized that they were made for each other.

The big day finally arrived on November 15. The day was bright and clear, but the temperature was only in the mid-forties. The ceremony was a short, modest one, conducted in the parlor of the Sample home. The Reverend John Elder, the Presbyterian minister, performed the rite in formal solemnity. All the members of both families and their neighbors were present, filling the inside of the home and the porch.

Immediately following the ceremony, the celebration commenced. All the foods of the season were available for consumption. An ample supply of liquor was on hand to ward off the chill. When everyone had the opportunity to eat their fill, the musical instruments were brought forth and the merriment reached a fever pitch. All in attendance enjoyed jigs, hornpipes, folk dances and minuets. The merriment was dampened only by the fact that several men had to forsake the celebration and stand guard, even on a special day such as this. So that everyone had the opportunity to partake of the joyous occasion, the men traded the guard positions on the hour.

About the bewitching hour of midnight, the newlyweds slipped away from the merriment and quickly made their way to their own little cabin. It was located on the opposite side of the barn, so it was somewhat isolated, and isolation and solitude were exactly what they desired.

They prepared for bed slowly and deliberately. Robert suddenly realized that he was frightened about what was to take place, and he assumed she felt the same way. Eventually they arrived on their bed in the only room apportioned off from the rest of the cabin.

Robert saw a real enchantment, for Annie's eyes opened wide and looked up into his, and he kissed her softly and gently on the neck and then on the lips. A forgotten magic was at work within him, something he had not experienced in over seven years. He had completely forgotten that he had ever felt like this, but he never put those thoughts into words.

Afterwards he stroked her hair and whispered, "You have given me the first pleasure I have had in many years."

She kissed him for that. Tears hovered on her eyelids, making a rainbow dazzle in the reflecting fireplace firelight. After she had fallen asleep, he watched the flames flicker in the fireplace, then catch and blaze upward. Annie's hair gleamed in the firelight; her naked body seemed so white next to his. He dared no more than glance after that; it was time that he allowed his new bride to sleep and rest.

When daylight began to peek through the cabin's east window, he arose, placed some more logs on the fire, and slipped out the door to answer a call of nature. Just as he was about to go back inside, she threw open the door. She stood with only a blanket pulled over her shoulders. He flung his arms around her and pressed savage kisses down on her hair and face, searching for her lips. Suddenly she raised her head and gave her lips to him in a hungering kiss. They clung together, swayed, and fell backward into the softness and warmth of their bed. He had her now to do as he wished, as it also was what she wished as well.

An hour later, her body leaped towards his once more, and he answered her passion with as fierce a flame. Afterwards they just held each other close. Eventually she spoke in a soft, barely audible voice. "I'm so glad you came back and let me love you. You bring me so much joy and happiness, more than I ever dreamed of having. I never thought loving you could be so fulfilling."

From outside on the porch they heard the rustle of feminine voices rising in the air. They looked at each other in alarm and frustration; they knew that their special night of nights was over. There would never be another one to match what they had just experienced.

"Listen to that gaggle of silly geese," Annie said. "They're jealous of me. Of course, how could they even guess as to the night that we had? God, I love you, Tay!"

Robert was silent for a moment, frowning abstractedly, and when he began to speak, she thought at first that he had not heard what she had said. "When I was a small boy I used to spend a great deal of time on the banks of the creek, often just listening to the birds. In the fall and spring, the geese would always be the noisiest, and you're right, those females do sound just like a silly gaggle of geese.

"You are right about me coming back. It was the right thing to do, the only thing to do. God had it planned this way, for us to become one. Another thing you were right about, you told me that I would learn to love you. And I have and I do love you, and I always will."

"Truly the world is full of surprises, but this is no surprise to me. I prayed and plotted for you to love me. I thank God every day and night for allowing this to happen."

It had happened so simply, inevitably. "Stay with me here," he whispered, "if only for another hour or two. Your friends will understand."

She gave no sign in answer; her eyes were dancing with merriment. "Just lie quietly and they will go away; then I'll give you one more hour." Then she was upon him, blotting out his look of amazement with passionate kisses.

Within an hour, a larger delegation made up of both sexes made their presence known, and this time they were unrelenting in their desire to see the newlyweds. Reluctantly, the new Mr. and Mrs. Robert Taylor met their friends and neighbors for their first luncheon as man and wife.

CHAPTER TWENTY FIVE

The Paxton Boys

A mood of discontent surrounding Pennsylvania's attempts to protect the citizens of its frontier regions emerged in the close vicinity of the Swatara, and without a doubt it included some of the Taylors' neighbors. Many of these Scotch-Irish immigrants were quite upset over the Quaker-dominated Provincial Council's inattention to continued attacks by the Indians. The majority of the inhabitants of Pennsylvania's frontier were greatly alarmed at the number of Indians of various tribes involved in the depredations and cruelties against white settlers and the lack of ammunition to defend the frontier.

In addition to the ill feelings towards the Provincial Council, many of the Scotch-Irish settlers in this region were upset by the British Parliament's passage of the Proclamation Line of October 7, 1763. They could not believe that the region between the Alleghenies and the Mississippi was not open to settlement.

The hotbed of this unrest was the neighborhood of Paxton Presbyterian Church in the village of Paxton. Reverend John Elder had begun his tenure as the pastor of this church in 1738. As the frustration, tension, and agitation manifested, it was just a matter of time until the settlers took the situation into their own hands, and they too became marauding savages. The inhabitants of Donegal and Paxton townships had requested that the government of Pennsylvania remove the Indians from the region, but the government chose not to take any action.

To many, the natives were looked upon as being bloody barbarians. "They are not human beings! They must be infuriated demons! They are beasts of prey! The bloody barbarians have exercised the most unnatural tortures, and butchered the white settlers in some pagan ritual."

When Reverend Elder was informed of the upcoming attempt to cut off the Conestoga Indians, he sent a warning to Magistrate Forster. "What you men are about to embark upon is cruel and unchristian in nature. The consequences could be severe prosecution and perhaps even capital punishment. I am thoroughly convinced that the Conestoga Indians have an ardent desire to live in peace with us. If vigorous measures are not enacted to deter the frontier vigilantes from murdering the Indians, the consequences may be disastrous."

Elder's actions were to no avail; he simply attributed the attacks to some hot-headed and ill-advised persons, and especially as someone who had suffered much in the late Indian war.

Many of the Paxtonians believed that some of the professed friendly Indians were guilty of treachery. They asserted, "Have not the bloody barbarians exercised on our fathers, mothers, brothers, sisters, wives, and children, inoffensive as they were, the most unnatural and leisurely tortures, butchered some in their beds, in the dead hour of the night, at their meals, or in some unguarded hour?"

The Paxtonians lent a deaf ear to Pastor Elder. One of them, Matthew Smith, said, "The preacher has gone soft on the savages. If the Provincial government refuses to solve the Indian problem in our valley, we'll solve the situation ourselves, even if we have to take the law into our own hands."

Reverend Elder did everything in his power to dissuade them from committing any rash acts against the Conestoga Indians. He decided to make one final effort to divert the Paxton Boys from their rash act. Elder mounted his horse and rode as hard as his horse would allow in an attempt to cut off the enraged men from Paxton.

When he finally overtook the mob, he blocked the narrow road with his own horse and body. "Men, you must listen to reason. I know you and your neighbors, friends, and relatives have suffered severely at the hands of the natives, but you must allow the law to handle their transgressions. I know all of you. You are good Christian men and law-abiding citizens. Do not allow innocent blood to stain your hands.

"I have urged the provincial government to move the Conestogas away from our frontier region, but to no avail. The pacifist Quaker-dominated government has taken a staunch defensive stance involving our concerns about Indian raids on our settlements. They seemingly cannot believe that the Moravian mission Indians are capable of trading with the Delawares and aiding them in their aggressive actions against us."

Matthew Smith pushed his horse through the throng of horses until he came face-to-face with the preacher. Smith looked squarely into Elder's eyes. "Pastor, you and I have been friends and neighbors for over fifteen years. I have sat in your church and listened to numerous sermons over the years. Most of us in this group have ridden with you just recently against the Indians further up the Susquehanna. Many of us affectionately refer to you as the 'Fighting Parson,' due to your esteemed role in organizing the Paxton Rangers during Pontiac's Uprising. There is no one who does not respect you and your principles. But I warn you, if you don't remove your horse from the middle of this road, I personally will blow the very life out of you with my own rifle."

For a matter of moments the two men stared at each other; the others in the group held their breath, hoping that Smith would not commit such an impulsive act. Slowly, Elder nodded. "Yes, Matthew, I do believe you would perform such an impetuous act of homicide. It appears you have been relieved of all your reasoning powers. I will not attempt to halt your endeavors any longer. Nevertheless, I certainly will spend the rest of this cold night in prayer, asking God's forgiveness for the dastardly acts that it appears you are so obstinately set on committing. I'll pray for all your wayward souls."

At daybreak the next day, Wednesday, December 14, 1763, the Paxton Boys mounted on horseback and, led by Matthew Smith, attacked the Conestoga village in Manor Township. Not all the Conestogas were at home in their village when the attack was unleashed.

Six of the village members were quickly massacred. The chief, Shaheas or She-e-hays, George or Wa-a-shen, Harry or Tee-kau-ly, Ess-ca-nesh, the chief's son, Sally or Te-a-won-sha-I-ong, and Ka-ne-un-qu-as were eliminated in this first attack. The assailants set fire to the victim's homes, and most of them were destroyed.

The Conestogas who were not in the village at the time of the attack were quickly lodged in the jail at Lancaster as a place of safety. Any of the personal effects of the survivors were removed for safekeeping as well.

Opinions ran high concerning the actions taken by the Paxton Rangers against the Conestogas. Robert Taylor realized that eventually he would be coerced into taking a stand on the issue. From time to time, he listened to citizens of the Swatara Valley and the vicinity, and Robert was concerned and appalled at the threats that some alleged Christians made against Indians that he considered to live peaceful and Christian-like lives.

As far as Robert was concerned, there was no one in this valley who had suffered more than he had at the hands of the Indians. Nevertheless, he was inclined to judge the natives as individuals, rather than lump them all into one category.

He had had good Indian friends living in this valley when he was a young lad, and no one treated him better than his Tuscarora neighbors from the village of Lacken in the Tuscarora Valley.

During his captivity both of his adopted families had treated him as an equal once he passed certain tests and won their respect. As much as Robert hated and despised Shingas and King Beaver and many of their followers, his ill will did not extend to all Indians.

He did not consider himself an Indian-lover, but he certainly was not an Indian-hater. It was difficult, if not impossible, for him to comprehend the concept that "the only good Indian was a dead one."

On their way home from church on the third Sunday in December, he couldn't help injecting his feelings and sentiments into a discussion he overheard on the outskirts of the church property.

Two neighbors, Keith Murray and John Collier, became involved in a deliberation over the Conestoga slayings. "I just can't believe that they murdered those poor, defenseless people," asserted Collier.

"What do you mean, 'poor people'?" countered Murray. "They're nothing but bloody savages! They massacred my brother and his family up in the Wyoming Valley. As far as I'm concerned, they got what they had coming."

As more people left the church, they joined the circle of people who were witnessing the exchange between the two neighbors. Many of these people began to make comments supporting either Collier or Murray, and the situation began to get out of hand.

Matthew Smith, one of the alleged leaders of the attack on the Conestogas, pushed his way to the front of the crowd. "John Collier, if you don't like what we defenders of this valley have done, then you ought to head back east and live among these pacifist, Indian-loving Quakers." Spying Robert on the fringes of the crowd, Smith turned his anger towards Robert. "What about you, Robert Taylor? You haven't helped our cause any."

Robert couldn't contain himself any longer. "I happen to believe that Reverend Elder's viewpoint is the correct one. The Conestoga Indians can't be much of a threat to us. Most of them are old men, women and children. To assault those Indians in Lancaster would be nothing but murder and unchristian in manner. The Indians who have plagued our frontier recently were under the influence of Pontiac. Pontiac's power has been diminished; it's almost nonexistent.

"No one in this valley has lost more or suffered more than I." Robert then removed his hat. "I want you to take a good, long look at this scar on the side of my head. I collected that little reminder on June 11, 1756, at Fort Bigham located in the Tuscarora Valley. Some of you have probably had a grand time poking fun at my unusual hair style. That was a gift from my captors in the Ohio and Allegheny Valleys.

"I spent almost two years living among the natives. What I observed is that they are just like us whites. There are good Indians, and there are bad Indians. Just like there are good whites and bad whites. If I were to return to Western Pennsylvania, I would perhaps be reacquainted with some natives who would welcome me as a friend and a brother. On the other hand, there are some out there who have warned me that the next time I see them, they will gladly lift my scalp.

"If you really must spill the blood of Indians to satisfy your need for revenge, then go west and join Colonel Bouquet's army as they move against the Indians in the Ohio Valley. Somehow, I don't think many of you have the intestinal fortitude for such an endeavor. It's much easier to attack someone who can't defend himself."

"Are you calling me a coward?" demanded Matthew Smith.

"I never used those words. Those are *your* words. People can make their own assumption about you."

"You're nothing but a damn Indian lover. I bet you even slept with a squaw out on the Ohio. You damn squaw-lover!"

"Anytime you want to press the issue, I'm available. Just be willing to back up your words face-to-face, but not in the dark of night, or from ambush. I'm ready anytime, anywhere, and now is as good a time and place as any."

Smith looked around for support from the crowd, but it did not materialize. Eventually he said, "This is the Lord's Day, a day of rest. Therefore, I have more important things to attend to than worry about a squaw-lover. There will be another time."

"I'll be here on the Swatara for at least another three or four months, if you desire to back up those words some day."

On December 14, 1763, Matthew Slough, the coroner of Lancaster County in Manor Township, conducted an inquisition.

The outcome of the inquest was that a person or persons unknown to the members of the inquest had killed the six Indians. The findings of the inquest were sent to Governor Penn in Philadelphia.

Governor John Penn issued a proclamation on December 22, offering a reward for bringing the perpetrators of this dastardly deed to trial to be dealt with according to the laws of the province. The governor called upon judicial, civil, and military officials to take action against these culprits in Lancaster County.

The Paxtonians disregarded the governor's proclamation. At approximately two o'clock on December 27, 1763, a sizable number of men, fifty or sixty, armed with knives, tomahawks, and rifles, under the leadership of Lazarus Stewart, rushed into the town of Lancaster and attacked the workhouse where the surviving fourteen Conestogas had been confined for their own safety.

The sheriff, John Hay, the coroner, and several other citizens attempted to oppose the assailants, but they were unable to provide protection for the unarmed Indians. The unfortunate inhabitants were unarmed, unprotected and completely helpless. As the slaughter began, the groveling Conestoga men, women, and children avowed their innocence of any attacks upon whites, and declared their love and obedience to the English Crown and the Province of Pennsylvania.

The assertions of three old, defenseless, unarmed men, three women, five little boys, and three little girls, fell upon deaf ears. The Conestogas were butchered in a shocking and repulsive manner. Brains were blown out, legs and hands chopped off, and heads were spilt open or scalped. Later the mangled bodies were buried at Lancaster.

Governor John Penn issued warrants for the arrest of the perpetrators on January 2, 1764, but this judicial order was not carried out due to the sympathetic views of many other residents of frontier Lancaster County.

The malcontents of Lancaster County were not sufficiently content with their felonious actions and next set their sights on the Moravian Indian settlement in the town of Bethlehem. On January 4, 1764, in order to avoid a massacre in Bethlehem like the one that had occurred in Lancaster, some of the Moravian missionaries moved the Moravian Indians to Philadelphia for safety.

An attempt was made to move the Moravian Indians to New York by sloop where they would be under the protection of the British army stationed in New York City. Just before the Indians were to embark on the sloops, a message arrived from the Governor of New York that not one Indian should set foot in New York. The Indians were then sent to Province Island near Philadelphia.

The Paxton Boys were incensed that the provincial government would continually refuse to allocate tax money to protect people on the frontier, but found it quite expedient to use tax money to protect these Indians. In late January, a group of between six hundred and fifteen hundred Paxton Boys began a march on Philadelphia, not only with the objective of eliminating the Moravian Indians, but to demand equal representation with the other counties of the province.

The authorities placed the Indian refugees under an armed guard in the garrison and sent an armed force of six foot companies, one artillery company, and two troops of horse to meet the Paxton Boys at Germantown. Some one thousand of the inhabitants of the city volunteered to render assistance to the troops should they fail in their attempt to halt the advance.

Dr. Benjamin Franklin led a group of Philadelphians to meet with the leaders of the exasperated multitude from the interior counties of the province. The marchers stated their avowed purpose to dispose of the Moravian Indians, but strongly presented their concept of "equal representation" in the Colonial Assembly.

The Quaker stronghold of the three eastern counties of Chester, Philadelphia, and Bucks had twenty-six representatives. The five interior counties of Lancaster, York, Berks, Northampton, and Cumberland had but ten representatives. It was the interior counties inhabited by the Scotch-Irish, German, and several other minority groups who had suffered the Indian attacks and were the true defenders of the frontier and the province.

Matthew Smith and James Gibson proceeded to Philadelphia to relay their grievances to Governor Penn and the Colonial Assembly. The majority of the marchers returned to their homes peacefully. While in the City of Brotherly Love, Smith and Gibson were placed on trial for the killing of the Conestoga. The two men were found "not guilty" and returned to their homes in Lancaster County.

Unhappily for the Paxton Rangers and their spokesmen, the only demand on their list that received any affirmative action was the passage of a bounty on Indian scalps. Soon other problems presented themselves to the people attempting to survive on Pennsylvania's frontier, and the Paxton Boys were all but forgotten.

CHAPTER TWENTY SIX

Bouquet's Expedition, 1764

After defeating the Indians at Bushy Run, Colonel Henry Bouquet remained at Fort Pitt until January 1764. When Bouquet was unable to accomplish his mission with undisciplined provisional militia, he returned east to raise enough troops to invade the region of the Ohio west of Fort Pitt.

Finally, on August 10, 1764, his army marched from Carlisle and arrived at Fort Loudoun on the 13th. The army followed the Forbes Road over the mountains and arrived at Fort Pitt on September 17. In late September, troops from Virginia arrived at the fort and gave Bouquet a force of nearly fifteen hundred troops.

Bouquet had sent a message to the Indians that he would pay no attention to the peace made by the Shawnees and Delawares with Colonel Bradstreet, believing that the Indians were not sincere in their actions. He also stated that he planned to move against the Indians immediately and that they should speedily agree to Bouquet's conditions of peace.

The invading force left Fort Pitt on October 4. By October 15, they had progressed into the heart of the Indian Territory, spreading terror among the population along the way. On October 17 and 20, Bouquet met with the chiefs of the Mingoes, Shawnees, and Delawares.

Bouquet's stance against the Indians was a bold and different approach. He chose to treat them with contempt and not as equals, and charged them with cruelty and perfidy. He let it be known that his troops were seeking revenge and possessed the power to destroy their tribes.

When the councils terminated, Bouquet took hostages from the Senecas, Shawnees, and Delawares to ensure the safe delivery of the captives who were to be returned within twelve days to the town of Wakatomica. To further impress and dismay the Indians, Bouquet marched his army thirty-two miles deeper into Indian country to the forks of the Muskingum, arriving near the forks on October 25. In a move to keep the Indians off balance, Bouquet insisted upon bringing the captives to this site instead of Wakatomica.

A total of 206 captives were brought to Bouquet's camp from October 25 to November 9. On November 12 and 14 Bouquet met with the chiefs of the Shawnees. The colonel demanded that the Shawnees hand over six hostages to be kept until the remainder of the captives were released. Due to the oncoming winter, these remaining captives would not be delivered until the next spring.

On November 18, Bouquet's army, with his white captives, began their march back to Fort Pitt. The army arrived at the Forks of the Ohio on November 28. Some of the captives were reunited with their families at Fort Pitt, while others were returned east to Carlisle and Lancaster. Along the way, several of the captives managed to escape and returned to the Indians.

The next spring, on May 9, 1765, the Shawnees kept their word and turned over the remaining captives to Deputy Indian Agent George Croghan at Fort Pitt. As in the past, many of these captives were unwilling to be emancipated, and many had to be bound when delivered to keep them from escaping back to their Indian families.

CHAPTER TWENTY SEVEN

The Return of the Innis Children

Word of the success of Bouquet's expedition to the Ohio Country spread eastward promptly. Once again, the hopes of many frontier families were raised that their loved ones who had been carried away during the earlier Indian uprising that began in 1755, and during the more recent troubles of 1763, would be returned to their homes.

Robert Taylor, although absent from the Tuscarora Valley in the fall of 1764 and the winter of 1765 when the newly surrendered captives began to arrive in Carlisle and Lancaster, immediately traveled to Lancaster to view first-hand the arrival of the captives.

As in the past, he scrutinized each child in Robbie's and Elizabeth's age group. Robert's hard luck continued its run; no child in any of the returning groups matched his missing children in age or physical characteristics.

Robert had felt for sure that Francis and Margery Ennis would have journeyed to Lancaster to examine the returnees, just as he had done. For some reason the Ennis family was not there. Their absence concerned Robert. He was tormented by the sight of one boy and girl who had been claimed by a man from Philadelphia. There was something oddly familiar about the pair, but he couldn't put his finger on the exact mannerism that activated his vexation. Those captives who were not claimed were taken to Philadelphia.

Later he lamented to his wife, "I know it's been over eight years since Jane and Nathaniel were carried away from Fort

Bigham and that immense changes would have incurred in that time span, but there was something about the girl's demeanor that reminded me of Jane."

Robert had difficulty sleeping that night. The image of the young girl swirled over and over in his mind. He just couldn't accept the fact that these two children had been reunited with their rightful parents.

Upon arising in the morning, Robert announced, "I'm going to attempt to contact Francis and Margery about the possibility that Jane and Nathaniel were matched up with the wrong parents. I know I could be stirring up a hornet's nest over mistaken identity and agitate broken dreams and heartaches. I just know that if the shoe was on the other foot and someone thought that he or she recognized Robbie and Elizabeth, I would want to know.

"I'm going to contact the officer in charge of yesterday's exchange and secure the name and address of the man from Philadelphia, just in case Francis and Margery want to pursue the identities of the two children."

After obtaining the information from the officer, Robert sent an urgent message to Carlisle to be relayed across the mountain to the Tuscarora Valley and the Ennis family. Nearly three weeks later, a return message was received from Francis. He explained that Margery was expecting another child and was not in very good health. That was why they had been absent from the exchange of captives. Francis was due to arrive in Lancaster in the near future and would inform Robert of his arrival so that they could review what Robert had observed during the captive exchange.

About ten days later, the message arrived that Francis would call upon the Taylors within a day or two. When Francis arrived at the Taylor farm, he and Robert spent several hours catching up on news before they tackled the reason for Francis's journey to the east.

Robert methodically described what he had observed in Lancaster and his convictions that the young pair was indeed

Jane and Nathaniel. "I hope and pray my suspicions are correct and that I am not leading you down the pathway to more heartache and disappointment."

Francis looked Robert straight in his eyes. "Robert, it's been over eight years since the attack, and I've never given up hope that my children would be returned. I know that you have the same feelings about your children as well. Anything is worth a try. Sure, I'll be disappointed if it isn't they, but I have to see with my own eyes. The man from Philadelphia, a Mr. Williamson Oliver, can't do more than order me off his property.

"I have one more favor to ask, Robert. Will you go with me to Philadelphia?"

"Most certainly I'll go with you! After all, I'm the one who got you to come this far. What kind of a friend would I be if I abandoned your cause at this point? I'll be ready to travel when you are. Let's head for Lancaster tomorrow and talk to the authorities about what kind of obstacles we could run into."

The two friends and former neighbors left for Lancaster shortly after sunrise. The meeting with the authorities didn't materialize until after midday the next day. This meant that they spent two nights in Lancaster, but they were on their way to Philadelphia the second morning.

As in the past, Robert was able to utilize the relationship that he had kindled and built with the John Taylor family of Thornbury Township whom he had visited on several previous excursions to Philadelphia.

The John Taylor family was delighted to see Robert again and to make the acquaintance of Francis. When the Taylors were informed of their mission, they were full of suggestions as to how to approach the subject. "I don't think you should barge right into their home unannounced. Let's draft a letter and inform Mr. Oliver of our concerns that a mistake has been made, and that we desire an audience with him in several days."

The letter was immediately composed and sent by a courier that very afternoon. The courier returned with an answer the next day. They could deduce by the curtness of the reply that Mr.

Oliver was troubled by the insinuation of a mistake in identity. Nevertheless, Mr. Oliver was agreeable to convening to establish legally his claim to the young boy and girl he had procured at Lancaster. The conference was to be held in two days at John Bartram's farm overlooking the Schuylkill River.

John Taylor decided to use some of his influence. "I'm going to secure the services of my attorney in this matter and request that he accompany us just in case we require any legal advice."

The Ennis and Taylor entourage arrived at the site overlooking the Schuylkill with some consternation. After the preliminary introductions and niceties, Francis began to state his case by explaining the circumstances of his family's abduction in June of 1756, and by giving a short summary of their time in captivity, his and Margery's release, and their tribulations since their return to the Tuscarora Valley.

Mr. Oliver expressed sympathy over the Ennis family's ordeal. "My family also has suffered great loss. We also lost our children, but now we have been rejoined through the efforts of Colonel Bouquet and his victorious army. During our children's more than eight years of captivity, they have forgotten much of what life was like for them. I intend to make amends for those lost years and build a better life for them. I will never take them into the frontier area where they would be subject to abduction again."

Francis replied gracefully, "All I want is to be certain that the young people you now have in your custody are not my children. Once I have the opportunity to observe them and speak with them, and cannot ascertain that they are indeed my children, I will take leave of you and beg your pardon for any inconvenience that I have caused you.

"I request one small consideration. I would ask that I be allowed to describe one physical attribute of the young boy, and if such a private mark be found upon his body, that he would be duly delivered to me as my rightful son."

Oliver's supporters looked at one another. Finally, Williamson Oliver cleared his throat and nodded meekly.

The bewildered boy was escorted into the room, nervously tugging at the brim of his hat. Everyone smiled and greeted him warmly in an attempt to place him at ease.

Francis began quite apprehensively, "When Nathaniel was three years of age, he was beset with a case of the boils. To relieve his pain and suffering from two huge, red, pus-filled swellings on the lower portion of his back, we sterilized a knife and removed the hard-core infection. The lanced skin did not heal properly, and ever since, Nathaniel has had two prominent marks on his lower back. If the young man in front of us possesses such marks, I claim him as my lawful son. Surely, you are a man of reason and do not want to keep a father and son apart."

Oliver nodded in agreement. "As much as I desire to have a son to call my own, I do not want to deprive a man of his own son. Please remove the boy's shirt and inspect his back for such a mark as described by Mr. Ennis."

Francis awaited the moment of truth. Slowly the young boy, soon to be a man, turned his back to the gentlemen within the room. Francis gasped, "My God, the marks are there. He's my Nathaniel! Oh, thank God!"

He ran across the room and threw his arms about the boy. The young boy was now completely confused. He was at a complete loss as to what had unfolded.

Francis stroked the young man's head. "Your name is Nathaniel Ennis, and I am your father. A mistake was made when you were exchanged at Lancaster. I'm here to take you home to your mother.

"Now, Mr. Oliver, what about the girl? Is she on the premises as well? I would like to examine her as well. If the two have been traveling together, it's quite possible she is my Jane. Would you please bring her into the room?"

"Yes, she is in the next room. Please have the girl brought into the room immediately."

A young girl entered the room with a puzzled look on her face. She examined the faces of the men staring at her and brightened when she came upon a familiar one.

"You're my father! You are Francis Ennis! I would know you

anywhere. I've thought about you every day since I was taken. I just knew that some day you would come and get me."

She surveyed the rest of the room. "There's Nathaniel! My brother Nathaniel! I never really lost track of him over the years. I didn't see him all the time, but occasionally I would see him." She ran first to Francis and then to Nathaniel.

Mr. Oliver attempted to be as gracious as possible under the circumstances. "I guess I made the wrong decision back in Lancaster. They were almost the same age as my children. I just wanted to have my family back so badly." Then he began to sob. "What am I going to tell my poor wife? This will just kill her."

They led Mr. Oliver out the door and placed him in his carriage. One of the men in his group climbed up on the seat beside the distraught man and began to drive him home.

On the other hand, the Ennis and Taylor group were delirious with happiness. They thanked Mr. Brantram for his hospitality and said good-bye. The celebration began immediately and continued in intensity once they arrived at the John Taylor household.

Several days later, when Francis and his family left Robert for the return to the Tuscarora Valley, Francis expressed his gratitude. "There's no way I can ever repay you for your efforts in reuniting our family. I just feel guilty that I'm so fortunate and you haven't had any luck at all."

"I don't want you to think that way. For a short period, I had Ann back. Now I'm fortunate to have another wonderful woman to share my life. I can't continue to look backward, but only forward. In a short period, the Robert Taylors will be returning to the Tuscarora Valley permanently. I will need your assistance in building a new cabin and reclaiming my fields from Mother Nature. Good luck to all of you, and please give my love to Margery and James. I forgot, there soon will be another Ennis to grace the Tuscarora Valley—give him or her my love also. See you again, and soon."

Soon after the joyous reunion in the Tuscarora Valley, the Ennis family grew to be six in number. Francis Jr. joined his newly returned brother and sister and his brother James, who had been born during captivity in Montreal.

CHAPTER TWENTY EIGHT

Return to the Valley, 1765

Colonel Henry Bouquet's successful campaign in Ohio in the fall of 1764 obliged the Indians to return to a peaceable way of life. Many of the people who had settled north of Carlisle had been driven from their lands during Pontiac's Uprising and chose to return to their holdings after Bouquet's victory. Some of these returning frontiersmen were shocked when they returned and found that during their absence their lands had been surveyed to others. Many of these unfortunate souls simply moved on, but in some cases, they bought out the squatter claims of other earlier settlers.

Application for warrants and surveys increased tremendously in the years of 1764 to 1768. It quickly appeared that most of the more desirable land would be claimed if a person did not act immediately.

With the alleged return of peace to the frontier of Pennsylvania, the other Taylor brothers decided it was about time for them to venture into the Kishacoquillas Valley and for Robert to return to the Tuscarora.

Robert Taylor and his new bride joined in the flurry of land acquisitions that unfolded in the Tuscarora Valley along the Tuscarora Creek in the area that soon would become part of the new township of Milford. Robert's father and, later, Robert himself had claimed land in this area just downstream from the Indian village of Laken.

These earlier Taylor claims had been made in the 1750s, prior to the outbreak of hostilities now known as the French and

Indian War. This period of warfare and, later, Pontiac's Uprising had caused Robert to vacate the valley and his claims during most of the period of 1756 to 1764.

Robert and William Bell, John Johnson (also known as the "White Hunter"), James Armstrong, Alexander Maginty, Ralph Sterrett, James Sample, Thomas Harris, James Mayes, John McKee, and Robert Taylor were landholders along the Tuscarora Creek about two or three miles above the mouth of the Tuscarora where it flows into the Juniata River.

Many of these landholders had moved into the valley before July of 1754 when the area was purchased from the Indians. John Johnson had a tract of land on the west side of the Tuscarora Creek located between the lands owned by Robert and William Bell. On November 10, 1755, the White Hunter sold this claim for the sum of eight pounds to James Sample and Thomas Harris of Lancaster County.

Later Sample and Harris sold the White Hunter's claim to James Mayes. Mayes in turn sold this Tuscarora Creek property to Robert Taylor on September 15, 1766, for "eight pounds lawful money of Pennsylvania."

On the 28th of this same month, Robert continued his acquisitions by warranting a tract of 296 acres located toward the back of the William Bell property. The next day, Robert Taylor entered a caveat (a legal notice given to a law officer or some legal authority to take no action until the person giving notice can be heard) against the James Armstrong survey of one hundred and fifty acres on the bend of the Tuscarora Creek.

Robert Taylor claimed, "The Armstrong survey included the best of the land necessary to support his improvement." A hearing was held regarding the caveat, but to Taylor's disappointment, the authorities ruled in favor of Armstrong and confirmed Armstrong's title. Furthermore, they informed Taylor to fill out his claim by extending back on the ridge. The primary argument in this case was that Robert Taylor had fooled his time away by not securing a warrant and having his claim surveyed. (Eventually, Robert Taylor bought out the Armstrong heirs and had that property patented under the name of "Taylor's Hope" on October 6, 1802.)

In 1803, Robert Taylor's dream of erecting a mill on a piece of property which had been surveyed out of the Bell tract for a mill-seat extending over the creek was blocked by John Patterson, at a location that later became Pomeroy's Mill, when Patterson built a mill at that site.

Robert Taylor's second wife, Anne, made a bold move, for a woman, by warranting 258 acres on November 28, 1767, above the Harris and McKee claim. These are but a few examples of the wheeling and dealing of land in the valley immediately following the return of the settlers to the valley after Bouquet's success in the Ohio territory.

While Robert was reestablishing his land claims in the Tuscarora Valley, his four brothers also became involved in the real estate business. Eventually all five Taylor brothers would patent land on some of the land warranted by their father in February 1754, or land near to it.

Robert Taylor's eldest brother, Henry, warranted a piece of property of one hundred acres in the Kishacoquillas Valley in 1764. After his first wife, Isabel, died, Henry married Rhoda Williamson, also of Lancaster County, in 1769, and shortly afterwards they moved to the banks of the Kishacoquillas Creek. Here they built their first log home and later constructed a gristmill on the creek. Adjacent to Henry's holdings were two parcels of land that had been warranted by his father, Robert Sr., on February 4, 1755.

Attached to the northern corner of the elder Taylor brother's claim, John, the fourth son of Robert Sr., warranted property on December 27, 1768. Between John's claim and the creek, Colonel John Armstrong had warranted land on February 3, 1755.

William, the second son of Robert Taylor Sr., settled on a tract of land to the east of his brother Henry. This three-hundred-acre tract was a section of the parcel warranted by his father in 1755 and was conveyed to William on November 9, 1767.

On the western border of William's tract, brother Robert was conveyed a parcel on November 9, 1768, thus giving the Tuscarora Valley inhabitant a claim in the Kishacoquillas Valley as well.

The youngest of the Taylor brothers, Matthew, and his wife, Sarah, established their log home opposite the Big Spring by the Kishacoquillas Creek with a warrant of land in 1772.

When Robert Taylor was convinced that it was safe to return to the Tuscarora Valley, he decided to make the first trip without Anne in order to select a new site for their cabin. The old cabin, constructed back in 1755, was in disrepair. Not only would it have needed extensive repairs, the cabin harbored too many memories of his departed family. He wanted to start life anew, but still live near his old haunts.

Robert selected a location nearly one-half mile downstream from the original cabin. Again, the main consideration was an adequate fresh water supply. He had remembered a small spring that fed into a small feeder stream of the Tuscarora, on a slight rise overlooking the Limestone Ridge. If you gazed above the intruding ridgeline, you could still observe the upper regions of the Tuscarora Mountain. He had decided that for a long time to come, he wanted to be able to cast his eyes on that mountain. It held a magical spell over him.

Upon returning to the Swatara, he made immediate plans to return to the Tuscarora and begin the construction of his new home. Not much had changed in building techniques since he had raised his first cabin, so it was going to be another painstaking endeavor. At least this time he knew what obstacles he was facing, and what major tools and instruments he needed before embarking on this new construction project.

CHAPTER TWENTY NINE

The Reverend Charles Beatty

The return of the settlers to the Tuscarora Valley brought about a renewed interest in bringing the Gospel of the Lord to the frontier inhabitants. The man chosen to promote Christianity among the frontier dwellers and to introduce the faith to Indians to the west of the Allegheny Mountains was the Reverend Charles Beatty.

Charles Beatty was born in Ireland about 1715 to the wife of an officer in the British army. The young Beatty immigrated to the American colonies in 1729. He received much of his education as a theology student at Log College (the forerunner of Princeton) under the tutorship of William Tennet. On December 1, 1743, Beatty was ordained into the ministry and undertook a congregation at Warwick, Pennsylvania.

During the course of the French and Indian War, Beatty toured North Carolina as a missionary and served as a chaplain on several military expeditions. In 1766, he and Reverend George Duffield were appointed as missionaries to the frontier settlements in the new purchase and to the Indians on the Ohio.

His appointment to this new position came through the synod of New York and Philadelphia. On August 12, 1766, Beatty and his interpreter, Joseph Peppy, a Christian Indian, began their 122-mile mile journey to Carlisle, where George Duffield joined them. They arrived at Carlisle on Friday, August 15, and were lodged at the quarters of Colonel Armstrong.

After Beatty preached for Duffield on the Sabbath of the 17th, they began their journey to Sherman's Valley the next day. That night they slept at the home of Thomas Ross, who lived about four miles into Sherman's Valley. The second night in the valley was spent at Fergus's after they delivered a sermon at a location where the settlers had begun to construct a log house of worship five miles down the valley.

On Wednesday the 20th, they crossed the south foot of the Conococheague Mountain.

Then they spanned the Tuscarora Mountain, utilizing Bigham's Gap on the Trader's Path. Once they came upon the Tuscarora Creek, their journey continued eastward on the Tuscarora Path, until they passed the ruins of Fort Bigham. One of the guides pointed out the ruins and related the tales of the two attacks upon the site.

"Reverend, what you are observing at this site is the remains of Fort Bigham. The original fort was constructed about 1749 and was attacked and destroyed on June 11, 1756. The survivors were herded to Kittanning and eventually many of those people either escaped or were freed. Some of those survivors have returned to the valley and still reside here. In the next several days, you will meet some of these plucky people.

"The fort was reconstructed in 1760, but during the most recent Indian troubles, it was attacked and destroyed the second time on July 10, 1763. Luckily, the fort's inhabitants had evacuated the site before it was attacked.

"The people who inhabit this valley are mostly Scotch-Irish and Presbyterian, a very determined and enterprising lot. That's why you are going to be welcomed so enthusiastically. They desire to be a churched people, with their own minister to live in their midst."

After delivering the sermon that evening, they traveled on to the home of William Graham. Unfortunately, on July 10, 1763, the party of raiders that had attacked the homes of Robert Campbell, William Anderson, the Collins family, and James Scott also set fire to the William Graham dwelling. The abandoned Graham residence had been burned down to its joists. Since then, repairs had been made, and without being informed of the attack, one would not have noticed any outward destruction.

William Graham greeted the travelers eagerly. "Reverends Duffield and Beatty, it is a great privilege to have you in the heart of our valley. We all enjoyed your message tonight and look forward to hearing you deliver the Word to us again tomorrow."

The next morning the party traveled along the bend of the Tuscarora Creek that constitutes the lower portion of what is commonly called the Half Moon, and crossed the creek along the path that Robert Taylor used to travel to reach his now abandoned cabin.

Behind the slight ridge dividing the bottomlands that had once been part of the site of the Indian village of Lackens from the main section of the valley, and before arriving at the Herringbone Ridge, the inhabitants of the valley had begun to build a house of worship before the war. This house of worship had been destroyed by fire during the war, but now the people were enthusiastically planning to replace the destroyed structure.

This site was located on the piece of property that Robert Taylor Sr. had sold to Samuel Waddle on June 1, 1754, just over a month before the Penn family purchased this land from the Indians at Albany. (This house of worship is presently known as the Lower Tuscarora Presbyterian Church at Academia.)

Reverend Duffield preached a stirring sermon to those people assembled at this location on August 21, 1766. His sermon was based upon this premise: "O sinner, stop and consider the fearful danger that you are in. In order to live a godly life here in this valley, you should consider three important concepts. One, from whence you came. Secondly, where are you going. And last, to whom you must account."

Afterwards, Charles Beatty addressed the people about their plans and aspirations for the construction of a permanent house of worship in the Tuscarora Valley. In order to build a better relationship with the people of the valley, Charles explained his background and position:

I offer you greetings from the Presbyterian leaders in the City of Brotherly Love. These good leaders have recognized your need and desire to establish a house of worship in your midst. Reverend Duffield and our good Christian Indian interpreter, Joseph Peepy, are carrying the Cross into these frontier regions to awaken a new spirit of Christianity, to make sure that no souls are lost to Satan.

Most of us share several common bonds other than religion. I, like many of you, have my roots in the Old Sod of Ireland. I was born there and immigrated to these good shores in 1729. During the recent Indian uprisings, I served as a chaplain on several expeditions and know the ravages of a cruel and barbarous enemy. I have witnessed destruction and horrid scenes, just like many of you. I realize that you have suffered much from the war and face many difficulties in beginning life anew.

You and I face tremendous challenges in establishing a living church in this valley. Unfortunately, we will be able to visit with you this one short day, but in so doing, it is our task to plant the seeds for the growth of a living, viable church in this beautiful valley that our Creator has provided for you.

I am quite certain that given the opportunity many of you will carry on God's good work in the absence of an ordained minister until the population of this section of the valley warrants the appointment of a permanent minister. In the meantime, we will highly recommend that a traveling minister, a circuit rider, be appointed to fill some of your Christian needs.

William Graham then stood and addressed the ministers and the congregation:

At the present time, I would estimate that there are approximately eighty-four families in this valley who propose to construct two houses for worship. One church will be located at this site, and another close to the Juniata River, but on the other side of the river.

Since our present financial circumstances will not allow

us to undertake supporting the Gospel on our own, we are proposing that we join with the people on the other side of the Juniata and share a minister.

Then it was Robert Taylor's turn to speak:

I feel it is most inconvenient for us to assemble in the open air, subject to the inclement weather. Our God has carried us to this beautiful valley, and we have built our houses and provided necessaries for our livelihood. Now it is time for us to construct a convenient house for God's worship. Once this objective is reached, we can turn our attention to construction of roads, bridges, schools, and a civil government for our valley. The building of a house of worship on this site is the first step in bringing civilization among us.

William Bell then rose and asked to be recognized. "Most of us are desirous of having the Gospel settled in among us. I believe that we should move forward and secure the needed land to construct a parsonage so that we can secure a minister for our valley. Whether we do this alone or share a minister with those people on the north side of the Juniata probably is not our decision."

Bell's announcement was met with pro and con comments, from, "I agree!" and "Now's the time, we can raise the money" to "Where's the money going to come from?" and "Let's not do anything hasty."

George Armstrong's deep voice penetrated the group. "We can't make any decisions today anyway. In the meantime, let's set up a committee to explore the possibilities. Reverend Beatty knows how we feel and can report back to Philadelphia and a decision can be made."

Reverend Beatty added, "Tomorrow, when I travel across the Juniata, I will be able to ascertain how those people feel about the situation, and then I will send my recommendations to Philadelphia."

After delivering the sermon, the Beatty party rode about eight miles, crossed the Juniata River, and arrived at Captain Patterson's fort. At Patterson's, they met Levi Hicks, who had spent his youth as a captive of the natives. Hicks was able to give Beatty some valuable information about the venture they were about to undertake.

On Friday, the 22nd, they once again preached in the woods at the site that later would house the Cedar Spring congregation. Afterwards they returned to spend the night at Captain Patterson's, and remained there the next day to rest.

The Sabbath found them preaching near the mouth of the Tuscarora Creek to a rather large congregation made up of people from the Tuscarora settlement that they had preached to earlier, the people from the Cedar Spring area, and people from farther east.

Unfortunately, the service was interrupted by a heavy summer shower, which was accompanied by high winds and thunder and lightning. Luckily, just a short distance up the creek there was a small house, where as many as possible crowded into the shelter while Reverend Beatty finished his sermon.

Reverend Duffield decided to split from the party and travel to Path Valley, the Great Cove, and the Little Cove. The plan was that the two would rejoin at Fort Littleton.

Early Monday morning they left the shelter of Patterson's and headed upriver towards the infamous Long Narrows. The former captive, Levi Hicks, accompanied the small group. Beatty disclosed this opinion of the narrows. "A rocky road bounds so close upon the river as to leave only a small path along the river for the most part, and this, for about ten miles, very uneven: at this time also encumbered by trees fallen across it, blown up from the roots, some time ago, by a hard gale of wind, so that we were obliged to walk some part of the way, and in some places to go along the edge of the water."[7]

Monday turned out to be a lengthy day, in that they finally reached Thomas Holt's after a twenty-one-mile journey. They rested at Holts', rode past the ruins of Fort Granville, and eventually found refuge in a small house where they were entertained quite well.

Beatty preached to a considerable number of people on Tuesday, and on Wednesday, after baptizing a small child in the morning, he delivered another sermon. On Thursday, the 28th, they crossed the Juniata at the mouth of the Aughwick Creek and passed what remained of Fort Shirley. After another long day in the saddle for thirty-one miles, just before nightfall they arrived at a public house at Fort Littleton operated by a Mr. Bird.

As planned, George Duffield rejoined the group at Fort Littleton. From Fort Littleton they headed westward through Fort Bedford and Fort Ligonier, and arrived at Fort Pitt on September 5, 1766.

Soon after Reverend Beatty's visit, a house of worship was constructed out of round logs and covered with clapboards. It was built at the site of the church that had been burned by accident during the latest Indian uprising where the Reverends Beatty and Duffield had held a service on August 21, 1763. This building had no floor and was heated by a large fireplace located at the one end.

CHAPTER THIRTY

The Black Boys of Fort Bedford, 1765

Pennsylvania failed in its attempts to regulate the Indian trade within its borders, even after passing laws and issuing proclamations seeking to license traders and control their abuses. The provincial assembly passed a stronger Indian trade act in 1758 that banned the sale of liquor to the Indians, created a monopoly of all trade west of the mountains, and named commissioners to supervise the trade. George Croghan disregarded Pennsylvania's law, stating that General John Stanwix had given him the right to trade with everyone.

Beginning in the early 1760s, the British government had attempted to enforce trade laws more strictly in order to stimulate English trade and industry, to provide additional revenue, and to bring the American colonies under closer supervision. The government levied new taxes so that the American colonies might defray part of the cost of the earlier French and Indian War as well as the maintenance of the British troops still stationed in America.

The king and his advisers, who controlled Parliament, seemed unaware that their policies of closer imperial control were beginning to stir up a hornet's nest in some parts of the American colonies. One example of this colonial unrest occurred in the vicinity of Fort Bedford and was led by the former Indian captive James Smith.

James Smith, like many other former captives, slowly reestablished his life in on the frontier of Western Pennsylvania. The valleys here continued to be harassed by skulking Indian parties until the spring of 1763 when the region ran red with blood as the natives struck viciously under the leadership of Pontiac. Much of the region was depopulated as terror-stricken settlers headed back east to the safety of Carlisle, York, Lancaster, and as far east as Philadelphia.

While many of the settlers of the region west of Shippensburg, particularly in the Fort Loudoun and Conococheague Valley, abandoned their tracts and fled for their lives, James Smith refused to leave. Instead, he enlisted a force of men to serve as rangers and scouts and assumed the title of Colonel. As he went on his recruiting rounds, he informed the men that their method of warfare would not be conventional.

"We will dress as our adversaries do. We will wear breechclouts, leggings, moccasins, and green shrouds. Our enemies paint their faces red and black, and we will do likewise. Hats only get in our way, so we will cover our heads with red handkerchiefs instead. Our frontiers will be defended using Indian tactics. Hit and run! Ambush! We will not fight out in the open like the British."

As the news of the success of Smith's ranger force spread, James was offered an ensign's commission in the Pennsylvania line. He eventually resigned his commission. However, in the fall of 1763 he was called back into active duty by General Armstrong to participate in a campaign against the Indians of the West Branch of the Susquehanna.

The next year, when Colonel Bouquet began his operations west of Fort Pitt against the Indians on the Muskingum, James Smith was given a lieutenant's commission. Upon completion of that campaign, Smith returned to his home region.

Pontiac's power had almost disappeared after the fall of 1763, but Indian raids continued to be carried out against the white settlers on the Pennsylvania frontier. Much of the activity of the Indians was due to the continuing efforts of some unscrupulous traders to supply the marauders with goods, especially powder, lead, knives, and tomahawks.

The white settlers were incensed over the continuing illegal trade activity, and the settlers communicated their displeasure to the commander of the British garrison stationed at Fort Bedford. The requests of the settlers fell upon deaf ears, and they were informed that the garrison's responsibility was simply to safeguard the settlers in the surrounding valley.

The issuing of the Royal Proclamation of 1763, better known as the Proclamation Line, which positioned a boundary on westward expansion for the American colonies in October of 1763, further displeased the inhabitants of the Pennsylvania frontier.

The time was ripe for an incident to occur on the Pennsylvania hinterlands that would drive a wedge between the frontiersmen and the British government.

During 1764, the Indians again began to stir up troubles by stealing horses and killing people on the frontier. The inhabitants of the frontier were on edge. It was only a matter of time until a situation would arise that would lead to violence.

In March of 1765 the trading company of Boynton, Wharton, and Morgan of Philadelphia conveyed a seventy-packhorse convoy of illegal goods to Henry Pawlins of the Conococheague Valley near present-day Greencastle. The goods were headed for Fort Pitt and as far west as the Illinois Country. This type of trade activity was unlawful and extremely dangerous to the settlers of the Pennsylvania frontier, and sent alarms throughout the valleys.

On March 6 William Duffield and a force of fifty armed men intercepted the packhorse train near present-day Mercersburg. Duffield and his men attempted to persuade the leaders of the train to turn back. "Men, we insist on you to halt your advance and store the goods and await additional orders from your employer in Philadelphia. The goods that you are carrying will lead to more bloodshed on the frontier. The blood of the inhabitants of these valleys will be on your hands."

The traders and packers greeted Duffield's request with jeers and hoots. "We have a job to do; and we're going to do it. You clods have no authority to stop us. We're packing legal goods, and only the army has the authority to halt our activities. You're nothing but a pack of nitpickers, jealous that someone else might make a pound or two out of this enterprise." After this malevolent exchange, the train continued westward towards Fort Bedford.

The settlers continued to shadow the train over the mountains to the valley called the Great Cove and on to the current site of McConnellsburg. Once again, Duffield attempted to reason with the traders and packers. "What you are doing is an example of great impropriety, especially the transporting of powder and lead to the Indians to the west of us. Already the tribes have been making raids on isolated settlements and cabins. Your actions are placing all of us in this region in grave danger. Presently, the Indians have little ammunition, but what you are carrying on your packhorses will lead to a huge escalation of hostility and bloodshed. You, sirs, are completely insensitive to our needs and desires. It is inhumane to carry these goods to the tribes."

As before, the members of the pack train made game of the frontiersmen. "These goods are from His Majesty to His Majesty's children among the western tribes. For you to attempt to halt our passage with these valuable gifts is a crime against the Crown.

"Maybe you ought to get your womenfolk to do your fighting for you. At least maybe they would show some backbone and initiative."

When James Smith, the original leader of the "Black Boys" that had gained prominence two years earlier under his leadership during the Pontiac Uprising, heard of the incident, he became angry. Smith collected some of his original men and again had this citizen army paint their faces red and black, and dress in the Indian manner.

Under the cover of night, Smith and his men quickly moved westward to Sideling Hill, where they camped for the night. The next morning Smith issued his instructions. "Men, I want you to scatter out about forty rods along the path. I want every two of you to work as a team and you should stick together about every eight or ten rods behind a tree.

"Always keep a reserve fire; one of you do not fire until your comrade has loaded his rifle. In this manner, we keep up a constant slow fire, from front to rear. It should take a goodly toll on the packers."

The pack train came along shortly, and the Black Boys used their old Indian tactics and opened fire on the train from the cover of the trees. Several of the packhorses were killed, and the traders quickly decided to change their plans.

Smith bellowed, "Unload those horses and arrange the goods in a pile. Get back over the mountains and don't come back. Those goods are illegal, and we don't want to see the likes of them or you again!"

Once the traders were out of sight, the Black Boys set fire to the goods, which consisted of lead, beads, wampum, blankets, tomahawks, and scalping knives and destroyed them. The traders retreated to the walls of Fort Loudoun and reported the destruction of goods that they claimed were for the defense of Fort Pitt and the Ohio Valley. They further claimed that the culprits were common robbers and had committed high crimes against the Crown by taking the gifts for their own use.

The commander of Fort Loudoun, Lieutenant Grant, sent out a squadron of his Highland soldiers and arrested a number of citizens of the valley simply on the grounds of suspicion, and without consulting any of the local magistrates or obtaining any civil papers giving them the authority to make the arrests. The prisoners were placed in the guardhouse of the fort.

The news of the imprisonment of these men spread rapidly throughout the surrounding valleys. Immediately, runners were sent out to inform their fellow frontier neighbors of the injustice of Lieutenant Grant's unwarranted imprisonment of these men. From other sections of the Conococheague, Sherman's Valley, the Tuscarora Valley, Cumberland Valley, the Great Cove, and Path Valley, angry and armed frontiersmen swarmed to the vicinity of Fort Loudoun.

On May 10, three hundred volunteers who encircled the fort joined Smith and the Black Boys. This group was referred to as the "Sideling Hill Volunteers."

Smith addressed his men briefly:

If it comes down to a shooting match, and I pray to God it doesn't, I want you to remember the Holy Trinity of Shooting. First, rely on quick loading. Second, aim accurately. And third, squeeze gently.

Men, I know that some of you have never aimed a rifle at a man, especially a white man. It's not going to be easy to draw a bead on one of your own, so if any of you have any qualms about this, now's the time to decide whether this endeavor is not for you and if not, bow out. No one will think any different about you; this is a tough situation.

With that said—and apparently no one has any problems with their conscience, we need to address some important tactics. First off, we're going to dress as the Black Boys have in the past. We'll paint our faces red and black and wear handkerchiefs on our heads. Our dress and fighting tactics will be just like our Delaware and Shawnee adversaries. As time goes on, we'll address that in more detail.

What I'm most concerned about is our ability or accuracy in shooting. So let's start with the problem of misfiring. From my experience, nearly all the instances when a gun fails to fire, it's the shooter, not the gun, that is at fault. It's imperative that you start with a clean rifle, making sure that the barrel, lock, pan, frizzen, and touchhole are free of dirt, grease, moisture, or powder residue.

Alcohol is cheap and evaporates quickly, giving a clean, dry surface. Don't make the mistake and blow on your flintlock. Blowing on it, especially the action, can leave moisture and cause a misfire. Another common mistake is to overfill your pan with priming powder. To make sure only a little priming powder seeps into the touchhole, simply bump your rifle near the action.

It's never a good idea to load your weapon directly from a powder horn. To avoid a leftover spark in your barrel from igniting the powder as it pours down the barrel and creating an explosion with your powder horn, use a small powder measure and keep it to the side of your muzzle.

Make sure that the ball is seated properly on the powder at the base of the barrel. You don't want an unseated ball becoming an obstruction, because that can cause a barrel to explode or burst.

Keep your weapon as clean as possible. If possible, give it a good cleaning at night, and check it again in the morning. You don't want to have to use your gun as a club without ever having the opportunity to fire a shot.

I know that what I have just told you is old hat to most of you veterans of the frontier, but there are a few of you that might fall into the category of being a greenhorn. In addition, some of you men can't shoot very accurately. Don't raise you hands to indicate who you are, but when you load, place some shot in your barrel and tamp it up with your ball. I know this doesn't seem like a fair way of carrying out warfare, but we've learned that the enemy doesn't always go by the alleged rules of warfare as followed in Europe. Out here on the frontier, anything goes.

As time went on, the Black Boys had more British Highlanders as prisoners than Grant had settlers in the guardhouse. Soon a flag of truce was flying over the fort, and after a period of negotiation, the prisoners were exchanged. The irate settlers, which included Robert Taylor and many of his Tuscarora Valley neighbors, eventually dispersed. However, a precedent had been set; the frontiersmen did not fear the power of the British frontier army.

Before Robert Taylor and his neighbors headed up the Tuscarora Path, Robert reintroduced himself to James Smith. "James, I'm Robert Taylor. A few years ago I visited your plantation while seeking information concerning my wife and children, who had been abducted by the Delawares under the Beaver King back in '56. I was more than happy to ride to your aid and will do it again, anytime, anywhere."

"Certainly, I remember you. We thank you immensely for your response. I hope that we won't have any more incidents of this nature, but I have this gut feeling that this travesty of justice is just the beginning of more British oppression. Thanks again for your aid; maybe we'll meet again but hopefully under more peaceful conditions."

The trading of illegal goods was brought to a halt for a short period, but soon the desire or greed for huge profits would overcome the actions of the settlers to keep powder, lead, guns, knives, and tomahawks from the hands of the Indians on the frontier.

Governor Penn and General Gage filled this brief interlude with legal activities. Governor Penn issued a *supersedeas* that removed William Smith from the magistracy and a writ to apprehend James Smith.

In this regard General Gage wrote, "I have been informed by sundry persons that the rascally parts of the Conococheague are determined, and are now laying a plan to do you (Bayton, Wharton and Morgan) some piece of injury by either stopping, or destroying, some part of your last cargo that yet remains with the carriers in that neighborhood...."

The issue of transporting questionable supplies and goods into the Western Pennsylvania and Ohio Valley frontier would not be resolved for many years to come, and the situation would lead to additional confrontations in 1769.

CHAPTER THIRTY ONE

Additions to the Taylor Family

On a hot, sultry morning in mid-July of 1766, Anne approached her loving husband with a playful grin on her face. "Tay, do you think that this cabin is large enough for three people?"

The message that she was attempting to convey to her husband passed right over him. "I don't see why not. Actually, I think this cabin could house four or five people quite easily. Who's coming to visit?"

"It isn't a visitor, but it is someone who will become a permanent member of our household. Wake up! I'm trying to tell you that you're going to be a father."

"You're pregnant? That's the best news a husband can ever receive."

Robert moved swiftly across the width of the cabin and embraced his wife, picked her up, and swung her around. "I guess I'd better be careful. I don't want to harm you or the baby. When is the baby due, Annie?"

"My calculations would have her arriving in early- to mid-February. Not a good time weather-wise, but this cabin is snug and warm. I'm good and strong, so I don't envision any problems."

"You said 'she.' How can you be so sure that the baby will be a girl?"

"It will be a girl because I need an ally against the stubbornness of you. We will be able to gang up on you and keep you under control."

"I don't care whether the baby is a boy or girl. Either one will bring a great deal of joy and happiness to this cabin. It makes me feel good all over my body. I'm ecstatic. Thank you for making me such a delighted and proud husband."

On February 11, 1767, the first child of Robert and Anne Taylor was born in the Tuscarora Valley. She was named Ann, without the "e." Her brother, Robert, named after his grandfather and father, joined Ann on July 3, 1769. It appeared that once the Taylors began to raise a family, they couldn't have enough children.

James joined the family on July 28, 1771, followed by Mary on April 27, 1774; Henry on July 8, 1776; Jane on August 21, 1778; Matthew on June 24, 1781; John on May 5, 1783; Sarah on September 15, 1785; and finally Elizabeth on August 21, 1788.

With the continuing increase in the Taylor household it became necessary for the Taylors to move further down the creek to a good ever-flowing spring and construct a two-story log house, eventually covered with chestnut siding.

This substantial expansion of Robert's family would have a profound influence on how he observed the events of the late 1760s and early 1770s that lead to the Revolutionary War. It also would influence his decision about whether to leave the Juniata Valley and join the Continental Army of George Washington or volunteer for the militia of Cumberland County.

Later, throughout the war, and during and after one childbirth after another, Anne Taylor did not neglect her personal appearance. Repeatedly, she would tell her busy, hardworking husband, "Just because we live an isolated life and I'm seldom seen by my neighbors or friends doesn't mean I shouldn't care about my appearance.

"I believe that I should be clothed in a condition to be seen by strangers without any mortification and without an expenditure to embarrass you, my dear husband."

There was little thought of Anne being able to "live prettily" in the beauty of the Tuscarora Valley. Although Robert's labors on the farm varied with the seasons and were performed for the most part amid the beauties of the great outdoors and his militia duties took him away at times, Anne's kitchen duties differed little from one season to another.

Even during the trying times of the war, for mental and physical relaxation, the ladies of the valley continued to organize quilting parties, spelling bees, and once in a great while, a tea party. British tea was not to touch their lips; they always consumed homemade brews, usually of sassafras.

At these sessions, the weary ladies received a new lease on life. They were able to discuss the news of the day, although it usually was several weeks old by the time it reached the remote Tuscarora Valley. Besides the war, they examined fashions, morals, and the probabilities of future matrimonial alliances. Sometimes those expounding would degenerate into plain old nosiness and gossipy exchanges. Nevertheless, these gatherings served a great social purpose and sent the ladies back home with something new to think about.

As the Taylor family continued to grow in numbers, Anne strove to find activities that would provide recreation and intellectual stimulation, often derived from scarce books. After the men had retired from the fields and woods for the day and had eaten a hearty supper, there was no flopping down around the fireplace to spend the evening in glum silence broken only by snores in the Taylor cabin.

Anne Taylor firmly believed in the concept of "let them sing; let them converse." She thought that amusements were essential to a balanced life, although she stood unequivocally against overindulgence in liquor and gambling. Luckily for Robert, Anne understood that, from time to time, her husband needed a refreshing swig from a jug of his own squeezings from the family still. It was an Irishman's right and privilege to gain resuscitation from such an endeavor after a hard day's labors.

Mrs. Taylor advocated that the children of a farmer or a frontiersman should be taught the social graces. She often quoted Solomon's mention of "a time to dance" and urged Robert to aid in teaching their children how to square dance and do jigs. Robert was not too fond of this activity, but to keep his wife happy, he indulged in these dance sessions from time to time. The dance spells came in handy when one of the young couples of the valley tied the knot and a huge celebration followed the ceremony.

Anne Taylor was not an obscure woman but instead was a powerful female, leaving her mark on her children, her church, and her country. She needed to be strong, because it was a troublesome period on the frontier. A lesser woman would not have been able to endure the numerous childbirths, the isolation and loneliness when her husband was away on militia duty, and the tremendous amount of labor it took to run a household and a farm.

She was a remarkable woman, one who made Robert Taylor very proud.

CHAPTER THIRTY TWO

The Stump Case, 1768

Opposition to British authority on the frontier increased on the Pennsylvania frontier in the same manner it grew and spread on the Atlantic seaboard. The halting of the pack train and the confrontation with Captain Grant, the commander of Fort Loudoun in 1765, was followed by another provocative challenge to authority on the outer limits of Cumberland County in 1768.

On January 10, 1768, a wintry Sunday in Central Pennsylvania, an event occurred that raised an immense apprehension of a new period of Indian unrest, and another example of resistance to British and Pennsylvanian authority.

Frederick Stump lived in Penn Township, Cumberland County, on Middle Creek at Stump's Run. Several Indians left the Big Island on the West Branch of the Susquehanna River and built cabins on Middle Creek. They were on friendly terms with their neighbors, and in January 1768, they visited with Stump's neighbor, William Blyth, and then went on to Stump's cabin.

Among the Indians were John Campbell, Jones, White Mingo, Cornelius, and two squaws. They allegedly arrived at Frederick Stump's on January 10 in a drunken condition. Stump and his servant, John Ironcutter, attempted to persuade the Indians to leave his premises. The Indians refused to leave, and Stump feared that they intended to harm him. Stump and Ironcutter murdered the six Indians and thrust their bodies into Middle Creek through a hole in the ice. The next day, fearing retaliation from the Indians, Stump and Ironcutter went to a cabin fourteen miles up the creek and killed a squaw, two Indian girls and a child, and burned the cabin to conceal the evidence.

About February 27, 1768, James Thompson found one of the bodies, minus its scalp and both ears, in the Susquehanna River in Allen Township in Cumberland County. Once Governor John Penn, the Provincial Council, and Sir William Johnson were informed of this atrocity, a reward of two hundred pounds was offered for the apprehension of Stump and Ironcutter. To keep the Indians from breaking the peace, the governor promised to sentence the two men to death.

The Delaware chief Newahleeka, who lived at Great Island, sent a message to the governor through Billy Champion. Newahleeka complained that five white men had been observed marking trees and surveying land in an area that had not been purchased by the colony.

On January 12 William Blyth gave a sworn deposition regarding the incident, with all the details provided by Stump himself.

When Captain William Patterson, who resided on the Juniata, heard of the incident, and without orders from the authorities, he led a party of nineteen men and arrested Stump and Ironcutter. Patterson delivered the two to Sheriff John Holmes in Carlisle of Cumberland County on Saturday, March 23. Captain Patterson was aware that the Indians would be angered over the murders and notified the Indians of the arrest of Stump and Ironcutter.

The Provincial Council ordered that warrants be issued for the arrest of Stump and Ironcutter and that they be brought to Philadelphia before His Majesty's Justices Oyer and Terminer. In the meantime, in a move similar to what occurred on the Conococheague, runners were sent out to the surrounding valleys to inform the public of the plight of Stump and Ironcutter. Due to previous actions by Indians in this region, many of the white settlers displayed great sympathy for the two accused of the crime. Some, of course, did not view their actions as a crime but as a form of vigilante justice.

Many settlers in the outreaches of Cumberland County objected to the attitude of the government. They felt that the government displayed a greater concern when a white killed an Indian, than when the Indians killed many whites.

The location for the trial also became a controversial issue. It was felt that the two would not be tried fairly if the trial were to be moved to Philadelphia, because their peers in Cumberland County had a very different perspective on Indian-White relations than the peace-seeking inhabitants of the City of Brotherly Love who had never had to fear the wrath of Indians.

On Friday the 29th at about ten o'clock, the day before the two men were to be taken to Philadelphia, a number of men armed with rifles and tomahawks and allegedly led by a John Davis and a John McClure, surrounded the jail.

"Sheriff, there's no way you're going to keep these two boys in your jail if you intend to move them to Philadelphia," shouted John Davis.

"There won't be any justice if we let them be taken to Philadelphia," screamed another voice from the crowd. "Those Injun-loving Quakers will have these two strung up by their necks before they know what's happening."

"We're liberating these two fine gentlemen in the name of frontier justice," Mcclure told the sheriff, who replied, "I recognize you, John McClure and John Davis. You two and the rest of this mob will pay dearly when we get our hands on you. You can't take the law into your own hands this way."

McClure laughed heartily. "There's no way you'll ever get your hands on anyone from over the mountain. If you do, they'll be free in no time."

To a chorus of shouts, threats, and rejoicing the mob released Stump and Ironcutter and quickly left Carlisle. Off they rode, heading for Croghan's Gap and Sherman's Valley. The armed men were followed for a short distance. Then a posse pursued them into Sherman's Valley on Monday and again on Tuesday, but to no avail.

Every avenue was explored to retake the prisoners and to punish those who aided in their rescue. The magistrates of Cumberland County issued warrants for some twenty or more men who allegedly played a role in the endeavor.

The alleged culprits were never re-arrested even though increased rewards were offered for their apprehension and arrest. It appears that the two left the boundaries of Pennsylvania and spent the rest of their days in Virginia.

In the aftermath of this incident, a great wave of excitement spread throughout Pennsylvania and beyond its borders, in that the authority of the colony and British law had both been challenged and the challengers had escaped punishment. The sheriff and the jailer of Cumberland County were reprimanded by the governor for their passive conduct in advising the retention of the prisoners in Carlisle instead of delivering them to Philadelphia.

Captain William Patterson was rewarded for marching to Middle Creek, apprehending and arresting Frederick Stump and John Ironcutter, and escorting them to the Cumberland County Jail in Carlisle. He was appointed a justice of the peace, the first such position west of the Tuscarora Mountain.

This incident in early 1768 is just one that would demonstrate contempt for the authority of the colonial government of Pennsylvania and British authority. The action by the settlers in freeing the two men was an event that shook the provincial government to its very core and helped set the scene for what would soon occur in Philadelphia.

To help solve the issue of the pressure on Indian lands, a great conference was held at Fort Pitt on May 9, 1768. This council led directly to the Treaty of Fort Stanwix on November 5, 1768, in which the Iroquois conveyed to the Penns a large piece of land extending from the New York line on the Susquehanna River, up the West Branch of the Susquehanna, over to Kittanning, then down the south side of the Allegheny and Ohio Rivers to the mouth of the Tennessee River.

This marked the last purchase made by the Penn family. The Shawnees and Delawares were upset with this transaction because their hunting grounds on the Ohio were sold out from under them.

CHAPTER THIRTY THREE

The Black Boys Again, 1768

Even with the new treaty signed in November of 1768, the Indians, especially the Delawares and Shawnees who were upset with the loss of their hunting grounds, began to make incursions on frontier settlements once again. In early 1769, as in 1765, the Indian marauders were receiving illegal goods that could be used for war purposes. The settlers appealed to the British army stationed at Fort Bedford, but as before, the army was reluctant to halt the activities of the influential and wealthy Philadelphia-based merchants who continued to trade with the Indians.

A small force of citizen vigilantes took it upon themselves to halt the menacing pack trains and successfully destroyed a large quantity of powder and lead. The British forces succeeded in reinforcing the settlers' contention that the British army was more interested in protecting the merchandise of the wealthy and influential merchants and the Indians than protecting the lives and property of the settlers. Shortly after the destruction of the gunpowder and lead, several settlers were apprehended and placed in irons in the guardhouse of Fort Bedford on suspicion of destruction of the merchants' property.

James Smith once again saw this confinement by arbitrary or military power as a violation of the basic rights of British citizens and vowed to right this wrong, even at the expense of his own freedom. Smith contended that the men placed in arms weren't even involved in the halting of the pack train and destruction of the property.

The Black Boys leader appealed to his old force of men, and a small, elite group of them responded to his call to arms. They marched swiftly against Fort Bedford to confront the British commander and demand the release of the prisoners.

James Smith had some advice for them. "If you were to get into a shooting match with the British garrison and were captured and sentenced to death for treason, you shouldn't be overly impressed with their marksmanship. You will suffer much less if the method of execution were to be hanging instead of a firing squad. If they were to muster a firing squad from the ranks, half of them would miss you and the other half would make much a mess of you that you would have to be dispatched by the provost marshal's pistol in order to carry out the sentence of death."

This last dispatch of information was greeted by robust laughter from the men who had joined James Smith in his endeavors to seek justice on Pennsylvania's frontier.

With information gathered by William Thompson about conditions within the fort, they arrived at Fort Bedford after a night's forced march from Juniata Crossing. Under cover of a blanket of fog and mist, the Black Boys struck at dawn. They moved swiftly through the gates and knocked over the stack of guns, completely catching the garrison off guard. After the prisoners were removed from their irons and released from the fort, the Black Boys returned the fort to Captain Swanson and his startled troops.

Swanson and his garrison attempted to capture James Smith and punish him for his role in the Fort Bedford takeover. During the attempt to apprehend James, a man by the name of Johnson was shot and killed, and James Smith was accused of pulling the trigger. James Smith was later taken into custody and transferred to Fort Bedford, and then secretly moved to the jail in Carlisle.

Word of the incarceration of the Black Boys' leader spread swiftly throughout Cumberland County. Soon a force of nearly six hundred sympathizers and supporters from the Sherman's, Conococheague, Tuscarora, Cumberland, Kishacoquillas Valleys, and elsewhere crowded the confines of Carlisle.

This mob of Smith partisans was focused on one objective, the release of its popular hero, legend, spearhead, and mentor. The situation was an explosive one; this upwelling of affection and devotion could easily lead to an attempt to forcibly release Smith from his detention.

Smith quickly assessed the volatile situation and persuaded the sheriff to allow him to address the unruly throng. It took him some time to quell the multitude of well-wishers, and eventually they quieted and were able to hear his message, his plea.

He began in earnest. "Friends, neighbors, fellow Black Boys, fellow Irishmen, and all of you that believe in justice, please hear me out. The worst thing we could allow to happen here on the frontier is to sanction the use of mob rule to handle our disputes.

"You all know, and I certainly know, and I suspect the British army authorities also know, that I'm innocent of these murder charges. If you break me out of this jail, it will look as though I've committed the act of murder with which I'm charged. So, relax, go home, and allow the judicial system to run its course. Under the law, I am guaranteed a trial by a jury of my peers. You are my peers, so don't taint or pressure the minds of the body of men that will constitute my jury by resorting to violence. Just allow my trial to take place, and I'll be found innocent and will be back in the Conococheague Valley before you know it."

The multitude of frontiersmen and women weren't happy to be dispersed in this manner, but they knew James was right. They returned to their homes and waited four long months until the next Supreme Court session was to be held. When the trial terminated, the jury of James Smith's peers found him innocent of the charge. Smith was released from the Cumberland County Jail and returned home to the Conococheague and his wife and family.

This incident marked the third example in which the frontiersmen of Cumberland County openly challenged the royal and state governments prior to the mid-1770s. The stage was being set for an overall confrontation that would lead to strife, bloodshed, and complete independence. All that was needed was a spark from a hotbed of opposition to ignite an all-out rebellion.

CHAPTER THIRTY FOUR

The Death of Pontiac
April 20, 1769

On the second Sunday of June in 1769, the God-fearing people of the Upper Tuscarora Valley met at their newly constructed log church near the gap in the Herringbone Ridge and welcomed a circuit-rider pastor from Carlisle whose duty it was to spread the Lord's Word on the frontier.

The pastor began the service with a lengthy prayer. Then he announced, "Before I get into the main text of today's sermon, I want to bring to you some good news from out in the Illinois Territory concerning our old adversary, Pontiac.

"After Pontiac failed to take Detroit back in 1763, he lost most of his power and prestige among the Illinois Confederacy. Since that time, the Ottawa war chief visited the Illinois Confederacy on numerous occasions, attempting to persuade the chiefs of the Confederacy to join him in one more effort against the British.

"Pontiac's main adversary is, or was, Chief Makatachinga, or Black Dog of the Peorias. Several years ago, Pontiac and Black Dog became entangled in an argument, and Pontiac attacked Makatachinga and stabbed him in the shoulder. Pontiac added further insult by threatening to destroy Black Dog's domain, Cahokia, in the spring.

"On April 3rd of this year, Makatachinga convened the confederated Illinois tribes at a grand council at Cahokia. Black Dog stated that his objective was to seek revenge and eliminate Pontiac. The chief choose his nephew, Pini, to eliminate the threat to the unity and power of the Illinois Confederacy.

"Pini used Pontiac's fondness for liquor as a ploy to initiate the assassination plot. First, Pini gained the friendship of Pontiac and his two grown sons, Otussa and Kasahda. Pini carried only his skinning knife and war club, which were not considered formidable weapons.

"When Pontiac became angry over his inability to secure whiskey or rum from the trading post, Pini produced a flask of rum from his pouch and gave it to Pontiac, further bonding the two men. While Pontiac was concentrating on the contents of the flask, Pini jerked his war club from his belt and brought the club down on the back of Pontiac's head. Pini was upon Pontiac before he hit the ground, and plunged the blade of his skinning knife deep into the chief's chest, piercing his heart."

While the pastor was communicating his account of the assassination, he swung his clenched fists as though he were wielding the club, and then thrust his right fist in a downward motion, simulating the entire assault, blow by blow.

The entire congregation sat spellbound. Finally, in a gesture unseen on the American frontier, the entire congregation rose as one, and applauded. It was a time of celebration in the Tuscarora Valley.

Once the congregation had regained its composure, the pastor continued, "We should be thankful that our Lord has seen fit to eliminate this menace from our midst. No longer must we live in fear that this Ottawa chieftain will assemble his horde of warriors to threaten the peace and tranquility of our beautiful valley. Thanks be to God for delivering us from Pontiac's wrath."

Like all his neighbors, Robert Taylor welcomed the news of the death of the Ottawa leader who had been the scourge of the frontier during the summer and early fall of 1763. However, he cautioned his neighbors, "Even though we're rid of a major source of terror, we have to keep in mind that he was just one of many. There are many other potential leaders of uprisings against us whites, it's an ongoing threat that we have to be aware of. It will be many years, if ever, before we will be able to let down our guard against the possibility of hit-and-run attacks from the natives to our west and north."

No one wanted to hear such a assessment of the situation; it spoiled their sense of euphoria and celebration. But everyone knew that Robert Taylor was a realist.

Marker for Rice's Church-located in Church Hill Cemetery along Route 75 in Turbett Township just outside of Port Royal, Pennsylvania.

Groninger Homestead-located along Groninger Valley Road in Milford Township, Juniata County, Pennsylvania, next to the Tuscarora Creek, built in 1823.

James Taylor Homestead-built in 1790, located on River Road between Mifflintown and Port Royal along the Juniata River in Pennsylvania.

Lower Tuscarora Presbyterian Church located in Academia, Pennsylvania, Juniata County, as described on page 229.

Port Royal Lutheran Church (as it looked in early 1900s) located on the corner of Fourth Street and Market Street in Port Royal, Pennsylvania.

Port Royal Presbyterian Church (1911) located on the corner of Fourth Street and Main Street in Port Royal, Pennsylvania.

Lower Falls of the Genesee River in Letchworth State Park in New York.

Upper Falls of the Genesee River in Letchworth State Park in New York.

Middle Falls of the Genesee River in Letchworth State Park in New York.

View of the upper and middle falls of the Genesee River in Letchworth State Park in New York.

LAND TRANSACTION BETWEEN ROBERT TAYLOR AND WILLIAM BELL-MADE ON DECEMBER 1, 1786 AND RECORDED ON APRIL 12, 1796

234 Entered April the 12th. AD. 1796. recorded and compared.

Saml. Postlethw. Ro.

This Indenture made the first day of December, on the year of our Lord, one thousand seven hundred and eighty six, and eleventh year of American Independence, by and between Robert Taylor, of Millford Township, Cumberland County, and State of Pennsylvania, farmer, of the one part, and William Bell, of the County and State afsd. farmer, of the other part. Witnefseth that the said Robert Taylor for and in Consideration of the sume of three hundred pounds, current money of the State of Pennsylvania, to me in hand paid by said William Bell, the receipt of which I do hereby acknowledge, Have bargained, sold, aliened and confirmed, and by these Presents Doth grant, bargain, sell, alien and confirm unto the said William Bell, and to his heirs and assigns for ever, all my right, claim and interest of, in and to a certain lot or parcel of land, situate in Millford Township, Containing three hundred acres, be the same more or less, held by Location, bearing date in Philadelphia, and adjoining land of Robert Taylor on the East, and also William Bell lands on the South, and the land of Clement Horrells heirs West and a ... Carson ridge on the North. Together with all my rights, hereditaments, rights and appurtenances thereunto belonging, and all my right, title, interest and demand whatsoever of, in and to the said Mefsuage and Premises, unto the said William Bell, to the only proper use and behoof of him the said William Bell, his heirs and assigns for ever, Subject to the payment of the residue of the purchase money, Interest and quit-rents thereupon due, and to become due to the Honourable the Proprietories of the said State, or Lord of the Soil, the said Robert Taylor and his heirs, the said premises hereby granted, or mentioned or intended to be granted, and all ways, waters and water courses, woods and underwoods, with the appurtenances, unto the said William Bell, his heirs and assigns, against him the said Robert Taylor and his heirs, and against all persons claiming or to claim from or under him, them or any of them, shall and will warrant and for ever defend by these Presents; In Witnefs whereof the said Robert Taylor have hereunto set his hand and seal, the day and year above written.

Signed, sealed and delivered in presence of

Arthur Bell
John Christy

Robert Taylor [seal]

Received the day of the date before signing the sume of three hundred pounds, it being in full the consideration above mentioned, I say received by me.

Robert Taylor

Cumberland County, fs.

Personally appeared before me the subscriber one of the Justices of the peace of the Court of Common Pleas for the sd. ... the sd. Robert Taylor, and acknowledged the above Indenture to be his act and deed and desired that the same may be recorded as such; Witnefs my hand ... the 6th day of January AD. 1788.

David ...

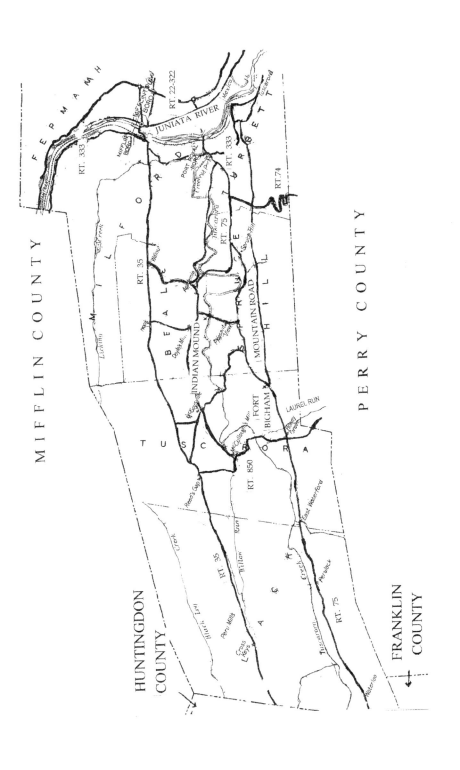

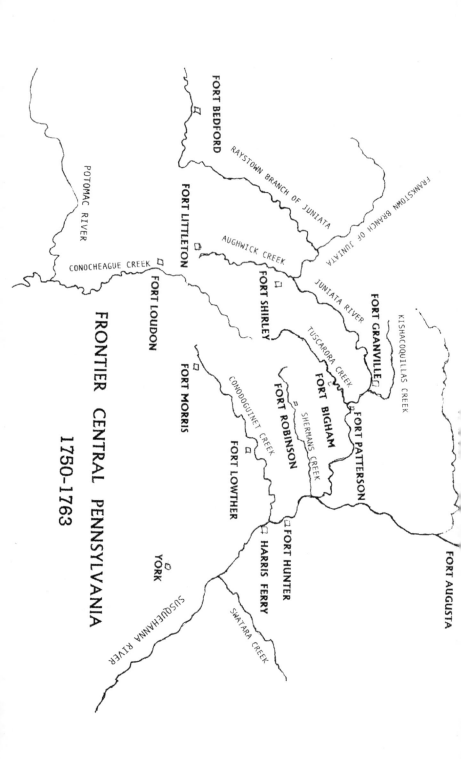

FRONTIER CENTRAL PENNSYLVANIA
1750-1763

POTOMAC RIVER

FORT BEDFORD

RAYSTOWN BRANCH OF JUNIATA

FRANKSTOWN BRANCH OF JUNIATA

FORT LITTLETON

AUGHWICK CREEK

CONOCHEAGUE CREEK

FORT LOUDON

FORT SHIRLEY

JUNIATA RIVER

FORT GRANVILLE

KISHACOQUILLAS CREEK

TUSCARORA CREEK

FORT MORRIS

CONODOGUINET CREEK

FORT BIGHAM

FORT ROBINSON

SHERMANS CREEK

FORT PATTERSON

FORT LOWTHER

FORT HUNTER

HARRIS FERRY

FORT AUGUSTA

YORK

SUSQUEHANNA RIVER

SWATARA CREEK

LAND CLAIMS IN THE KISHACOQUILLAS VALLEY
1755-1775

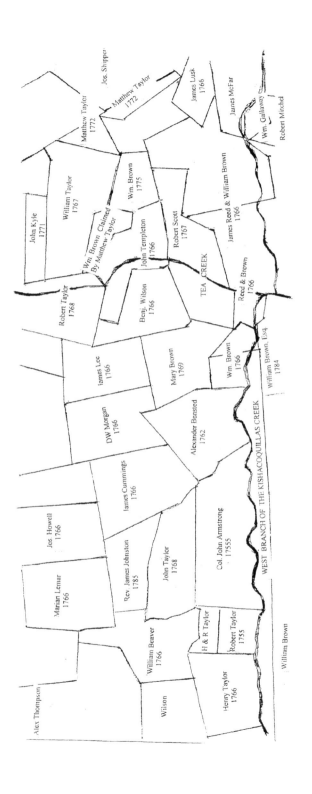

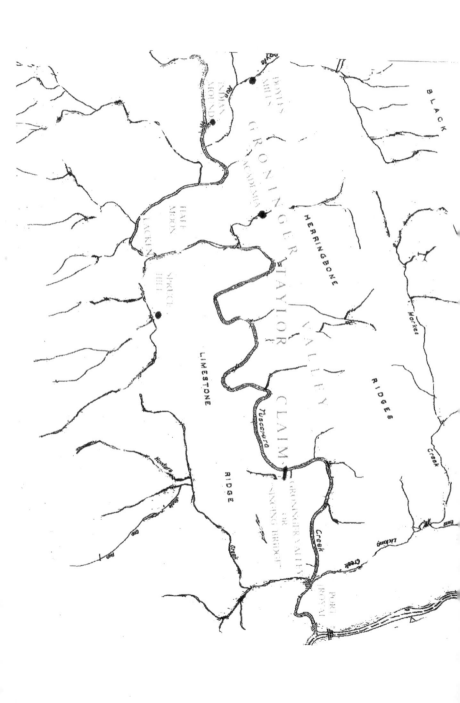

WAR ON THE IROQUOIS FRONTIER

Fort Anne

Fort George

Schenectady

Albany

Hudson River

Mohawk River

Schoharie Creek

New York

West Point

Morristown

Fort Stanwix

German Flats

Cherry Valley

Delaware River

Easton

General James Clinton 1779

Chemung River

Wyoming Valley

General John Sullivan 1779

Lehigh River

Wilkes-Barre fort

Fort Oswego

Catherine's Town

Newtown

Fort Jenkins

Fort Augusta

Oswego River

Cayuga

Cayuga Lake

Chemung

Tioga

North Branch of the

Susquehanna River

Fort Freeland

Seneca Lake

LAKE ONTARIO

Canandaigua

Canadasaga

Cohocton River

Canisteo River

West Branch of the Susquehanna River

Chenussio

Genesee River

Fort Niagara

LAKE ERIE

Fort Presqu' Isle

Canewango

Colonel Daniel Broadhead 1779

Fort Le Boeuf

Venango

Fort Pitt

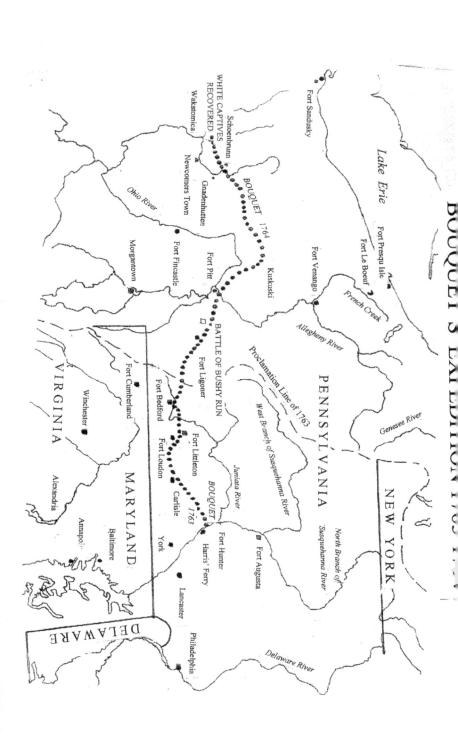

BOUQUET'S EXPEDITION 1763-1764

Lake Erie

Fort Sandusky

WHITE CAPTIVES RECOVERED
Schoenbrunn
Wakatomica
Newcomers Town
Gnadenhutten
BOUQUET 1764
Ohio River
Kuskuski
Morgantown
Fort Fincastle
Fort Pitt

Fort Presqu Isle
Fort Le Boeuf
French Creek
Fort Venango
Allegheny River

BATTLE OF BUSHY RUN
Fort Ligonier
Fort Bedford
Fort Littleton
Fort Loudon
Carlisle
BOUQUET 1763
York
Harris' Ferry
Fort Hunter
Fort Augusta

Proclamation Line of 1763
West Branch of Susquehanna River
Juniata River
North Branch of Susquehanna River
Genesee River

PENNSYLVANIA

NEW YORK

VIRGINIA
Fort Cumberland
Winchester
Alexandria

MARYLAND
Annapolis
Baltimore
Lancaster
Philadelphia
Delaware River

DELAWARE

EARLY COUNTIES OF PENNSYLVANIA

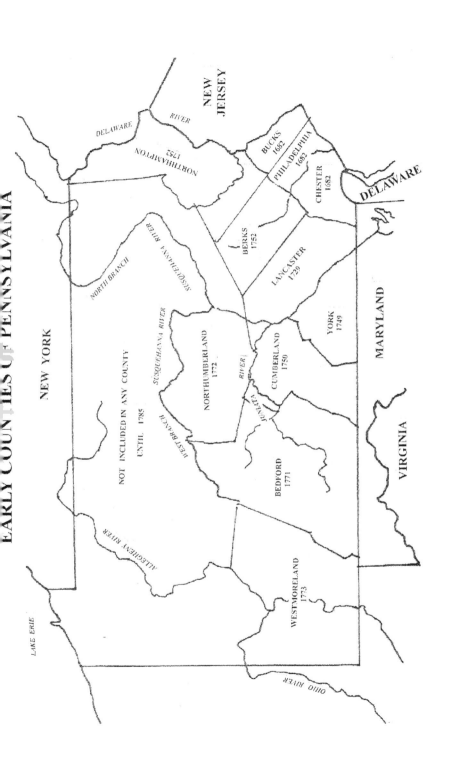

PROCLAMATION LINE OF 1763

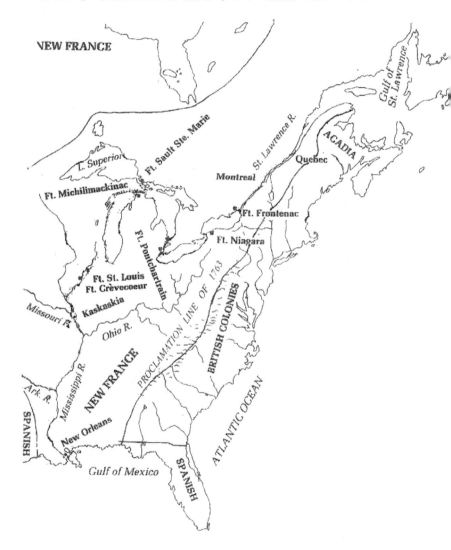

LEONARD GRONINGER'S PATH INTO CAPTIVITY--FROM BUFFALO VALLEY TO CHENUSSIO IN THE GENESEE VALLEY

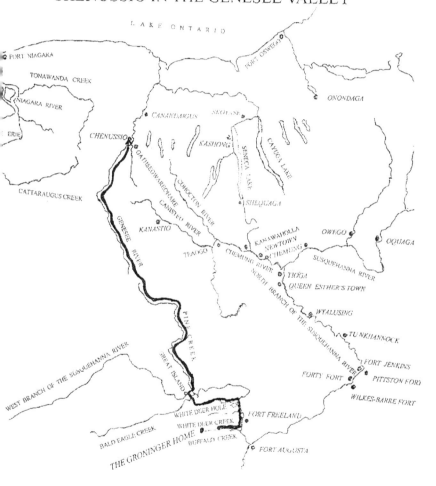

LEONARD GRONINGER'S ESCAPE
FROM CHENUSSIO TO
FORT AUGUSTA

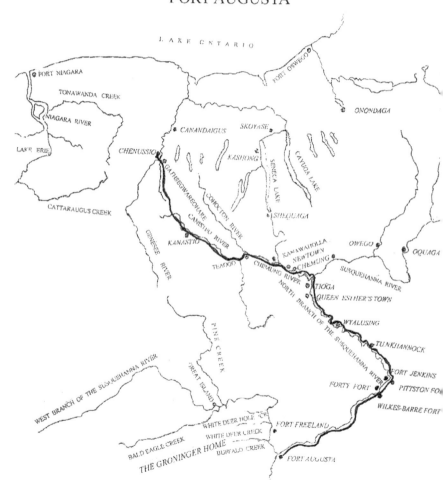

CHAPTER THIRTY FIVE

The Gray Litigations

After church on a bright Sunday morning in June 1770, Robert Taylor was approached by another Fort Bigham survivor, Hannah Gray.

"Good morning, Robert, it's good to see you again. I think the last time we saw each other was in Carlisle several years ago."

"And a good morning to you, Hannah. You're right, it's been over a decade since we've been able to have a friendly little chat."

"Yes, they have been very busy years in which many changes have taken place. Thank heavens these last ten years have gone better than the earlier years in the valley. You and I have so much in common. We both were fortunate to survive captivity and return to the Tuscarora Valley. Unfortunately we both lost our spouses and had to go through the ordeal of returning without our children."

Robert nodded. "I often reflect on those days of captivity at Kittanning and Fort Duquesne. From time to time I think of George Woods. He was so attracted to you. Do you ever hear from George?"

"George was very dear to me and treated me with great kindness and understanding. Sometimes I wonder how things would have turned out if I had taken him up on his offer and stayed with him, instead of being taken to Canada. Janie would never have had to leave my side if I had stayed with George. You know that I got my Janie back, don't you?"

Robert noticed how Hannah avoided his question concerning George Woods, but it was her question that left Robert quite uncomfortable. Robert had been told in great detail by Francis and Margery Innis that the girl known as Janie Gray was not really Janie. Rumors persisted that the Janie Gray now in residence in the valley was instead a German captive that Hannah had claimed as her missing daughter in Philadelphia after Bouquet had forced the Indians to surrender numerous captives in 1764. It was asserted that this Janie was about the same age as the real Janie.

As the alleged Janie grew, she did not possess the traits and characteristics that would have been expected. Instead most of her neighbors considered her gross and unbecoming in stature, quite awkward in her manners, and most distressing, loose in her morals. An elderly Mrs. McKee would describe Janie as "a big, black, ugly, Dutch lump."

Robert pushed these thoughts aside and answered, "You were very fortuitous in getting your Janie back. Fate was not as kind to me, as I had no luck in getting Robbie and Elizabeth back. On the hand, Providence has allowed me to find another beautiful and loving wife. We have been blessed with three children, with another due shortly."

"Enoch Williams has become my new partner in life and a father to Janie," Hannah said. "My departed husband John's will stipulated that his sister Mary would receive one half of his plantation, which he had warranted on February 8, 1755, once she paid John's nephew a given sum and forgave John's debt to her. The other half of the plot was to be divided between Janie and me, share and share alike.

"Mary has relinquished her right to my half of the tract, and I have paid her John's debt plus interest, which I don't think I was legally obligated to do, but I feel better that I did. We are coexisting with the Grays as friendly neighbors and everyone considers Enoch and me to be the owners of John's estate. Since Enoch and I have not been able to have any children, Janie is our only heir to the plantation.

"I'd like you to meet my Janie," Hannah said, beckoning to the young woman. "Janie, come here, I'd like you to meet Mr.

Taylor, who survived the attack on Fort Bigham just like you and me."

"It's a pleasure to see you once again, Janie," Robert said. "The last time I saw you was at Fort Duquesne back in '56. You've certainly grown up since then."

The young woman seemed ill at ease in Robert's presence, but managed to say, "It's nice to meet you, Mr. Taylor."

Janie quickly excused herself and returned to the group of young people who were involved in a game which Robert did not recognize. As he watched her walk across the clearing, the rumors of her background swirled in his mind. She didn't resemble either of her parents. John had been gaunt and thin, almost frail. Even today Hannah was not the least bit obese; she possessed a full figure and had gained a few middle-aged pounds, but she was not overweight.

On the other hand, the young woman who had just stood before him was rather squat and stout. Robert didn't necessarily agree with Mrs. McKee's assessment, but he had to concur that Janie was big. She was much larger than most of the women of the valley; perhaps she was not of Scotch-Irish descent.

Robert realized that he did not have time to dwell upon Janie's background at this moment, because he did not want to insult Hannah, an old friend.

"I'm so happy that everything is working out so well for you, Hannah," he said instead. "Hopefully the dark clouds of war will pass us by and we can live in peace in our beautiful valley. I believe that we are entitled to some years of peace and prosperity. It's been good talking to you, Hannah. Please give my regards to your husband, Enoch."

The two former captives parted company, not knowing that the piece of land that they were discussing, John Gray's warrant of February 8, 1755, would become one of the most celebrated pieces of land in the future Juniata County.

(AUTHOR'S NOTE: The good relationship between the Gray and Williams families would slowly disintegrate into disenchantment with Hannah living's arrangement with Enoch Williams, and the growing perception that Jane wasn't really John and Hannah Gray's biological daughter, even though she was considered the heir to the Gray plantation. Mary Gray was to have been the executrix of her brother John's will, but she never qualified as the executrix.

About 1789, John Gray Jr., the nephew of the deceased John Gray and the son of James Gray, sought to secure the Williamses' land. Young Gray gained some valuable information from George Woods and others concerning the true identity of Jane Gray, who by now had married a Mr. Gillespie. This information, if proven true, might disallow Jane Gray Gillespie as heir to John Gray's plantation. In 1791 Enoch Williams was appointed administrator of the former John Gray estate.

Somehow young John Gray was able to get possession of a house on his Aunt Mary's land. Young John persuaded his Aunt Mary to give him a deed for her half of John Gray's plantation in 1803, which renewed the claim of Mary Gray to John Gray's property.

In the meantime, on July 11, 1803, Hannah Williams sold to David Beale all her rights as vested in her by the deed of trust that she had taken out on November 6, 1796. Beale pressed an ejectment suit against John Gray Jr., and placed David and John Fredericks as tenants on the place. Gray followed with an ejectment suit against the Fredericks. This led to a trial in 1815, followed by an appeal in 1817.

To further confuse the issue, Enoch Williams died. Under Enoch Williams's will, his half of the land was sold to satisfy a judgment for his lawyers. Once the lawyers got tired of waiting, the land was vested in Zachariah and David Williams and then bought by lawyer Hale, who deeded it over to John Norris. Now Norris and Beale became the interested parties in the suit, while John Cummin replaced John Gray who had died.

In May 1823 the case was tried again, with the verdict being appealed and taken before the State Supreme Court at

Sunbury in June 1823. The case was taken to the Circuit Court in the May term of 1827 and again in May 1832, which ended in a compromise and terminated the contest for the Mary Gray half of the plantation.

The Gillespies had sold the property they inherited from Hannah Gray Williams to a clergyman, William McKee of Washington D.C., who in turn sold it to his nephew, William McKee of the Tuscarora Valley. William McKee instituted an ejectment suit against John Frederick and Samuel Kirk in 1817. This case went to trial in May 1823 and was retried in March 1825. The verdict gave McKee the Mary Gray half and half of the other part.

A new trial was granted and in June 1829 the case was removed to the Circuit Court. The final decision came on May 3, 1833, in favor of the defendants. David Beale had died in 1827 and in his will had authorized the sale of the property in the event of a favorable verdict. Beale's sons then sold the undivided half to William Okeson, and John Norris sold his half to the same man.

This transaction terminated the most celebrated land litigation known as *Frederick et al versus Gray,* in what was, by 1833, Juniata County. The author would like to apologize for any misinterpretations in his summation of the famous Gray Land Litigations. The cases covered over fifty years of suits, trials, and appeals, and it is simply mind-boggling for anyone, legally trained or not, to understand all the nuances of the case.)

Later that night Robert couldn't get the image of Janie Gray out of his thoughts. He finally mentioned his consternation to Anne. "I think Hannah Gray Williams made a huge mistake in claiming that girl as her daughter Jane. Hannah has unleashed a huge storm in this valley. I think that the Grays and Williams family can coexist for a short time, but before long someone is going to have second thoughts about that fine piece of property falling into the hands of someone who has no biological connection to it. Without a doubt, when Hannah passes on, the younger Grays will seek legal possession of their deceased uncle's property."

"Tay, it's not really a concern of yours," Annie replied. "I know that you and Hannah have a special bond because of what you experienced back in the '50s, but she made the decision on her own and she will have to live with it. I know that sounds hard-nosed, but we have no recourse in the situation."

"I know, I know, but I just hate to see people get hurt. We've enough strife in this valley, and we don't need any more hard feelings between kinfolk. I guess I should turn my attention to the schism developing between the colonies and Britain instead of worrying about my neighbor's mistakes."

CHAPTER THIRTY SIX

The First Movement to Independence

With the defeat of France and the subsequent Treaty of Paris of 1763, France was obliged to relinquish its North American territories and turn Florida over to its Spanish allies. This war, known as the French and Indian War in the colonies and as the Seven Years War in Europe, ultimately contributed to the movement for American independence.

Militarily, the war had given the American military forces from various parts of the colonies the opportunity to unite and to be successful. Leaders of the colonial forces gained invaluable insight into military strategy and acquired confidence in their military prowess.

The threat and competition of the French in the St. Lawrence Valley, the Great Lakes Region, and the Ohio and Mississippi River Valleys had been removed. The American colonists no longer needed as much protection as they had once thought necessary, although the Indian menace still existed in those old French-held territories. Since protection was no longer paramount, the British military role switched from guardian or protector to that of a separate controlling factor.

The war with France had proved to be extremely expensive. The coffers of the British Empire were almost empty. To remedy this financial predicament, the British government chose to increase taxation of the American colonies to help pay for the war.

Upon the conclusion of the French and Indian War, the British government embarked on a new concept in which the

Crown not only increased taxes in the American colonies but also attempted to tighten its control over the governments of the individual colonies.

Since the 1600s England had pursued an economic policy aimed at benefiting the mother country by regulating the economic life of the colonies. To achieve this, Britain, like many other nations of Europe, adopted a policy of mercantilism. Under this policy, money was considered the most favorable form of wealth, and a favorable balance of trade the surest method of increasing the supply of money. Colonies were established to furnish raw materials and buy the mother country's manufactured goods and thus secure a favorable balance of trade. Colonies were forbidden to manufacture goods that would compete with those produced in the mother country.

In accordance with these objectives, beginning in 1651 Britain began to pass a series of Trade and Navigations Acts, which were indifferently enforced due to various wars with France. With the ending of the war in 1763, Britain was able to devote her full attention to the rigid enforcement of the old laws and to begin placing political restrictions upon the colonies.

To rectify the situation of a huge debt, about half of it incurred in defending the American colonies, Lord George Grenville, the First Lord of the Treasury and Chancellor of the Exchequer, introduced the Sugar Act in 1764. This act heavily taxed molasses that was imported from non-British countries and their colonies, and threatened to end New England's lucrative rum industry and to curtail her commerce and shipping.

The next year the Stamp Act hit the pocketbooks of all classes of people in all the colonies. This act stipulated that all newspapers, pamphlets, and legal documents, and many instruments of business were to pay this new tax. The act imposed a levy on about fifty items, including bills of lading, diplomas, playing cards, dice, and marriage licenses. The revenue was to be expended exclusively for the purpose of "defending, protecting, and securing" the colonies. The act passed Parliament in March 1764 with little opposition.

This act was to have immediate reverberations in the colonies. In the Virginia House of Burgesses, Patrick Henry, after a fiery speech, introduced resolutions, one of which declared, "that the general assembly of this colony have the only and sole exclusive right and power to lay taxes and impositions upon the inhabitants of this colony."

The Massachusetts House of Representatives issued a call for a meeting to be held in New York to form a united opposition to the new taxation policy. The Sons of Liberty were organized throughout the colonies. They staged demonstrations and intimidated stamp agents. Their rallying cry became "Liberty, Property, and No Stamps." In Massachusetts, the activities of the Sons of Liberty culminated in the destruction of the home of Lieutenant Governor Hutchinson.

Many Americans striving to wrest a living from the frontier wilderness were deeply alarmed. They felt that they were already paying substantial local taxes as approved by their own colonial legislatures. The new actions undertaken by Parliament aroused the prospect of double taxation. The frontiersmen's dreams of owning their own land did not include the reality of taxation of those lands.

In the Tuscarora Valley, that reality came home as the county government out of Carlisle extended its tax rolls to include those people who warranted and patented land to the north of the county seat.

For a long time the inhabitants of the frontier, including the Tuscarora Valley, had not protested against the custom duties levied by Parliament. Those earlier taxes were indirect taxes, paid at the customhouses and passed on indirectly to the consumer as higher prices on merchandise.

The new Stamp Act was a direct tax, levied specifically on the consumer, primarily to raise revenue and not to regulate trade. Although the Stamp Act was admittedly a light tax, the feeling was that once it was accepted, it would lead to more taxes that were ruinous.

"Taxation without representation is tyranny" was a cry

voiced by thousands of Americans. The people of the Pennsylvania frontier had expressed this concept in response to the reluctance of Pennsylvania's government to protect the inhabitants of the frontier since the first Indian incursions in 1755. Matthew Smith and James Gibson, the leaders of the Paxtang Boys, on February 13, 1764, had voiced the concern of frontier grievances when they met with colonial authorities in their "Remonstrance of the Distressed and Bleeding Frontier Inhabitants of the Province of Pennsylvania."

In October 1765, twenty-seven delegates from nine colonies met in New York, drew up a statement of their rights and grievances, and requested the King and Parliament to repeal the legislation.

What the American colonials really wanted was a return to the "good old days" prior to the French and Indian War. Before the war, the navigation laws had been poorly enforced, and the colonies had suffered taxation only at the hands of their own colonial legislatures. The Americans were unwilling to grasp the idea of shouldering the new responsibilities that were thrust upon them as citizens of a great global empire.

England was hard hit economically. After a stormy debate, Parliament in 1766 reluctantly repealed the Stamp Act. At the same time, it passed the Declaratory Act. This measure reaffirmed the right of Parliament to legislate for the colonies.

The repeal of the Stamp Act masked the impact of the sweeping Declaratory Act. William Pitt took office as prime minister soon after the repeal of the Stamp Act. Pitt became ill and crippled with gout. As a result, he seldom attended Cabinet meetings and only nominally presided over the Cabinet. The key leadership was thrown into the hands of Charles Townshend, the Chancellor of the Exchequer.

Charles Townshend was a gifted and aggressive but erratic statesman. He was dubbed "Champagne Charley" because he was noted for delivering brilliant speeches in Parliament while drunk. The hope of relieving the British taxpayers at the expense of the colonies did not disappear easily. Townshend rashly promised to pluck feathers from the colonial goose with a minimum of squawking.

In 1767 Champagne Charley persuaded the Parliament to pass the Townshend Acts, which were designed to be external taxes, as opposed to the Stamp Tax, which the colonists opposed because they felt it was an internal tax. The most important of these proposed regulations was a light import duty on glass, white lead, paper, painter's colors, and tea. Although these taxes were not high, they had been placed on commonplace articles and therefore raised the cost of living.

To most colonists, the import duty on tea was extremely irksome. It was estimated that one million persons drank "the cup that cheers" twice a day. Even the Native Americans had been introduced to tea and used it when firewater was not available.

On the frontier of Central Pennsylvania, the tea tax did not have a great impact. Many of the inhabitants simply passed off the tax, saying, "Tea tax? Who can afford imported tea? We brew our own from sassafras or herbs. That tax won't affect us, but the principle of the tax certainly irritates us, especially since we in the colonies have no say in England.

Many colonists considered other features of the Townshend Acts to be far more dangerous. These features called for the reorganization of the customs service, with courts of admiralty being established in the colonies to expedite cases of smuggling. The money raised from this source was to be used to pay the expenses of the royal governors and judges in America. This feature was considered excessive in that it removed the control of the purse strings from the colonies.

New York was singled out, and the colony's assembly was suspended because it had refused to comply with a law of 1765 that required the adequate quartering of soldiers in the colonies.

The major objection was that part of one of the acts reaffirmed the legality of writs of assistance. These writs were general warrants permitting customs officials to enter private premises in search of smuggled goods. Although these writs were thought to be effective in preventing smuggling, they were also considered exceedingly offensive and dangerous to personal liberty. The British had first used the writs of assistance during the French and Indian War in an attempt to curtail trading with the enemy.

The citizens and merchants throughout the colonies implemented economic boycotts in the form of nonconsumption and nonimportation agreements. This attempt at economic boycott was not just a voluntary movement; it became backed and encouraged by many colonial legislative bodies.

John Dickinson of Pennsylvania urged in his *Letters from a Farmer in Pennsylvania* that the colonists "behave like dutiful children," but clearly emphasized that if Britain maintained her rights to tax imports, "the tragedy of American liberty is finished."

Two regiments of British troops landed in Boston in 1768 to deal with the breakdown of law and order in that city. Unfortunately, many of the soldiers were drunken and profane characters. The liberty-loving and ever more rebellious colonials resented the presence of the red-coated ruffians. They dubbed the soldiers "lobster backs," and began to taunt the soldiers unmercifully.

British imports into New England and the middle colonies dropped considerably in 1768-1769. Eventually Parliament became convinced that it was an unwise policy to tax its own goods sold abroad. In April 1770, all the duties of the Townshend Acts were repealed except the one on tea. This exception was a matter of principle in order to assert the power of the British government to tax the colonies.

The struggle of the Irish for the rights of Irishmen also played a role in opposition to the British government in America due to the great influx of Irish or Scotch-Irish immigrants to the American colonies. Consistently throughout the early eighteenth century, the Irish had asserted that they had a natural right to independence. The Irish arguments were of little avail against the facts of English control, but they were gaining momentum in America, especially in the frontier regions.

Eighteen months of continual friction between the British soldiers and the Bostonian citizens culminated on March 5, 1770, in the "Boston Massacre." A clash between the two opposing groups was inevitable. On the evening of the fifth, a crowd of nearly sixty townspeople began to goad a squad of ten soldiers beyond endurance, after a sentry on guard at the customhouse who had been repeatedly bullied and snowballed, called for assistance.

One of the soldiers was hit by a club, and another was knocked down. In retaliation, the squad, acting apparently without orders, fired a volley into the mob of citizens. The volley killed or wounded eleven Bostonians. Captain Preston, the commander of the guard, immediately surrendered to the civilian authorities, and the other members of the squad were arrested.

In the subsequent trial, John Adams and Josiah Quincy Jr. defended the squad members. Only two of the soldiers were found guilty of manslaughter. The two were branded on the hand and released. The Boston Massacre, which was essentially a skirmish, further roused the colonists against the British, especially after the spread of the conviction that the Americans were wholly unoffending.

Paul Revere played a prominent role in this form of propaganda by producing and distributing a fanciful engraving depicting a line of British soldiers firing a volley into a "peaceful" group of demonstrating citizens. He followed this up with the little dilly "Unhappy Boston! See thy sons deplore Thy hallowed walks besmear'd with guiltless gore."

Massacre Day, March 5, was observed as a patriotic holiday until 1776, when the date was eclipsed by the more glorious Fourth of July.

Samuel Adams of Boston seized every opportunity to keep the revolutionary spirit alive in the colonies. He stated, "When our liberty is gone, history and civilization alike will teach us that an inhabitant's will be but an increase in slaves." In 1772, he was successful in having a Boston town meeting vote to create Committees of Correspondence to exchange views and information with other towns in the colony.

The concept of the Committees of Correspondence grew in acceptance, and soon a network of Committees kept the leaders in each colony acquainted with the latest political developments. These intercolonial groups were supremely significant in stimulating and spreading united action sentiment that eventually evolved into the First Continental Congress.

The British East India Company became the next unwitting villain on the colonial scene. The British Parliament in May 1773 authorized an arrangement that granted the company a virtual tea monopoly. The company was permitted to send its tea directly to the colonies in its own ships and to retailers through its own agencies. This eliminated the British and colonial importer. This allowed the company to undersell both the honest tea merchants and those who smuggled tea.

Samuel Adams summoned a mass meeting that unanimously adopted a resolution stating that tea should not be unloaded and the duty on the tea should not be paid. On the night of December 16, 1773, a group of men disguised as Indians boarded the ships in Boston's harbor and dumped 342 chests of tea in the harbor. The East India Company's tea also met with opposition in the other colonies.

In the spring of 1774, Lord North requested that Parliament pass the infamous Intolerable Acts. The Boston Port Bill went into effect in June 1774, which closed Boston's harbor until damages were paid and order could be assured. The Massachusetts Government Act swept away many of the chartered rights of the colony. Under the Administration of Justice Act, officials who killed colonials in the line of duty were sent to England to stand trial, by order of the governor. The Quartering Act revived the old Quartering Act of 1765 that allowed the governors to requisition certain buildings for the use of British troops in all colonies. Parliament also extended the old boundaries of the Province of Quebec southward all the way to the Ohio River.

The most important response to these "Intolerable Acts" was the summoning of the First Continental Congress in 1774 in Philadelphia to consider ways of redressing colonial grievances. This Congress deliberated for seven weeks, from September 5 to October 26, 1774.

The Congress adopted a no-intercourse agreement that recommended that after December 1, 1774, no goods be imported from Great Britain, and after September 10, 1775, no exports be shipped except rice to the British West Indies. This became known as the "American Association." In addition, "A Declaration of Rights and Grievances" was drawn up, which stated the political theory of the colonists and condemned the recent acts of Parliament. A petition to the king appealing for a redress of grievances was enacted.

The Congress adjourned in late October and was scheduled to meet again in May of the next year if their grievances were not redressed. The controversy would pass from petitions and addresses to the field of battle before the next Congress could assemble.

In May 1774, the British army had undergone a change of command in Boston. The mild-mannered and conciliatory General Thomas Gage was appointed as Chief of the Armed Forces in America and as the Governor of Massachusetts, with instructions to enforce the acts of Parliament.

On the night of April 18, 1775, Gage dispatched about seven hundred men to destroy military stores that had been collected by the radicals at Concord and to arrest two of the radical American leaders, Samuel Adams and John Hancock. Paul Revere and William Dawes warned the rebel countryside of General Gage's intentions. The Patriots, who had been waiting for such a move by the British, intercepted the British regulars at daybreak at Lexington. A brief skirmish ensued; eight of the minutemen were killed and ten wounded. The British pressed on to Concord and destroyed the stores that had not been removed and then fought another skirmish at Concord Bridge. The British were harassed during their long retreat to Boston, and the militia directed a deadly fire from behind every rock, tree, and fence.

The minutemen closed in on Boston, resulting in a siege of the city that would last for eleven months. Thus, after long years of controversy, a clash of arms between English brethren erupted that would eventually lead to American independence.

The news from Lexington spread rapidly and strengthened

the spirit of revolt. On May 10, 1775, the Second Continental Congress assembled at Philadelphia. The Congress assumed responsibility for the troops located in the vicinity of Boston. On June 15, the Congress appointed George Washington as commander-in-chief of the Continental Army and approved an expedition against Canada. Another petition was addressed to the king, which he refused to receive.

The Continental Army that the Congress needed to create had to be a European-style regular army, but there was no standing patriot army anywhere in the colonies. The local militia of New England that quickly rallied and marched to Boston was a collection of "embattled farmers," not trained soldiers.

The army that George Washington took command of on July 2, 1775, did not represent any existing nation, but a loose alliance of separate colonies. The newly appointed commander quickly set about transforming the inhabitants of the encampments into a unified and disciplined army.

One of his most pressing problems was that most of the men under his command had only short-term militia enlistments. The first body of troops from outside New England arrived on July 25. This was a corps of rifle-wielding frontiersmen whose enlistment had been empowered by the Second Continental Congress.

These men were distinguished by their frock-like hunting shirts, leggings, and round hats. However, what stood out more were their peculiar-looking weapons: long guns with rifled barrels. These weapons gave the wielders tremendous accuracy and distance. Unfortunately these frontiersmen were prone to brawling, and soon started a riot.

One popular myth about the typical American Revolutionary War soldier was that every man was handy with a gun. This soon proved not to be the case in that some soldiers were town dwellers who had rarely handled weapons. In addition, many farmers lived in areas near large settlements and lacked opportunities to hunt and use firearms.

John Dickinson and Thomas Jefferson penned a stirring

"Declaration of the Causes and Necessity of Taking Up Arms." In this document, they stated, "We have not raised armies with ambitious designs of separating from Great Britain, and establishing independent states." Later Jefferson would write that "in July 1775, a separation from Great Britain and the establishment of a Republican Government had not yet entered any person's mind."

This feeling would change dramatically during the next year as events unfolded that would not allow an amicable settlement. In January 1776, Thomas Paine published his famous pamphlet, *Common Sense,* in which he set forth his arguments for complete independence.

In this clarion call to separate from the mother country, Paine wrote:

> The sun never shined on a cause of greater worth... O! You that love mankind! You that dare oppose not only the tyranny but the tyrant, stand forth!... Freedom had been hunted round the globe. Asia and Africa have long expelled her. Europe regards her like a stranger, and England hath given her warning to depart. O! Receive the fugitive, and prepare in time an asylum for mankind.

This forty-seven-page pamphlet sharply accelerated the movement toward independence. Thomas Paine advocated an immediate break from Britain, and Congress heeded his words and advised the colonies to establish themselves into states.

On June 7, Richard Henry Lee of Virginia moved that "these United Colonies are, and of right ought to be, free and independent States; that they are absolved from all allegiance to the British Crown; and that all political connection between them and the state of Great Britain is, and ought to be totally resolved." The Congress accepted Lee's resolution on July 2, and two days later, July 4, 1776, adopted the Declaration of Independence, almost entirely the work of Thomas Jefferson.

It became a source of inspiration to revolutionary movements everywhere. Known familiarly as "a shout heard round the world," this Declaration became a call to arms throughout the colonies, which, with the adoption of this document, now became states.

CHAPTER THIRTY SEVEN

Loyalists or Tories

Throughout the colonies, those opposed to the Crown's policies depicted Gage and his Redcoats as "massacrers of innocent people," "butcherers," and "the agents of tyrannous despoilers of liberty."

There was widespread opposition to English policies, but the majority of the colonists did not consistently support the Revolution. One English historian stated, "The American Revolution, like most others, was the work of an energetic minority who succeeded in committing an undecided and fluctuating majority to courses for which they had little love, and leading them step by step to a position from which it was impossible to recede."

The American War for Independence was a war within a war. Colonials loyal to the king, known as Loyalists or Tories, fought the American rebels, known as Patriots or Whigs. The Rebels or Patriots fought both the Loyalists and the British Redcoats.

John Dickinson of Pennsylvania sneered at the conservative Americans who remained loyal to the king, "This word, Rebellion, hath froze them up, like fish in a pond," he wrote.

One loyalist feared that the "dirty rabble" inflamed by violence would break out of control. "If I must be devoured," stated another Tory, "let me be devoured by the jaws of a lion, and not gnawed to death by rats and vermin."

The Loyalists were usually the most numerous in strongholds of the Anglican Church and in the Quaker sections of Pennsylvania. The Patriots were most numerous where

Presbyterianism and Congregational churches were entrenched. Later, invading British armies expressed their anger and contempt for these churches by using their church buildings as pigsties and stables.

Nicholas Cresswell, a Tory diarist, complained, "The Presbyterian clergy are particularly active in supporting the measures of Congress from the rostrum, gaining proselytes, persecuting the unbelievers, preaching up the righteousness of their cause, and persuading the unthinking populace of the infallibility of success."

In Pennsylvania, great landholding families such as the Whartons, Penningtons, and Pembertons of Philadelphia did not forsake their loyalty to Great Britain. In the opinion of one Loyalist, "the Revolution was a conspiracy and the conspirators were an infernal, dark-designing group of men...obscure, pettifogging attorneys, bankrupt shopkeepers, outlawed smugglers,...wretched banditti,...the refuse and dregs of mankind."

It appears that only in Massachusetts and Virginia were the masses in favor of revolution from the very beginning of the movement. The regions of New York, eastern Pennsylvania, and New Jersey were almost hostile territory to Washington's army until the British made the mistake of using Hessians. In early campaigns in these areas, Washington felt that he was fighting in "the enemy's country."

The hostilities that engulfed the Loyalists and their Patriot neighbors amounted to a civil war, and civil wars are inevitably bitter. Jonathan Boucher, a slave-owning Anglican clergyman, was so disdainfully Loyalist that he resorted to violence. On one occasion, he encountered a blacksmith who was armed with a stick and gun and felled him with one punch. He stated, "For more than six months I preached, when I did preach, with a pair of loaded pistols lying on the cushion; having giving notice that if any man... threatened to drag me out of my own pulpit, I should think myself justified before God and man in repelling violence by violence."

George Washington called the Loyalists "pests of society" and thought that they ought to commit suicide or be hanged. Frank Moore of Pennsylvania joined in his disdain for the Tories, of whom he wrote, "Who prevailed on the savages of the wilderness to join the standard of the enemy? The Tories! Who have assisted the Indians in taking the scalp from the aging matron, the blooming fair one, the helpless infant, and the dying hero? The Tories! Who advised and who assisted in burning your towns, ravaging your country, and violating the chastity of your women? The Tories!"

Not everyone shared this view. On the eve of the revolution, some frontier observers felt that a Scotch-Irish or Presbyterian Loyalist was unheard of, especially in the Juniata Valley of Pennsylvania. Sadly, for Robert Taylor and his fellow supporters of the Revolution, some frontier dwellers remained loyal to King George III and felt no obligation to fight and die for colonial independence.

The first instance of Tory activity occurred in Tyrone Township of Cumberland County, now known as Perry County. On February 19, 1776, Clefton Bowen swore before George Robison, a justice for the County of Cumberland, "that some time in the month of January last, he, this deponent, was in the house of John Montgomery, in Tyrone Township, in company with a certain Edward Erwin, of Rye Township, and this deponent says he then and there heard said Edward Erwin drink damnation and confusion to the Continental Congress, and damn their proceedings, saying they were all a parcel of damned rebels, and against spring would be cut off like a parcel of snowbirds, and more such stuff."

On February 11, 1777, the General Assembly of the newly formed state of Pennsylvania enacted legislation that declared what actions would be considered treason and what various other crimes and practices against Pennsylvania would be imprisonment for treason.

Thomas Kerr, one of the leading farmers of Lack Township of the Tuscarora Valley, was charged with treason under the act of 1777 and found guilty in the court at Carlisle in October 1778.

On March 6, 1778, the legislature of Pennsylvania passed a more stringent law concerning Loyalist or Tory activity. Under this law the Supreme Executive Council of the State was given the power to confiscate the estates of those who practiced internal dissension and continued to support the king. The measure also required the appointment of agents to operate throughout the state to report and give testimony about those considered to be enemies of the State.

Major Robert Taylor and his fellow militiamen, even in their worst nightmares, would never have dreamed that in the upper end of the Juniata Valley resided nearly as many Tories as Patriots. Not only did these unpatriotic persons inhabit the Juniata Valley, they attempted to concentrate a formidable force of Tories and Indians at Kittanning on the Allegheny River.

Beginning in 1777 the Tories who resided in Aughwick, Hare's Valley, Woodcock Valley, Shaver's Creek, Warrior's Mark, and Canoe Creek began to hold secret meetings that were attended by Tory emissaries from Detroit. This conspiracy also extended from Path Valley, through Amberson and the Tuscarora Valleys, and up the Juniata Valley to the previously mentioned locations. The conspirators elected John Weston, who lived above Water Street, as their captain. Jacob Hare and John McKee aided Weston in his leadership of the Tory expedition.

Early in the spring of 1778, the force left Weston's home and headquarters under cover of darkness and attempted to avoid all settlements on their line of march. They skirted Brush Mountain and followed the path to Kittanning. Although they attempted to employ the utmost secrecy, Major Robert Cluggage, along with his company that had been recruited chiefly out of Bedford County, was well aware of their activities. The major employed Captain Logan, a Cayuga Chief, to spy upon the Tory force as they moved westward.

Colonel John Piper of Yellow Creek and George Woods of Bedford wrote to President Wharton of the Supreme Executive Council of Pennsylvania to inform him of the Tory threat on Pennsylvania's frontier. Terror and alarm spread throughout the

Juniata Valley; many settlers retired to the local forts, and an appeal was made to Captain Thomas Blair of Path Valley to overtake and punish the Tory force.

Within forty-eight hours after the Tories under Weston had departed for Kittanning, Captain Blair had a force of thirty men ready to march to apprehend the Tories. At least twenty of the militia were from Path Valley, while the rest of the militia were recruited from units between there and Standing Stone. Brothers Gersham and Moses Hicks joined the company at Canoe Valley and acted as scouts and interpreters. Since the Hicks boys had spent nearly seven years in captivity, they knew the Indians and the area quite well.

The Tories plan was to join the Indians from Kittanning, then cross the mountains to Burgoon's Gap. At the gap, the force would divide. One party was to march through the Cove, and move through the Conococheague and Path Valleys into the Cumberland Valley. The other force was to follow the Juniata River Valley and eventually join with the other force at Lancaster.

Along the way, they were to kill all the inhabitants of the settlements. The fine farms and plantations along the route were to be divided among the marchers, while their Indian allies were to divide all the movable property. This was quite an undertaking for such a small company.

In late April, the expedition neared Kittanning, where they halted, and John Weston and Jacob Hare approached the town under the protection of a flag of peace. The Indians returned with Weston and Hare to greet the rest of the force and escort them back to town. The Indians employed great caution, and all went well until McKee ordered his men to "present arms." The Indians misinterpreted the movement, and believing that this order was an aggressive action, reacted by firing a volley into the Tory force.

John Weston and at least eight of his men were killed, and Weston was immediately scalped. Hare and the survivors fled in terror and great haste in their attempts to return to the Juniata Valley.

In the meantime, Captain Blair and his men were also advancing on Kittanning. When they arrived on the path where it crosses the headwaters of Blacklick Creek, they came face-to-face with two of Weston's survivors. The immediate impulse was to shoot them, but Captain Blair practiced mercy as the two piteously begged them to spare their lives.

The two men claimed they had been totally deceived by John Weston and produced a supposedly true statement as to what had transpired. When the two Tories reached the settlements, they were taken into custody by Samuel Moore and Jacob Roller and eventually taken to Fort Bedford. From Bedford they were transported to Carlisle to appear before the magistrates.

Blair's men began to retrace their path back to their homes, but along the way they suffered greatly from hunger and inclement weather. The unfortunate Hicks brothers were once again taken captive by the Indians and taken westward all the way to Detroit. The rest of Blair's men made it back to civilization. Although most were quite ill, they eventually recovered to serve their country again.

Jacob Hare made the mistake of spending a night at a location about three miles from Concord in Path Valley. His presence was soon discovered, and he was taken into custody. The news spread throughout Path Valley and the upper Tuscarora Valley, and a large number of settlers gathered and became quite rowdy in proposing various punishments for the Tory. A rope was thrown around Hare's neck and the end of it thrown over a beam, in preparation for hanging him.

Suddenly, William Darlington stood up, waving a large case knife with a hacked blade. "We're wasting time with this scoundrel! Hold his head and I'll make sure he never has to listen to us good Patriots speak of independence and of slandering the good King."

Three husky men followed William's suggestion and grabbed Hare around the neck and shoulders. Darlington showed no remorse as he executed his self-proclaimed sentence by sawing off Hare's ears as the crowd cheered him on. Hare's head bled profusely where the ears had been. Eventually two women stepped forward, stemmed the flow, and saved the Tory's life.

Tory Hare finally made his way back to his home in a small isolated valley about a mile south of Jack's Narrows on the Juniata. Here he loaded his effects upon his packhorses and left the country. It was later reported that he grew his hair long in order to disguise his lack of ears.

Richard Weston was apprehended when he attempted to return to his home. Weston was sent to Cumberland County jail in Carlisle on April 27, 1778, to await the decision of the Supreme Executive Council of Pennsylvania concerning his role in the Kittanning affair.

As Captain Blair and his men traveled through an area known as Pleasant Valley, they came upon another known Tory, John Hess. The militia took him into the woods, strung him up on a hickory sapling, and let him swing. The men became upset as they watched the man struggling to maintain his life that they cut him loose. Hess was so thankful that he swore allegiance to the State and the United States and joined the militia.

Later, on October 30, 1778, the State's Supreme Executive Council issued the following proclamation regarding the Tory activity involving Weston and Hare:

> John Campbell, William Campbell, James Little, Edward Gibbons, and James De Long, yeomen, all now or late of Amberson Valley; and Andrew Smith and Robert Nixon, yeomen, both now or late of the township of Lack; and Joseph King, yeoman, and William Wright, dyer, both now or late of the township of Path Valley; and Dominick McNeal and John Stillwell, yeomen, both now or late of the township of Tuscarora; all now or late of the county of Cumberland; and Richard Weston, yeoman, now or late of the township of Frankstown; and Jacob Hare, Michael Hare and Samuel Barrow, yeomen, now or late of the township of Baree; all now or late of the county of Bedford; beside many others, have severally adhered to and knowingly and willingly aided

and assisted the enemies of this State and of the United States of America by having joined their armies within this State. It was provided that unless they surrendered themselves for trial, they should, after the 15th day of December next, stand and attainted of High Treason, to all intents and purposes, and shall suffer such pain and penalties and undergo all such forfeitures as persons attainted of High Treason ought to do.[8]

Under the Act of March 6, 1778, George Stephenson, John Boggs, and Joseph Brady were appointed as Agents for Forfeited Estates with the power to report guilty and persons suspected of treason on May 6 of the same year for Cumberland County. A year later Alexander McGechan received the same appointment.

On December 10, 1779, George Stephenson sent the following letter from Carlisle:

I do not find mementoes the names of six men who left this County some time after the British army got possession of the City of Philadelphia, and joined them there; soon after my appointment as an agent, I wrote to his Excellency, Thomas Wharton, Esq'r, all I knew concerning those men; as this was about two years ago, and before the Act of the Assembly for the Attainder of Traitors was made, 'tis probable my letter might have been mislaid or forgot, or I may not have seen their proscription; their names are Alexander McDonald, Kennet McKinzie, and Edward Erwin, all of Rye Township, farmers; also William Simpson, William McPherson, blacksmiths, and Hugh Gwin, labourer, single men, all of Tyrone Township. Thomas McCahan, of Tuscarora Valley, went off afterwards, to New York, as I am informed; he was an unmarried man, rented out his farm, and I think he ought to be proscribed.[9]

CHAPTER THIRTY EIGHT

The Role of the Clergy

Many of the Scotch-Irish settlers followed the concept that they had nothing to begin with, for few of them had any appreciable assets, so they had nothing to lose. They felt that they owed no allegiance to the arbitrary actions of colonial or English governments. They were prepared to fight Indians, pacifistic Quakers, or British bureaucrats and soldiers.

Numerous settlers in the Juniata Valley had grown to believe that revolts against authority were morally justifiable, as evidenced by the actions of James Smith's Black Boys and the reaction of the Sherman's and Tuscarora men to the jailing of Frederick Stump. Through the experiences that they had gained during the French and Indian War, these restless people had developed the ability to adapt their military expertise to the battlefield of the frontier wilderness.

They had learned to accept that at some point in their lives they should expect harsh and bloody conflict as a way of life. The men had grown accustomed to the idea that they were expected to fight. On the frontier, every able-bodied man was considered a member of the local militia.

The frontier women knew that their men were expected to fight, and that they would be required to run the farms while the men were away fighting. The risk of raiding parties was a constant threat, a form of terrorism that they accepted, and they rose to the challenge of protecting the farm and family.

The Scotch-Irish who inhabited Cumberland County of 1774 were early responders to the aggression of the British against the colonies. On July 12, 1774, some defenders of colonial liberties met in the First Presbyterian Church of Carlisle to deliberate on the rousing events occurring elsewhere in the colonies and to offer their indignation and protests against British authority.

The delegates to this assembly addressed the plight of the inhabitants of Boston under the yoke of the infamous Boston Port Bill, stating that the people of Boston "are suffering in the common cause of the colonies."

The assembly displayed their staunch belief in the cause of liberty by appointing delegates to Philadelphia to meet with delegates from other counties about the dire need for an assembly of like-minded men from all the colonies to meet and discuss their options. This, of course, led to the formation of the First Continental Congress that met in Philadelphia on September 5, 1774.

It appears that the entire population of Cumberland County was inspired and aroused by the able leadership of its outspoken Presbyterian clergymen. Reverend John Steel of the First Presbyterian Church of Carlisle, Reverend John King of the Upper West Conococheague Presbyterian Church of Mercersburg, Reverend Robert Cooper, pastor of the Middle Spring Church, Reverend William Linn, and Reverend John Craighead, pastor of Big Spring and later the pastor of the Rocky Spring Church on the Conococheague, were all classic examples of the pastor leading his flock into the throes of extreme patriotism.

Another influential voice from the pulpit was that of Reverend George Duffield. Duffield had joined Reverend Charles Beatty in 1766 in his excursion into the Tuscarora Valley. After his return from the west, he became the pastor of the Big Spring and Carlisle churches. In 1772, Duffield had accepted the call to become the pastor of the Third Presbyterian Church of Philadelphia. When the conflict broke out, Reverend Duffield was chosen chaplain of the Continental Congress and was often found following the Continental Army, extending comfort and encouragement to the soldiers.

The historian Edward Bancroft observed, "We shall find that the first voice publicly raised in America to dissolve all connection with Great Britain came, not from the Puritans of New England, nor the Dutch of New York, nor the planters of Virginia, but from the Scotch-Irish Presbyterians."[10]

To inspire the members of his congregation who were enter into the conflict, Reverend John King of Mercersburg stated, "The cause of American Independence and Liberty, which has now called you to go forth to the scene of the action, is indeed a cause in which it will be glorious to conquer and honorable to die."[11]

The patriotic pastors who occupied the pulpits of the various valleys of Cumberland County during the Revolutionary War period had a tremendous influence on their congregations. Often they asserted that the people of these valleys had a right to rebel against a government that confiscated their property and money. They preached the values of liberty or death, which had a profound impact on many young men, who showed tremendous enthusiasm for military glory and the virtues of independence by joining either the Continental Army or the militia.

Robert Taylor of the Tuscarora Valley and his neighbors listened to several itinerant pastors at the Lower Tuscarora Presbyterian Church, which had been established in the center of their valley in 1766. The theme varied little from one pastor to another, as the clergy attempted to motivate the inhabitants of the valley to defend themselves against the injustices of the British colonial system. Within Lack Township, two other Presbyterian congregations also existed: Upper Tuscarora and Middle Tuscarora. These congregations heard the same revolutionary theme again and again and eventually most of their members responded and supported the new nation.

In 1771, a Reverend Rhea was called as the first pastor to the Lower Tuscarora Church in conjunction with the Cedar Spring Church, but he was never installed as the pastor. The combined congregations at Cedar Springs and in the Tuscarora Valley repeated their supplications for a regular pastor and for supplies.

For a short period, the two congregations had Reverend Samuel Kennedy as their pastor, but the Presbytery refused to recognize Kennedy as a minister. This created divisions and a great deal of trouble in both congregations. The Presbytery endeavored to reestablish stability by sending a moderator to read a paper to that effect. A melee almost resulted when the paper was snatched from the hand of the moderator, who promptly fled the scene. This left the situation unresolved and the region without a pastor.

In 1773, twenty acres of land were set aside for a log church that became known as the Lower Tuscarora Presbyterian Church.

In 1776 Reverend Hugh Magill was sent as a supply minister for ten months, and afterwards he received a call to serve the two churches. Reverend Magill was installed as the first pastor of the Cedar Springs and Lower Tuscarora Churches on the fourth Wednesday of November 1779 in the midst of the War for Independence. Magill continued to serve both churches until April of 1796, when he resigned from the Lower Tuscarora Church but continued to serve at Cedar Spring until his death on September 4, 1805.

Prior to the installation of Reverend Magill in 1779, church services were held at the Lower Tuscarora Church when the Presbytery of Donegal was able to send itinerant pastors or missionaries to this isolated frontier settlement. It became quite popular to hold four-day camp meetings at the church several times a year.

Repeatedly Robert's ears heard the same theme from the pulpit:

> How much longer can we exist in a peaceful situation where peace is maintained at the expense of life, liberty, and property? Blessed is the defender of his country; blessed is the brave soldier who destroys his enemies. The sword should be consecrated to God, and our cry should become 'to arms'!

> You may conclude that in these inland parts of the country we are as yet unmolested by the calamities that have

unfolded on the seaboard and are not of our real concern, but I assure you that this sense of security is unfounded. Many of us remember all too well the savage shouts and whoops of the Delaware and Shawnee, as they were unleashed against us in the late war against the French. Since the alleged conclusion of the war in 1763, the traders and the king's representatives have aided the natives by loading them with presents and have not only sought their support but have taught the natives to the west of us to despise us and look upon us as easy prey.

We may expect the Indian revenge and thirst for blood to be continued, this time not headed by the French but by the British. This time we must stand our ground. We will not desert our remote settlements as we did in the past. This time we will not allow our strength to be weakened by a vast loss of men and arms.

Is it not our duty, in the sight of God; is it not our work to take up arms for the defense of our country, our homes, and our families?

All of you that love your friends and relatives, Enlist! Do not allow all those who are dear to you be enslaved or butchered before your eyes. All of you young and hardy men, you that have been formed by God and nature to be good soldiers, Enlist!

Those of you that yet do not have the burden of a young family and have no one depending upon you for subsistence, Enlist!

You that love your country, Enlist! Honor will follow you in life or death in such a glorious cause.

These sermons did not fall upon deaf ears. They were a tremendous influence in shaping the sentiments against British colonial polices. Soon men from the Tuscarora, Sherman's, Kishacoquillas, Aughwick, and Conococheague Valleys joined their brethren on the other side of the Blue Mountains in the cause of independence.

Anne Taylor had listened to the sermons and understood the pressure on her husband. She decided to address the issue. "Tay, I know our country needs you, but so do I and our children. You're the father of four children, four young children who need your guidance and love. I don't want you to neglect your duty or turn your back on our patriotic cause, but I think you have to consider where you might do the most good.

"It's not fair for you to run off to defend Boston or attack Montreal, which many of our men are doing. I believe what we really need is for many of our own men to remain in our valley to ward off the threats of Indians and the Loyalists. Not all of you men can abandon us in favor of supporting the Continental Army.

"Our local militia needs every able man it can muster; the whole frontier just can't be depopulated of all its able bodied men. In addition, there is the factor that an army travels on its stomach. Someone needs to remain on the farms to raise staple crops to feed and maintain an army.

"Oh, I could give you a dozen good arguments for serving in the militia, but I know you, you've made up your mind a long time ago, and no matter what I say you'll do whatever you have your mind set on doing. I'm sorry, but I am a good wife and mother, and I want us to be protected here at home."

Robert smiled for a long time before responding to his mild wife's outburst. "I've been mulling this over in my mind for over a year, ever since the first Continental Congress convened. I figured pretty well how you felt; besides that many of us men have been discussing our options.

"I'm not exactly a young man any more, and like you said, I do have quite a family to protect and provide for. I'm not going off half-cocked, and I'm not about to repeat my mistakes in judgment—although I'm not going to discuss my history of mistakes.

"I've discussed my situation with Colonel Thompson at Carlisle, and he cut me off. He told me in no uncertain terms that my biggest contribution to the cause of Independence would be to serve as a battalion officer in the Cumberland County militia.

"Colonel Thompson has offered me a commission as a major involved mainly in recruitment. He felt that there would be an immediate rush to volunteer to serve under Washington in the Continental Army in New England, which would drain our county's manpower. One of the difficulties facing Pennsylvania will be to establish an organized militia to guard our frontier against those who remain loyal to the king and the natives who would support the king for revenge and financial reasons.

"In essence, I'll be serving my country, but here close to home. I'll be gone for lengthy periods, but I won't be that far from the Tuscarora Valley. I hope that we'll be able to recruit enough manpower to deter the Tories and Indians from considering taking any action against us. That's probably wishful thinking, so we will have to be prepared for anything at anytime. This preparation needs to start at home. Everyone is going to undergo some training with weapons and to understand an escape plan.

"Unfortunately, I think the good colonel is afraid to allow me to seek active duty because of what occurred at Fort Bigham. He brought up the subject, but I told him that was a long time ago and really didn't pertain to the present situation. I guess he is reluctant to allow me to be placed in a situation where my freedom could be taken away from me again."

Anne threw her arms around Robert and held onto him for a long time. "I'm so relieved. I know all of us could be in danger, but knowing that you'll be in the vicinity will allow me to rest much easier."

CHAPTER THIRTY NINE

Reverend Fithian's Visit

As this period of turmoil unfolded within the colonies, the Reverend Philip Vickers Fithian visited Path Valley and the Tuscarora Valley, and later the Kishacoquillas Valley, in the summer of 1775. Reverend Fithian was a graduate of the College of New Jersey (Princeton University) in 1772, and received a license to preach from the first Presbytery of Philadelphia on November 6, 1774. Since there were no vacancies near his home, he received a commission to visit Central Pennsylvania to serve as a supply minister to the many scattered churches of that region. Reverend Fithian kept a detailed journal of his travels, which was addressed to his sweetheart, Miss Elizabeth Beatty, the daughter of the Reverend Charles Clinton Beatty. Reverend Beatty had traveled through the Tuscarora in 1766.

Of special interest is his description of his journey from Path Valley to the Juniata River, and then to the banks of the Susquehanna River at Sunbury:

Thursday, June 22, 1775. This valley is in many places not more than a mile wide; it is level, and the land rich; the mountains are both high and so near, that the sun is hid night and morning an hour before he rises and sets. I rode on to one Elliot's (Francis Elliot, at whose house the Reverend Charles Beatty stopped in 1766, on his return from Ohio); he keeps a genteel house with good accommodations. I saw a young woman, a daughter of his, who has never been over the South Mountain, as elegant in her manner and as neat in her dress as most in the city. It is not place, therefore, but temper makes the person. In this valley, we have many of the sugar tree; it is very like a maple; the bark is more rough and curled. It grows in a low, level, rich land. They told me there has been a frost here two mornings this week.

Friday, June 23. Expenses at this tavern, 4? shillings; distance from Philadelphia computed, 160 miles west. We passed from this valley by the Narrows, (This is the gap at Concord and opening out toward Waterloo), into Tuscarora Valley, a most stony valley; two high mountains on every side. The passage so narrow, that you may take one stone in your right hand and another in your left and throw each upon a mountain, and they are so high that they obscure more than half of the horizon. A rainy, dripping day, more uncomfortable for riding among the leaves. On the way all day was only a small foot-path, and covered with many sharp stones. After many circumlocutions and regradations through the woods, it raining all day, we arrived about five in the evening, although be soaked, at one James Gray's, in a little hamlet in the woods. (James Gray of Spruce Hill Township, a brother of John Gray, whose wife was carried off by the Indians in 1756). He was kind, and received me civilly; he had good pasture for my horse, and his good wife prepared me a warm and suitable supper. Forgive my country! I supped on tea! It relieved me, however, and I went to bed soon. Distance rode today, 28 miles; course N. N. W.; expenses at small tavern, 1s.

Saturday, June 24. Before breakfast came in a Scotch matron with her rock and spindle, twisting away at the flax. The rock is a long staff on the end of which is her flax, like a distaff; the spindle is a peg about 8 inches long, sharp at the end where the thread is twisted, and large at the other where it is rolled on. Expenses here, 2s. I rode on after breakfast to Mr. Samuel Lyon's, twelve miles yet in Tuscarora. (Samuel Lyon, Esq., third son of John, lived on the John Kelly place, in Milford.) He lives neat, has glass windows, and apparently a good farm. (Houses with glass windows were yet a rarity in this region.) Here I met Mr. Slemons on his way down. From Mr. Lyon's I rode to the Juniata, three miles, forded it and stopped just on the other side at John Harris, Esq. (founder of Mifflin). He lives elegantly. In the parlor where I was sitting are three windows, each with twenty-four lights of glass.

Sunday, June 25. — Cedar Springs, Cumberland County. A large and genteel society, but in great and furious turmoil about one Mr. Kennedy, who was once their preacher. (The "genteel society" was the Presbyterian Church, near the residence of David Diven.) Poor I was frightened. One of the society when he was asked to set the tune, answered "that he knew not whether I was a Papist or a Methodist, or a Baptist or a Seceder." I made him soon acquainted with my authority. It is now sunset, and I am sitting under a dark tuft of willow and large sycamores, close on the bank of the beautiful river Juniata. The river, near two hundred yards broad, lined with willows, sycamores, walnuts, white oaks and a fine bank—what are my thoughts? Fair genius of this water, O tell me, will not this, in some future time, be a vast, pleasant, and very populous country? Are not many large towns to be raised on these shady banks? I seem to wish to be transferred forward only one century. Great God, America will surprise the world.

Monday, June 26. I rose early with the purpose of setting off for Sunbury. I had an invitation to a wedding in the neighborhood, but my business will not permit me. After breakfast I rode to one Mr. Bogle's, a well-disposed, civil and sensible man. (This was Joseph Bogle. He lived on the tract called "Hibernia," which he owned and where McAlisterville is now located. The Bogles left that section in 1778.) He entertained me kindly and acquainted me largely with the disturbance with Mr. Kennedy. I dined with him and his wife. She looks very much in person and appears in manner like my much-honored and ever-dear Mamma. Thence I rode onward through a dark, bleak path, they call it a 'bridle-road,' to one Mr. Eckert's, a Dutchman. (German). He used me with great civility and politeness. Distance rode today, 25 miles; course N.E. I met on the road a tinker on the way to what is called the 'New Purchase.' (The region embracing the valleys of the North and West Branches of the Susquehanna had been purchased from the Six Nations in 1768.) He has been at Cohansie. Knew many there, at Pottsgrove, Deepel, and New England Town. He told me that he had been acquainted in Seven Colonies, but never yet saw any place in which the inhabitants were so sober, uniform in their manners, and every act so religious as at New England Town, and Mr. Ramsey was his favorite preacher. He spoke of religious matters with understanding, and I hope with some feeling.

Tuesday, June 27. Rode from the clever Dutchman's (German-Eckert) to Sunbury over the Susquehanna, fifteen miles. I think the river is a half a mile over, and so shallow that I forded it. The bottom is hard rock. Sunbury is on the northeast bank. It is yet a small village, but seems to be growing rapidly. Then I rode on half a mile to one Hunter's (Colonel Samuel Hunter), within the walls of Fort Augusta. Then I rode onward to Northumberland about a mile, but on the way crossed the river twice.[12]

Reverend Philip Fithian continued his journey up the West Branch of the Susquehanna to Muncy, to Bald Eagle (Flemington), Bald Eagle's Nest (Milesburg), and into Penn's Valley. Fithian made his way across the Seven Mountains and into the Kishacoquillas Valley. He visited throughout the Kishacoquillas Valley from Tuesday, August 8 until Monday, August 21, 1775. Standing Stone, or Huntingdon, was his next stop. From there he turned down the Juniata River to the valley of the Aughwick, visited Fort Shirley, and then back to the western end of Path Valley.

Reverend Fithian finally returned home to New Jersey. On October 25, 1775, he married his twenty-three-year-old sweetheart, Miss Elizabeth Beatty. In June of 1776, he followed the footsteps of many members of the Presbyterian clergy, and became a chaplain in the Continental Army. Fithian served in Colonel Newcomb's battalion of New Jersey. He continued to keep up his journal until after the Battle of Long Island, with this last entry written on Sunday, September 22, 1776: "Many of our battalion sick; our lads grow tired and begin to count the days of service which remain." Unfortunately, Fithian became ill, and on October 7, 1776, he succumbed to dysentery at Camp Fort Washington.[13]

CHAPTER FORTY

Cumberland County's Militia

The men of Cumberland County who answered the call of independence faced a major quandary in that they were threatened by the British forces to the east and the Indians to the north and the west. Congress authorized the raising of six companies of expert riflemen in Pennsylvania on June 14, 1775. The first rifle battalion (1st Reg.) was formed on the same day. Pennsylvania was directed to raise two more companies within the same month.

Lancaster County doubled its quota; thus, Pennsylvania's battalion included nine companies commanded by Colonel William Thompson of Carlisle. One of these companies was composed largely of men from the townships of Cumberland County north of the Blue Mountains (Mifflin, Juniata, and Perry County today).

This company was led by Captain William Hendricks of Carlisle, who would lose his life while leading his men during General Benedict Arnold's attack on Quebec. Those men of Hendricks's company who survived the attack were forced to surrender. On August 7, 1776, most of these men were paroled and exchanged, and many later reenlisted.

In January of 1776 the first Pennsylvania Regiments of the Pennsylvania Line were formed. This famous Pennsylvania Line, thought by some to be the best fighting unit in the Continental Army, was mainly manned by Scotch-Irish volunteers.

By July of 1776, the Pennsylvania Associated Battalions were organized in Cumberland County, and sometimes referred to as

Flying Camps. Their main objective was to serve as a reserve for the Continental Army.

On July 31, 1777, the militia was organized to ensure sufficient manpower since it wasn't possible to attract enough volunteers. It then became a necessity to draft all able-bodied men between eighteen and fifty-three years of age.

Cumberland County included twenty-two townships, and those townships were divided into eight battalions of militia. These battalions were then organized into eight companies. A company usually consisted of fifty men. These companies could be utilized against the Indian threat, the Tories, or the British. The townships that would later comprise Juniata County were Fermanagh, Greenwood, Lack, and Milford, and the members of this militia were organized into the Fourth Battalion of 1777 and later the Seventh Battalion of 1780.

The three top officers of the Fourth Battalion of 1777 were Colonel Samuel Lyon, Lieutenant Colonel Thomas Turbet and Major Robert Taylor, all of Milford Township. John Taylor's name would be found on the register of the Seventh Battalion of 1780. In the Fifth Battalion of the townships of Armagh and Derry, Henry Taylor, brother of Robert Taylor, would serve as a captain.

Many of the militia's leaders were early settlers who had shown themselves to be competent leaders or good soldiers during the French and Indian War. In some cases, they were survivors of Indian captivity during the same war, as was Major Robert Taylor.

One of the major obstacles facing the militia was their command structure, which was somewhere between loose and nonexistent. All too often the officers looked upon their men as equals and hoped that their commands would appear wise and practical so that they would be followed.

One of Major Robert Taylor's duties was to attempt to inspire his fellow valley inhabitants to join the ranks of the Fourth Battalion of the militia. As he traveled throughout the settlements, he often would choose to repeat some of the themes that he had heard from the pulpit of the Presbyterian Church in the middle of the Tuscarora Valley.

He would urge the frontiersmen to consider some of these concepts:

> We fight not for glory or conquest, but to protect our own rights and freedoms. Our cause is a just cause, for the preservation of our liberties.
>
> We have to take up arms for the protection of our property acquired by the honest industry of our fathers and ourselves. We shall lay down our arms when hostilities cease on the part of the British aggressors and all danger is removed.
>
> We are seeking males who are not suspected of being an enemy to the liberty of America, and sadly you and I know that there are enemies in our midst who do not believe in our just cause. You must be at least eighteen years of age, and of great courage and principle.
>
> I urge all of you of-age males to join us in training for the day when the threat of the British army, and those among us who remain loyal to those known as Tories, or the natives to the west and north of us will move to destroy us and take over our lands.

Robert Taylor and his counterparts were untiring in their efforts to recruit the manpower to defend the expanses of Cumberland County. A messenger system was established so that any commands or orders coming from the Continental Capital could be sent to Carlisle, and then be dispersed westward to Shippensburg, Chambersburg, Fort Loudoun, and across the mountains. The word also was sent across the mountains to Fort Robinson in Sherman's Valley, then across the Tuscarora to the Tuscarora Valley, to the Kishacoquillas Valley and beyond. Not a quick and efficient method, but given enough time, effective.

When the Fourth assembled to drill, they were not a very impressive unit. Slowly they became somewhat cohesive, and when the time came, they would pose a considerable threat.

The uniforms worn by these loosely knit fighting units were either caped hunting shirts, leggings, or breeches constructed of buckskin; or homemade linen breeches and linen blouses reaching to their knees and belted at the waist. Most wore a rawhide belt from which hung essential equipment, such as buckskin to mend their calf-length moccasins. In their pouchy shirtfront, they stored bread and johnnycakes, jerked meat, flax fibers for cleaning their rifle, along with a waterproof deer bladder to keep their gun's lock dry. On their neck strap they carried a knife, powder, and priming horns. Most carried a leather pouch that held spare flints, patches, rifle balls, and tools for repair. Other rations, ammunition, and bedrolls were carried on their backs or in necessary bags.

There was a great variety of weapons as well. Tomahawks and knives were standard frontier weapons borrowed from the natives. The principal weapon of these pioneer soldiers was the Pennsylvania rifle developed by German gunsmiths. Usually these weapons were of a small bore in order to conserve lead and powder. The rifling, or spiral grooves, gave a spin to the round ball and increased its accuracy. Some unfortunate frontiersmen had to rely upon smooth bored guns that lacked accuracy. One such weapon was the standard-issue infantry firearm of the British army in the 1770s, the fourteen-pound, thirty-nine-inch-long Brown Bess, which made up for its inaccuracy by being easy to load.

Due to the problems of communication, transportation, and geography the Fourth Battalion did not become completely organized until July 31, 1777.

The militia was organized in a much-decentralized fashion, because they concluded that the region would not face any large ground threats from the British that would force them to keep their units concentrated. By being spread out, the militia could exert control over a much larger geographic region.

In the event of hit-and-run raids by the Indians, it would be easier and quicker to deploy men from nearby areas to counter the Indian attacks, and to pursue the raiders and punish them for their actions.

Robert Taylor, like most of the men of the Fourth Battalion and the Fifth Battalion in which his brother Henry was serving, had little or no prior military background. These were green, untrained troops. When the Fourth was first organized, they drilled and trained constantly for several weeks and learned basic commands, formations, and tactics.

The Fourth's base of operations varied, but normally they used the Lower Tuscarora Presbyterian Church.

The Fourth Battalion was divided into companies drawn from eight geographic regions. Captains John Williams, John Elliot, and John Hamilton commanded the men from Milford Township. Jonathan Robison and James McConnell led the recruits from Lack, while John Fouts and Philip Mathias led those from Greenwood, and Robert McTeer was in charge of the men from Fermanagh Township.

In late fall 1777, Major. Robert Taylor observed his captains as they directed their raw recruits, most dressed in their buckskin garb, through another frustrating session of drills and commands. The recruits didn't drill smartly or go through their paces with the smooth precision of the French soldiers he had observed at the various French forts where he had been a forced visitor during the French and Indian War.

Even if the quasi-military volunteers were clumsy and inept at first glance, something else stood out: these men had an extraordinary spirit, an *esprit de corps*. They had a can-do attitude.

Captain John Williams approached Robert, and they exchanged salutes. "Major, I seek permission to allow each man to fire three rounds in order to assess his ability to handle his weapon."

Robert had discussed this exercise with his commanding officer, Colonel Samuel Lyon, prior to the men assembling this morning. Gunpowder could be obtained from Carlisle, and although not in great supply, it was adequate. Lead, on the other hand, was at a premium on the frontier.

Robert remembered that when he first arrived in the

Tuscarora Valley in 1755, rumors abounded that the natives were aware of a lead mine in the vicinity. Unfortunately, no amount of persuasion, no amount of bribery or alcohol had been successful in loosening their tongues and exposing the location of the legendary lead mine.

About 1763 a major source of the necessary and valuable mineral was discovered farther up the Juniata River Valley in what is known as the Sinking Valley. In April of 1777, General Daniel Roberdeau stated that he proposed to erect a stockade fort in the neighborhood of a working lead mine near Roller's Fort, where he had discovered a new vein of ample supply.

Roberdeau planned to have the fort completed early in 1778 to guard against the incursions of the natives and any Tories in the vicinity. He planned to construct a furnace, using bricks made and burned on the scene, to produce an ample supply of lead for the Continental Army.

In the fall of 1777 the construction of Fort Roberdeau was still off in the future. In the meantime, General Roberdeau was well aware of the need to conserve lead and powder. "I know the men need to practice to develop a degree of accuracy, but we have to limit the firing process. The colonel gave me orders to allow each man to fire his weapon twice. I know for some men that is inadequate to develop their skills, but that's the best we can do for the moment. Hopefully, our lead supply will improve by spring, and then we can step up our practice sessions." In the meantime, the men practiced priming and loading.

Colonel Samuel Lyon signaled for all the companies to form up within earshot and to stand at ease. At Lyons's request, Major Taylor addressed the battalion:

Men, as the activities of the enemy spread, we will be obliged to call the whole of the battalion immediately for action. Your readiness to turn out will convince both our enemies and our friends of your commitment and determination to be free.

We must be prepared to cheerfully turn out with the utmost speed. Keep your arms and blankets at the ready, and be prepared to remain in service for six weeks if needed.

Be prepared to utilize the Indian method of fighting because it has a surprising effect upon the enemy if they are not acquainted with it.

It is expected that you gentlemen, as friends of the common cause and lovers of your county's welfare, will dispatch as rapidly as possible and in sufficient numbers to repel the enemy.

The enemy is on their way, undoubtedly not the Redcoats in our vicinity, but either the Tories or the Indians who present a formidable threat to our settlements. Nothing will save us but that spirit which induced us to resist from the very beginning.

Before the men of the Fourth dispersed, the messenger system for spreading messages was reexamined so that there would be no wasted time and effort in assembling the militia to meet a threat from the enemy, be they native, Tory, or British regulars. With each mustering of the troops, there appeared a growing confidence that if a crisis arose, the men of the Fourth could respond to the challenge.

On the same date, July 31, 1777, that the Fourth Battalion was being formed, the Fifth Battalion, comprised of volunteers from Armagh and Derry Townships of the same county, was organized.

Arthur Buchanan of Derry Township was appointed as the Fifth's colonel, while Alexander Brown was its lieutenant colonel, and Alexander McIlhatten the battalion's major. The Fifth Battalion was divided into eight companies, but only two were designated to be on active duty at any one time. Accordingly, each militiaman was called to duty only once or twice each year, allowing him to spend the remainder of the year with his family and to take care of his farm or business.

Robert Taylor's brother Henry was appointed captain of the Third Company. In June of 1777, almost a month before the Fifth Battalion was organized, Henry Taylor participated as a volunteer under Captain Arthur Buchanan against a band of British and

Indians operating out of Detroit. These invaders had attacked the northern extremes of Cumberland County at Standing Stone on the Juniata River and down into the Kishacoquillas Valley. Buchanan led his volunteers against the enemy at Frankstown and drove the marauders from the area for the time being.

The Taylor brothers did not have much contact with each other during these difficult times. There were several times when they served on active duty at the same time, with their assignments taking them into the same area. After a lengthy separation, they reunited in the spring of 1780.

The first thing that Robert noticed about Henry was that Henry did not have the normal use of his left hand. "What happened, Henry?" he asked.

"Late in the summer I led my company north to Penn's Creek Valley against a band of Tories and Indians who had been ravaging the beleaguered inhabitants of the valley. In an ensuing engagement, I came face-to-face with a British officer. I came out on the short end of things. The area where the ball entered severed the lower joints of my index and middle fingers, and they became infected. The doctor made the decision to amputate those two fingers in order to save the rest of my hand.

"I know it looks rather grotesque, but luckily it isn't very painful. I can still perform my duties as an officer and most of my work around the farm. If it had been my right hand, I would have been handicapped a lot more.

"We were successful in driving the Tories and their Indian allies from the valley. I'm afraid it was just a temporary victory; we hear reports that the Indians are back in the Susquehanna Valley in full force. It will probably be just be a matter of time until they return to our area.

"Rumor has it that our battalion is to be reorganized this summer. If that occurs, I'll probably resign my commission and attempt to eliminate the six years of neglect of my farm."

Robert shook his head. "I'm sorry you were wounded in such a manner. If there is any way that I can help you with your farm work, just let me know. I'd be glad to bring the family along, and we could all pitch in and help."

During one of Major Robert Taylor's forays along the Juniata just north of the mouth of the Tuscarora Creek, the major made an amazing discovery about the Taylor clan of Cumberland County.

As Robert's company was moving upriver about three miles from the mouth of the Tuscarora Creek, he came upon a man and his servant struggling to remove a stubborn stump. Robert and his men offered to give the farmer a hand with the stump, which the farmer quickly accepted.

Robert approached the farmer. "Good afternoon, squire, I am Robert Taylor from farther up the Tuscarora Valley, and I am at your service as a major in the militia of Cumberland County."

The farmer laughed heartily. "I've heard there was another Irishman by the name of Taylor in the valley. I'm James Taylor, farmer, and as of June 9, 1777, the justice of the peace of Fermanagh Township."

"James Taylor, well, I'll be damned! I'd heard rumors of other Taylors, but there was some confusion because all my brothers live in the Kishacoquillas Valley, in Armagh Township, which used to be part of Fermanagh Township."

"I secured this land on July 21, 1769, but I didn't move here until later," James Taylor explained. "Look around you. I have visions of establishing a town in this vicinity in the near future. If you observe the river, there is a real good ford right at the end of the path that goes right down to the river from my cabin.

"Notice those two big red oaks? Just down from them about twenty yards I have plans of constructing a two-story stone house. This will be a solid stone house that will last for years. Yes, I'm full of dreams, like all Irishmen. I would imagine that Robert Taylor has all kinds of dreams also. When this sordid war is over, you and I will have to sit down under a shade tree and enjoy a good jug and discuss our wild Irish dreams."

Realizing that he had to get his company of men moving, Robert took leave of his new Taylor acquaintance. "It has been a pleasure meeting you, James. We will have to meet again when peace arrives in our valley. Until then, be wary, my new friend. These are dangerous times that we live in."

CHAPTER FORTY ONE

The War, 1776–1777

Boston had become the formidable fortress of the rebellion, but for the time being, appeared to be lost to the British. The British then employed a new approach to the war. They turned their attention to two places where Tories abounded: South Carolina and New York.

New York City was a critical prize in that whoever controlled the city and the harbor controlled the Hudson River Valley, a principal route into the northern American interior. The British plan was to occupy New York City, spread their control up the Hudson River, thus isolating New England from the rest of the colonies, and create communication and transportation problems for the Continental Army and Congress.

Beginning in June of 1776, General William Howe opposed General Washington in the battles of Long Island, Manhattan, and White Plains. Howe employed superior numbers, guns, and equipment to defeat Washington, but fortunately for the Americans, Howe never exploited these victories and Washington escaped with the bulk of his army.

With the loss of New York City, Washington retreated to New Jersey with an army low in morale and resolve. After he was further forced to cross the Delaware into Pennsylvania, Washington chose to go on the offensive, to offset his losses.

On Christmas night 1776, Washington crossed back over the Delaware and surprised the Hessian mercenaries at Trenton. On the morning of January 3, Washington won another startling victory at Princeton. The Americans then went into winter quarters at Morristown after these two stunning victories.

On February 28, 1777, General "Gentleman Johnny" Burgoyne inaugurated a three-pronged attack against the remainder of New York. A principal force would advance from Canada through Lake Champlain and the Upper Hudson. A smaller force would move forward from Fort Oswego and strike through the Mohawk Valley. These two maneuvers would be coordinated with Howe's third force imposing its way up the Hudson Valley to isolate New England from the other colonies.

Fortunately for Washington and his meager army, Burgoyne's grand scheme to seize New York State and divide and conquer the colonies collapsed and all but disintegrated in the backcountry of Vermont and New York.

In the meantime, General William Howe was lured by the prospect of capturing Philadelphia, the capital of the alleged independent United States and the center of colonial wealth, commerce, and culture. It was the second largest city in the British Empire and the stronghold of loyalty to King George III and his government.

If successful, Howe's strategy to capture the City of Brotherly Love would be a devastating blow to the rebel movement. Obviously, Washington would have to throw the majority of his forces into the defense of the capital city.

Luckily for Washington, Howe took a roundabout route to the city, which enabled Washington to assemble and move his army into a defensive position. The banks of placid Brandywine Creek became the scene of an American disaster and defeat on September 11, 1777, as General Washington attempted to defend Philadelphia from British occupation. Washington mistakenly left many of the upstream fords of Brandywine Creek undefended, and Howe's men approached from the Americans' right rear. The Americans fought fiercely, but panic and confusion overcame them, and Washington suffered great losses, due to casualties and men taken as prisoners.

Nearby resided the German immigrant Zachariah Rice, who had gained prominence as a millwright since his arrival in America in 1751. Robert Taylor had visited Rice and his family in the summer of 1758 when he had been subpoenaed to appear before the Provincial Council in regards to treason charges against Lawrence Burke. In the intervening period since Taylor's visit in 1758, Rice's reputation as a gifted millwright, skillful mechanic, builder, and farmer had spread throughout Pennsylvania and into the surrounding colonies, now states.

Zachariah Rice had immigrated to Pennsylvania from the Lower Palatinate in Bavaria, Germany, aboard the ship *Edinburg* on September 16, 1751. Maria Appolonia Hartman, better known as Abigail, had arrived in Philadelphia on the ship *Royal Union* on August 15, 1750, from Wurttemburg, Germany, with her parents, Johannes and Margaret Hartman.

The Hartmans and Zachariah Rice eventually settled in Pikeland Township in Chester County. At the age of sixteen, in 1757, Abigail Hartman became the wife of Zachariah Rice. This marriage was blessed with the birth of twenty-one children, seventeen of whom would walk in her funeral procession in November of 1789.

In the aftermath of the Battle of Brandywine, General George Washington retreated across the Chester Valley into the vicinity of Yellow Springs. His path of withdrawal led past the home of Abigail and Zachariah Rice. The general and his staff halted at the Rice home and partook of essential refreshments. Several of the Rice children distributed cool drinks and appetizers to the general and his staff. Abigail blended a concoction of water, sugar, rum, and spice into a liquid refreshment called flip, a popular drink. When Abigail presented the mixture to General Washington, she respectfully addressed him as "My Lord."

The general smiled softly at his hostess and replied, "Mrs. Rice, we have no titles here. We are all brothers. My heart is heavy with the thought of my fallen men who lie on the battlefield at Brandywine. The use of titles like you called me is one of the reasons we fight for freedom."

Washington always had a fondness for children, and as the Rices' daughter Susan scampered by, the general whisked the little girl off her feet and lifted her on his horse in front of his saddle. Susan giggled and laughed at the attention, although at her age, she had no idea of the importance and power of the tall, handsome soldier who showered his attention upon her.

Later that night, when Susan was saying her prayers before she went to bed, she asked her mother. "Momma, who was that big man who stopped for refreshments today?"

"Susan, that was General George Washington from Virginia. He is leading our soldiers in fighting against the British in order to gain our freedom."

As in all battles, once the able-bodied soldiers abandoned the battlefield, the wounded were left behind to recover. Abigail Rice immediately volunteered to do her part in aiding the wounded at the Yellow Springs Military Hospital a few miles from her home. She soon became known as an angel of mercy for her acts of charity and kindness that she bestowed upon the recuperating soldiers.

Unfortunately, her kindness and charity led to her undoing. During her frequent visits to the hospital, she contracted typhus fever, which ran rampant among the wounded men at the hospital. Sadly, Abigail succumbed to the fever on November 6, 1789, at the age of forty-eight. She was laid to rest near the Lutheran Church at Pikeland.

Washington withdrew to Chester, where he positioned himself between the British army and their objective, Philadelphia. As Howe's army advanced to the outskirts of Philadelphia, Alexander Hamilton's persuasive power finally convinced the members of Congress to vacate the capital on September 18 for Lancaster. Later the Congress moved farther westward to the village of York.

The woes of the American army continued at White Horse Tavern and Malvern Hill. The real disaster struck at Paoli, which became known as the Paoli Massacre, due to the manner in which the British bayonets mangled the bodies of the fallen Americans.

Sadly, on September 23, Lord Cornwallis marched two Hessian and four British units unopposed into Philadelphia. On October 4, the Americans suffered another disaster at Germantown.

In a move that would offset these American disasters, on October 17, 1777, British General John Burgoyne formally surrendered his forces to General Horatio Gates at Saratoga, New York. This eventually would be considered the turning point of the war and would finally convince the French to make a full alliance with the United States.

At the end of 1777, George Washington faced the dire prospect of getting his ill-clothed and poorly fed army through the winter. Washington chose to winter at Valley Forge on the west side of the Schuylkill River, because he felt it was easily defended and centrally located.

Washington's small and beleaguered army suffered terribly at Valley Forge throughout the winter of 1777–1778. The government officials who were responsible for supplying the army proved to be corrupt and incompetent, and the army spent the winter huddled in makeshift huts. About 2,500 out of the complement of 10,000 lost their lives during six horrible months of encampment.

CHAPTER FORTY TWO

The War on the Frontier

On the eve of the American Revolution, colonial America was composed of three diverse geographical areas: the commercial North, from the ports of Maine to the Chesapeake Bay; the tidewater region from Maryland to Georgia; and the indefinite frontier, that stretched from Canada southward, bounded on the east by the earlier settled areas and on the west by the Allegheny Mountains.

The majority of the inhabitants of the frontier favored the American cause. No social or economic ties bound them to England. They resented the political, social, and economic domination of the seaboard aristocracy, made up of merchants, Anglican clergy, and professional men in New England, the Quaker oligarchy of Philadelphia, manor owners on the Hudson, and the planters of the tidewater region.

The American Revolution was largely fought in a series of engagements in the coastal areas, from the outbreak of hostilities at Lexington in April 1775 to the British surrender at Yorktown in October 1781. Only a small percentage of the 2.4 million colonists in 1775 had ventured beyond the safety of the coast and into the inland valleys of the Alleghenies.

Ever since the frontier was stunned by the news of the actions of the British government on October 7, 1763, when the Proclamation Line was issued limiting white settlement to the region east of the Appalachian crest, most pioneers did not need the cry of "No taxation without representation" to motivate them to hold the British government in contempt and push them towards the side of rebellion.

At the outbreak of the revolution few of the English colonists could be found in the region of the Old Northwest (this was the region between the Great Lakes and the Ohio River and between the Appalachian Mountains and the Mississippi River), except in the vicinity just west of Pittsburgh. The nearest English forces to this region were the British troops occupying strategic posts along the Great Lakes that had been taken from the French at the conclusion of the French and Indian War.

If campaigns were to be conducted in the West, they would have to occur over long distances through hundreds of miles of wilderness to attack a few unimportant western settlements, a rather profitless endeavor from the British perspective. The British did find it desirable to harass the western fringe of the colonies to necessitate the use of American troops to protect the frontier, troops that could have been used for more important operations on the coastal area.

The Indian tribes remained quiet until the colonists arose in rebellion. The eastern tribes had intensely desired a dike-like frontier to hinder colonial expansion across the Alleghenies, but with the commencement of hostilities, the contenders pressed the Indians to take sides just as they had during the French and Indian War.

Rather than use large numbers of British troops on the frontier, the British sealed alliances with some of the Indian tribes and used them as an effective weapon against the western settlements. The Indians were encouraged by British officers, such as Henry Hamilton, to attack any settlers within their reach, similar to the encouragement earlier Indians had received from the French. These tribes were reinforced by the Loyalists or Tories that remained loyal to the king.

The frontiersmen found themselves exposed to constant Indian attacks at the very beginning of the Revolution. Behind the hostility of the Indians could readily be seen the influence of the British. The American frontier was ablaze during much of the war. The Indian allies of the British were busy with torches and tomahawks. The British agents who egged on the natives were branded as "hair buyers" by the Americans, as the agents allegedly paid bounties for American scalps.

A debate raged in Parliament as to whether the British should use the Indians to their advantage, but in the end, the large percentage of the Indians became a terror to the American colonists on the frontier. In the Declaration of Independence the colonists complained that George III had "endeavored to bring on the inhabitants of our frontiers, the merciless Indian Savages whose known rule of warfare is an undistinguished destruction of all ages, sexes, and conditions."

Later in the war, in the summer of 1777, General "Gentleman Johnny" Burgoyne issued a proclamation intended to intimidate the American rebels. The general cautioned that he would unleash thousands of his savage allies to hunt them down. The rebels could expect "devastation, famine, and every concomitant horror that a reluctant but indispensable prosecution of military duty must occasion."

Burgoyne addressed his Indian allies before they began their campaign towards Albany. "Warriors, you are free—go forth in the might and valor of your cause—strike at the common enemies of Great Britain and America—disturbers of public order, peace and happiness, destroyers of commerce, parricides of state...."

Personal friendships generally forged alliances during the Revolution. Long before "the shot heard round the world," William Johnson had formed a personal and political alliance with Joseph Brant of the Mohawks, the most powerful of the powerful Iroquois confederation. Johnson's bravery during the French and Indian War and his marriage to Degonwadonti, or Molly Brant, had earned him great prestige among the Mohawks.

William Johnson died in 1774, and his son, Guy, continued the relationship with Joseph Brant. Brant and the Mohawks persuaded the Senecas, Cayugas, and Onondagas to side with the British. The other members of the confederation, the Oneidas and Tuscaroras, aligned themselves with the Americans. These two tribes were also supported by the Mohicans, who were also known as the Stockbridge Indians. Splits also occurred within the tribes on both sides.

The American frontier of Virginia, New York, and

Pennsylvania was on the verge of panic by September 1776. Numerous loyalists who had been evicted from their properties took advantage of the panic in the Mohawk Valley by disguising themselves as Indians and raiding the rebel settlers. New York's Tory governor, William Tryon, urged the British to "loose the savages against the miserable Rebels in order to impose a reign of terror on the frontiers."

By 1777, it was seen that Iroquois fought and killed Iroquois, shattering the league that had been formulated in 1677. Hit-and-run raids became commonplace activities along the Pennsylvania and New York frontier. No quarter was given as people were scalped, mutilated, and burned. One raid would be followed by counter raids; revenge became the order of the day. Much of the horror was performed in the Mohawk, Cherry and Wyoming Valleys, and down the north Branch of the Susquehanna River.

In the spring of 1778 , Major John Butler of the British army organized a force of four hundred Tories and seven hundred Senecas and Cayugas into a guerrilla force known as Butler's Rangers at the Indian town of Tioga. Their target was the Wyoming Valley of northern Pennsylvania.

Further north, Joseph Brant and his force of 450 Indians and Tories attacked the Cherry Valley of New York. The Seneca Chief, Gu-cinge, took four hundred warriors and began to attack settlements along the West Branch of the Susquehanna. Meanwhile, Butler constructed boats to float down the Susquehanna River.

The Wyoming Valley had been settled by Moravians in 1742, and rivals from Connecticut and Pennsylvania had disputed the valley's ownership, but by the outbreak of the revolution, the settlers from Connecticut appeared to be in control. The beautiful Wyoming Valley was defended by a collection of forts; most were merely fortified log-houses that didn't afford much protection. Adding to the problem of defense was the fact that many of the able-bodied men of the area had left to join the Connecticut Line of the Continental Army under George Washington.

Large numbers of settlers of the back country realized that

they were no match for the Tories and Indians and had gone downriver in 1776 and 1777. The decimated frontier population continued to be a source of supplies for the American Army, and Butler's Rangers were motivated to put an end to that.

Wintermoot's Fort and Fort Jenkins capitulated on July 1 and 2. On July 3 occurred the infamous Wyoming Massacre at Forty Fort. The fort was garrisoned by about 450 Continental troops and militiamen, mostly old men and boys, and commanded by Colonel Zebulon Butler who was home from his duties with the Continental Army. Unfortunately the settlers were outnumbered nearly three to one, and a slaughter without mercy ensued. Those who surrendered were subject to the cruelest types of torture.

One of the most gruesome debacles occurred at a place that became known as Queen Esther's Rock or Bloody Rock. At this site, sixteen survivors were arranged around the rock and Queen Esther Montour, a granddaughter of Madam Montour, wielded a tomahawk to bash the brains out of each defenseless white man.

Others were shot trying to escape in the river, while still others were simply butchered. When the smoke of battle cleared, only about sixty of the men survived. It was estimated that the Indians collected 227 scalps, which netted them ten dollars each. The Indians continued to scalp, rob, burn, and plunder throughout the night.

Many of the terrified survivors fled the scene under cover of darkness. The massacre that occurred at Forty Fort was repeated at Pittston Fort and Wilkes-Barre Fort. Joining the fugitives from these forts in a mad dash for safety were the inhabitants of Shawnee Fort, Rosecran's Blockhouse, and Stewart's Blockhouse.

The Tories and the Senecas were bent on plunder, torture, and destruction. They laid waste to houses, mills, barns, and fields; livestock was driven north, and anything of value was carried away as well.

The terrorizing news quickly spread down the North Branch of the Susquehanna and over to the West Branch as well. Both branches of the great river were evacuated; the only hope these people possessed was to flee downriver to safety.

Besides horseback and foot, every type of watercraft that could be utilized was observed floating downstream on the river. Canoes, rafts, hog-troughs, keel boats, and bateaux made up the armada coming down the river. This mass movement of humanity that was fleeing for their lives became known as the "Great Runaway."

Various militia units were sent out to destroy Indian towns and villages in retaliation for the raids in the Wyoming and Cherry Valleys. Some new forts were constructed in the Susquehanna Valley shortly after the Great Runaway.

Colonel Samuel Hunter commanded a small stockade on the Susquehanna known as Fort Schwartz, which was constructed during 1777-78. Hunter observed on July 9, 1778, that both branches of the Susquehanna were nearly evacuated, and Sunbury would be the frontier in less than twenty-four hours. On July 12, Colonel Hunter wrote to the president and the Executive Council and strenuously urged that "a few hundreds of men, well armed" be immediately sent to relieve the people.

The Executive Council heeded Hunter's advice and redirected Colonel Brodhead, who was on his way to Fort Pitt, to march into the West Branch of the Susquehanna. By July 24, Brodhead had arrived at Fort Muncy and sent a captain and twenty-four men to help protect General Potter and the reapers of Penn's Valley. Afterwards, Brodhead resumed his march westward to Fort Pitt.

In the meantime, Colonel Thomas Hartley and his small force of men were sent to replace Brodhead. Hartley arrived at Fort Augusta on August 1 with his regular army recruits, along with about two hundred militiamen.

Out of Carlisle, Lieutenant Carothers, who commanded sixty men, set off through Sherman's and Tuscarora Valleys and up into Kishacoquillas Valley and its smaller neighboring valleys. His orders were to remain for a period of time to protect the people who were attempting to harvest their crops.

Even with the deployment of more troops in the Juniata and Susquehanna Valleys, burning, murdering, and pillaging continued to plague the inhabitants who did not flee for their lives.

In an attempt to thwart the attacks of the Indians on the north Branch of the Susquehanna, Colonel Hartley led an expedition up the river to attack Tioga. He left Fort Muncy on September 21 with about two hundred men and enough provisions to last them twelve days. They were successful in burning Tioga, Queen Esther's Town, and returned to Fort Augusta on October 5, after covering nearly three hundred miles.

Again, the expedition had little effect upon the Indians, and by the beginning of November, they had returned to the bloody business of terrorizing the North Branch as far south as Nescopeck.

In July of 1778, the Fourth Battalion of Cumberland County's militia was activated into service to meet the threat of Indian activity. When Colonel Samuel Lyon, Lieutenant Colonel Thomas Turbet, and Major Robert Taylor convened with their counterparts from the other battalions, Colonel Frederick Watt, the commander of the Seventh Battalion, which was manned for the most part by men from Sherman's Valley, enlightened them about the recent defection of Simon Girty.

Colonel Watt began his revealing update of the former Sherman's Valley resident by first directing several questions to Robert Taylor.

"Major Taylor, if my memory serves me right, you were once a resident of Kittanning, were you not?"

"Yes, Colonel. I spent from mid-June to early September of 1756 on the banks of the Allegheny River at Kittanning, as a result of being taken captive at Fort Bigham, thanks to King Beaver."

"Then I assume you were there when the survivors from Fort Granville were brought to Captain Jacob's stronghold and that you became acquainted with the infamous Girty family?"

"Yes, I had the distinct pleasure of sharing living space with the four Girty boys and their mother. They took to Indian life quite readily. Their stepfather, John Turner, was the one who opened the gates at Granville and invited Captain Jacobs and his warriors inside. What they did to Turner still turns my stomach when I stop and think about it."

"Simon Girty was born on Sherman's Creek on January 16, 1744, a day we will rue forever," interjected Colonel Watts. "It seems like Thomas Girty is the only one of the Girtys who will amount to anything, since he was liberated at Kittanning by Armstrong.

"The other three were divided up among the various tribes. Simon was adopted by the Senecas and given the name of Katepacomen. He easily became a native in habits, dress, and language. George was adopted by the Delawares, while James was accepted by the Shawnees. They found Indian life quite agreeable."

"Simon was commissioned an officer of militia at Fort Pitt when the Revolution broke out, probably because of his role in Lord Dunmore's War, his actions as an Indian agent after the war, and his friendship with Colonel William Crawford.

"On March 28 of this year (1778), Simon, accompanied by Matthew Elliott and Alexander McKee, became a turncoat and joined the British. It appears that he is under the direct influence of the British commander at Detroit, Henry Hamilton, better known as the "Hair Buyer." It didn't take long for Simon Girty to gain the nickname of "White Savage." His atrocities are causing many frontiersmen to tremble with fear.

"In June, Pennsylvania officially labeled Simon Girty a traitor to the American cause and placed the reward of eight hundred dollars upon his head. The White Savage was delighted to learn how much he was worth.

"It appears that George and James Girty have followed in their brother's footsteps, and have left our cause and joined the British as well. They are quickly gaining reputations for their blood-thirsty raids on the frontier, just like their brother."

Robert sadly shook his head. "You could see that type of attitude formed at Kittanning and Fort Duquesne. Now many unsuspecting settlers will feel their wrath. They will use this war as an excuse to kill and plunder. I'll be willing to wager that when this war comes to an end, their path of blood, death and destruction will not end.

"It is baffling to try and understand how a man born in our

own county, Sherman's Valley to be exact, and taken hostage at neighboring Fort Granville in July 1756, basically one of us, could become so involved in bringing harm to his old friends and neighbors."

It was difficult, almost impossible for any of these militia officers to comprehend why, not just one of their own, but three could turn their backs on their former friends, neighbors, and family members, and now wage war against them.

CHAPTER FORTY THREE

The Capture of Leonard Groninger

George Washington authorized a massive campaign of retaliation against the Iroquois who supported the British. In 1779 General John Sullivan led a force of twenty-five hundred men up the Susquehanna to the New York border, while General James Clinton with fifteen hundred men moved through the Mohawk Valley, and Colonel Daniel Brodhead took six hundred men from Fort Pitt up the Allegheny River. These frontier armies devastated the Indian settlements and caused great hardship and starvation among the British allies.

Pennsylvania faced one of the severest winters ever during the winter of 1779-80. One heavy snowstorm followed another, and this winter became known as "the winter of the deep snow." The woods and mountains lay under a mantle of snow measuring as deep as four feet by February.

The Iroquois who had their towns and food supplies destroyed by Sullivan's expedition starved and froze to death during this terrible winter. The snow cover prevented the Indians from mounting any retaliatory raids until mid-March of 1780.

The Delawares, Shawnees, and Wyandots struck Western Pennsylvania from their stronghold in the Ohio Country, before the Six Nations, especially the Senecas that had been bloodied by General Sullivan and Colonel Bradford, were able to recover and spread terror to the upper Susquehanna Valley.

Although Sullivan had spread havoc in the Chemung, Genesee, and North Branch of the Susquehanna Valleys in the previous late summer and early fall, the Indians and Tories reentered the Wyoming Valley by late March and began to inflict terrible suffering on the remaining inhabitants of that area.

To help counter the substantial bounties offered by the British and Tory commanders at Detroit and New York to their Indian allies for American scalps, President Joseph Reed of Pennsylvania, on April 7, 1780, informed Colonel Hunter, "The council would and do for this purpose authorize you to offer the following premiums for every male prisoner whether white or Indian, if the former is acting with the latter, Fifteen Hundred Dollars, and One Thousand Dollars for every Indian scalp."[14]

Four days later Reed informed Colonel Jacob Stroud of a similar arrangement: "We have therefore authorized Lieutenant (no name given) of the county (Northampton) to offer Fifteen Hundred Dollars for every Indian or Tory prisoner taken in arms against us, and One Thousand Dollars for every Indian scalp."[15]

The activities of Tories and their Indian allies in the region just north of the junction of the North and West Branches of the Susquehanna River had a tremendous impact on the settlement of the Tuscarora Valley after the conclusion of the Revolution.

One such incident in 1780 that impacted the development of the Tuscarora Valley in the aftermath of the Revolutionary War began in the Buffalo Valley, which is drained by the Buffalo Creek, a tributary of the West Branch of the Susquehanna River.

The Buffalo Valley was just one of the small valleys of Central Pennsylvania that had felt the wrath of marauding Indians since the early days of the Revolution. It had been hoped that the Sullivan expedition in the late summer and fall of 1779 would have saved the West Branch of the Susquehanna from additional Indian raids after many of the Indians had been deprived of their subsistence by Sullivan's scorched earth policy. Unfortunately, this was not the case. In April of 1780 the Indian assaults were renewed opposite Warrior Run and near White Deer Mills.

These renewed incursions motivated seventeen-year-old Leonard Groninger of the Buffalo Valley, known on the rolls as Lenheart, to enlist on April 8 in the company known as the Northumberland County Rangers, led by Captain Thomas Robinson. To halt or at least stifle Indian activity, Captain

Robinson built a blockhouse at Deerstown to protect the settlers of the surrounding region.

Leonard Groninger's older brother, Joseph, had enlisted on September 26, 1776, under the command of Captain John Clark. Two other Groningers, Henry and George, had enlisted in the company led by Captain Benjamin Weiser.

By July, the forays infiltrated into the Buffalo Valley and the Penn's Creek area. Captain Robinson sent Rangers Himpleman, Groninger, and Moore to search along Penn's Creek for signs of Indians in the vicinity.

As the trio skirted the edge of a cornfield, Groninger exclaimed, "Himpleman, be on the alert. Your dog's acting mighty peculiar, like it might be sniffing out an Indian."

"Yah, he does act like he's winded something."

With that the dog wheeled around and ran straight back to his master.

The three rangers looked around in bewilderment. Suddenly a barrage of rifle fire was discharged from the underbrush along the creek bank.

Himpleman screamed in terror and clutched his chest as a bright red river discharged from the left side of his chest. He collapsed to the ground and lay still. Leonard suddenly experienced a red-hot sensation in his left hand, and screamed in agony. He fell to one knee and grabbed the throbbing extremity with his opposite hand, attempting to extricate the cause of the pain.

Groninger glanced at his lacerated hand and quickly recognized that he was a very lucky young man. Even though he was in agonizing pain, he could move all his fingers. The ball had passed through the middle of his palm and apparently had not struck any bones or major tendons. At most, it was a major flesh wound; if he kept it clean, he should not suffer any complications. But at the moment, that was not his major concern; fleeing for safety was.

Moore did not break stride once he heard the deafening roar of the discharging Indian weapons, and soon outdistanced any pursuers. Eventually Moore arrived back at the blockhouse and reported to Captain Robinson the plight of Himpleman and Groninger.

Once Leonard gained his senses, he jumped to his feet and sprinted hard for the woods. Soon, with the loss of blood and the pain, he could not continue his pace and had to sit down on a log to rest. This, of course, was his undoing, as the warriors quickly overtook him and prepared to finish him off.

One of the attackers raised his tomahawk, poised to deliver one last deadly blow to split Groninger's skull. The older and more athletic member of the attackers yelled an order, and the brave held back the fatal blow. The leader then approached Leonard and in broken English inquired, "Are you hurt bad? Can you travel?"

Leonard answered immediately, "I can travel. My hand will heal."

The leader slapped him on the back. "Good, we go now." He then grabbed Leonard by the uninjured arm and lifted him to his feet, shoving him forward away from the creek.

Along the way, they added insult to injury, as they backtracked to Leonard's family home and quickly set it ablaze. Leonard was unable to stop the act, as flames completely engulfed his family's cabin and all its belongings.

The raiding party and its wounded captive quickly traveled down the creek to its mouth, before turning north and following the Susquehanna River. Soon they passed the mouth of White Deer Creek and entered the White Deer Hole Valley. Here they turned westward and up over North White Deer Ridge.

Darkness had settled in, but this proved to be no deterrent to the marauders. They entered the Nippenose Valley and followed it to its head. Then they passed through the gap in Bald Eagle Mountain and struck McElhattan Creek. They stuck to this creek until it flowed into the West Branch of the Susquehanna. At the mouth of the creek they turned slightly southwest and proceeded along the banks of the mighty Susquehanna until they came to the village located on Great Island in the middle of the river.

Over the past several years, this village had been the scene of numerous attacks by white soldiers under the command of the

English during the late war, and now led by Pennsylvania militia and Continental Army troops. Still, the village managed to flourish, though in a diminished capacity.

Leonard and his captors spent the remainder of the night at Great Island. All the captives spent a miserable night on the island as their hands were tied behind their backs, and their legs were bound also. Leonard's wounded hand throbbed and burned throughout the long night, making sleep next to impossible. The leader of the raiders barked an order to one of the squaws to treat Leonard's hand, and she did so reluctantly. The middle-aged woman cleaned the wound thoroughly, applied a type of salve to it, and wrapped it in a piece of cloth. Early in the morning the party was joined by other Indians and several of their unfortunate captives. When they left Great Island, they crossed over to the north bank of the river and headed downriver.

Within five or six miles they arrived at the mouth of a broad creek, and the party left the banks of the Susquehanna and turned north to follow the new creek. This was Pine Creek. Even in Leonard's painful condition, he soon recognized that he was traveling through one of the most beautiful, uncompromised, extensive wilderness regions he could ever imagine.

None of the white captives had ever witnessed such an abundance of natural beauty. In the early going, the creek had to be crossed several times to avoid mountain shoulders and overhangs. Once they passed a stream that flowed in from the east, Little Pine Creek, and then continued on the east bank.

Soon they noticed a high-pitched buzzing din. As they continued upstream, it amplified to an incessant, piercing, almost earsplitting crescendo. The warriors appeared not be perplexed or dismayed by the commotion that was interrupting the peace and quiet of the beautiful gorge known as Tiadaghton.

As the white captives began to look around for the source of the ungodly disturbance, slight smirks or smiles slowly erupted on the faces of the braves. They were enjoying the discomfort of their white captives.

Finally, the whites were led off the path and herded closer to the banks of the creek. In front of them they observed a section of the stream where it abruptly flowed eastward and surged into the side of an enormous rock or overcrop that jutted into the stream. The change in direction of the creek and its gushing into the rock wasn't the source of the din, but what was located on the rock certainly was.

The entire surface of the rock appeared to be one squirming, shifting, coiling and recoiling, thrusting mass of reptiles. Yes, a monstrous, nightmarish, open den of poisonous serpents basking in the sunlight, all seemingly attempting to rattle their tails louder than their coiled neighbors.

It was unbelievable that so many rattlesnakes could congregate in one spot. It was a scene that Leonard Groninger would carry to his grave. He wanted to be as far away from this spot as soon as possible. He wanted to move upstream with utmost speed to once again be able to hear the insects and birds that inhabited the gore, or even to hear the water again. It took over an hour before the horrific sound stopped reaching his ears.

About two or three miles from Rattlesnake Rock, they arrived at the mouth of another sizeable stream flowing in from the east, Babb Creek. Here they halted their journey and made camp for the night. The captives were given some dried venison and corn, just enough to keep up their strength to continue their travels. Leonard removed his bandage and cleaned the wound as well as he could. Again, their hands and feet were bound, making any attempt at escape impossible.

Upon breaking camp the next morning, the group beheld a valley that was now a definite gorge, quite narrow. For most of the next sixteen or seventeen miles, the mountains ended right at the edge of the creek. The stream itself became a series of long, quiet pools interlaced with moderate rapids, which mostly created mild whitewater. They found one exception about two miles before they left the main gorge and entered into a wide floodplain. This section of about three or four hundred yards was where the gradient dropped rapidly and created an aggressive flow over some submerged and around some exposed rocks. Also, the creek slammed into some outcropped rocks on the right bank. All this fast-paced activity created what appeared to be some large waves and bouncy chutes in the water.

The mountain slopes were covered with firs, hemlocks, spruces and cathedral-like maples, oaks, chestnut, and hickory. On the steeper inclines were spectacular waterfalls cascading to the creek below. On some of these extreme gradients, towering palisades and dramatic rock outcrops graced the skyline of the gorge.

The stream appeared to abound with trout, but it also proved to be a haven for eagles, hawks, ravens, and crows. Wildlife was quite abundant, with beaver, otter, mink, and muskrat appearing frequently on the banks of the creek. Large animals such as deer, bear, elk, and wildcat were also sighted.

They observed osprey roosting in trees lining the creek and they were thrilled to witness the hunting rituals of these graceful birds. (Osprey are easily distinguished, as they soar on wings that have a noticeable kink or crook, as opposed to the flat wings of the bald eagle.) Their white bellies flashed in the sunlight as they swooped down onto the surface of Pine Creek and extracted sizable trout from the stream with their sharp talons.

Leonard was a mesmerized witness to the continuing drama of survival of the fittest as an osprey gracefully grabbed a trout, turned the fish's head forward into the wind, and gained altitude to return to his nest high on the side of the mountain. Suddenly, a much larger bird with a white head and white tail plunged out of the sky and collided with the osprey, knocking the trout from the osprey's talons. As the fish plummeted, the bald eagle snatched it out of the air and headed upstream, leaving behind a stunned osprey who struggled to maintain his balance and continue in flight.

The gorge eventually melted away into a flat floodplain. There the stream which they had been following almost straight north from the Susquehanna, Pine Creek, digressed almost ninety degrees and therefore now bore directly westward. A smaller stream, Marsh Creek, joined Pine Creek from the northeast.

Buffeted with cliffs and bluffs, the creek continued to flow down a scenic mountain valley. For about the next twelve or thirteen miles the path continued on an almost directly westward course until Pine Creek branched and the path followed the main branch that once again flowed out of the northwest.

At this junction, the party halted for the night, again tying up the captives.

Shortly after daybreak they were back on the trail. After nearly five miles the path left the banks of Pine Creek and followed its tributary, known as Genesee Fork which flowed directly from the north. The path stuck to the Genesee Fork for almost three miles; then it veered northwest up Cushing Hollow. At this point the path became steep as it climbed out of the headwaters of Pine Creek and over the mountain into the headwaters of the Genesee River.

The Genesee begins as a tiny torrent that steadily descends over a series of short, rocky, and cobbly riffles. As the river flows north, it merges with smaller brooks and streams. Within about nine miles it is joined by the west and middle Branches of the Genesee, which boost its volume slightly. Even so, the Genesee remains a small, gently flowing stream coursing through a rich, forested valley.

The party soon passed through the small village of Genesee. About three miles later they came to Shongo, another small and insignificant village. At Shongo, they halted and discussed what route to follow. From what Leonard could determine, some of the warriors wanted to continue down the Genesee, which would be the shorter route. Unknown to Leonard, farther down the Genesee was the Genesee River Gorge, a seventeen-mile gorge with walls as high as six hundred feet.

Those who opposed the shorter Genesee route wanted to head northeast on what was known as the Forbidden Path, to the village of Passigachkunk, or Canisteo, on the banks of the Canisteo River. This path passed over Beech Hill, crossed Dyke Creek, and then kept on high and broad ridges until it reached the village of Canisteo. From Canisteo it followed the Canisteo River to its headwaters. After crossing several high ridges, the path followed the Canaseraga Creek to the village of

Gathesegawareohare. The creek flowed into the Genesee River after less than an hour's journey from the village. A little farther down, Little Beard's Creek flowed into the Genesee, where the village of Chenussio was located.

The decision was made to continue the journey following the Genesee. Within a few miles, several of the braves went into the underbrush on the banks of the river and uncovered a small flotilla of framed canoes covered with birch bark. The crafts proved to be quite agile and swift moving, and the miles were rapidly negotiated.

Leonard absent-mindedly heeded the dip-dip of the paddles, not fully comprehending that with each stroke he was being transported farther and farther away from the Buffalo Valley. He was not required to engage in the methodical task of paddling the canoe in which he was a passenger, and had he not been a hostage, he might have enjoyed the spectacular scenery.

They came to the small village of Caneadea, where a party of warriors on their way south to the frontier settlements of Pennsylvania also camped for the night. Later the two groups appeared to be holding a council, and Leonard perceived that he was the key subject of their meeting. Nothing was done to him that night. The young German assumed that he had passed some test, and his running of the gauntlet was postponed until another day.

The next morning, after the party had paddled steadily for about two hours, the scenery underwent a transformation, and the velocity of the river increased. They were entering a gorge that reminded Leonard of the Pine Creek Valley, which they had traversed earlier.

Like the Pine Creek Gorge, the Genesee Gorge is about seventeen miles long. The Genesee cuts deep into the shale, limestone, and sandstone, above a section known as Middle Falls, creating precipitous walls about four hundred feet across and nearly six hundred feet in height.

Near the southern end of the gorge is a section known as Portage Canyon. As they entered this section, the paddlers broke their rhythm and braced their paddles on the right side of the canoes to steer them quickly to the bank. Leonard quickly figured out the reason for the abrupt change in paddling technique and their haste to land the canoes.

Within this area, the Genesee River roars over three major waterfalls. Middle Falls, which is about 107 feet high, was called "Ska-ga-dee." Leonard later learned that the Senecas called the land around this canyon "She-ga-hun-da," or the "Vale of the Three Falls."

The waterfalls were circumvented by a treacherous portage which didn't seem to phase Leonard's captors in the least. It appeared to be just another small irritation on their journey back home. Leonard was extraordinarily impressed with the plunge and spray of the magnificent and breathtaking waterfalls.

After the portage and the return to the canoes, Leonard and his captors left the gorge and its mountains with its abundant foliage over their heads and entered into a broad river valley. Suddenly a scene unfolded before his eyes that he could never have imagined in his wildest dreams. He had been transported into an oasis of open space that contained richly cultivated fields. This was a valley that he judged to be about twenty miles long and about four miles across.

Here and there he observed dark islands in stark contrast to the lush vegetation. These areas he recognized as old orchards that had probably been growing for generations, judging from the size of the stumps of the apple, peach, plum, and cherry trees. Many of the trees had been hacked to the ground by Sullivan's force last September. Some of the trees had been torched, and others had been girdled, but it was evident that the American army had destroyed the majority of the orchards no matter which method they employed.

Incredibly, a few of the trees had survived on this flat river plain and were on their way to producing a rich profusion of fruit.

As they progressed into the valley, it became evident that acres and acres of the once-lush grain fields were not in a productive state in this growing season. Many acres still were blackened and scorched. Instead of what had been tall, ripe grass and cornfield after cornfield as far as the eye could see, the scars of a scorched earth policy presented a stark contrast to the beautiful, surrounding wilderness.

Some cornfields had not been set afire; instead, the stalks had been simply uprooted. Apparently, there had been too much corn to destroy, so that uprooting or cutting the stalks wasn't sufficient. So Sullivan's men had pulled off the ears and tossed them into the creek. Not all of it was wasted or destroyed, however; the army took some of it.

Leonard began to realize that his captors were experiencing a wave of apprehension and consternation as they approached the banks of the stream that, up until last September, had boasted an example of unsurpassed civilization that most white men could never have envisioned

The first destroyed village that they entered was Gathesegawareohare; loosely translated, it meant "a spear laid up." It was situated on a beautiful site on the banks of the Canaseraga Creek, just before it flows into the Genesee River. Observing the remains of the charred log homes, Leonard surmised that there probably had been about twenty-five well-built homes in the village prior to its destruction. Here and there, a few pitiful huts had been reconstructed out of the remnants of the former homes.

The warriors were not content to linger among these woeful huts and moved downriver about a mile and a half to a much larger village positioned between the Genesee River on the east and Little Beard's Creek on the west. This was Chenussio, which in the Seneca language meant "Beautiful Valley."

Up until mid-September of last year this village had not been misnamed. Sullivan and his men considered it the largest and finest Indian village they had ever seen. They had been greeted by an incredible sight when they entered the town. An enormous Seneca longhouse constructed of peeled logs, laid two stories high and painted bright red, was the centerpiece of the town. Positioned around this impressive longhouse were about 128 elegantly constructed homes.

This extraordinary Seneca town had been Sullivan's final objective, and it had been left undefended by the Senecas, as had been Gathesegawareohare. When Sullivan's army left the banks of Little Beard's Creek on September 15, 1779, the "Beautiful Valley" no longer existed. The town and all its incredible cornfields, well-tended orchards, and superb grasslands had been ravaged, although it had not been an easy task to accomplish.

Sullivan's overall objective had been to bring total ruin to the Indian settlements and destruction of their crops, hoping to generate famine, disease, and great suffering among the British allies on the upper Susquehanna frontier. They hoped this expedition would put an end to the Iroquois excursions into the Wyoming Valley and beyond.

Those Iroquois who had not abandoned this valley and did not pass the winter within the confines of Fort Niagara suffered severely. Sullivan's forces had done an admirable job destroying the Iroquois' food supplies, and many Iroquois starved and froze to death during what was probably the severest winter in the history of our country, "the winter of the deep snow."

Leonard Groninger knew little of the particulars of the Sullivan expedition into the Genesee Valley, which had occurred the fall before his forced visit. All he knew was that he was observing the results of a tremendous wave of ravaging destruction.

Many of the Senecas had returned to the charred remnants as soon as the snow left the ground in April and began to reconstruct their once-thriving and beautiful town. Already several log homes had been replaced, while most of the inhabitants were living in hastily constructed, temporary huts. The centerpiece of the town, the two-story log longhouse, was in the process of being replaced, although the logs were still at the first-story level.

Suddenly, Leonard was startled from his reverie, as he was shoved onto his knees and kicked in the ribs as he went down. From his kneeling position he observed that the inhabitants of the town were forming two long lines facing each other, and each individual was reaching for, or already was grasping, a club, tomahawk, spear, or stout stick. He had heard about this ritual, and he realized that the next few minutes could well be the last minutes of his life or at least the most painful that he had ever endured.

The Seneca participants began to chant, projecting a shrill howling, seething, screeching yelp or shriek. Leonard shivered at his fate. He quickly assessed his chances as slim and realized he had to run faster than he had ever run in his life, keep his hand and arms up to protect his head, and above all, not allow himself to be tripped or knocked off his feet.

Two large braves grabbed his arms and jerked him to his feet. They dragged him and his companions to the head of the line, and using sign language, conveyed the message that their captives were to run to the end of the line that ended just in front of the longhouse.

Leonard was the second to run the gauntlet. As he began his run, he concentrated on staying on his feet. To stumble and fall would bring an avalanche of blows to his head and body, from which he probably would not survive. He took short, quick strides while bringing his knees up as high as possible, and kept his feet churning. In no way was he going to look ahead to the end of the line; all he was concerned about was dodging or blocking the blows raining down on him.

Suddenly, he stumbled and almost went down, but he struggled and regained his balance, although he probably absorbed several additional blows during that instant. He kicked out at his attackers, and on several occasions, landed some solid boots on the participants.

Then, as quickly as it had begun, it was over. He had survived! He had run the length of the gauntlet and absorbed blow after blow, arriving at the end of the line, bleeding, bruised, slashed, punctured, and exhausted, but still alive.

There was no time to celebrate his good fortune. Several brawny warriors grabbed him by his shoulders and slammed him against the log wall of the longhouse. He felt as if his lungs were going to explode, but he sucked in some air and regained his balance. The braves began to drag Leonard back to the head of the line to make him run the gauntlet a second time.

His spirits sagged; there was no way he could survive a second running of the gauntlet. If they wanted to kill him, why didn't they just bludgeon him with a tomahawk and put him out of his misery? Leonard attempted to regain his composure and summon enough strength and energy to face his adversaries once again.

Out of the corner of his bleary left eye, he saw a slightly overweight squaw approach his tormentors. She began to shake her right index finger in their faces while screaming in a high-pitched squeal. The warriors recoiled, released Leonard, and retreated to the other side of the gauntlet.

Leonard was utterly confused over his sudden good fortune and glanced around for an explanation. The squaw now approached Leonard, and she gently patted him on his right shoulder, motioning for him to follow her. As he complied, another younger woman stepped forward and in very broken English explained, "Tatamee wants to adopt you so you can replace her only son who was killed by the Americans while fighting for the British at Oriskany."

The young German had no idea what adoption would entail, but it had to be better than being clubbed to death while running the gauntlet the second time. He continued to follow his savior until they arrived at a small, crude hut near the bank of the creek. Tatamee motioned for him to sit, and she entered the hut. She quickly returned with some small bowls, a few utensils, and several pieces of cloth.

She began to cleanse his wounds, even the one he had received when he was captured. After the cleansing, she applied salves made from herbs and roots to his wounds. They burned his skin, but Leonard didn't allow himself to react to the stinging effects of the herbs. The motherly squaw returned the bowls and utensils to the hut and this time brought out some dried venison and a type of johnnycake for him to eat.

When night came, Tatamee invited Leonard to sleep inside

the hut. He hurt terribly as he spent his first night of captivity in his new home in the revitalized Seneca town of Chenussio on the banks of the Genesee River, far to the north of his home in the Buffalo Valley of Pennsylvania.

It wasn't long into Leonard's captivity that he learned why his life had been spared. In order for these Indians to survive the coming winter they desperately needed to resurrect their cornfields and vegetable gardens. There weren't enough squaws to perform this typical women's work, so they were employing slave labor—white captives.

CHAPTER FORTY FOUR

Groninger's Captivity

Late one hot humid August afternoon, two young Seneca women approached Leonard and another white captive named John Reigert. The women were all smiles and making no effort to hide their amorous intentions. The girls offered the nearly dehydrated white captives a drink from an earthen urn, which they accepted readily.

The two youths attempted to relay their thanks by using sign language and some broken Seneca phrases that they had absorbed during their stay in Chenussio. The capricious maidens persistently made intimate and sensuous gestures, using body language which the young men appreciated. Suddenly, an old squaw appeared, uttering what were undoubtedly threats to all four of them. The maidens hurriedly departed. The gnarled old women shook a stout stick at the two white men, who understood that she meant for them to return to work hoeing the cornfields, and not to bother the young girls.

Two evenings later, right after the young men had consumed their meal, the young maidens sauntered beguilingly past Tatamee's hut to the creek bank and entered the water. The maidens commenced to frolic in the stream, splashing and dunking each other in a wanton and lewd fashion.

They waved to the two captives and beckoned for them to join them in the water. Leonard and Reigert looked at each other and shrugged, took off their moccasins, and impulsively slid down the bank and into the water to join the impish girls. Soon the boys were enjoying intimate body contact with the maidens. All four young people were oblivious to their surroundings, so immersed were they in their provocative activities.

Abruptly, the same ancient squaw who had interrupted their first encounter in the cornfield arrived on the bank of the creek and released an ear-splitting bellow. All four youths froze. The girls dropped their heads and scrambled up the bank of the creek as fast as their nimble legs could carry them. Again, the squaw threatened the captives with her stick, glowered at them, and turned away.

Three evenings later, at dusk, the boys heard what sounded like a raven behind their hut towards the creek. Both of them recognized that in no way was the noise made by a raven. They stepped outside and strolled towards the creek. There waiting in the semi-darkness were the two merry maidens.

The older girl took John by the hand and led him down the creek away from the village and prying eyes. The other girl flashed a naughty and playful glance at Leonard. Leonard knew the intentions of the impish girl, but he played dumb, and acted as if he knew absolutely nothing about the opposite sex.

Try as she might, the young maiden could not motivate Leonard to participate in her sexual scheme. Later, when the other couple returned from their encounter, they were all smiles. On the other hand, Leonard's companion stomped her feet, muttered an apparent oath, and left with a nasty scowl on her face.

Later, that night, John asked Leonard, "What in the world did you do to that girl tonight? She was in one nasty mood when she left."

"That's just it. I didn't do anything," he answered. "I'm pretty sure I knew what she had in mind, but I'm not going to plant my seed in some dusky Seneca maiden. I've got the right girl picked out for me when I get back to the Buffalo Valley."

John looked skeptical. "First off, how do you know that we're ever going to escape from here and be able to return to our homes? Just who is this lucky, chosen young lady?"

"Well, I haven't met her yet," Leonard said sheepishly. "There are several young girls in our valley who are pleasant to look at and who would make good wives."

"Huh! You're wasting your time! They'll never fall for the likes of you. They always have a hankering for the older boys. By the time we get out of here, they'll be hitched and have a whole brood of kids."

"Just you wait and see. I'll win one of them yet…if we ever get back."

"I'll be willing to bet you that when fall arrives and the weather turns colder, that young Seneca maiden is going to look a lot more inviting. It gets awfully frigid up here in the winter. You might be willing to try anything to keep warm."

"I don't plan to be here in the fall," Leonard said. "Sooner or later my chance, our chance, for escape will come. Just be patient, it will happen."

From time to time, Leonard and some of his fellow captors discussed the possibility of attempting to escape and return to their home in the South. Several factors stood out in their escape plans. The Genesee River and most of its tributaries were of no use to them. The Genesee flows north, and they wanted to head south. For them to retrace Leonard's journey from the headwaters of the Genesee would be folly also, for Leonard remembered all too well the obstacles presented by the Genesee Gorge and its waterfalls.

Leonard took into account the discussion among his captors at Shongo. His captors had debated whether to use the Genesee River or to cross over and use the Canisteo River and the Canaseraga Creek path. It appeared to Leonard that he should head up the Canaseraga Creek and then over the ridges and mountains to the headwaters of the Canisteo River in order to float down the Susquehanna to Fort Augusta.

The young German did not mention the possibility of this escape route. If he decided to use this path to freedom, he did not want to risk jeopardizing his strategy by sharing it with other captives who might divulge his plans.

All the captives were well aware of the consequences that awaited them if their break to freedom failed. They had witnessed the brutality dealt those who failed in their attempts to reach civilization. One of the most common modes of torture was for the captors, often women, to prepare wooden splinters about the thickness of an arrow and taper them to a sharp point at one end. The splinters were soaked in turpentine or pitch. The saturated splinters were then randomly embedded into the naked body of the bound captive. This alone caused excruciating pain, but to magnify the agonizing pangs of discomfort and to expedite death, the splinters would be set afire. Most victims died shortly afterwards, but there were occasions where some lived in that condition for several hours.

With this in mind, Leonard vowed to bide his time until the conditions were ripe for his success.

What Leonard Groninger and his fellow captives experienced in the Genesee Valley served as evidence that Sullivan's campaign of the previous year had failed to eliminate the Indian troubles in the upper Susquehanna River Valley. The Indians under Joseph Brant, the Great Captain of the Iroquois, appeared to have needed only the past winter to recover from Sullivan's autumn destruction of their villages and farmlands.

The Iroquois had been forced to nestle under the British protection of Fort Niagara while they suffered terribly throughout the winter of 1779-80. The Iroquois who survived Sullivan's wrath would have perished without British aid. When spring came, the survivors sought revenge against the Americans to their east and south. Consequently, most of the warriors were absent from the villages throughout the summer, and the adoption of Leonard Groninger was postponed until autumn when most of the men returned from the warpath.

When the warriors began returning in late summer and early fall, the lifestyle that the captives had enjoyed in Chenussio changed drastically. One day in mid-October, Leonard was approached by several young, athletic braves. The most powerfully built youngster held a piece of bark that had some ashes on it. He dipped his fingers into the ashes to establish a firmer grip and methodically commenced to pull the hair out of Leonard's head. It was a painful process, but Leonard knew that he was expected not to exhibit any pain.

Finally all of his hair was removed except for an area about three or four inches square on the crown of his head. The warriors cut this remaining hair, except for three locks, one of which they wrapped with a beaded garter, while the other two were plaited. Next, they bored small holes in his nose and ears and inserted ear rings and a nose ring. They ordered him to strip off his clothes and dressed him instead in a breechclout (loincloth). The young warriors then escorted him to the banks of the creek, where four young women took over Leonard's transformation.

The young squaws led him into the shallow water and began to scrub him profusely. Afterwards, they led him back onto the bank of the creek. Here three other squaws painted his head, face, and body in a variety of colors. He was led to the building which served as the council-house, since the original one had been destroyed by Sullivan and his men.

Inside the council-house Leonard was presented with new clothes and a pair of moccasins. The chief, who had just returned from a summer of waging war on the Americans, took Leonard's right hand and delivered a lengthy speech, of which Leonard recognized only a few words.

When the chief finished, he placed Leonard's right hand in Tatamee's and stated, "You are now a member of the Seneca tribe. You have been made one of us by strong law and custom. You are now to consider yourself as one of us."

After the ceremony was concluded, a huge feast was held in Leonard's honor. In the meantime, a new name, 'Chickaton," was given to the newest member of the Senecas of the village of Chenussio.

The adoption ceremony led to a change in the amount of freedom allowed Leonard, now Chickatom. He could now roam freely and fish and hunt with bow and arrow, spears, and traps. Guns were scarce, and the Senecas probably didn't trust him enough to turn over one of their prized possessions.

Chickatom was introduced to a new method of fishing and hunting from a dug-out canoe at night. The Senecas would drift the dug-out down the river or creek close to shore. The deer would come to the stream to drink their fill. The hunters would carefully build a fire out of pitch pine in the middle of the canoe. One brave would be stationed in the stern to steer the canoe; several others would kneel in the bow, prepared to shoot at the deer as they drifted their way. This was usually a successful method of securing meat for the village.

The same method was used to fish for eels, shad, bass, pickerel, and trout. The firelight seemed to attract the fish and made them easy prey. On some occasions the braves would hunt for deer or other animals and fish on the same trip.

The winter of 1780–81 began in early November and proved to be bleak and arctic, with interminable snow squalls, heavy snows, and blizzards bombarding the landscape. The Genesee was frozen solid early in the winter, and it did not relinquish its frozen cover until early April.

The horrible, biting cold created food shortages that plagued the village. Even with all their diligence the villagers had not amassed sufficient food supplies. From time to time, foraging parties were sent out, but they would return, suffering the effects of mental and physical fatigue and with little food to show for their efforts.

"No meat, no meat" was the cry uttered by the squaws as they complained about their plight. Leonard and the men struggled against the elements to provide meat. Most of the larger animals had disappeared from the valley. Raccoons, beavers, and squirrels were easily obtained, but they did not provide much meat.

Leonard never could adjust to the huts filled with smoke due to the lack of chimneys, and his eyes were constantly red, bleary, and bulging. He suffered much anguish over the absence from his home and family.

Many villagers left to seek the sanctuary of Fort Niagara, some in the search of rum or whiskey to ward off the cold and misery. Numerous young, old, and feeble Senecas did not survive the onslaught of winter. When spring eventually arrived, the numbers of the village had lessened considerably.

As soon as the snow and frost left the ground, the villagers began preparing the ground for spring plantings. They all knew that in order to avoid another winter like the one that they had just survived, they desperately needed to increase their production of foodstuff. Leonard and the rest of the captives were once again put to work in the cornfields and garden patches. It was the same monotonous, dreary, dusk-to-dawn, grueling labor, with no respite available. In the meantime, other warriors had left the village to once again begin the raiding of English settlements to the east and south of the Genesee Valley.

Finally, Reigert decided that he had had enough. One evening, as the squaws were busily engaged in preparing the nightly meal, Reigert and Leonard left the edge of the cornfield and entered the woods. Reigert threw down his hoe. "I can't take any more of this; I'm not hoeing another hill of corn. You can waste more of your life here in this valley or take a chance of making a run for it right now.'

It didn't take Leonard more than a few seconds to toss his hoe down and follow Reigert into the woods. "I'm with you. I've been wanting to do this for several weeks, ever since the weather broke. I'm like you; it's now or never."

Between them they possessed a knife and a tomahawk. They each had a small pouch in which they carried a portion of food that would see them through the first night. After that they would have to forage to stay alive.

They never looked back at the village to see if anyone had observed their break for freedom. All they could hope for was that they wouldn't be missed until the start of the evening meal. By that time, darkness would mask their movements. There weren't any healthy warriors left in the village to attempt to track them tonight. By the time any warriors returned, the two escapees would be well on their way to the tributaries of the Susquehanna—and home.

CHAPTER FORTY FIVE

The Escape

At this location, the Genesee River is about one hundred feet wide, fairly swift, but providential, only about waist-deep. The two defectors plunged into the waist-deep water and swam as noiselessly as possible to the opposite bank of the river.

As they made their break, they discussed their possible course to freedom. Leonard quickly summarized the plans that he had been formulating for the nine months that he had been in captivity. He emphasized their need to head southeast and find the headwaters of the Canisteo River, which is a tributary of the Tioga River. The Tioga joins the Cohocton River at Teaog to form the Chemung River, which in turn flows into the Susquehanna.

The Susquehanna was their goal, their highway to freedom. But before they arrived on the banks of this mighty river, they had to journey over unknown territory with all manner of obstacles and challenges. Their first major challenge was to head east to find the Canaseraga Creek, and at the same time avoid the village of Gathesegawareohare.

They located the creek about two miles above Gathesegawareohare before the night turned pitch dark; then they stumbled and blundered up the creek towards its headwaters. They lurched, sprawled, and staggered over slippery rocks, logs, and submerged trees. The going was worse than they ever imagined, but they realized there was no turning back.

Implanted in their minds was the memory of those unfortunate souls who had unsuccessfully attempted what they were undertaking, especially those who had undergone the pine splint torture. It would be better to die along the way than to turn back or be overtaken by braves from Chenussio. They had to avoid any contact with any other villages or Indians. To be discovered meant death.

Luckily, there was an early-rising three-quarter moon that produced enough illumination for them to continue long into the night. Finally hunger and fatigue took their toll on their bodies, and before the moon set, the defectors left the embankment of the ever-diminishing creek.

"Try to avoid stepping in any soft areas or mud," Leonard advised. "Step from rock to rock. I doubt if anyone from the village is pursuing us, but we can't take any chances and leave any tell-tale signs. There's a stand of hemlocks near the crest of the ridge. That appears to be a good spot for us to hide and sleep part of the day."

Pangs of hunger awakened them after about five hours of much-needed sleep. They returned to the creek and were successful in grabbing a few crawfish and scooping out several of the abundant native trout that populated the languid pools of the stream. The famished men devoured their catch as they continued their ascent of the increasingly steep mountainous terrain.

The creek dwindled to a mere trickle, but the elevation of the mountain did not diminish, and it challenged their lungs and legs as they continued their assault on the mountain. Just before dark they reached what they assumed was the crest of the elevation. They took a short break, then began descending the opposite side of the mountain.

The eastern slope proved to be more of a challenge than had its western counterpart. At first, the route they chose was strewn with rocks and boulders. Then it was shrouded with forests of incredibly thick hemlock, spruce, and pine. The density of the evergreens made it difficult to penetrate their branches, so the pair decided to sleep until sunup and then pick their way down to the river valley.

When they arose, the sun was finding its way through the boughs, but it was still extremely difficult for the men to make any headway. The struggle slackened when they came to the slanted gradient of a ravine. Well below them, the stream cascaded, a sight that lifted their spirits, because they hoped that this rivulet would flow southward into the Canisteo or Cohocton Rivers.

They began to probe the crest of the ravine for an animal path that would give them a safer access to the depths of the hollow and the stream of water, hopefully one of their couriers to the Susquehanna. After about two hundred yards they discovered a worn pathway that slanted in an easterly direction.

The trail was crisscrossed with additional paths, and at times it was difficult to ascertain the main one. The animal path maintained its slanted gradient until it intersected the rivulet; then it flanked the stream as it continued its plummet to the river.

After what seemed like several miles, the terrain leveled out, and the slightly enlarged creek entered a swampy region. The evergreens gave way to dense thickets of elders and willow scrub. Before entering the swamp, the two men retraced their steps for several hundred yards and located a hidden sleeping spot among the hemlocks. Once again the runaways sought a meal of crawfish and small fish from the stream before falling into an exhausted sleep.

Acknowledging that they were leaving a dissected plateau and had arrived in a river valley, they recognized that they would have to be constantly vigilant to avoid contact with Senecas or Mohawks residing in the region.

Unbeknownst to the two white men, they had reached the Canisteo River, which means either "Pickerel" or "Head of Water," a tributary of the Tioga River. This was the watery route that they were hoping to reach, because this river represents the northwestern reach of the watershed of the Susquehanna River. The Canisteo was approximately fifty-five miles in length, although the tributary that Leonard and John had followed from the mountain merged with the river about ten miles into its southeasterly course.

Once they reached the banks of the Canisteo, caution—extreme caution—became their byword. They could encounter the enemy at any bend in the river. "I know that we're completely blind in regards to the lay of the land and the river," Leonard admitted. "Maybe we would be better off traveling at night. At least we could observe the cooking fires of the Indians and have some knowledge of what and where to avoid."

John agreed. "We won't be able to travel as fast, but at least we shouldn't blunder into a raiding party heading south to do its dirty work, or one returning with its captives and plunder."

They spent the rest of that day assembling a small raft from dried pine logs joined by grapevines. They made three stout poles ten to twelve feet in length to thrust the raft downriver. They also fashioned two crude paddles to aid in propelling the raft.

That night, well after darkness had descended, they shoved their raft into the slow current of the Canisteo. It was good strategy that they waited until nightfall to begin their float. Shortly before midnight they smelled smoke. They had come upon the remains of the village of Canaseraga. Although they did not know this village by name or of any of the other villages and towns along their journey, they all spelled out the same thing—danger.

Hazards lurked throughout each night's float. Submerged logs and trees, small and large boulders, overhanging tree limbs, and small riffles and rapids posed threats to the unstable watercraft. Since the river was not very wide, the pair would not have a lengthy swim to the nearest bank if disaster struck.

The raft was not only unstable, but it was extremely slow. At best, they were probably cruising at three to four miles an hour. Progress was slow, but at least it was steady. When the sky became streaked with the first signs of daylight, they steered the unsteady craft to the safest-looking refuge. The ideal sanctuary was a haven sheltered by overhanging branches or reeds and water plants that grew into the water's edge.

After safely skirting Canaseraga, they passed two uneventful nights until again they smelled smoke wafting upriver and voices just a few hundred yards away. They were nearing the village of Canisteo. As they had done when they passed the first village, the men slipped off the raft into the water opposite the village and continued safely downriver.

Nearly twenty miles later and midway through the next night, the raft gained momentum when the waters of the Canisteo River merged with those of the Tioga River flowing in from the west. The Tioga River rose in the uplands of north central Pennsylvania and flowed northward into New York. About five miles after merging with the Canisteo River, the Tioga River confluenced with the Cohocton River flowing from the north to form the Chemung River.

Near this confluence, the fleeing white men had to be wary of the village of Teaogo. Employing the previous tactics, they passed the village unimpeded.

The Chemung River was a large transportation artery for the Iroquois long before the appearance of white men in North America. It was a relatively large river approximately forty-five miles long that flowed through a wide valley farmed extensively by the Iroquois and bordered by low, heavily forested mountains before emptying into the Susquehanna.

General Sullivan had laid waste to the villages and farmland in this area during the late summer and early fall of 1779. Some of the area had been resurrected, but for the most part, it still showed the effects of Sullivan's scorched earth policy. Due to the destruction of the area, the population had diminished, lessening the threat of detection for Groninger and Reigert.

Shortly after passing the nearly abandoned village of Teaogo and before the two rafters had to deal with the larger village of Kanawaholla, they spotted an empty bark canoe floating near the south bank.

"Well, well," John said. "It looks like we are about to receive an early Christmas gift. Now we'll be able to travel much faster, even if our paddles aren't in very good shape."

"Not only that, it will be much safer and drier," Leonard agreed.

"I'm not sure of that safer part. I've seen some white men go for an unintentional swim when they don't have the skills to handle one of these."

"We'll learn quickly. I've done enough swimming the last few nights."

The Chemung River was now relatively wide and flat, but blessed with a strong current which aided the two escapees. Its modest gradient flowed over gentle and well-spaced riffles which offered no real threat to the novice paddlers. With these advantages, the canoeists began to float much faster than they had upon the raft on the Canisteo and Tioga Rivers.

At the mouth of the Newtown Creek was located the relatively active Cayuga village of Kanawaholla. The name of this village signifies "A-Head-Stuck-on-A-Pole."

To avoid detection, John and Leonard decided to paddle to the south bank and hide the canoe and themselves until nightfall. When the village bedded down for the night, the men reentered the river. They hugged the right shoreline, lay hidden in the bottom of the canoe, and allowed the strong current between the larger of the two islands and the southern shore to take them downriver.

They had no time to rest; about five miles south of Kanawaholla they came upon the slightly restored village of Newtown, which had been the scene of a battle in which the entire force of Iroquois, British, and Tories had been put to full flight. Newtown had been plundered and reduced to a pile of ashes by Sullivan's troops.

Cautiously, the two men steered the canoe past Newtown and around Baldwin Island and two smaller islands downriver from the village. This was a challenge in the dark, but disaster was avoided, and they continued towards the Seneca village of Chemung.

In the Iroquois language, Chemung means "Big Horn" or "Horn in the Water." Chemung had been a sizeable village until August 14, 1779. It was comprised of nearly forty well-constructed, hewn-timber and log homes and as many as fifty or more large wigwams. On that morning in 1779, the Senecas abandoned their village and avoided a major skirmish with Sullivan's forces. The entire village was consumed in a conflagration, and all its grain and vegetable fields were destroyed.

The men used extreme caution in floating through this region, because the Senecas had returned to the area hoping to raise crops in abundance, as they had done before Sullivan's invasion. Ahead were the resurrected remains of Tioga and Queen Esther's Town, where the Chemung flows into the Susquehanna.

Nearly a dozen miles downriver, on a narrow peninsula formed by the junction of the Chemung and Susquehanna Rivers was Tioga, one of the most important villages of the Iroquois until the fall of 1778. In August of 1779, Sullivan and Clinton had rendezvoused before they turned north to lay waste to the Iroquois countryside.

Unbeknownst to Reigert and Groninger, John Johnson's Royal Greens and Joseph Brant's Indians were again sweeping up and down the Mohawk Valley and the Upper Susquehanna Valley, burning and destroying everything in their path. Knowledge of this activity would have had no effect on their attempts to return home.

The canoe slipped noiselessly past Tioga on the peninsula and Queen Esther's Town on the western shore of the Susquehanna. Colonel Thomas Hartley had destroyed Queen Esther's Town and Tioga in the fall of 1778. These two villages had been the staging areas for Colonel John Butler prior to his invasion of the Wyoming Valley settlements.

The fragile canoe floated into a treacherous section of the Susquehanna. The river was encumbered with an array of small islands that created deceptive crosscurrents, especially where the currents rejoined at the downriver end of the islands. The young canoeists learned the hard way, by trial and error, and somehow survived.

After spending their first night on the western shore of the Susquehanna, they came upon a larger island, aptly named Bald Eagle Island. Here, as when Hartley and, later, Sullivan had moved against the Iroquois, nested several bald eagles.

Then disaster struck. Maybe the men had become too complacent or overconfident about their improving canoeing skills, but whatever the reason, they were now in big trouble. As they were passing under a grove of trees with overhanging limbs while looking for a safe and easy place to land to look for food, Reigert was struck by a tree limb and knocked overboard. Leonard struggled to maintain his balance and keep the canoe afloat, but the current took hold of the stern and the boat went over, spilling Leonard into the swift current to join John. All they could do was fight their way to shore and safety, and sadly watch the canoe disappear into the undercurrent of the mighty Susquehanna.

After spending the night on the western shore, they struck out on foot. Because they were no longer able to use the river's current as an easy conduit to the safety of Fort Augusta, their journey decelerated and took a tremendous toll on their energy and strength. They were consuming enormous amounts of calories, and their progress became laborious.

The banks of the Susquehanna did not possess much in the way of forage this early in the year. The men used their knives to dig for roots, but even what they managed to scavenge didn't do much to satisfy their expanding appetites.

They arrived at the mouth of a small creek and followed it for a few hundred yards. Luck was with them, for they were able to spear several small shad with a pole they had sharpened with a knife. Their spirits buoyed, they headed downriver on foot once again.

At first this section of the Susquehanna flowed through a mile-wide valley bordered by low mountains. Soon the mountains gained in height, and the valley began to narrow and deepen like a canyon. Sandstone-tiered cliffs towered over the great bends.

Between the mouths of Sugar Creek and Towanda Creek were two islands. In a narrow channel between the two islands, good fortune smiled upon Leonard and John. Bobbing along in a small eddy was a dug-out canoe about fifteen feet in length. The men quickly swam out to the canoe and clambered abroad, exhausted by their efforts.

Nearly three miles later, they floated past the mouth of Wysox Creek. Another three miles later brought them to an area known as Standing Stone. Sometime long ago, a huge, elongated rock had plunged down the mountain, flattening all the vegetation in its path, and embedded itself upright at the river's shore. A portion of the stone, about three feet thick, fourteen feet wide, and nearly twenty feet high, protruded out of the water—an impressive sight.

The men considered spending the night at this location, but wondered if it was a better strategy to float at night. In the end, they gave in to their exhaustion. After floating only about two miles, they went ashore, hid their canoe, and collapsed in the vegetation high on the bank.

Not wanting to waste a whole day waiting for nightfall, they commenced their float the next day. Shortly, the river made two large bends before they came to the village of Wyalusing at the mouth of Wyalusing Creek. This was the site of a former Moravian mission known as Friedenshuetten, established by David Zeisberger in 1756 and abandoned in 1772. This had previously served as a meetingplace for hostile Indians and Tories. Both Colonel Hartley and General Sullivan had occupied the remains of the village.

About two miles below Wyalusing, Sugar Run Creek joins the waters of the Susquehanna. In this area the two canoeists received a tremendous shakeup. Neither of the men was concentrating on his surroundings. Suddenly they heard shrill voices coming from the eastern shore of the river. They immediately braced right toward the west bank. Once they beached the canoe, they jumped out, dragged it up the bank, and scrambled for cover in nearby vegetation.

The canoe had just barely been concealed when three canoes filled with braves paddled briskly against the current near the eastern shore. The native canoeists didn't appear to have seen the white men, for they quickly paddled out of sight.

"That's it," Leonard declared. "We're back to traveling at night. We might go slower, but at least we aren't as apt to have company on the river."

"I'm with you," John said. "That was too close for comfort." The two men lay beside their canoe for a lengthy period before they had enough confidence to begin their daily foraging for food. After consuming their unappetizing meal of bitter roots, the two dropped into an exhausted sleep.

That night, when they returned to the water, the Susquehanna made a huge bend to the east, then another to the west immediately. The river continued its serpentine course until it was joined by the Lackawanna River.

Several nights later the canoeists floated past the mouth of the Lackawanna River and Scovell Island. Then they glided between the Jenkins's Fort, a stockade constructed in 1776 above the west bank, and Pittston Fort, nearly opposite. Both these forts, along with Wintermoot's Fort, had fallen to the Indians in July of 1778. When John and Leonard drifted between these forts, they failed to notice that efforts were underway to restore and repopulate these stockades. Apparently, the smoke from the fires within the stockade did not descend to the river.

A series of islands presented some challenges to the men's paddling skills. One of these islands, Monocanock Island, was quite large. The men spent a day resting deep within the foliage of this island. That night they floated by the walls of Forty Fort, which stood on the high west bank where it had a commanding view of the river. Begun in 1770, it was surrendered to the enemy on July 4, 1778. It was not destroyed and was occupied by this time.

A few miles later they whisked past the remains of Wilkes-Barre Fort, which had been abandoned and destroyed during the attacks in the Wyoming Valley in July 1778. This fort had been situated on the east bank of the river.

This section of the river flowed southwestward and was joined by Harvey's Creek below the former village of Nanticoke. In this vicinity the canoe was bounced and jolted over a chain of wavelets called Nanticoke Falls. Farther along, steep and forested mountains escorted the river past Shickshinny, Wapwallopen, and Nescopeck.

At Nescopeck the men were again challenged when they came upon a huge drop in the river that amounted to an actual falls. The noise from the drop warned them of an abrupt change in the current. They made the wise choice to beach the canoe and inspect the terrain. They chose to float down a less dangerous channel near the west bank of the river, and with some tricky maneuvering they managed to stay afloat.

Just below Nescopeck, disaster struck again. Out of nowhere, without any warning, a severe storm engulfed the river. One moment there was no breeze; the leaves on the trees were barely stirring. Then a tremendous gust of wind swept down the river, accompanied by a horrendous crashing of thunder. All along the banks the wind snapped trees and scattered limbs and branches down on the river and the canoe. John and Leonard paddled with all their might to reach the protection of trees overhanging the west bank of the river.

Suddenly a limb from a tree broke off and struck Leonard in the left calf, embedding itself in his flesh and muscle. The pain, though not immediate, quickly became agonizing. The two men labored to remove the huge splinter of wood. Once they succeeded, blood oozed out from the wound and covered the floor of the canoe. Reigert tore a segment off his ragged shirt, soaked it in water, and tried to clean out the throbbing wound. The men packed the lacerated calf in a poultice of mud like one they had seen Tatamee apply on a similar wound. Then they wrapped the wound with the tattered remains of the shirt.

Leonard was in horrific pain through the rest of the night and into the next day. He could put no weight on his leg, because it began to swell and turn a pale, sickly white. He soon developed a fever. Obviously he was unable to forage for food. John returned from scavenging with a meager stock of tea-berries and sassafras leaves. He looked over at Leonard and said matter-of-factly, "You're not going to survive, so I'm not wasting food on you."

Leonard quickly became so weak and disoriented that he could no longer share the paddling. Reigert decided not to wait until the next nightfall, but to shove out into the current and paddle at his own pace.

By dusk, Reigert was completely exhausted and not as cautious as he should have been. He headed for a location on the western shore that looked promising as a haven of sleep for the night, for a large rock jutted out towards the shore. John beached the canoe and struggled to aid Leonard in dragging himself under the rock.

They had barely reached the rock shelter when the nightmarish sound of a highly agitated rattlesnake broke the silence. Both men reacted as one and scrambled and crawled out of the overhang and back into the safety of the canoe. John shoved them off into the current, and they drifted throughout the night.

John was now too exhausted to care anymore, and Leonard was so engulfed by hunger and fever that he was delirious and unconscious. When daylight sifted into the valley the next morning, several inhabitants of Fort Augusta sighted the canoe and assumed it was unoccupied, for it was drifting aimlessly down the river.

Fortunately for Reigert and Groninger, two young boys decided that it might be worth their efforts to bring the canoe ashore. The youths were astonished when they grabbed the craft by its bow and observed two white men sprawled on its floor.

With great effort the boys managed to beach the canoe. They immediately broke the news of their find to their elders. the two lucky fugitives from Chenussio were back in civilization and not too far from home.

Reigert recovered quickly from his ordeal and was on his way home within a few days. Leonard, on the other hand, almost succumbed to his wound, along with dehydration and malnourishment. It took three days for the fever to break, and then he regained consciousness and began his way back to good health and robustness.

Everyone rejoiced at Reigert and Leonard's successful escape and return to civilization. While Leonard was being treated by the good people of Fort Augusta, a courier was sent to Deerstown and the Buffalo Creek Valley to inform his family of his appearance at the fort and his disabled condition. While he convalesced, his family arrived to return him to the valley once he was able to travel.

One day, as Leonard was describing to an audience his treatment by his captors, one of the men interrupted him. "Son, you don't know how close you were to being recaptured or, worse yet, shot and killed by the savages. Johan Swartz left this fort on horseback and headed upriver the very morning you turned up here at the fort. A day later he was found shot and scalped just about two miles from here."

Joseph, Leonard's brother, joined his father, Leonard Sr., and his mother, Elizabeth Deishman Groninger, in escorting the younger Leonard back to their home in the Buffalo Valley near Deerstown.

Joseph filled Leonard in on many of the happenings in the valley that occurred while Leonard was in captivity. "One thing you will have to adjust to is that right after you were captured, the Indians burned our cabin to the ground. Our new home is built very close to the old site, and you'll notice that the new version is an improvement."

The Groningers returned to Buffalo Valley where the elder Leonard would live out the rest of his days. Young Leonard would eventually meet a young German maiden, Maria Barbara May, and make her his wife in 1788.

CHAPTER FORTY SIX

The End of the War

In Cumberland County in August of 1780, it was assumed that due to favorable weather and rainfall, there would be a plentiful harvest in the county, especially of corn and fruit. Adam Smith, the commander of the armed forces in Carlisle, called for volunteers on the north side of the Blue Mountain to assist the inhabitants of areas in distress while they attempted to save their harvest in the late summer of 1780.

One of Smith's major concerns was that the frequent Indian activity, which had led to a great loss of manpower among the disbursed militia, would cause many of the remaining militia members to ignore his orders to turn out and defend the frontier country. Cumberland County also faced a scarcity of ammunition. And it was difficult to secure wagons, teams, and wagon masters to transport sufficient quantity of lead, flints, and powder. Money to pay for these desperately needed supplies was another challenge for Smith.

The settlers of the Juniata Valley, including the northern sections of Cumberland County, were much troubled by Indians as late as 1780.

The following is a copy of an agreement relative to protecting the frontier:

May 21, 1780

Terms proposed to the freemen of this company for granting some assistance to our frontier, as follows, viz: That four men be raised immediately, and paid by this old way, per month, during the time they shall be in actual service, and also provisions. The time they shall engage to serve, one month, and the method for paying the men aforesaid shall be by levying a proportionable tax on all and singular the taxable property of each person residing within the bounds of Captain Minteer's company: and if any person shall so far forget his duty as to refuse complying with his brethren in the aforesaid necessary proposals, he shall be deemed an enemy to his country, and be debarred from the privileges of a subject of this State by being excluded the benefits of all tradesmen working for him, such as millers, smiths, &c. [16]

We, the subscribers, do approve of the above proposals, and bind ourselves by these presents to the performance of and compliance with the same. In witness whereof we have hereunto set our hands this 21st Day of May 1780. N.B.— Wheat to be 51, Rye and Corn 31 per bushel. We also agree that Captain Minteer's company shall meet on Wednesday next, at William Sharon's.[17]

The war on Pennsylvania's frontier did not change much as the struggle dragged on. However, beginning in late 1778, much of the focus of the war moved to the southern states; thus, this stage of the Revolution is often referred to as the southern phase. The arrival of the French fleet in 1778 to aid the Americans drove the British from Philadelphia. The British hoped for strong Loyalist support in the South. They were immediately victorious at Savannah, Georgia; Charleston, South Carolina; and Camden, South Carolina.

The turning point of the southern phase occurred in October of 1780, when an army of backwoodsmen overwhelmed a thousand Loyalists at King's Mountain, North Carolina. This was followed by another defeat of the British at Cowpens in January of 1781.

The Americans under General Nathanael Greene maneuvered the British army under Lord Cornwallis northward through North Carolina, pushing him farther away from his supply base at Charleston. While the Americans were turning the tide in the South, beginning in 1779, General George Rogers Clark led a small band of resolute frontiersmen down the Ohio River and captured the British outposts of Kaskaskia, Cahokia, and Vincennes. This broke the power of Colonel Henry "The Hairbuyer" Hamilton, and essentially brought the Ohio Country under American rule, although England continued to control a few posts on the Great Lakes.

George Washington feigned an attack on New York City; then, with lightning speed, he moved nearly sixteen thousand troops from New York, across New Jersey to boats that ferried them to Virginia. While Washington was moving his troops southward, French Adm. François de Grasse held off the British fleet at the mouth of the Chesapeake Bay, which could not relieve Cornwallis from the trap.

The combined French and American forces under Rochambeau and Washington attacked and isolated the British army at Yorktown, Virginia. On October 19, 1781, seven thousand British soldiers became prisoners of war as their commander sent General Charles O'Hara to surrender on behalf of Cornwallis who allegedly was ill.

The jubilant news of the surrender of Cornwallis was carried by courier to the Congress at Philadelphia and arrived there on October 23. This significant information was rapidly spread throughout Pennsylvania and the rest of the new states. The realization that the inhabitants of the long-suffering colonies, now states, were independent would not occur immediately.

On the frontier the news circulated from one militia company to another, from Carlisle across the mountains. It took nearly two weeks until the news reached the Tuscarora Valley. It spread from cabin to cabin, from farm to farm, like wildfire. Like so many times in the short history of the valley, the Lower Presbyterian Church became the center for a wondrous victory celebration.

The residents of the valley arrived at the log church in an ecstatic mood. At the beginning of the festivities, Reverend Hugh Magill addressed the tumultuous throng, some whom had already begun their celebrating by imbibing several good-sized mugs of flavorsome liquor that had recently been squeezed from this fall's abundant corn crop:

> This is a most glorious day for our new nation. The word that we have received from the siege at Yorktown on the shores of Virginia is what we have been praying and hoping for since the first shot heard round the world in April of 1775. The times that try men's souls have ended.
>
> The theme from the ramparts at Yorktown is "the world turned upside down," and for the British, their world is exactly that. General Washington has exhibited the brilliance of his strategic skills in combining a land and sea offensive to force Lord Cornwallis to surrender.
>
> I now ask all of you to bow your heads in a prayer of thanksgiving and praise to the Lord our God for making it possible for our independence to become a reality.
>
> Dear Lord, we your humble servants of this beautiful valley reverently thank you for guiding us through these turbulent and strife-ridden times. We all are aware that nothing is possible without your guidance and blessing. Without your guiding hand General Washington and his staff would not have been able to outwit the British hierarchy and achieve our tremendous victory.
>
> We offer our thanks to you for enabling the Continental Congress to secure the financial resources that were required to continue the struggle, and the alliance with France that helped to change the tide. We thank you for giving us the strength and will-power to carry on the fight, sometimes against seemingly overwhelming odds.
>
> Now that peace appears to be with us, we ask that you guide our government leaders in establishing a great republic in which we have no privileged classes or organizations. That all men are truly equal. Make us a God-loving and God-fearing nation that will spread your ideas and values to all men everywhere.
>
> Again, we offer our thanks for leading us to victory and independence!

A spontaneous and thunderous "amen" reverberated through the tranquility of the leafless forests and rebounded off the Herringbone Ridge just to the north.

Despite all the celebrating, reality still prevailed among some of the valley's citizens.

Captain Daniel McClelland pointed out to all who would listen (and many didn't want to hear any discouraging news on this day of festivity), "We are going to have to continue to keep an army in the field. The Loyalists and British army located in the South are not about to give up so easily or quickly. Greene and his men still face some tough times."

Major John Elliot chimed in, "Things are far from over here on the frontier. It could be years before we enjoy real peace here in the Juniata Valley. The Tories and the Indians are not going to accept the loss of their lands just because of a ceremony down in Virginia. Raiding and plundering have been a way of life for the Indians for so long that it will take a complete change in their lifestyles to quell their warlike nature."

Elliot noticed Robert Taylor listening with keen interest. "Major Taylor, what is your take on the frontier situation?"

"I agree with you, John. British traders will continue to support the Indians in their resistance to American settlement. The spirit of battle will not be easily extinguished on the frontier. It will continue to flame fiercely to our west, especially in Ohio and Kentucky. This could spill over into the Juniata Valley at any time. We will have to remain vigilant for some time to come."

These revelations did nothing to dampen the festive atmosphere of the autumn day.

The reveling and rejoicing continued until the sun began to set behind the ridge. Numerous merrymakers utilized pine-pitch-covered pole torches to light their way back to their cabins and farms. Morning came too soon for many of those who had imbibed in the home-distilled whiskey that made the rounds at the celebration. Headaches and turbulent stomachs were common complaints throughout the Tuscarora Valley.

CHAPTER FORTY SEVEN

The War Continues on the Frontier

Cornwallis's surrender of his army in Virginia did not end the hostilities; General Nathanael Green continued his campaign against the British and Tories in the South. By December 9, 1781, the British were confined mostly to Savannah and Charleston. They evacuated from Savannah on July 11, 1782, and from Charleston on December 14, 1782. Green moved his army into Charleston where, in August 1783 he received the good news about the signing of the Treaty of Paris of 1783.

The war continued on the frontier as well. The settlers of upstate New York discovered that General John Sullivan's campaign of destruction in the summer and early fall of 1779 had merely inflamed the Indians. After Colonel Daniel Brodhead had carried out a month-long campaign against the Indians of the Allegheny valley in 1780, Sir John Johnson and Joseph Brant descended upon the Scoharie Valley and Mohawk River Valley, burning every American house or building in their path.

General Robert Van Rensselaer and Colonel Marianus Willett carried out skillful and vigorous attacks against the Tories and Indians. When Walter Butler was fatally wounded, the raiders dispersed. Joseph Brant was unsuccessful in recruiting a segment of Delawares known as the Moravian Indians, because they had been Christianized by Moravian missionaries. The British authorities ordered the Moravian Indians to move to the Ohio County and by early 1782, due to a winter famine, the Moravian Indians had settled on the Tuscarawas River.

Unfortunately for the Moravian Indians, the Mohawks and Delawares had just concluded a brutal campaign against the

Americans. Colonel David Williamson was dispatched by Colonel Brodhead to punish the raiders. Williamson attacked the Moravian Indians at Gnadenhutten, Ohio, believing that they had participated in raids in the area. There was no resistance, and the Indians surrendered with no hostile action.

Williamson explained to the Indians, "We are going to bind your wrists and take you to Fort Pitt where you will be protected from any harm. I have sent runners to Salem to bring those missionary Indians here to join us in our journey to Pitt."

About fifty natives arrived from Salem, and their wrists were also bound.

The frontiersmen then decided that the whole population should be executed. In the morning Williamson indicated that his plans for the Indians had changed. He announced to the nearly one hundred Christian Indians, "Since your Delaware brothers have wreaked havoc on our Allegheny and Ohio frontier, killing and destroying everything in their path, all of you will be put to death as punishment for what they have done."

On March 8, 1782, the captive men were led to the cooper shop, where they were whacked to death with tomahawks and mallets. The women and children were led into the church and suffered the same fate. Two boys managed to escape and spread word of the massacre. The Indians were outraged at Williamson's unjustified execution of these innocent, defenseless Christianized Indians, and they answered with a massive retaliation against the American frontier.

Colonel William Crawford responded to the Indian's massive vengeance raids by launching the purported Second Moravian Campaign to eliminate hostile Indian settlements. Crawford's force was a ragtag rabble, a disorderly command. The unruly command was ambushed by a force of Delawares and Shawnees, and the undisciplined militia panicked, broke ranks, and fled from the battlefield.

The breakdown of discipline led to the death or capture of about fifty men and the wounding of another twenty-eight. Among those captured was Colonel William Crawford. Captain

Pipe, or Hopocan, was the leader of the band of Delawares that captured him. Captain Pipe matter-of-factly pronounced the colonel's fate: "The white dog will be burned at the stake."

Crawford's only hope of escaping his death sentence was to appeal to his old friend, the Delaware chief Wingenund. The chief dashed any of Crawford's hopes. "It is not within my power to spare your life. If you had not been with that murderer of women and children, Williamson, I might be able to intercede. It is our belief that you have traveled here to commit more outrages against our people. It is our will that you must pay the extreme penalty for what Williamson has committed against our people. Enough has been said. You will die as prescribed by Hopocan."

With tears streaking down his cheeks, the old chief turned and left the scene so that he would not have to witness the terrible death of his old friend. Also about to witness this horrible spectacle was Simon Girty, at one time a close friend of Crawford. By this time Simon Girty had earned the reputation as the "White Savage." Since his desertion to the British in 1778, he had become a blood-thirsty raider of the American frontier.

The Moravian missionary the Reverend John Heckewelder described Girty in this manner: "Never before did any of us hear the like oaths, or know anybody to rave like him. He appeared like a host of evil spirits.... No Indian we had ever seen drunk would have been a match for him." Others who came in contact with Girty saw him as a "wild beast in human form," or "the very picture of a villain."

On June 11, 1782, Colonel William Crawford met his end in a most gruesome manner. He was tied to a pole by a long rope. Then his tormenters gleefully shot charge after charge of gunpowder into his body. Two powerful braves held his head, as a third severed his ears with two swift slices of his knife. Several other braves apparently enjoyed running the points of their knives across the colonel's chest, down his back, legs, and arms, causing him to bleed profusely. Next they pressed burned splints and coals against his skin.

By this time, Crawford was in excruciating pain, and he

began to cry, begging his old friend, Simon Girty, "Please, please have mercy on me. Put me out of my misery. Please take your rifle and shoot me in the head. Please…please…"

Simon Girty merely grinned and continued to enjoy the militiaman's continuing agony, which persisted for nearly four hours before Crawford finally fell unconscious. Then his scalp was ripped off his head and burning coals were poured on his bleeding skull. Somehow he staggered to his feet, took several unsteady steps, emitted a screeching groan, and gave up his fight for life.

William Crawford's mutilated corpse was pulled back to the base of the pole, and the embers of the fire were stirred up and more tinder and dry wood were placed under and over the body. Soon the conflagration consumed what remained of the colonel.

When the flames had done their best to turn Crawford's remains to ashes, Simon Girty turned away from the smoke and ashes with a fiendish sneer.

When the news of William Crawford's horrific death and Simon Girty's role in it filtered back to Cumberland County, many people were aghast that one of their own could be involved in such a horrific undertaking.

Robert Taylor shook his head in disbelief. "I knew when I first met the Girty boys that some of them would be trouble. To turn against your own people and fight for the British like Simon, James, and George did is one thing, but to participate in the slow roasting to death of a friend is unspeakable, completely appalling. Someday Simon Girty should be held accountable for such an abominable and repugnant perpetration. Hopefully, his soul will never know any rest."

Indian outrages continued in Western and Central Pennsylvania throughout 1782. On May 13, 1782, Barnard Dougherty wrote from Standing Stone to President William Moore of Pennsylvania's Supreme Executive Council concerning the state of affairs on the Central Pennsylvania frontier:

I beg leave to inform your excellency that a company of

Cumberland County militia, consisting of thirty-five men, arrived here yesterday on their way to Frankstown garrison, where they were joined by Captain Boyd's ranging company. The people in the frontiers of this county are mostly fled from their habitations. Also it is strongly rumored here that depredations have been committed in Penn's Valley, and that upwards of twenty of the militia have fallen. [18]

Afterwards, on May 18, Dougherty sent a second message to President Moore from Bedford, stating that unless money was forthcoming for paying the militia, the garrison at Frankstown "must inevitably be evacuated."[19]

The victory at Yorktown did little to alter or alleviate the pressure from the Indians on the frontier. Many people of the Central and Western Pennsylvania frontier were greatly alarmed over the massacre of the Moravian Delawares at Gnadenhutten, suspecting that the natives would resume their vigorous and incessant depredations against the white population in the region in retaliation for the vile actions of Colonel David Williamson.

Later, George Rogers Clark gathered a substantial militia force and pursued the Indians. The Indians eluded Clark and his men, so to drive home Clark's point, the militia destroyed many Shawnee towns and their vital stores of corn. This led to starvation and famine during the winter of 1782–83, which caused the Indians to halt their raiding of the frontier until springtime.

In 1783, Arthur Lee journeyed to Pittsburg, and described the scene:

Pittsburg is inhabited almost entirely by Scots and Irish, who live in paltry houses and are as dirty as in the north of Ireland, or even in Scotland. There is a great deal of small trade carried on; the goods being brought in at the vast expense of 45 shillings per cwt., from Philadelphia and Baltimore. The place, I believe, will never be very considerable.

With the signing of the peace treaty, England ceded the Old Northwest region to the United States, which was really under the control of the natives. The treaty did not end Indian-white warfare in this frontier area, but it did bring temporary peace to a region where the ravages of war had been cruelly felt.

The British and American commissioners who drafted and signed the Treaty of Paris in 1783 stated nothing about the Indians and their problems. The Indians, in turn, ignored the provisions of the Treaty of Paris. To further confuse matters, the Indians became a pawn in the struggle between the new national government and the states for the control of Indian affairs.

The land between the Appalachians and Mississippi River would not be secured from Indian's transgressions until after the War of 1812. The British traders would continue to support the Indians in their resistance to American migration and settlement. The Indians learned the hard way that the passage in the Declaration of Independence, "that all men are created equal," did not apply to the natives.

CHAPTER FORTY EIGHT

Our New Government

On May 10, 1775, delegates from twelve colonies, excluding Georgia, met in a Second Continental Congress at the State House in Philadelphia. This was a revolutionary body that assumed the functions of a national government and declared that the thirteen colonies were independent. It also directed the joint efforts of the thirteen colonies through the six years of war.

Congress's governmental functions included raising an army and navy, commissioning George Washington as commander in chief, exercising executive authority, advising the colonies in the organization of separate state governments, and drafting the Articles of Confederation. Congress also appointed ministers to foreign nations, signed a military alliance with France, and raised funds by printing paper currency and by borrowing.

The creators of the new American government during the Revolutionary War were wary of giving too much power to a central government. The Revolution was being fought to eliminate the tyranny of a similar government.

In 1777, the Second Continental Congress adopted the Articles of Confederation, which can be considered the first constitution of the United States. It was not ratified until 1781, because Maryland withheld ratification until all states having claims to portions of the Northwest Territory agreed to transfer these claims to the new central government. The Articles of Confederation created a "firm league of friendship" and not a united nation with a strong central government.

The states shared their sovereignty with a central Congress in which each state had one vote. Congress was charged with declaring war, making peace, conducting foreign policy, maintaining an army and navy, and other necessary responsibilities. Congress lacked the power to levy taxes or control commerce. The document did not create an executive or judicial branch. Therefore, Congress had no means of enforcing the laws or directives it passed and had no means of interpreting the laws.

How the Articles of Confederation held the thirteen newly formed states together during the course of the Revolution was almost miraculous. The government managed to bring the Revolutionary War to a successful close, and it concluded a very favorable treaty of peace.

The Treaty of Paris was ratified and formally signed on September 3, 1783. Under the terms of this treaty, Great Britain recognized the independence of the United States, acknowledged its boundaries, and ceded all English territory up to the Mississippi River and south of the Great Lakes. It gave Americans the right to fish off the banks of Newfoundland and Nova Scotia. All legal debts would be honored by each country. The Mississippi River would be open to navigation by the United States and Britain. All remaining British troops would evacuate the territory of the United States. Loyalists whose property had been confiscated during the war by the Americans would be compensated.

The news of the treaty caused mixed reactions in the Tuscarora Valley. John Patton was elated over the extension of the new nation's western boundary to the Mississippi River. "At least we aren't restricted in moving westward into the Ohio Territory like we were under the Proclamation of 1763. Right now the only power to stop us moving there will be the natives."

Joseph Gordon was unhappy with the section of the treaty that concerned the property of the Tories or Loyalists. "I can't believe Ben Franklin, John Adams, and John Jay allowed that term to be included in the treaty," he complained. "Why shouldn't their property be confiscated? They made the choice to continue to support King George. We can't help it if they chose the losing side. Now, I don't believe in lynching Tories like they did in the South, or tarring and feathering them as performed in New Jersey, but I can't support restoration of confiscated property or compensating Loyalists for their losses."

"I agree with you, Joseph," Robert Taylor said, adding, "Nor can I support allowing previously disqualified Tories to regain the right to vote, hold public office, or practice law. I guess we have to examine what Ben Franklin wrote several months ago: 'In my opinion, there never was a good war or a bad peace.' In time, maybe we will find that Ben was correct in his assessment."

Eventually the spirit of moderation spread throughout the states. It took time to heal the wounds left by the war. In a few years many of those who had supported the Crown were forgiven by their neighbors; even Jacob Hare returned and had his property restored to him, although nothing could be done to restore his ears.

One major success in asserting the authority of the national government under the Articles of Confederation was the enactment of the Northwest Ordinance on June 13, 1787. This measure specified how territories and states were to be formed from the western lands known as the Northwest Territory won during the Revolution.

The close of the Revolutionary War removed the common danger that had forced the thirteen states to cooperate to achieve victory and independence. Immediately after the war there followed a critical period during which local animosities and economic and political chaos threatened to destroy the newly formed nation. The relationship between the thirteen states was permeated with petty jealousies and quarrels.

The fundamental defects in the Articles of Confederation and the unstable relationship among the states contributed to economic and political weakness and to impotence in the conduct of foreign affairs. Unable to tax, Congress was unable to meet current expenses or to pay interest on the national debt.

Since the government was unable to execute or enforce laws, it was powerless to quell riots staged by disgruntled soldiers in 1783. The most famous incident occurred in Massachusetts in 1786.

The years from 1783 to 1787 were filled with economic problems, and farmers, small retailers, laboring men, and debtors often found themselves unable to meet their financial obligations. The possessions of these indebted people passed into the hands of tax gatherers and creditors through foreclosure and seizure, and sometimes the people themselves were thrown into prison.

In some cases, drastic measures were taken, sometimes leading to acts of violence. In Windsor and Rutland Counties in Vermont, mobs tried to prevent courts from holding sessions. At Plymouth, New Hampshire, the courthouse was burned. In Rhode Island the struggle over paper money produced a significant judicial decision which became the forerunner of the principle of judicial review.

A major uprising flared in western Massachusetts in 1786. In that year a new tax of twenty dollars for every household of five was instituted to help pay off the state's Revolutionary War debts. This tax fell heavily on the farmers, and in many cases the amount was more than what many could afford to pay. As a result, thousands of debtors lost everything, and the jails overflowed with prisoners confined for debt.

Beginning in August, insurgents seized courthouses, prevented courts from sitting, or forced them to adjourn in a number of towns throughout Massachusetts. When an insurgent force led by Daniel Shays, who had fought at Lexington, Bunker Hill, Saratoga, and Stony Point, forced the adjournment of the court at Springfield, the governor dispatched General Benjamin Lincoln with a force of four thousand troops to quell the rebellion.

Several skirmishes followed, with the loss of three lives, but Lincoln was successful in quashing the uprising by February 4, 1787. The creditor class wanted the rebels to be severely punished, and Daniel Shays was condemned to death. Later the legislature granted amnesty to all those involved, including Shays, who was pardoned.

Law and order had triumphed, but many saw that the government of the United States was really a government in name only. There was now a strong movement to create a stronger central government.

For residents of the Tuscarora Valley, civil strife in other areas of the new nation was accepted as a way of life. Some of the inhabitants of the valley had served in the Continental Army and had seen firsthand the effects of the Continental Congress's inability to provide proper clothing and food or compensation for the soldiers.

There was a general grumbling about Pennsylvania levying a tariff on goods brought into the state from other states, with a higher tariff yet on goods imported from Britain post war, thus increasing the cost of those goods. Inflation ran rampant, taking a terrible toll on the citizens of the frontier, and taxes jumped at alarming rates.

After church services on a Sunday late in March, a serious discussion ensued concerning the direction the nation was headed under the Congress of the Articles of Confederation.

Robert Taylor observed, "It appears that the states are going in thirteen separate ways. I've been told that you should not accept money issued from another state; most of it is worthless. I can see why Daniel Shays and his followers took the law into their own hands; it wouldn't take much for similar action to take place in Pennsylvania. It appears that it is time to replace the Articles with a different form of government, or before we know it, all our sacrifices in winning independence will have been in vain."

Clement Horrell commented, "I don't know what is wrong with some people. They should be cheerfully repaying their own private debts and contributing their portion to support our government."

"It appears that some of those leaders in New England are nothing but sots or bankrupts that have gambled away their property," added William Beale.

"I think that they ought to release all imprisoned debtors," James Chambers declared. "It makes no sense to me to place a man in jail for nonpayment of debts. How will you ever get your money from a man if he's in jail? Imprisonment seems counterproductive to me."

Horrell joined back in. "Something has to be done to redress debtors' grievances and at the same time protect the courts. We just can't allow people to resort to anarchy. We need a strong central government, but not so powerful that it would lead to tyranny."

While these men were discussing those problems, the Congress of the Confederation requested that the states send delegates to a convention in Philadelphia to revise the national government.

Fifty-five men attended the meetings at Philadelphia, which were scheduled to begin on May 14, 1787, but didn't commence until May 25. These men were highly competent, and many of them had already distinguished themselves in the service of their respective states.

Pennsylvania's delegation was an elite group that represented the propertied interests of the state. Benjamin Franklin led Pennsylvania's representation. Other outstanding Pennsylvanians were James Wilson, Gouverneur Morris, Thomas Mifflin, Robert Morris, Jared Ingersoll, Thomas Fitzsimons, and George Clymer.

Throughout the hot, humid summer, the delegates held secret deliberations and did not complete their task until September 17. They soon recognized that only a whole new plan of national government would give the thirteen states the effective government they needed.

The new document that became the Constitution was a bundle of compromises. The major compromises provided for a president to be named by a college of electors; a Congress of two houses; and a Supreme Court and such inferior courts as Congress might create.

The strengths of the new federal government were defined in the powers given to the Congress. Particularly important were such powers as taxation, control of the army and navy, regulation of interstate and foreign commerce, and supervision of foreign relations. The Constitution limited the power of the states in some areas and denied certain powers to the states completely.

Benjamin Franklin, summing up the situation, declared, "It was the best we could do at the time." Franklin and his fellow delegates from Pennsylvania favored adoption of the new Constitution, and they became known as Federalists. Those opposed to adoption became known as Anti-Federalists.

In the hinterlands of Pennsylvania, the Constitution was looked upon with great suspicion, and most of the delegates from the less settled counties, such as Cumberland County, opposed ratification of the document.

In the Tuscarora Valley, as elsewhere, the battle for ratification was a hot topic of discussion during the autumn of 1787.

Charles Stewart spoke against the ratification. "I oppose the new Constitution simply because it was secretly fashioned by the representatives of a propertied aristocracy. All those men have deliberately set out to feather their own nests."

"You are absolutely correct," agreed William Maclay. "Their holdings are going to sharply increase in value under a strong central government."

"I look at the new document in a different manner," Robert Taylor stated. "First, the delegates went beyond their powers in writing a new framework of government. They gave the national government far too much power and reduced the states to dependent provinces. The rights of man were deemphasized, while property rights were enhanced. But more important, the document makes no attempt to provide a bill of rights to protect the average citizen against the type of tyranny we just rebelled against.

"The major problem we face is that we have no vote concerning ratification. I know of no one from this valley who was selected as a delegate to the ratification convention. Someday, this situation has to change. It's too late for us to seek to gain representation at the upcoming convention. What we need to do is take steps to become a new county. We have the population and the prosperity that are the main criteria for seeking division into a new county. We better move on this before people above the long narrows do, or we'll become second-class citizens to our neighbors to the north."

Both the Federalists and the Anti-Federalists bombarded the citizenry with speeches, pamphlets, letters, and newspaper articles. In November 1787, the state of Pennsylvania held a convention to decide whether to ratify the Constitution. The debates were lengthy and bitter. In Carlisle the agitation between the two groups erupted into a violent encounter:

> In December, 1787, a fracas occurred between the Constitutionalists and the Anti-Constitutionalists. A number of citizens from the county assembled on the 26th (at Carlisle), to express, in their way, aided by the firing of cannons, their feelings on the actions of the convention that had assembled to frame the Constitution of the United States, when they were assaulted by an adverse party; after dealing out blows they dispersed. On Thursday, the 27th, those who had assembled the day before met again at the courthouse, well armed with guns and muskets. They, however, proceeded without molestation, except that those who had opposed them also assembled, kindled a bonfire and burned several effigies. For that temerity several, styled as rioters, were arrested and snugly lodged in jail. They were subsequently, on a compromise between the Federalists and Democrats, liberated. The Federalists were the Constitutionalists.[20]

On December 12, 1787, Pennsylvania became the second state to ratify the new Constitution by a vote of forty-six to twenty-three. Delaware was the first to ratify on December 7, and thereby became known as the "First State." On July 2, 1788, the Congress of the United States announced that the ninth state had ratified the document, and the Constitution had become the new frame of government of the new republic.

On Independence Day of 1788, most towns and villages throughout Pennsylvania celebrated the advent of the new government. Philadelphia held its largest parade and celebration in the city's short history. There were a few exceptions to the festivities. In one town where the Anti-Federalists were in the majority, a Federalist celebration provoked a situation where several copies of the new Constitution were seized and thrown into a bonfire.

CHAPTER FORTY NINE

The Rices Move to Tuscarora Valley

The new ship of state sailed with the first congressional and presidential election in 1788. The First Congress met in 1789, while George Washington was inaugurated as president on April 30, 1789, in New York City, after being unanimously chosen president by the Electoral College. John Adams was sworn in as the first vice-president. The cabinet contained only three full-fledged department heads under Washington in 1789. Thomas Jefferson was the logical choice for Secretary of State. Alexander Hamilton was eminently well qualified for the position of Secretary of the Treasury. Three-hundred-pound Revolutionary War general Henry Knox was entrusted to oversee the tiny army and navy as Secretary of War. John Jay of New York was appointed as the first chief justice of the Supreme Court, which met in New York City.

While these events were unfolding on the national scene and the new government was attempting to create a spirit of buoyancy and confidence under an ambitious new program, the political scene in the Juniata Valley was undergoing a transformation.

One aspect of this transformation resulted from the actions of one unscrupulous, dishonest, and deceitful man prior to the American Revolution—a man named Andrew Allen. In our journey through the history of the development of the valley drained by the Tuscarora Creek, we have twice come in contact with the German immigrant Zachariah Rice, of Pikeland in Chester County. The first time we were introduced to this millwright of great renown, Robert Taylor visited his mill and farm in July of 1758 on his return from Philadelphia and his appearance before the Provincial Council of Pennsylvania. Our second encounter occurred in September 1777 in the aftermath of the Battle of Brandywine, when George Washington paused at the Rice household to partake of refreshments.

Zachariah Rice employed his tremendous carpentry skills and patriotic desires to help construct a much-needed hospital for the sick and wounded at Yellow Springs. Zachariah's wife, Maria Appolonia, known as Abigail, was a frequent visitor on errands of mercy.

During the dark days of the Revolution and the period immediately after the war, Zachariah's remarkable skills and abilities and his untiring efforts provided him with the financial wherewithal to purchase the farm comprised of 205 acres on which he lived. On May 22, 1786, Zachariah had bought at Sheriff's Sale another 110 acres and allowances from his adjoining neighbor, Francis Sole.

The Rice family grew until it numbered seventeen living children, and they lived quite happily until the spring of 1789. Then the unthinkable occurred; the farm was seized by foreclosure of an old English mortgage.

Pikeland Township had passed through a succession of owners beginning in William Penn's time, until it was owned by a rich London merchant named Samuel Hoare. Hoare then sold the Pikeland tract for a small sum to a Philadelphia merchant, Andrew Allen, giving Allen a mortgage for the balance. Allen then divided the huge tract of land into 200- and 300-acre farms. When the unsuspecting German immigrants arrived in Philadelphia, Allen systematically sold the farms to the land-starved Germans.

Andrew Allen was a prominent business man, later a member of the Continental Congress—a man above reproach, never to be suspected of any fraudulent actions. However, this did not prove to be the case. After the Revolution had begun and the fortunes of war had swung in favor of the British, and General Lord Howe had captured Trenton, Allen turned traitor. He crossed the

Delaware River and placed himself under the protection of the British army and Lord Howe. Later in the war, like many Loyalists or Tories, he fled to London and eventually died there.

After the Americans emerged victorious from the Revolution, Pennsylvania established its own system of laws and courts. In Chester County, the sheriff of the county, Ezekiel Howard, was given the task of selling out the entire Pikeland tract under a foreclosure of the Hoare-Allen mortgage dated August 26, 1789. The naïve, unsuspecting German immigrants—114 of them—lost their properties, even the St. Peters Church, which they had constructed, all to satisfy the greed of the English merchant Samuel Hoare who foreclosed on Allen's mortgage. The Germans had merely accepted the papers from Allen and never questioned their legality; therefore they conducted no back searches for titles.

All their hard work of over thirty years was swept away with no warning and no legal recourse. This was a complete disaster, because most of the 114 Germans were left without any property.

A second disaster struck the Rice family on November 6, 1789, when Abigail Rice passed on to her reward at the age of forty-seven, two months, and two days, from the typhus fever which she had contracted at the hospital at Yellow Springs. She was buried at the St. Peters Lutheran Church at Pikeland, with seventeen of her children in attendance. The following was allegedly inscribed on her tombstone: "Some have children, some have none; Here lies the mother of twenty-one."

With the loss of his property and his wife, Zachariah Rice left Chester County with seventeen of his children. His five older children, who were now married, joined their father in search of inexpensive land west of the Susquehanna River. They loaded all their household effects into wagons and journeyed to what had become Harrisburg where they took a ferry across the Susquehanna.

Zachariah remained optimistic, "I remember back in '58, a young Irishman by the name of Taylor visited us for several days, because he wanted some information about the construction of mills and mill races. His home was in a valley north of Carlisle and the Blue Mountain. If I remember correctly, it was the Tuscarora Valley.

"He spoke glowingly of his valley. Taylor bragged of its unspoiled beauty. According to the young Irishman, the valley had abundant sources of timber, plentiful game for hunting, productive farm land, and a bountiful supply of springs and streams.

"We're going to ferry the Susquehanna River and travel to Carlisle. Then we'll cross the mountains and explore the possibilities of the Sherman's and Tuscarora Valleys."

The Rice family was not alone in its quest for suitable new homes. Many of the other German families who had lost their farms, homes, and businesses due to fraudulent titles moved over the mountains north of Carlisle and into Cumberland County. Most notable of these were the Fuller, Hench, Saylor, Shull, Bower, Yohn, Landis, Hipple, and Hartman families, who intermarried with the Rice family.

Once Zachariah Rice arrived in the vicinity of Sherman's Creek Valley, he left his family there and resumed his travels across the Tuscarora Mountain to seek out his old acquaintance, Robert Taylor. By this time, people desiring to travel to the lower or eastern portion of the Tuscarora Valley no longer used Bigham's Gap. They instead followed Fort Granville Road, which utilized another gap known as Jennie's Gap, named after the widow of John McAfee. John McAfee had constructed a twenty-eight-foot-square house, with a chimney at each end, at the foot of the Tuscarora Mountain.

Zachariah found Robert in the fields overseeing his older sons hard at work clearing more land. Robert was surprised to see the German millwright and carpenter. "Herr Rice, I can't believe it's you. Little did I realize that my description of the fabulous Tuscarora Valley would motivate you to visit me."

Rice smiled. "I'm quite happy to see you also, Robert. However, this is not just a social visit. Unfortunately, all that I had labored so diligently to achieve was lost due to fraudulent deeds that I had foolishly purchased. Not only was I duped, but so were over one hundred of my countrymen."

Zachariah quickly presented the details of the financial disaster. "I'm not here looking for sympathy but rather for land that I can purchase at a decent price so that the Rices can begin life anew."

Robert scratched his head. "My neighbor, Lawrence King, mentioned that he might be willing to sell some of his holdings if the price was right."

(AUTHOR'S NOTE: The section of land that Robert Taylor was referring to was originally warranted by Richard Rankin and John Hunter back in 1755. Rankin and Hunter sold their warrants to Robert Campbell on February 6, 1759. This land was sold to John Campbell on July 29, 1790, and John then sold two hundred and eighteen acres of the lower portion to Lawrence King on June 23, 1792).

Robert continued, "This section of land begins on the banks of the Tuscarora Creek and extends south to the top of the ridge. The way Lawrence talked, he didn't need that much land, and if the right deal could be arranged, he might part with a segment of it. Let's go talk to Lawrence and see what kind of deal can be arranged."

Lawrence King and Zachariah Rice hit it off immediately. Before too long, Lawrence had agreed to allow Zachariah to settle and work almost the whole parcel, as the agreement called for the exchange of 199 acres and 153 perches. Eventually, in 1801, Zachariah paid off the mortgage for the sum of eleven hundred English pounds for the property. Zachariah named his new home "Spring Hill."

Robert Taylor joined the Rices and other members of the German population in the construction of Zachariah's home. Several weeks after its completion, Robert visited his good German friend.

Above the front door of the Rice house hung a sign written in German that caught Robert's immediate attention: *"Bleibe Bei*

Uns Denn Es Will Abend Werden."

"Knowing you, Zachariah, I would be willing to guess that the sign is a quote from the Bible," Robert said.

"Yah, it is from Luke 24:29. Do you know your Bible well enough to know what it means in English?"

Robert hesitated. "I think I remember that passage. During the winter of '59–'60, I read the Bible several times just to keep my mental senses, so I guess I became rather knowledgeable about the Good Book." He paused, studying the sign, then said, "Let's see…'Stay with us for it is toward evening'?"

"Goot, very goot. That's rather impressive for a backwoods Presbyterian."

Since the Germans who moved into the Tuscarora Valley at this time had no Lutheran church in which to worship, the Rices found themselves in the same situation as in the early days in Pikeland in Chester County when they traveled to St. Augustine's Lutheran Church at the Trappe in Montgomery County. In Chester County the Rices and Hartmans had to endure a journey of almost thirteen miles, but more formidable was the fording of the Schuylkill River. In 1771 the Lutheran church at Pikeland was constructed and ended the weekly treks to St. Augustine's. But once again they had to travel a considerable distance to attend church services.

When they settled in the Tuscarora Valley, the distance to the church that was going to be constructed in Loysville was a few more miles than what they had traveled in Pikeland. In addition to the fording of several lesser streams, the Tuscarora Mountain loomed as a major barrier between their home and their church.

The Lutherans in the Sherman's Creek region from 1780 to 1788 had the good fortune of enjoying frequent visitations from Reverend John G. Butler, pastor of the Lutheran church in Carlisle. Thereafter, Reverend John Timothy Kuhl of Franklin County began visiting the Lutherans of Sherman's Valley. In 1790, the team of George Fleisher of Saville Township transported Reverend Kuhl and his family to the site where Loysville is now located to make their new home.

The Lutherans were widely scattered throughout the valley, and Reverend Kuhl visited among them by preaching once every six weeks at each place. Until the Lutherans erected a permanent church building, Reverend Kuhl preached in barns, private homes, and in the open at different locations in the valley.

The German population of the area continued to increase and they were encouraged to erect a house of worship since they now had a minister living in their midst. In 1794 the first church was erected at Loysville and was known as the Lebanon Lutheran Church. It was a tradition in those days that the member who cut and delivered the first log on the date appointed was given the special honor of laying the first log. On that construction day, Zachariah had risen early and cut a very fine log from the area of his holdings known as the "Barrens." To Zachariah's surprise and chagrin, one of his neighbors was already at the building site with the first log when he arrived.

Zachariah protested vehemently, "It is not possible that Jacob could have cut that log early enough to have beaten me across the mountain. I urge you to examine the sap of the log and how it has penetrated the rings to determine just how long ago it was cut."

Five other members of the congregation were chosen to examine the log and the approximate time of its harvesting. All were in accord: it had to have been cut the previous day. Eventually Jacob confessed that he had not cut the log that day. Therefore, the elderly Rice was given the honor of having his log laid first in the wall of the new Lebanon Lutheran Church.

For several years the Lutherans of the Tuscarora Valley trekked through Jennie's Gap in the Tuscarora Mountain to attend services at the Lebanon Lutheran Church. Sometime before 1802 the Lutherans in the valley constructed a log church in the vicinity later to be called Church Hill. The congregation at this site received pastoral visits from Reverend William Scriba. When this Lutheran Church was erected, it was known as either "Rice's Church" or the "Lower Tuscarora Church."

CHAPTER FIFTY

The Riot Above the Long Narrows

Since the creation of Cumberland County in 1750 and the designation of Carlisle as its county seat, there had been a movement of emigrants over the Blue Mountains and into Sherman's, Tuscarora, and Kishacoquillas Valleys. This stream of people seeking free or cheap land abated amidst the Indian troubles during the French and Indian War, Pontiac's Uprising, and the Revolutionary War, but during the periods of peace, especially after the Revolution, large numbers of people expanded Cumberland County's far-reaching population.

In order to facilitate the counting of the population, in 1790 the United States Census Bureau counted the first census. Robert Taylor was reported to be living in Milford Township, and in the household there is one male listed over sixteen years of age, six males under age sixteen, and three females.

When the population of a certain area warranted it, new townships or counties were created. Bedford County was the first county to be formed out of the western stretches of Cumberland County in 1771. Northumberland County followed in 1772, Franklin County in 1784, and Huntingdon County was formed out of part of Bedford in 1787.

In the winter of 1788-89, petitions were sent to the Pennsylvania legislature to create a new county out of some of the townships north of the Tuscarora Mountain, which would include Lack, Milford, Fermanagh, Wayne, Derry, Armagh, Potter, and Upper Bald Eagle Townships.

Mifflin County was erected by an act of the Pennsylvania General Assembly on September 17, 1789. The preamble stated:

Whereas, It hath been represented to the General Assembly of this State by the inhabitants of those parts of Cumberland and Northumberland which are included with the lines hereafter mentioned, that they labour under great hardships by reason of their great distance from the present seat of justice and the public offices for the said counties, for the remedy thereof.[21]

John Culbertson was thoroughly upset over the erection of the new county, but more so over the selection of Lewistown as the new county seat. "I would rather travel over the Tuscarora and Blue Mountains to Carlisle than struggle to pick a trail among the rocks, boulders, and debris that obstruct the path through the long narrows."

Alexander Wilson of Lack Township expressed complete disdain over Lewistown's selection. "The people from Lack Township will have to travel over forty miles to conduct any business at the county seat. That is over twice the amount of mileage that anyone from above the long narrows will have to travel to arrive at the county seat. I would rather continue to do business at Carlisle."

David Glenn, also of Lack Township, stated that he had read an article in the *Columbia Magazine* that gave this account of the Long Narrows in 1788:

After crossing at Miller's Ferry, which lies a few miles from the mouth of the river and keeping up at midway to Standing Stone, a three-fold junction of the mountains is plainly perceived, being the Tuscarora, Shade, and Narrow Mountains. Through them, at this place, commences what is known by the name of Long Narrows, formed by one continued break through the above hills, and continues surrounded by astonishing crags for upwards of eight or nine miles, during which space the traveller has nothing to walk on for either himself or horse (which he is obliged to dismount for better security) than the piled rocks and stones that have from time to time accumulated by their fall from the surrounding parts. After passing through this miserable place, immediately upon the other side stands the town or settlement called Old Town, consisting only of a tavern and a few scattered hovels, and containing nothing worth notice.[22]

Glenn continued, "It doesn't take a very intelligent man to conclude that the author and anyone who reads the article would take immediate exception to the selection of Old Town as the new county seat. Just for us to overcome the obstacles described in the article to arrive at Old Town will be a feat in itself. The town portrayed in the magazine article is a fairly accurate one— 'containing nothing worth notice' is as true as it gets. It's an abomination for Lewistown to be selected as the county seat; John Harris's town would be a much more logical choice."

William Graham was adamant in his demands that an investigation be undertaken. "It appears to me that there is a degree of chicanery involved. It's the same old story just like before the revolution; those that have the money have the power, and they'll soon have more of both. For the moment, I can't see that this new government is much better than what we had before 1776.

"As far as I see it, John Harris's town, Mifflintown, is the most convenient and central location for our county seat. Pennsylvania's legislature surely must have been deceived into making their selection. If the selection of Old Town or Lewistown holds, I believe our only course of action is to petition for our own county to be located below the Long Narrows."

The concerns of the residents below the Long Narrows fell upon deaf ears, and the seat of government for the newly erected county of Mifflin was located in Lewistown.

Section Ten of the Act of Erection of Mifflin County provided "that the Justices of the Supreme Court and of the courts of Oyer and Terminer and General Goal Delivery of this State shall have the like powers, jurisdictions, and authorities, with the said County of Mifflin, as by law they are vested with, and entitled to have and exercise in other counties of this State;...[23]

The first session of the Court of Common Pleas was held in Mifflin County on December 8, 1789, in the house of Arthur Buchanan, and the court continued to hold session there until a courthouse was constructed. In 1790 a two-story, log, dual-purpose jail and courthouse was constructed. The court convened on the upper floor, and was reached by an outside staircase. At this first session the court heard no cases; it merely organized and admitted attorneys to practice in the courts.

On March 8, 1790, the first Court of Quarter Sessions was held before William Brown, Esq. and his associate. At this session the first grand jury was impaneled, with William Smith chosen as the foreman. Robert Taylor of the Tuscarora Valley was one of those citizens chosen to sit on this first grand jury. It was designated that the courts of Mifflin County would be conducted in this manner until December 1791.

On Monday, September 12, 1791, the court was preparing for its last term of court under the first jurisdiction. The president judge, William Brown, and his associate judges, Samuel Bryson and James Armstrong, met in the morning and waited until three o'clock for the arrival of Thomas Beale, the other associate judge, who lived below the Long Narrows in Milford Township.

When Beale arrived, he declined to join the others when they moved on to the courthouse to open the proceedings of the court. Due to the lateness of the day, the court adjourned until ten o'clock the next morning.

About an hour before the court was to return to session, word was received that a sizable crowd of men had assembled at David Jordan's tavern, located below the Long Narrows, with the alleged intention of marching to the courthouse in Lewistown and removing Judge Samuel Bryson from the bench—forcibly, if necessary. The mob apparently had spent the night, or at least part of it, imbibing the spirits trafficked by Jordan. The throng was presumably armed with pistols, rifles, and swords, and in a mood to harm the judge if they were successful in laying their hands on him.

When President Justice William Brown was informed of the impending breach of the peace, he approached James Horrel,

Robert Taylor, and John Elliot, who all lived below the Long Narrows and had served as officers in the Fourth or Seventh Battalion of Cumberland County's militia during the Revolution, and inquired of them as to the cause of the fracas.

"Men, I know the three of you reside below the Narrows and probably know all the members of the mob down at Jordan's tavern. Would any of you be aware as to the origins of their discontent?"

"Your honor," began John Elliot, "it all stems from an incident during the war involving Samuel Bryson, who had been a county lieutenant for several years. In that capacity he could confirm or refute the commissions of officers. The elements of two regiments elected two reputable men to serve them as the unit's colonels. For some despicable reason, Bryson chose not to validate the commission of these two men."

James Horrel chimed in, "When the people below the Narrows were informed of Bryson's elevation to Associate Justice, we...uh...they were appalled at the action. Many swore an oath that they would never allow Bryson to sit in the court as an associate justice."

"In other words," Robert Taylor said, "the good people of Lack, Milford, Fermanagh, and Greenwood Townships see Mr. Bryson sitting on the bench as an injustice. It might be prudent to have the deputy state's attorney, John Clarke, intervene and attempt to avert any violence or civil disorder here on the streets of Lewistown."

"Yes, yes, I'll see to it right away," declared the president justice, and he immediately went to confer with Clarke and the associate justices.

Once informed of the impending disaster, John Clarke took charge of the situation. "The Prothonotary Samuel Edmiston and Judges Beale, Stewart, and Bell should join with Sheriff George Wilson and proceed towards the Narrows and meet with the mob. The rioters should be informed that if their intentions are hostile, they should disperse and that the court is alarmed at their proceedings."

About two hours later the court opened its proceedings, and the grand jury was sworn in and impaneled. Immediately, a fife's piercing melody was heard, while guns were discharged, presumably in the air, and the riotous multitude led by three men on horseback appeared in the vicinity of the courthouse.

The officers of the court who had been sent to meet the unruly mob were held under guard at the rear of the mass of men. The court officers were released, except for Sheriff George Wilson. The court ordered deputy state's attorney Clarke to confer with the crush of men and explain the consequences of disobeying the court and removing Justice Bryson from his rightful seat on the bench.

The mob converged on Clarke. "March on! March on!" was their rallying cry. "Draw your sword on him!" someone urged from the rear of the crowd. "Ride over him!" cried another rebel.

John Clarke seized the reins of the horse of the sheriff's own brother, William Wilson, and ordered him to desist.

"Release my reins immediately," Wilson yelled as he drew his sword. "Release my horse, or I'll strike your hand and release the reins by force."

Suddenly, John Clarke faced another serious threat as none other than Judge Beale's nephew poked his pistol into Clarke's chest. At that point Clarke released the reins and walked in front of the crowd until he came to the stairs of the courthouse.

An altercation took place on the stairway when William Wilson, Colonel Walker and Colonel Holt attempted to climb the stairs, urged on by "March on, damn you; proceed and take him." Judge Armstrong met them head-on, screaming at the rioters, "You damn'd rascals, come on! We will defend the court ourselves, and before you shall take Judge Bryson, you shall kill me and many others, which seems to be your intention and which you may do."[24]

Just as Wilson and Beale were about to do the unthinkable to Clarke with sword or pistol, Clarke was able to appeal to their civilized side. "Please consider what you are about to do. Think about where we are, and who I represent. Just withdraw your men, and appoint two or three of you to meet with me in half an hour, and we'll try and figure out this dispute."

The rioters withdrew, and William Wilson, Walker, and Sterrett met with Hamilton and Clarke at Alexander's Tavern to discuss the various proposals, but nothing concrete was agreed upon. Clarke followed the group and inquired of Wilson, "Your object is that Judge Bryson leave the bench and not sit in court?" The answer was in the affirmative. "Will you promise to disperse and go home and offer him no insult?" Clarke asked. This also was met with a "Yes." The men gave their mutual pledge of honor in regards to the agreement.

Soon afterwards, Wilson and his men reappeared at the courthouse, and Clarke met them at the foot of the stairs. "Men, Judge Bryson has left for the evening, and your presence in this manner is a breach of your given word and a forfeiture of your honor."

Colonel Walker countered, "Many of our group do not support the agreement, and there is nothing I can do to change their minds."

"Yes, and now we're going to get that lowlife of a Bryson and give him a taste of our justice," snarled William Wilson as he attempted to push past Clarke and climb the stairs.

Clarke quickly blocked the passageway. He looked Wilson straight in the eyes and said, "If you remove your weapons and promise no harm, you may pass."

"I have an address to present to the judges," Wilson snapped, pulling a document from his breast pocket. "Observe, the article is all nice and legal. As you can see, it is signed by 'The People'—the people below the Narrows who oppose Samuel Bryson's judgeship."

While Clarke was occupied with examining the document, for the third time during the incident Young Beale drew his pistol from his belt and threatened Clarke by cocking the weapon and aiming it at the attorney's chest. "Under the circumstances, I think you should allow us to proceed up the stairs."

"I think not, Squire Beale. If you are so adamant about using that weapon or force to gain your way, perhaps you and I should settle the matter man-to-man with equal weaponry."

Beale's face turned pale, and Clarke knew that he had struck a nerve, for the man lost all his bravado when he didn't hold the upper hand and wasn't facing an unarmed man. Beale and Wilson retreated from the stairs and headed down the street, letting loose a nasty string of oaths as they withdrew to the safety of their numbers.

Colonel William McFarland marched into town at the head of his regiment the next day and offered his services to the court to restore order if necessary. President Justice Brown responded, "The court is genuinely appreciative of your superb military display and your fastidious offer; however, at the present time we see no need to accept your offer of assistance in maintaining order as no harm has been generated."

After the regiment had retired from the vicinity of the courthouse and the court convened, Judge Samuel Bryson delivered a statement that he had written: "I would desire that the course of action taken by the rioters during the incident of Monday, September 12, 1791, be recorded in the public record of this Court of Quarter Session for Mifflin County. Within that record should be described the ill-treatment that I as an associate justice received in my attempt to perform my duties. Let it be known that no threat of danger will ever prevent me from taking and keeping my seat as a member of this court."

The court was preparing to reconvene at two o'clock when a fracas erupted between Sheriff George Wilson and Judge Bryson. For some reason, Sheriff Wilson struck and kicked at the judge. Judge James Armstrong intervened and prevented Wilson from doing Bryson any bodily harm.

The coroner immediately assumed the duties of the sheriff, and Sheriff Wilson, by order of the court, was removed from the scene and incarcerated in the jail on the first floor of the courthouse.

The news of the sheriff's incarceration soon spread, and that night Colonel Holt and about seventy of his men reappeared.

Shouts of "Liberty or Death," "Down with Bryson," and "Free the Sheriff" were heard throughout the night.

Several voices bellowed, "We're coming to break you out, George! That jail isn't strong enough to hold you!"

Colonel Holt gave the order. "Just stand back, George. We'll have you out of there in a moment."

From within the confines of the jail, George Wilson, who had regained his wits, replied, "No, men, don't break any more laws and force open the jail. What I did was wrong. I violated my oath of office and I deeply regret my actions."

Express riders were sent down the narrows to Mifflintown, Taylorstown, and beyond to rally men to ride to the rescue of George Wilson. In the meantime, Major Edmiston spoke on Wilson's behalf, and permission was granted for the sheriff to be released from jail and to communicate with the members of the court.

Sheriff George Wilson addressed the members of the court, except Judge Bryson who did not attend the impromptu meeting. "I am contritely regretful for my unwarranted actions and attack upon Judge Bryson. This was completely contrary to my oath of office, and I should never have acted in such an impulsive and irrational demeanor. I beg your pardon and request that you exonerate me and allow me to return to my duties and to serve this court until the expiration of my commission."

Justices Armstrong, Brown, and Beale conferred for several minutes. Then Justice Brown addressed the sheriff. "We understand the tremendous pressure that was placed upon you by your friends, family, and neighbors in regards to the incident surrounding the court and the admittance of Judge Bryson to the bench. Therefore, we see no need to continue your incarceration, and you should be released and resume your duties. But I warn you, sir, if there are any more incidents of this nature, you will be imprisoned in the Mifflin County lockup for an extended period of time."

By the next morning, nearly three hundred men had collected below the narrows in preparation for the march on the courthouse and the forcible release of the sheriff and the prevention of Samuel Bryson from retaking his seat on the bench of the court.

Again, John Clarke moved to the forefront and addressed the explosive state of affairs. "I recommend that we send a delegation to communicate with the agitated crowd and inform them that the sheriff has apologized for his actions, has been released from jail, and has resumed his duties as an officer of the court."

Clarke's recommendation was immediately carried out. Once the crowd below the Narrows was informed of the sheriff's release and reinstatement, the men slowly dispersed and returned to their homes.

Since the crisis had ended and the business of the court was terminated, court was adjourned and the members of the grand jury were dismissed and began to return to their homes.

As Robert Taylor and the contingent from below the narrows rode towards home, Robert reflected upon the events that just had unfolded. "What do you think would have been the consequences if Young Beale had been foolish enough to have squeezed his trigger and blown a hole in John Clarke's chest and killed him?"

John Eliot had a ready answer. "There is no doubt in my mind that we would have had a Shay's type of insurrection on our hands, or maybe even worse, like they had in Massachusetts in 1787. After all, Clarke is a direct representative of the state government. If he had been harmed or murdered in the middle of a riot, reverberations would have been felt throughout the state and the nation, and the state militia would have been called up. The governor would have used troops from other regions of the state that would have no knowledge of the underlying causes of the disturbance, so that they would not have been prejudiced in handling the affair."

"Yes," agreed James Horrel, "we came about as close to a civil disaster as a government could. Thank God, no shots were discharged in anger, and no one was struck or run through with a sword. I think we all learned a valuable lesson from this incident, and I hope the people of our valley remember it."

Robert said, "This path, now unrealistically considered a road by some people, has been improved very little since I first traveled through this gorge in 1754, nearly a year before the Braddock disaster that changed this region forever. I have holdings and family in the Kishacoquillas Valley that I have to visit periodically, so I travel this route more than most people do. I often reflect upon Reverend Charles Beatty's depiction of the narrows in his journal of 1766.

The entry he was referring to was: "A rocky road bounds so close upon the river as to leave a small path along for the most part, and this, for about ten miles, very uneven: at this time also encumbered by trees fallen across it, blown up from the roots, some time ago, by a hard gale of wind, so that we were obliged to walk some part of the way, and in some places to go along the edge of the water."[25]

Robert continued, "Since the General Assembly of Pennsylvania has seen fit to locate the county seat in Lewistown on the other side of these narrows, I hope they see it expedient to appropriate funds to provide for the necessary improvements of this means of transportation. All we need is for some of those diligent members of the assembly from Philadelphia or Lancaster to have to travel this route through the gorge several times, and the funds will be quickly forthcoming."

John Elliot chuckled, "That will happen when hell freezes over. None of us will ever live long enough to see any major improvements in the road through these narrows. Those poor people from Lack Township face a terrible trip every time they want to buy or sell land, or conduct any state-related business. It just doesn't appear to be fair; they were better off traveling to Carlisle. Oh well, I guess we have other problems that will occupy most of our time."

James Horrell added, "At least it appears that we no longer face any threat from the savages. Most of the hostiles moved to the Ohio Territory and beyond, so we should be safe from unprovoked attacks."

In defiance of the situation that surrounded the civil

disturbance known by most people as the "Riot of 1791," it is recorded in the tax records of Milford Township for 1791 that Robert Taylor of Milford "made no return when demand was made by the assessor." [26]

CHAPTER FIFTY ONE

The Whiskey Rebellion

The Irish or Scotch-Irish brought to the American frontier from the Old Sod the custom or tradition of distilling their own whiskey. They considered whiskey a household necessity, using it as a cure-all or remedy for a variety of illnesses and afflictions. Whiskey and cider were utilized as friendly neighborly offerings when a guest paid a visit on the frontier. Whiskey flowed so freely on the frontier it often was used as money. One gallon was worth one shilling.

Nearly every frontier plantation possessed its own still, and tending the family still was as routine a daily chore as milking the cow, feeding the chickens, gathering their eggs, fetching wood for the fireplace, and carrying water from the spring or well.

The ability of the frontier farmer to grow barley, rye, and corn enabled them to easily have the raw materials on hand to manufacture their own mash to turn into whiskey.

Most Scotch-Irish frontiersmen would draw the line and refuse to supply the natives with distilled spirits. The natives' consumption of intoxicating beverages was a constant source of irritation on the frontier. All too often, unscrupulous traders would allow the spirits to fall into the hands of the natives, who would then perform lawless actions against the frontier families.

One of the major flaws in the first Constitution of the fledgling nation, the Articles of Confederation, was the failure of that document to provide the national government with the power to levy and collect taxes.

Throughout the course of the American Revolution and

during the period the United States attempted to exist under the Articles of Confederation, the national government incurred a heavy debt, which needed to be addressed by the new government under the Constitution.

In the new Constitution, Article I dealt with the legislative branch or Congress. Article I, Section 8, clause 1, stated that Congress should have the power to levy and collect taxes, thereby correcting a major weakness of the previous government.

The arduous task of establishing a national financial policy fell upon Alexander Hamilton, the first secretary of the treasury, when he took office in 1789. Hamilton was largely responsible for shaping the government's first tax policies.

On July 4, 1789, at Hamilton's insistence, Congress enacted a modest tariff bill that was a meager attempt to eliminate the huge national debt and to balance the budget. Congress made no effort to implement Hamilton's elaborate program to stimulate American manufacturing.

Secretary Hamilton conceived a Bank of the United States that would be a powerful institution in which the federal treasury would deposit its surplus monies. The bank would also print paper money intended to provide a sound and stable national currency.

Since additional sources of internal revenue were urgently needed to implement Hamilton's plan to create a federal budget, a tax was proposed to be levied on certain articles produced and sold in the United States. This excise tax was to be collected directly from the persons who produced and sold the articles.

Therefore, Hamilton's proposal for an excise tax on "spirituous" beverages was enacted by Congress in 1791. The new tax amounted to about seven cents a gallon.

The secretary apparently felt that the new excise law would also accustom the people to a direct tax by the federal government. Furthermore, the tax would extend the operations of the federal government throughout the nation and impress upon the remote frontiersman that a strong central authority had been established.

The excise tax on whiskey placed a heavy burden on the impoverished farmers of Central and Western Pennsylvania. The interior roads were so poor that the Pennsylvania farmers in this region found it more profitable to transport their corn or rye to market in liquid concentrate. Whiskey also brought a higher price than grain. Much of the liquor produced on the frontier was for domestic use, and the excise tax fell on the frontiersmen as a direct tax.

This federal excise tax on whiskey immediately created a controversy in Pennsylvania. The act of 1791 had divided the United States into fourteen districts of one state each, with the four western counties of Pennsylvania—Allegheny, Westmoreland, Fayette, and Bedford—comprising the fourteenth. The General Assembly of Pennsylvania responded with a resolution on June 22, 1791, declaring the collection of revenue by excise duty to be subversive of peace and liberty, against the rights of the citizen, and a violation of the fundamental rights of the government.

News of the passage of the excise tax by Congress aroused widespread opposition on the frontier. To pacify the frontiersmen, in 1792 Congress adopted additional legislation abolishing the tax on smaller stills. This modification did little to placate the frontier farmer, especially in Pennsylvania.

In the hinterlands of Pennsylvania, irate citizens composed resolutions, staged meetings and protests, and created democratic societies to air their grievances against the federal government and its policies. From the banks of the Susquehanna River to the Ohio Valley, frontiersmen were indignant over the excise tax on whiskey, whether you called it "moonshine," "white lightning," "corn squeezing," or "Old Monongahela rye."

Opposition slogans and descriptions came in many different forms: "The excise tax is an infernal one," was a common complaint. Some turned their wrath on Hamilton. "Hamilton is merely pursuing his purpose of strengthening the national government and increasing the national debt." People who used whiskey as a substitute for money saw it this way: "This is not a tax on a luxury, but a burden on an economic necessity and a medium of exchange." One of the stronger feelings against the collection was expressed in these words: "It shall not be collected, and we will punish, expel, and banish the officers who attempt to collect the tax." Some described the tax as "a capitalist device to enrich the wealthy and impoverish the poor."

Most frontier farmers refused to pay the tax, and many arrests were performed by federal agents sent to the region by Hamilton's authority. These arrests placed an even larger burden on the arrested farmers. Once arrested, the alleged offender had to travel all the way to Philadelphia to stand trial because the only federal court in Pennsylvania was located in the City of Brotherly Love. This trip of nearly three hundred miles one way was an extreme inconvenience for the summoned offender. Not only did he have to secure the necessary funds for such a trip, he would be absent from his farm for a lengthy period, and work on the farm could not wait until his return. All this would add up to considerable expense and losses of potential farm crops.

Then there were the legal ramifications. Could the alleged offender afford a lawyer to represent him, or would he have to represent himself in court? Under the new Constitution, an accused person was guaranteed a fair trial by a jury of his peers. Bringing the defendants back east also meant that jurors and witnesses would have to be transported to Philadelphia, greatly increasing the cost of a trial. How could a backwoods farmer possibly receive a fair trial?

These factors, along with many more, created a backlash against the federal government, which led to more tensions, grievances, demonstrations, and eventually violence.

Groups of men known as "Whiskey Boys" blackened their faces and wore rag masks as a form of disguise and then roughed up the revenue collectors. Standard treatment of the collectors entailed stripping the officer and burning his clothes, shaving his head, tarring and feathering him, taking him deep into the woods, or tying him to a tree and making off with his horse.

Those farmers who paid the tax or advocated obedience to the law would have their stills shot up or burned. Inspector John

Neville had his house and barn burned. David Lenox, who incensed the countryside when he began to serve scores of writs ordering defendants to travel to Philadelphia to stand trial, escaped down the Ohio River before he was done any real harm.

A good many tar-and-feather parties were led by David Bradford and a figure known as "Tom the Tinker." Not only did these Western Pennsylvania rebels vow death to revenue collectors, they also vowed to withdraw from the union if President Washington enforced the hated excise tax on whiskey.

President Washington requested Governor Mifflin of Pennsylvania to call up the militia to enforce the federal law. Mifflin declined to use only Pennsylvania troops because many of the state's militia refused to bear arms against men from their own state.

The sharp challenge to the authority of the new government erupted in southwestern Pennsylvania in 1794. The distillation of whiskey was probably more important in southwestern Pennsylvania than in any other region. It was estimated that about twenty-five percent of the active stills in 1794 were in southwestern Pennsylvania. Whiskey Poles, similar to the Liberty Poles of the anti-Stamp Tax reaction in 1765, were erected. The cry "Liberty and No Excise" reverberated throughout the mountains, hills, and valleys of frontier Pennsylvania.

Disturbances arose in Central Pennsylvania in protest against the draft. Bedford witnessed a mob of nearly three hundred men erecting a liberty pole in the middle of the town. The road to Bedford was allegedly lined with liberty poles every four or five miles apart.

A liberty pole was raised in Chambersburg, but eventually chopped down and removed. On one of the main corners of the town of Northumberland a pole studded with nails was erected. The town was held captive by the insurgents for several days. To make matters worse, the arsenal was entered and weapons were seized. Governor Mifflin sent a company of militia from Lancaster to restore order. Several of the ringleaders were arrested and escorted to Philadelphia to stand trial.

Some of the men from Sherman's and Tuscarora Valleys journeyed to Carlisle to display their opposition to the tax. On the evening of August 28, a group of men with blackened faces paid a visit to the tax collector and forced him to resign his position. The situation became livelier on the night of September 9 when a whiskey pole was erected in the town square with the slogan "Liberty and No Excise, O Whiskey" carved into it.

It is recorded that a young man, David Watts, from the section of Cumberland County that later became Perry County, supported the federal government and opposed the Whiskey Boys. Young Watts rode to the location of the whiskey pole and, unaided and unarmed, felled the pole with full knowledge of the consequences—bodily harm or death—because the Boys had vowed to shoot anyone who disturbed the pole.

The Whiskey Boys of Carlisle met that night and made a lot of noise erecting another pole. The whiskey pole became the rallying point for nightly carousing and revelry. Noise making, consumption of whiskey, and discharging of weapons were all part of the celebration. Peaceable citizens wisely remained indoors; those foolish enough to venture into the streets were often compelled to contribute to the purchase of more spirits for the mob.

Western Virginia, Western Maryland, and North Carolina were the scenes of other disturbances. In Maryland some of the riots were the result of opposition to the drafts to raise an army to quell the insurrectionists.

Things came to a head when the Whiskey Boys seized a federal mail carrier to determine what information was being disseminated by federal officials. This assault gave the president the excuse that he needed to utilize federal troops.

On August 7, 1794, United States Supreme Court Justice James Wilson decreed that regular or state court officers could not enforce federal law in Western Pennsylvania. The president ordered the insurgents to disperse. Secretary of War Henry Knox requested that the governors of New Jersey, Maryland,

Pennsylvania, and Virginia place thirteen thousand militia under federal control. Pennsylvania's quota was set at 5, 200 men.

A joint peace commission was created in an effort to avoid the use of military force against the Whiskey Boys. After observing mass meetings in mid-August, the peace commission talked with leaders of the uprising, and reported that there was no hope of peaceful settlement of the crisis.

On September 19, Pennsylvania's General Assembly reacted by passing a four-month draft law to meet the state's quota. Several young men of Cumberland County helped to fill the ranks of the state's militia quota. David Watts, who felled the whiskey pole, was among those reviewed by President Washington. Another member of the militia from north of the Blue Mountains was George Gibson. By October 4 the army had collected at Carlisle under the leadership of Virginia Governor Henry Lee and was joined by the president.

Before the army of fifteen thousand began its westward march, William Findley and David Redick arrived in Carlisle and informed the president and Governor Lee that the insurrectionists would comply with the excise law. Washington was not impressed and gave the order to march.

General Henry Lee's army reached Parkinson's Ferry on November 8. There the general issued a proclamation that all loyal citizens would be required to take an oath in support of the federal Constitution. The local justices of the peace lined their pockets by charging a fee for administering the oaths.

At the sight of such an overwhelming force, the rebellion merely died. The mutinous moonshiners were overrun, and either scattered or captured. Following a roundup of suspects conducted by the army, about twenty men were marched back to Philadelphia to stand trial on November 25. General Lee remained behind, and a general pardon was issued on November 29. The court found most of the defendants not guilty. Two men were sentenced to death because of treason—Phillip Weigel and John Mitchell—but President Washington pardoned both of them. The only rebel who did not receive amnesty for his role in the rebellion was David Bradford, and he fled to Spanish Louisiana.

The United States government was strengthened by the suppression of the small insurrection known as the Whiskey Rebellion. It now commanded a new respect. President Washington's opposition accused him of using too much force to subdue the defiant distillers. In the following years, the backcountry men of the West were taught a harsh lesson, but they would learn it well. They would forsake the whiskey poles and the tar kettles for the ballot box and support the political party of Thomas Jefferson.

CHAPTER FIFTY TWO

The Groningers Move to the Tuscarora Valley

As Robert Taylor progressed well into what was considered old age in the late eighteenth century, he recognized that the land holdings he controlled along the lower Tuscarora Creek were increasing in value. This prompted him to consider marketing some of the holdings so that he could pursue other ventures. The one business enterprise that he had considered since first arriving in the valley was the erection of a mill on the old Sterrett survey.

One of Robert's first speculative ventures occurred on December 1, 1786, when he entered into an agreement with his neighbor, William Bell. Taylor agreed to convey a parcel of three hundred acres to Bell. The parcel was bounded on the east by one of Robert Taylor's other holdings, another parcel of William Bell's on the south, the land of Clement Horrell's heirs on the west, and a high narrow ridge on the north. This land was within the realm of the Tuscarora Creek.

Robert Taylor personally appeared before Justice of the peace David McClure on January 8, 1788, to place his signature on the agreement. The three hundred acres changed hands for the sum of three hundred pounds. It was formally recorded on April the 12th A.D. 1796.

A second much more significant land transaction occurred in 1794. One of Robert's neighbors was aware of Robert's desire to sell additional acreage to raise funds for the construction of a mill farther up the Tuscarora and told others about it. The property was a desirable piece of land on a large curve on the Tuscarora Creek, where the creek leaves the border of the Limestone Ridge after paralleling the ridge for over two miles and flows north towards the Herringbone Ridge.

On one beautiful afternoon in early October of 1794, Robert Taylor was overseeing the picking of his abundant corn crop in a field adjacent to the Tuscarora Creek. It had been some time since the region had had any Indian problems; therefore, the Taylors weren't as alert as they might have been five years previous. None of the harvesters were aware of two approaching riders until after they had forded the creek and were climbing the slight grade up the creek bank. When the riders entered the perimeter of the cornfield, the family dog and Robert's next-to-youngest daughter, Sarah, noticed them.

She cried out, "Poppa, Poppa, we have company."

Robert turned to address the intruders, but not in the manner he would have assumed twenty years earlier. "Greetings! What brings you gentlemen to the valley of the Tuscarora? I'm Robert Taylor, the owner of this ample cornfield and the father of all these good workers." As he spoke these words, he advanced towards the two men. "Please join us for a refreshing drink, as we all could use a respite from our labors."

The two men dismounted and approached Robert. Robert shook hands first with the older man, who quickly introduced himself. "I'm George May, a former major in the Continental Army during the Revolution. This young gent is my son-in-law, Leonard Groninger. We reside in the Buffalo Valley near Deerstown along the Susquehanna River. Luck is with us, because you happen to be the very person we are seeking.

"We've received word that you might have a parcel of good bottomland that you would be willing to sell, and we are interested in purchasing the right farmland where we can move our families. Our neck of the woods is getting too crowded, so we're hoping to move farther west and start life anew."

Robert didn't want to appear too anxious to part with his property. Therefore, he remained somewhat elusive and didn't broach the subject of the land immediately. He wanted to feel the men out before he began the negotiation process.

"Squire May, you mentioned you were an officer in Washington's Army during the war for independence. I happen to have carried the same rank as you in the Cumberland County militia. Most of our duties were to guard the valley against the Indians and the Tories. Not the most exciting obligation, but at the time a very necessary one."

"I certainly agree with you, sir," replied May. "The Buffalo Valley and surrounding region of the Susquehanna Valley saw several incursions by the natives in the late seventies and early eighties. We had our hands full most of the time, and unfortunately we lost some mighty fine friends and neighbors.

"My duties took me out of the Susquehanna Valley to serve with General Washington. I led two companies of our finest men under Washington. My unfortunate men suffered greatly with the general at Valley Forge. Thankfully, most of them survived that terrible winter, and we were able to serve with distinction later in the war. As a matter of fact, towards the end of the war I was commissioned a colonel. Most of my acquaintances remember me as a major, so that is the rank that I use."

"I am sorry to hear about your trials and tribulations," Robert said. "Let's hope those times are all behind us and we can enjoy peace and prosperity forever."

Robert then turned his attention to the younger man. "Young man, you stated that your name is Groninger. That's a good German name, isn't it?"

"Yes, Groninger is German, and I'm proud of it. My family came to America in 1749 on the ship *Lydia* from Kuchen, Wurttemberg, Germany. In 1788 I married Mr. May's daughter, Maria Barbara. Barbara and I plan to migrate to this valley also if we are successful in purchasing some good farmland.

"Don't underestimate me, Robert Taylor," Leonard Groninger added flatly, "I'm a survivor, and this valley will not defeat me."

"Don't be offended young man," Robert said gently. "In all likelihood you will fit into the surroundings of this valley quite easily. But, I'm curious. Why did you choose to describe yourself as a survivor? Aren't we all survivors? Is there something special about you?"

Leonard thought for a moment. "In all honesty, I *am* a survivor. In the summer of 1781 I was captured by some marauding Senecas near my home in the Buffalo Valley. They took me north to the Genesee Valley in New York, where I spent nearly nine months in captivity. A companion and I were able to escape and float down the North Branch of the Susquehanna River to Fort Augusta at Sunbury. I was very lucky to persist because my leg became infected, and I was delirious for several days. So, you see, I consider myself to be an extraordinary survivor."

As Leonard Groninger finished his description, Robert Taylor's face broke into a smile. "Young man, I must congratulate you on your escape from the savages. You and I have a good deal in common. During the war against the French and Indians back in 1756, I suffered a similar fate. Just about seven miles west of our location on the other side of this ridge to the south of us, there was a private fort where many of us attempted to protect our families. The fort was overrun in June of 1756, several of the fort's defenders were killed, and the rest of us were taken captive.

"We were herded westward to the Indian town of Kittanning, and later dispersed among other villages. I won't bore you with all the details, but I was lucky like you and escaped down the Allegheny River. I spent almost two years in captivity. So you see, we have a certain bond, a camaraderie. Someday we will sit down and compare our experiences, that is, if it isn't too painful and upsetting to you."

"No, it won't upset me. If and when I move to this valley, it will be interesting to exchange information and share our stories of captivity."

Robert glanced at the sun which was slowly setting behind the Herringbone Ridge and Shade Mountain. "The hour is approaching for us to curtail our harvesting efforts and complete our evening chores. Why don't you gentlemen come home with us and share our evening meal? Although it will be somewhat crowded, I believe we can find a bed for you. So please come and spend the night and we'll discuss the details of a land deal."

The next morning Robert showed the two Germans the extent of his holdings and the section that he proposed to put up for sale. Robert could sense that they were impressed. The next phase, the negotiations or parleying, was the part that Robert dreaded.

The parcel of land up for sale had been surveyed years before, and the surveying markers were still visible. The creek served as the southern and eastern borders, so those boundaries were easy to ascertain, while two large white oaks served as two obvious markers for the western and northern boundaries.

Major George May divulged more about his background as the day progressed. "Right after the cessation of the war, I was grieved at the loss of my first wife, Catharina Dewalt. Upon her death I sold my farm and entered into the tavern business. My place of business is known as the Blymer Tavern. Recently I have become betrothed to the widow of Theobald Miller, Mrs. Mary Miller. The life of an innkeeper no longer appeals to me, and I desire to return to the role of a farmer and start life anew.

"I plan to bring my future wife to the valley, as well as my daughter, Barbara, and her fine husband, Leonard, my companion on this trip. My son, John, and his wife also plan to move here after we have constructed our log home."

"I believe that you and your family will find life quite pleasant here in this valley," Robert said. "Since the end of the war, more and more German families have migrated into this region. There is one particular gentleman that I will personally acquaint you with. His name is Zachariah Rice. He previously resided in Pikeland, Chester County, but due to a fraudulent land deal, he and over one hundred of his friends and neighbors lost their farms, homes, and businesses. Many of those defrauded Germans have moved to the northern section of Cumberland County and the southern region of Mifflin County. Zachariah is a remarkable carpenter, mechanic, and wheelwright. He is also a devout Lutheran, and I predict that he will soon be responsible for the establishment of a strong Lutheran church nearby."

Major May nodded, then returned to the subject of land. "I am impressed with the parcel of land that you have indicated that you would perhaps part with for the right price. Just how many acres are contained in that parcel?"

"The piece of property that we are discussing is bordered on the east and south by the Tuscarora Creek. It was formerly the property of James Armstrong, now deceased. That section of land contains 150 acres of prime bottomland. It is one of the most productive parcels in the valley and will make a lovely site for a home. It has the additional advantage of controlling the west bank of the ford on the path that leads to the crossing on the Juniata River about two miles distant, which you perhaps used to travel to my plantation."

"You don't have to persuade us on the location and apparent productiveness of this property," Major May said. "To be frank, I can't believe that you want to part with it. Nevertheless, I desire to own this acreage, and I am willing to offer you what I feel is a reasonable amount. Would the amount of 1,500 pounds be suitable?"

Robert grimaced. "It isn't exactly what I had in mind. I was thinking more along the lines of 2,500 pounds."

"I was afraid that you would be seeking more. How about 2,000 pounds?"

"Now that I think we can agree upon," smiled Robert.

The deal was concluded. On the eighth day of December 1794, the transaction that would eventually transform the valley of the Tuscarora between the Limestone and Herringbone Ridges was made official at the Mifflin County Courthouse.

Major George May with his, wife, Mary and several of his children, including Sarah or Sally who was born to the newlyweds in 1795, moved to Milford Township in 1796 shortly after their marriage. George's son, John, and his wife, Maria Margaret Strouse, followed the elder Mays to the banks of the Tuscarora Creek.

Shortly after the birth of their first daughter, Elizabeth,in

1796, Leonard and Barbara May Groninger, who had wed in 1788, moved to a little log house on the banks of the Tuscarora Creek, near the newly constructed double log house of Barbara's father.

Unfortunately, Major May did not live very long in his new home in Milford Township on the banks of the Tuscarora. George May died in 1798 and was buried in Kilmer Cemetery, a German cemetery about three miles from his new home. Major May had a large family that consisted of seven daughters and five sons; sadly, not all of them outlived their father.

With George May's death, an arrangement was made between John May and the Groningers to exchange homes. John moved to the little house at the creek, and Leonard and Barbara transferred their household to the double log house situated farther from the creek. This led to a shift in responsibilities, and Leonard assumed all the obligations to the other heirs in the May family.

This transfer of responsibilities and obligations would have a tremendous impact on the future of this section of the Tuscarora Valley. The line of inheritance of the May farm in Milford Township now transferred to the Groninger lineage.

CHAPTER FIFTY THREE

Taylorstown

In the spring of 1795 Robert Taylor found it necessary to journey to the county seat in Lewistown to conduct some urgent business. As much as he abhorred traveling through the Long Narrows, he couldn't postpone the trek. He decided to take a different route since the river was flowing at a low stage for this time of year. Robert stayed on the west or north bank of the Tuscarora to the point where Licking Creek joined the Tuscarora near the holdings of Robert Campbell. From there he followed Licking Creek to the end of the northern section of Herringbone Ridge. Then he headed east to the crossing or rope ferry on the Juniata River, which was controlled by James Taylor.

Although James Taylor was not a relative, Robert found him to be an intriguing character, with whom he had a lot in common. James Taylor bought a plot of land that containing 270 acres on July 21, 1769, from Frances West, who had purchased the survey when it was seized by the sheriff on June 3, 1757. This piece of property was bounded on the west by the Juniata River about three-quarters of a mile downriver from Harris Island.

James Taylor apparently moved to the Juniata River property shortly after he purchased it, because his name appears on the Cumberland County's tax roll in 1770 and 1772, where it was recorded that he had two hundred acres, one servant, and one horse.

In July 1776, before the adoption of the Declaration of Independence, James Taylor was appointed Judge of Election of the Third District of Cumberland County by the convention held at Carpenter's Hall in Philadelphia. On June 9, 1777, he was appointed Justice of the Peace of Fermanagh Township and served in that capacity until his death around 1808.

About 1789, James Taylor laid out a town on his plot of land and called it Mifflinburg, while others would refer to the town as Taylorstown. Mifflinburg was marked separately in the assessment roll of Fermanagh Township in 1790, and John McClure, Alexander Jackson, Samuel Jackson, and John Fright were assessed on lots located in the town.

In 1794, when Robert Taylor was involved in selling his parcel of land to George May, a petition was made for a road "through the town of Mifflinburg to John McClelland's ferry." The road received approval, and it was recorded that it started at Market Street on the northeast side of Mifflinburg.

A later deed documented "one lot of ground in the new town, called Mifflinburg (later called Mifflintown), laid out by the said James Taylor between the bank of the Juniata River and the Great Road leading up the river from the Susquehanna to Lewistown, thence to the new country westward."[27]

When the two Taylors first met, James informed Robert that he intended to construct a formidable stone house or mansion not far from the river. When Robert stood on the west bank of the Juniata River and began his crossing of the river, he looked east and was immediately impressed by the stone structure that filled his view. James Taylor had done himself proud; the house was indeed an impressive edifice.

Robert prodded his horse out of the river and up the east bank of the river. He slowly approached the house where a young man confronted him. "Howdy, mister, welcome to the home of James Taylor."

"Well, howdy to you, young man. Just who might you be?" Robert asked.

"I'm Matthew Taylor, the eldest son of James Taylor, the justice of the peace of Fermanagh Township."

"I'm very impressed, Matthew. Is your father at home?'

"Yes, sir, he is out in the next field with our hired hand. Just give me a moment and I'll fetch him for you."

"You do that, Matthew, and tell him that Robert Taylor is here to pay him a visit."

While Robert awaited the arrival of James Taylor, he made a cursory appraisal of the new stone dwelling, and it made him envious. He was dismayed by the commonplace and mundane façade of a log house or clapboard-covered log house. He vowed to himself, "If I continue to live in the Tuscarora Valley, I'm going to build a significant stone lodging."

James appeared on the scene and the two Taylors greeted each other warmly. "I must congratulate you on your construction project. It's quite a home," enthused Robert.

"Thank you, Robert. I anticipate enjoying the scenery of the Juniata River from my front porch well into my old age. The house isn't as luxurious as I had first wanted, but after a while, reality set in. It's still more that I ever dreamed about when I was a young man."

Realizing that he needed to be on his journey once again, Robert said, "I understand you have an ambitious undertaking of laying out a town here at the eastern terminal of your river crossing, and I congratulate you on that endeavor. I'm sorry that I can't tarry longer and discuss more of your plans, but I must be at the county seat by dusk. I'll try to visit longer on my next trip through the Long Narrows."

CHAPTER FIFTY FOUR

The Hot Water Rebellion

As the eighteenth century came to a close, Central Pennsylvania, the Commonwealth of Pennsylvania, and the United States of America experienced numerous transformations and challenges.

On the national front, another challenge to the authority of the federal government unfolded in Pennsylvania. This time it would not be in the hinterlands of the state as was the case in the Whiskey Rebellion of 1794, but in the southeastern counties, which had become the stronghold of a dominant German population.

The Congress of the United States passed a Direct House Tax on July 9, 1798, providing for "the valuation of lands and dwelling houses and the enumeration of slaves within the United States." The purpose of this tax was to raise two million dollars to create an endowment for a possible war with France. Pennsylvania's quota was $237, 177.

Since the inhabitants of Pennsylvania did not possess many slaves, the mainstay of taxes was to be raised by assessing dwellings and land. The value of the houses was to be determined by number and size of windows because glass was scarce and expensive, and windows were a sign of wealth.

Many of the German inhabitants of Pennsylvania did not read or write English and did not understand the nature of the law. Some were led to believe false rumors that the Direct House Tax was similar to the hated salt or hearth taxes that had been levied in Germany.

Ignorance of the law and the inquisitional nature of the counting of window lights created suspicion and fear, which turned into the use of violence. Reaction to the law in Northampton, Montgomery, and Bucks Counties was inflamed by a former militia captain and itinerant auctioneer by the name of John Fries.

Angry housewives threw hot water at the tax collectors from second-story windows. Some house owners boarded up, bricked, or stoned shut their windows in order to decrease the amount of tax they were required to pay. In some instances, tax agents were assaulted, and their tax records seized and destroyed. To counteract this civil disobedience, President John Adams declared that armed resistance to the federal government was an act of treason. The Federal District Court issued general warrants for the ringleaders of the insurgency. A United States marshal and his deputies arrested twenty-three men and incarcerated them in the Sun Tavern in Bethlehem, Pennsylvania.

On March 7, 1799, John Fries organized a group of nearly sixty men, which grew to about four hundred by midday. They traveled to Bethlehem and forcibly freed the twenty-three prisoners.

President Adams reacted on March 12 by giving the lawbreakers six days to disperse. The president's decree went unanswered; therefore, on March 20, Adams instructed the secretary of war to require Pennsylvania's Governor Mifflin to call out the militia to quell the uprising.

Governor Mifflin complied, and Brigadier General William MacPherson of the Pennsylvania militia was given the same rank in the United States Army and placed in command of the nationalized militia. The troops marched from Philadelphia into Northampton, Montgomery and Bucks Counties on April 4. Shortly thereafter, they captured John Fries in Bucks County by following his dog into the swamp where Fries was hiding. Later, the other leaders were rounded up and held for trial.

In late April, John Fries was indicted for treason, tried for his offenses, found guilty, and sentenced to death by hanging.

Political writer William Duane led a successful effort to obtain a new trial for Fries. In his second trial, held in April 1800, Fries was again found guilty and sentenced to death. That same month President Adams pardoned Fries, and a general amnesty was issued on May 21 for all those involved in the Hot Water Rebellion.

Once again, the constitutional authority of the United States government was upheld by the applied military force of the president of the United States. It proved that the Constitution could withstand substantial challenges to its authority and taxing power.

Robert Taylor and the increasing number of citizens of the Tuscarora Valley were skeptical of an all-powerful, national government but were relieved that the new government could keep the peace and solve most of their grievances and problems. Robert mused about the perplexity of the taxation issue. "I realize that the strains of 'No Taxation Without Taxation' still ring throughout the boundaries of this new nation," he said, "but we must learn to be patient. Taxation is a necessity, a way of life; there is no way of escaping it.

"If we desire to have the benefits of a civilized society, then we must shoulder the burdens and responsibilities that go with the blessings. Many of us must learn to utilize other methods of change besides force, violence, and military might. We have to adjust to the methods presented and described in the new Constitution: the rights of free speech, press, and petition; the right to use the ballot box to elect our officials to represent us in government; the right to use the courts in solving many of our differences; and many others too numerous to mention.

"We will adjust to our new way of life, but it will not happen overnight. I'm too old to live long enough to reap many of the benefits of our new nation, but my children and their children and a long line of Taylors will."

CHAPTER FIFTY FIVE

The End of Indian Problems in Pennsylvania

In the waning years of the eighteen century, Central Pennsylvania was no longer the frontier. This imaginary line where wilderness and civilization converge had shifted across the Allegheny Mountains and beyond Pennsylvania's boundaries, except in northwestern Pennsylvania. The outbreak of the Revolution had caused a temporary cessation of westward movement, mostly due to the increased Indian hostility in the West.

At the commencement of the American Revolution, there were very few English colonists in the Old Northwest—the region between the Great Lakes and the Ohio Rive,r and between the Appalachian Mountains and the Mississippi River. When the Treaty of Paris of 1783 officially ended the war and granted the United States title to the land westward to the Mississippi, a flood of settlers poured into the trans-Appalachian region.

The Northwest Territory faced several major problems, such as the conflicting claims of various states to western land, the problem of land disposal, and the question of Indian relations. The first two of these problems were addressed and solved partially by the Northwest Ordinance of 1787. The question of Indian relations would prove to be an ongoing problem.

The usual method of settling conflicts between Indians and white settlers was to buy the land in dispute and open it formally to white settlement. The main flaw in this method was that the Indians never fully understood the white attitude toward land ownership. To the Indians, there was no such concept as individual ownership and sale of land. The two sides never saw eye-to-eye concerning treaties.

As long as the whites continued to view Indian lands with covetous eyes, the frontier would remain in turmoil. At the end of the Revolution, the war continued for the Indians. The Congress under the Articles of Confederation maintained that since the majority of the Indians were British allies, they, too, had lost the war and hence had forfeited all claim to their land. This was a proposition that was impossible to maintain in fact.

In the South, the Cherokee, Chickasaw, Choctaw, and Creek tribes signed several treaties in 1785, 1786, and 1790, but they remained generally hostile to the whites. In 1784, the Iroquois at Fort Stanwix had promised once again to give up their western claims. Most of the northwestern tribes signed treaties agreeing to accept American sovereignty and to cede their claims to the Ohio Territory, but these treaties did little to change the situation in the West. Indians raids continued, and the natives showed little enthusiasm for keeping their agreements.

In 1785, Colonel Josiah Harmar endeavored to implement a policy that would eject all unauthorized white settlers in the Indian Country. This was similar to the policy that was employed by Pennsylvania nearly thirty years before, which led to the Burnt Cabins incident. Harmar's measure failed, as did Pennsylvania's in 1754; therefore, in 1789, Colonel Harmar tried to use force against the Indians. His operations were ineffective and disastrous. In early 1791, several other expeditions were sent against the Indians to halt their depredations, but were also unsuccessful.

President George Washington ordered Governor Arthur St. Clair to take personal command of the next campaign. St. Clair's efforts were calamitous, and the army gradually straggled back to Cincinnati, thoroughly beaten and demoralized after being ambushed on November 4, 1791.

Finally, one of Pennsylvania's finest Revolutionary War heroes, General "Mad" Anthony Wayne, was chosen to lead the next expedition against the Indians. When negotiations at Detroit failed, in late July Wayne led his army of 2,500 infantry, cavalry, and artillery from Pittsburgh down the Ohio to Fort Washington at Cincinnati and into the Ohio Territory to meet some 2,000 warriors. The army encountered the main body of thirteen hundred warriors near the rapids of the Maumee River, at a place called Fallen Timbers, on August 20, 1794. The attack resulted in a victory for Wayne, with the Indians retreating in panic to the gates of the British fort at Maumee. The British commander's promise to give the Indians sanctuary did not materialize, and Wayne's troops cut them down without mercy.

After Fallen Timbers, the Indians realized the futility of further immediate resistance, allowing the frontier to be freed of the menace of Indian attack for the first time in many years. This resulted in the signing of the Treaty of Greenville on August 3, 1795. It became the first and only treaty of its kind, because it was based on a thorough intimidation of the Indians.

With General Wayne's victory at Fallen Timbers and the signing of the Treaty of Greenville, Indian resistance in the Old Northwest ended for the time being, and the scene of conflict in the long war between whites and Indians shifted elsewhere.

The year of 1795 marked the end of a forty-year war in Pennsylvania that had begun with the defeat of Braddock on July 9, 1755, in southwestern Pennsylvania. Braddock's defeat had ended the period of peaceful relations that began with William Penn's treaty with Tamanend in June of 1683. Robert Taylor had lived through the attack on Fort Bigham on June 11, 1756, and his subsequent captivity before escaping. After Pontiac's Uprising in 1763, most of the Pennsylvania frontier was vacated as the people sought safety in Carlisle, York, Lancaster, and farther east. Then there was the Revolutionary War and the depredations by the Tories and their Indian allies instigated by British agents.

The last recorded Indian act of violence in Pennsylvania during this forty-year period of hostilities occurred between Fort Le Boeuf and Fort Presqu'Isle on May 22, 1795. Ralph Rutledge was killed and scalped about two miles from Presqu'Isle, during an apparent retaliatory attack after a party of ten white men attacked a family of friendly Indians on May 7.

When Robert Taylor was informed of General Wayne's victory and the signing of the Treaty of Greenville, he found it difficult to believe that he and his neighbors no longer had to live in constant fear of an attack on their homes at any time. Robert reflected, 'Peace! How good that word sounds. I never thought that it would be possible in my lifetime. It will take some time adjusting to this new way of life; I've carried my rifle in my hands for so many years it's become a permanent fixture.

"I hope my children and the generations to come never have to live through a period of chaos and turmoil as I have. I doubt if future generations will ever appreciate the sacrifices, the trials and tribulations, and the depredations and atrocities that my generation has experienced these last forty years. However, to be truthful, I don't think that I would have done it any differently. When I think of the horror stories that I heard as a youth about the living conditions in the Old Sod of Ireland, I'm glad I can claim to be a free man, a property owner, and a propagator of my family. Apparently, one can place a great deal of credence in the Taylor clan motto '*Consequitur Quodqunque petit,*' which translates as 'He Obtains Whatever He Seeks,' or 'He Hits Whatever He Aims At.'"

Anne agreed with her husband. "I know that our time is growing short, but we've enjoyed a good life in the Tuscarora Valley. I don't regret anything that we've experienced, although I once wondered about the size of our family. Now I know that the Taylor name should survive in the valley for generations to come, an accomplishment in itself."

CHAPTER FIFTY SIX

The Emerging Melting Pot

In the early 1750s, the first white settlers disregarded the fact that the land to the north of the Blue Mountain had not been purchased from the Indians and chose to move into the Tuscarora Valley. More settlers trekked across the mountains after the land was purchased at Albany in 1754. The majority of these early settlers in northern Cumberland County in the 1750s and '60s were Scotch-Irish or Irish in nationality and Presbyterian in religion. Some prominent names during that migration and settlement were Patterson, Armstrong, Gray, Hogg, Taylor, Woods, Bingham, Innis, McDonnell, Giles, McCachren, Adams, McKinney, McAllister, Cochran, Graham, Cunningham, Fitzgerald, Christy, Buchanan, Reed, Henderson, McKee, Stewart, Turbett, Wilson and many, many more.

Evidence of this constituency is found in the following:

> In a sermon now before us it is stated that at the same time of the early settlements (whatever period this comprehended) there were "no other people of any other nationality here (in Tuscarora Valley) except Scotch-Irish, and no people of any creed besides Presbyterians. All people of other national ancestors, or religious creeds, are importations made long since these times." As a matter of fact there were a few persons of other creeds from the earliest settlements.[28]

About the time of the outbreak of the Revolution, and during the war, a small group of German immigrants drifted into the

Tuscarora Valley. When the war terminated, the trickle of German immigrants into the valley escalated into a deluge. By the end of the century, about one third of the population of Pennsylvania was of German descent, and many of them had moved westward. These new settlers brought with them their German customs and traditions, but more importantly, their German language and Lutheran religion.

Although English was the universal language, the Germans spoke their own tongue. In the early days, they steadfastly adhered to the use of the German language in their homes, schools, and churches. There was no real direct clash of cultures between these new German settlers and the older, established Scotch-Irish or Irish, and they coexisted peacefully. Eventually the barriers broke down, especially when the young began to intermarry.

Some of the new names that cluttered the landscape and transformed the valley forever were Kilmer, Graybill, Groninger, Rice, Auker, Kepner, Boyer, Guss, Kolher, Hertzler, Hartman, Brackbill, Hench, Crozier, Weimer, Saylor, Suloff, Weishaupt, Strouse, Brant—and the list goes on.

One classic example of coexistence and cooperation was the establishment of the Lutheran church on Church Hill. Lawrence King sold a piece of land containing 199 acres and 153 perches to Zachariah Rice on April 13, 1801. This property was passed on to Jacob Rice, the son of Zachariah Rice. On January 1, 1803, Jacob Rice sold a parcel of one and a half acres to Valentine Weishaupt and Peter Rice, trustees of the German Lutheran congregation of the Tuscarora Valley, for the price of sixteen dollars.

While this land still belonged to Lawrence King, William Harris had made a survey of the property, and Harris's draft contained a picture of the church and specified its use "for a Burying Ground and a place of Worship for the use of the German Society."[29] Later, the Presbyterians helped to repair the church and were allowed to worship in the church on the unused alternate Sunday.

"The Rices, the two Kepners, Groninger, Weishaupt, Weimer, Suloff, Saylor and other families were the active members in erecting and sustaining the church on the hill."[30]

The Groninger family was a classic example of the melting pot concept through the marriage of Jacob Groninger's eleven sons and six daughters and their offspring to non-German spouses. Jacob was born on March 1, 1797, and was the first son of Leonard and Barbara May Groninger to be born on the banks of the Tuscarora Creek.

Jacob married Nancy Hench on May 25, 1819. Nancy was the daughter of Jacob and Susan Rice Hench. (Susan was the young Rice daughter who had helped to serve refreshments to General George Washington refreshments after the battle of Brandywine.) After giving birth to eight children, Nancy died on November 25, 1831, at the age of thirty-seven. A year later, Sidney Wilson, at the age of eighteen, became the second wife of Jacob Groninger. Sidney was the daughter of Philip Wilson and Philip and Catherine Strouse. This marriage produced nine children; thus, Jacob fathered seventeen children.

The young people born on the plot of ground brought by George May from Robert Taylor would gain insight and inspiration from the little log church at Church Hill. Eventually the little church would pass into the pages of history, being replaced by churches constructed in Perrysville, later to be named Port Royal in 1874. The Lutheran church would be located on the corner of Fourth and Market Streets, while the Presbyterian church would be a block away, at the corners of Fourth and Main Streets. The Groninger family would be staunch supporters and leaders of both churches.

As the years passed, the Groninger name spread throughout the United States. Jacob's offspring would play a prominent role in the development of the valley, the state, and the nation. In a few years the valley, from the mouth of Licking Creek westward beyond the Half Moon region and the site of the Indian Mound, became known as Groninger Valley, because so much of the farmland had passed into Groninger ownership. Much of the land claimed by William Bell, Robert Taylor, and James Armstrong became Groninger lands.

The population of the new republic was overwhelmingly rural. In almost all frontier communities, the business of making a living took precedence over other considerations. The American economy of 1800 differed little from that of early colonial days. The vast majority of the population still achieved their livelihood from agriculture, and the farmer's mode of life, his tools, methods, or habits had changed. Pennsylvania was one of the few locations where there was any evidence of agricultural progress.

One of the major differences that Robert Taylor recognized was that the world that he lived in allowed considerably more class fluidity than that found in Europe. The vast expanses of cheap land, the abundance of natural resources, the sparseness of population, the growing widespread notion that one person was as good as another, and the absence of inflexible class barriers made it possible for a person to climb the social ladder in America.

The movement from one social echelon to another was very noticeable in the Tuscarora Valley and in Pennsylvania by 1800. Some of Robert Taylor's neighbors and friends had started out with nothing, at the very bottom, when they arrived in the valley. Now, many of them owned vast amounts of acreage, had abandoned living in log cabins with dirt floors for stately dwellings, and held offices in the local government. Central Pennsylvania, all of America, was the land of opportunity for those ambitious enough to accept the challenges that this primitive land presented.

As Robert and Anne Taylor mulled over the events of their married life, at the end of the eighteenth century, what they contemplated could probably best be described by the words that had been written in the journal of the Reverend Philip Vickers Fithian on Sunday, June 25, 1775.

> ...It is now sunset, and I am sitting under a dark tuft of willow and large sycamores, close on the bank of the

beautiful Juniata River. The river, near two hundred yards broad, lined with willows, sycamores, walnuts, white-oaks and a fine bank—what are my thoughts? Fair genius of this water, O tell me, will not this, in some future time, be a vast, pleasant, and very populous country? Are not many large towns to be raised on these shady banks? I seem to wish to be transferred forward only one century. Great God, America will surprise the world.[31]

Yes, Reverend Fithian, America has surprised the world. Moreover, a great God certainly has blessed the valley and the newly emerging nation envisioned by men like Philip Fithian and Robert Taylor. While they pondered the future of the Tuscarora and Juniata Valleys, I would like to do the reverse of what Reverend Fithian contemplated and return to those days of the eighteenth century to enjoy the unspoiled beauty of this picturesque valley. However, I can only do what they did—dream and hope for a better and greater America.

BIBLIOGRAPHY

Addresses Delivered at the Historical Pilgrimage in Juniata County and the Dedication of a Marker and Tablet at Fort Bigham. Arranged by the Juniata County Historical Society. Port Royal, Pa.: Port Royal Times Print, 1934.

Bailey, Thomas A. *The American Pageant: A History of the Republic.* Boston: D.C. Heath and Company, 1966.

Bell, Raymond Martin. *Mifflin County, Pennsylvania Families and Records Before 1800.* Lewistown, Pa.: Privately Printed, 1987.

Busch, Clarence M. *Report of the Commission to Locate the Site of the Frontier Forts of Pennsylvania, Vols. I and II.* State Printer of Pennsylvania, 1896.

Groninger, Thomas R. ed. *The Groninger Family Record.* Lewisburg, Pa: Privately Published.

Hain, H.H. *History of Perry County, Pennsylvania.* Harrisburg, Pa.: Hain-Moore Company, Publishers, 1922.

Henry, Dale H. III. *Mifflintown: A Comprehensive History.* Port Royal, Pa.: The Times Publishing Company, 2004.

History of Port Royal and Vicinity. Compiled and edited by the members of the Class of 1950 of Tuscarora Valley High School. Port Royal, Pa.: Privately Printed, 1950.

History of Port Royal and Vicinity and Sesqui-Centennial Celebration July 24-29, 1962. Port Royal, Pa.: Times Print, 1962.

History of that Part of the Susquehanna and Juniata Valleys Embraced in the Counties of Mifflin, Juniata, Perry, Union, and Snyder in the Commonwealth of Pennsylvania, Vol. I. Philadelphia, Pa.: Everts, Peck and Richards, 1886; reprint Mt. Vernon, I. Windmill Publications, Inc. 1996.

Jones, U. J. *History of the Early Settlement of the Juniata Valley.* Harrisburg, Pa.: The Telegraph Press, 1940.

Klein, Philip S. and Ari Hoogenboom. *A History of Pennsylvania.* University Park, Pa.: The Pennsylvania State University Press. 1980.

Kniseley, Rev. John B. ed. *A Memorial History of the Port Royal Lutheran Charge Port Royal and St. Paul Churches.* Port Royal, Pa.: Privately Published, 1919.

Pennsylvania Archives, Vols. III and IV.

Pennsylvania Records, Vol. VIII.

Rice, Rev. Vernon. *History of the Rice or Reiss Family.* New Bloomfield, Pa.: Privately Printed, 1900.

Roberts, Rev. Robert J. *A Narrative History of the Lower Tuscarora Presbyterian Church, Academia, Pa.* Academia, Pa.: Privately Published, 1986.

Sipe, C. Hale. *The Indian Chiefs of Pennsylvania.* Lewisburg, Pa.: Wennawoods Publishing, 1997.

_____ *The Indian Wars of Pennsylvania.* Lewisburg, Pa.: Wennawoods Publishing, 1998.

Stewart, Harriet Wylie. *History of the Cumberland Valley, Pennsylvania.* Privately Printed.

Taylor, Wayne E. *Hope on the Tuscarora*. Tarentum, Pa.: Word Association Publishers, 2005.

Trebbel, John and Keith Jennison. *The American Indian Wars*. Edison, NJ: Castle Books, 2003.

Wallace, Paul A. *The Indian Paths of Pennsylvania*. Harrisburg, Pa.: The Pennsylvania Historical and Museum Commission, 1987.

ENDNOTES

1 *Pennsylvania Archives, Vol. IV,* 106.

2 *Pennsylvania Records, Vol. VIII,* 269.

3 *Pennsylvania Archives, Vol. III,* 745.

4 Sipe, C. Hale, *The Indian Wars of Pennsylvania* (Lewisburg, Pa.: Wennawoods Publishings, 1998), 421.

5 *Ibid.,* 421.

6 *Ibid.,* 429.

7 *History of that Part of the Susquehanna and Juniata Valleys Embraced in the Counties of Mifflin, Juniata, Perry, Union, and Snyder in the Commonwealth of Pennsylvania.* (Philadelphia: Everts, Peck and Richards, 1886; reprinted, Windmill Publications, Inc. Mt. Vernon, IN, 1996), 114.

8 Ibid., 115.

9 Ibid.

10 Stewart, Harriet Wylie, *History of the Cumberland Valley Pennsylvania,* 44.

11 Ibid., 45.

[12] *History of that Part of the Susquehanna and Juniata Valleys,* op.cit., 669-670.

[13] Ibid., 669.

[14] Sipe, *The Indian Chiefs of Pennsylvania,* reprint (Lewisburg, Pa.: Wennawoods Publishing, 1997), 517.

[15] Ibid., 517.

[16] *History of that Part of the Susquehanna and Juniata Valleys, op.cit., 811.*

[17] Ibid., 811.

[18] Sipe, *The Indian Wars of Pennsylvania,* 865.

[19] Ibid.

[20] Hain, H. H., *History of Perry County, Pennsylvania,* (Harrisburg, Pa.: Hain-Moore Co. Publishers, 1922), 189.

[21] *History of that Part of the Susquehanna and Juniata Valleys,* op. cit., 451.

[22] Ibid., 493.

[23] Ibid., 460.

[24] Ibid., 464.

[25] Ibid., 82.

[26] Ibid., 675.

[27] Ibid., 864.

[28] Ibid., 803.

[29] Ibid., 780.

[30] Ibid., 804.

[31] Ibid., 669.

Wayne E. Taylor

Wayne E. Taylor taught history in the schools of Juniata County for thirty-three years after graduating from Tuscarora Valley High School, Carson-Newman College while attending several graduate schools. His successful French and Indian War era historical novel *Hope on the Tuscarora* depicted the early settlement of his native valley. *Hope Rekindled* is a sequel to this novel and continues to trace the inhabitation of this region in the late Eighteenth Century. Taylor and his wife Lucille, his two children, and five grandchildren reside in the Licking Creek Valley which is a sub-valley of the Tuscarora Valley.